Christmas
Wish

ERIN GREEN was born and raised in
Warwickshire, where she resides with her
husband. She writes contemporary novels
focusing on love, life and laughter. An
ideal day for Erin involves writing, people-
watching and copious amounts of tea. Erin
was delighted to be awarded The Katie
Fforde Bursary in 2017 and, previously,
Love Stories 'New Talent Award' in 2015.
For more about Erin, visit her website
www.ErinGreenAuthor.co.uk or follow on
Twitter @ErinGreenAuthor.

A Christmas Wish

Erin Green

First published as an ebook in 2017 by Aria,
an imprint of Head of Zeus, Ltd.

First published in print in the UK in 2017 by Aria.

9 7 5 3 1 2 4 6 8

A catalogue record for this book is available from
the British Library.

ISBN (PB): 9781788541077
ISBN (E): 9781786697950

Typeset by Divaddict Publishing Solutions Ltd.

Printed and bound by CPI Group (UK) Ltd,
Croydon, CR0 4YY

Head of Zeus Ltd
First Floor East
5–8 Hardwick Street
London EC1R 4RG
WWW.HEADOFZEUS.COM

To Leo, my hero

1

24th December 2016
Flora

I'm driving. Not my usual tootle-around-town driving, but pedal-to-the-metal-with-power-ballad-blaring driving – the kind seen in plush car adverts. If I were driving in a snazzy commercial I'd have a backdrop of raging fire, tornados or cyclones looming over a dusky landscape to reinforce my mood. Instead there's a pitch-black night sky and a heavy flurry of snow pelting the windscreen creating a deep-in-outer-space illusion.

Like the car commercials, I have navigated many winding and twisting roads, but despite having a satnav with the destination entered, I have no idea where I am.

'Take the third exit at the roundabout,' orders the satnav lady.

I follow her instructions as I have for the previous two hours. 'Continue for one mile… arriving at your destination on the left.' The tiny screen depicts a chequered flag and a blobby image unrecognisable as my red Mini.

My stomach flips; I want to be sick.

Not the drunken sickness that Christmas Eve parties can deliver, I haven't touched a drop of alcohol, but that nervy tremor, butterflies-in-your-stomach kind of sick.

Within minutes, I arrive at my destination: St Bede's Mews, Pooley.

I indicate, park at the kerb and switch off the engine in front of a large church with stone angles and angels illuminated by spotlights strategically positioned amongst the tilting gravestones. The church looks empty and locked; I presume Christmas Eve Mass was earlier in the evening. Janet, my mum, always goes to church on Christmas Eve – though not this year.

Is this a bad idea? Should I stay or return home? I want someone else to decide – there's no chance of assistance; I'm on my own.

The church clock strikes half eleven.

I hadn't planned on driving here. I'm supposed to be dancing under neon lights at the Pink Coconut, laughing and joking alongside Lisa and Steph surrounded by tonight's selection of tall, dark and handsome Prince Charmings.

Was I right to dash off into the night? Did they manage to flog my Christmas Eve Extravaganza party invite to the ticketless crowd huddled by the club entrance?

I stare at my surroundings. Adjacent to the church is a row of Edwardian houses with steep stone steps leading to impressive doorways. A large archway is straight ahead, through which the road snakes before disappearing, linking the houses to a quadrangle of commercial buildings. The buildings edge a pretty cobblestone square freshly decorated with the flurry of snow and dominated by a community Christmas tree. On the far side of The Square, opposite the church, a noisy pub spews festive spirit from an open doorway.

My stomach convulses and my mouth unattractively dry gags.

'Don't puke,' I mutter, looking down at the red chiffon skimming my bare thighs. 'I haven't paid for it yet.'

I don't do tights, even in winter. I don't do spare plastic bags to act as sick bags stashed in glove compartments either.

I lower the window by an inch, allowing a whoosh of cold air to bathe my clammy forehead.

Breathe, just breathe.

I close my eyes.

This *has* to be the right decision. How many nights have I dreamt of seeing The Square?

It's not easy growing up being different. Different from every child in the extended family, your English class, Girl Guides or youth club. Everyone I know knows where they came from: job relocation from Newcastle, divorcing parents or social aspirations – they all knew how they'd arrived in the leafy suburbs of Bushey. Except me, because I am different. I'm special, as Janet says.

'*Special*' – not the most flattering of labels in today's society. 'Special' counts for nothing in the employment stakes, the education system or a long-term romance. 'Special' doesn't get you far in life outside the three-bedroomed detached belonging to Janet and David Phillips, my adoptive parents.

What would they say if they knew I was here? I peer into the Mini's tiny rear-view mirror where my sea-green eyes reflect a wave of guilt that snags in my throat. Was this the way to repay their kindness and love? Snooping behind their backs while they cruise the Bahamas escaping the British winter and celebrating an early Ruby wedding anniversary. What harm could it do? They'd *never* know. A quick look and I'd be starting the return journey towards Bushey within ten minutes.

The majority of the world were preparing for the fraught and frantic celebrations of a family Christmas, so why wasn't I? Because family is the Achilles heel of my life, through no fault of my own. Sadly, I seek answers to the complex curiosity or sheer spite of the seven-year-olds who taunted me relentlessly in a primary school playground.

I was destined to be different from day one. Different from

Steph and her infectious laughter, her overflowing confidence and in-control attitude. Or Lisa, with her delicate manner, her ditzy brain and her constant search for Mr Right. Or as Steph jokes, her 'Mr Right-Now'.

I snort at the very thought.

My Mr Right-Now had been Julian Wright who swiftly became Mr Has-been-and-gone two months ago by knobbing the blonde who serves in the local chemist. Before Julian, I swore blind Robbie Brookes was my Prince, but he stuffed it up on a stag weekend in Blackpool. Before him was Terry, Rikki, Seb, Jamie and...

Need I torture myself by continuing?

I open my eyes; the nausea has passed – much like the heavy snow flurry which has eased to a light sprinkle.

Reaching for my silver clutch bag on the passenger seat, I rummage for my purse and unzip the back pocket. Lisa keeps an emergency twenty tucked in hers. Steph an emergency condom. I keep a yellowing piece of newspaper.

I know the piece off by heart.

I carefully unfold my clipping and stare at the black and white image, gently stroking the baby's forehead, as if she can feel my touch. This was my beginning, my first photograph, technically the first entry in my baby record book, if I had one.

I carefully fold my newspaper cutting. I've treasured this clipping since the story was explained to me by Janet, amidst tears and gentle hugs, at the tender age of seven.

I've heard about The Square in Pooley, throughout my life.

Be it a scrubbed red tile, rough cement, or coloured block paving, *that* doorstep was the beginning of my story.

I might as well take a look. It won't hurt. I may never be *this* near again.

I haven't brought a coat so reach for the tartan blanket stashed on the rear seat, wrap it around my bare shoulders and make my way from the car, clutching my newspaper clipping.

Instantly, the snow permeates my strappy heels as I head for the row of Edwardian houses.

The houses in St Bede's Mews vary in original features and renovation work. Number three, the middle house, is in darkness like every other house; the occupants were obviously out enjoying themselves or early to bed awaiting Santa.

I suppose this is how burglaries occur.

If I was a burglar I could nip over the wrought-iron fencing, jemmy up the front window and be off with their presents from beneath their decorated tree. But I'm not a burglar; I'm a single, thirty-year-old who wasted an hour curling her hair and a hundred quid on a red dress to stand and stare at a doorstep on Christmas Eve.

I stand before their gate and stare at the pathway of tiny black and white tiles lightly covered in snow.

If the tiles are original, and they definitely look original, then my birth mother walked along them, twice.

I gulp.

Never before have I been in close proximity to anything that my birth mother had touched.

Clutching the tartan blanket beneath my chin, I place the yellowed clipping in my lap as I crouch down, passing my hand through the swirls of wrought iron to touch the snow-frosted tiles that *she* walked upon.

My eyes fill with tears.

I can touch something that my birth mother touched – *this* is a first.

The church bells strike midnight; immediately an explosion of coloured fireworks fills the night sky.

'I may be a little old to make Christmas wishes, but let's hope this one brings me some happiness and festive cheer.'

Joel

I depress the radio button.

'Officer 4402 to control. We have a lone female acting suspiciously in St Bede's Mews just off The Square at Pooley – we'll investigate and report back, over.'

A crackled acknowledgement is received from control.

'She'll be drunk,' says Scotty, my partner in crime, from the driving seat.

'We'll see.'

I step from the patrol car, grabbing my hat and notebook as the church bells strike midnight and fireworks burst across the snowy night sky. Since when did fireworks belong to Christmas Eve?

'Merry Christmas, mate,' I say cheerily, leaning back into the patrol car.

'Same to you, it can't be any worse than the last one, hey Joel?' laughs Scotty, showing his fillings.

He's not wrong.

'You git,' I mutter, as the face of Veronica, my ex, flashes before my eyes. The image of her blue eyes and blonde highlights wasn't the issue. It was the unexpected reminder. 'Are fireworks now compulsory for every celebration?' I ask, quickly changing the subject. I know what I should say but can't bring myself to ask how he and his dad plan to spend Christmas without his mum.

'I know, every weekend since Halloween I've heard the same routine after dark. It's probably a birthday celebration for a family on the estate. Pound to a penny *she's* drunk,' he scoffs, nodding towards our crouching figure. 'She's probably been dumped by her fella and downed a bottle of vodka.'

'*Maybe.*'

Slamming the patrol car door, I stride across The Square towards the Edwardian houses – my size ten boots disturb the picturesque snow scene around the giant Christmas tree.

He's got a fair point; we've patrolled this area long enough to know. Thanks to the extended licencing hours, the streets were always deserted while the revellers were squashed inside the pubs and the Liberal Welfare club celebrating finishing work for the holidays. So, an hour ago, we'd pitched our patrol car in the small car park facing the church, knowing we had a short time before the drama started. Experience had taught us that we'd only be needed once kick-out occurred and then the booze-induced fights and the rowdy behaviour would erupt.

The figure is crouching beside the gateway.

We'd watched her silhouette for nearly thirty minutes.

'She's parked on double yellows and hasn't even noticed,' said Scotty, as we observed her actions.

'Just watch. We'll pounce when necessary, but right now she's only sitting there – hardly a crime.'

'It's the most we've seen tonight.'

'Be grateful then... or can't we handle a lone female on Christmas Eve?' I'd laughed, knowing the waiting game was killing Scotty.

'I dread this shift every year. We always get the dodgy folk when huge fights kick off and spend extra hours booking them into custody when we should have clocked off and gone home.'

'Stop moaning and think of the overtime,' I said, my eyes fixed upon the red Mini.

She'd spent several minutes composing herself before climbing from the vehicle with a blanket slung around her shoulders.

'Now, she's definitely parked illegally, go!' urged Scotty.

'Seriously, would you nick her... tonight of all nights?'

'Yeah! She shouldn't be parked on double yellows.' He answered without hesitation.

'Nah.' I pulled a face at my partner. He thinks he's mighty tough and an advocate for by-the-book policing but I know deep down he's kinder than that.

'Seriously, I would,' he continued. 'There's a perfectly good car park provided... as proven, *we're* parked in it.'

Eleven years in the police force has taught me to give people the benefit of the doubt. You'd be surprised how wrong you can be by making snap judgements. I keep telling Scotty, you can't predict. She may be drunk, in which case she'll be breathalysed and cautioned. But there may be a reasonable explanation.

'She's not a local,' I'd added before radioing the station and climbing from the patrol car.

'We'd know her name, entire family tree and her employment history – if she were local, Joel,' laughed Scotty. 'Plus, she wouldn't be parked on double yellows in front of the church.'

He was right, there was an advantage to being raised in the neighbourhood – we knew all the yokels.

As I approach, she's bent double by the gate; one hand reaching through the metalwork, her long curls have fallen forward, covering her face.

Trust me to get the first sick job of the night.

I scan the pavement as I near – there's no vomit, but that doesn't mean anything nowadays. I've seen many a young lady vomit into her own lap, or handbag.

'Excuse me, Madam – is everything all right?' I stop short of her position.

She flinches as I speak, snatching her hand back through the wrought-iron gate.

'Sorry... I was...' she turns, her hair parting around her slender face, her almond-shaped eyes widen.

'Is everything all right?' I repeat, as she straightens up, one hand clutching at the draped blanket. A fold of paper falls to the pavement. I'm relieved to see her red dress is clear of vomit.

'How embarrassing... I was just... I thought...' She falls silent under my gaze. I scour the pavement around her. No wine bottle, no shot glass, no vomit. I step forward and sniff the air. Not a hint of alcohol, but just to be sure.

'Have you been drinking this evening, Madam?'

'Are you *bloody* joking?' Her temper flares now she's risen to her full height; five foot three is my guess.

Here we go, Scotty will be pleased.

This isn't unusual, the general public are all politeness and goodwill one minute. The next, they're charging at my uniform with a smashed bottle and a knuckleduster.

'Madam, please... myself and my colleague are parked across the way...' I proceed to explain what we've witnessed.

'Whoopi-bloody-do, a sodding parking offence – haven't you got anything better to do?'

Great, a feisty one. Just what I need to start the Christmas holidays.

I do the usual routine, ask Madam to take a step backwards, ask her to refrain from shouting and to calm down. I'm only trying to ascertain that no harm has come to her. Sadly, Madam's having none of it.

'Madam... please.' I'm usually pretty good talking to irate females. I do the whole gently, gently routine knowing Scotty's probably killing himself laughing.

She steps closer, her perfume filling my personal space.

'Don't you *Madam* me in that patronising tone... you think I'm drunk, don't you? Well, I'm not. I've got a good reason to be here... I have every reason to be here... in fact I have more...' She stops dead, looking round frantically. 'Where's my clipping?'

'As you stood up...' I say, remembering the slip of paper that fell to the pavement, but she's not listening.

9

'Oh no, I can't lose it,' she cries, turning around frantically, scouring the ground.

At the same time, we spot the folded paper lying against the fence post amidst a smattering of snow. Instantly, we bend and grab for the paper in a swift synchronised move. Crash! Her forehead collides full force with the bridge of my nose.

I hear the break.

The pain registers and my eyesight blurs to a pool of red as I double over in agony.

'Sorry, I was only trying to grab... my clipping. I didn't mean to...' she stutters.

I hear the slam of the patrol car door and the rumble of black boots – Scotty's size elevens soon fill my line of vision along with the snow-flurried cracks in the pavement.

'Lady, you're coming with us. I am arresting you on suspicion of assaulting a police officer, you do not have to say anything but it may harm your defence if you do not mention when questioned something you later rely on in court...'

Amidst the whoops and bangs of fireworks overhead, I hear the cuffs snap on her wrists as Scotty continues his spiel and my fingers curl tightly round her folded clipping.

2

Flora

My tea steams in a white polystyrene cup. I'd give anything for a Massimo latte with chocolate sprinkles but I assume the beverage menu is limited at Pooley police station. On arrival, they'd confiscated my tartan blanket as a personal possession and provided me with a larger cream-coloured blanket, which remains draped around my shoulders. They'd also confirmed the charge of assaulting a police officer, so I'm not about to complain about my tea.

My fingers gingerly lift the flimsy cup, squashing its wide mouth to a quivering oval. I tentatively sip under the watchful glare of two officers: my arresting male officer and a willowy framed female, whose strawberry blonde hair is snared in a severe ponytail. The hot tea scalds my tongue, so I quickly replace the wobbly cup on the tabletop.

It's as you see on TV: a room with minimalist decor, a black-topped table, a few hard-backed chairs and a recording machine. To my left sits the duty solicitor, a tiny bloke in a cheap nylon suit, no taller than me, supplied courtesy of my rights. I've never been involved with the police before so why would I have a family solicitor?

I refused my chance to call someone; I'm not selfish enough to ruin my parents' cruise.

The male officer, whose lower jaw is defined by his shaving shadow, unwraps the cellophane from two blank tapes before loading and pressing the machine's record button.

My stomach quivers with nerves.

Is this step one towards prison? A deadbeat life of slop buckets and grey boiler suits? Or a life on the run with a Mafia-style existence in Marbella?

'Officer Scott Hamilton and Officer Kylie Brown at Pooley police station interviewing at 2 a.m. on the twenty-fifth of December 2016. The accused was arrested for assaulting police officer Joel Kennedy in the vicinity of St Bede's Mews shortly after midnight. Duty solicitor Mr Jonathan Green is also present.'

The officer coughs and clears his throat before staring at me, his chest and biceps strain against the fabric of his shirt.

'Could you state your full name and address please?'

'Flora Eloise Phillips of thirty-one St Edith's Crescent, Bushey, Hertfordshire,' I answer, knowing full well that his official eyebrow should be raised given my distance from home.

'Occupation?'

I cringe.

'I'm currently without employment.'

The male officer smirks, the female simply stares before writing notes on her lined pad.

They think I'm a dosser who can't keep a job so I fill my time by headbutting coppers. Why couldn't I be answering 'a receptionist for the family furniture maker of Wright, Wright and Wright'? Ahhh yes, because their beloved son Julian Wright cheated on me, forcing me to up sticks and move on from relationship, residence and employment – one stone, three direct hits.

'What brings you to the area, Flora?'

I hesitate, pull the cream blanket tightly over my shoulders, nervously glancing between his staring gaze and her bored expression.

'I...' In my head the words flow in neatly formed sentences which eloquently explain everything, but I know the reality will be a tsunami of stuttering. How pathetic will I sound admitting to two officers and an aged solicitor that life's not good. Actually, I'm feeling a bit down. Not your usual everyday under-the-weather down or an emotional wobble but a full-blown, life-long crisis that's been on the cards since 1986. An emotional, deep-seated feeling of being unloved, unwanted and, ashamedly at thirty years of age, a total failure in the game of life. I can't hold onto a boyfriend, or a job, and am currently staying at my parents' house and kipping in their spare bedroom. I can call it house-sitting while they're on a cruise sunning themselves – I've failed to create an excuse for the previous two months.

His dark eyebrow lifts, her nude mouth purses. My solicitor's hand hovers, his biro suspended in mid-air above his yellow legal paper – they're waiting for an answer.

'It's private,' I mumble, reaching for my tea.

She hastily writes down my words.

'*Private*?' I can hear the sarcasm in his voice. 'That may be so, Miss Phillips... but given the circumstances and charge, you need to outline the reasons for your presence outside St Bede's Mews.'

I slurp my tea as a distraction but am instantly reminded that it's too hot to drink so return the flimsy cup to the table.

I begin to pick at my left thumbnail.

'Miss Phillips?' urges the male officer.

I avoid his stare by focusing upon my thumbnail.

These guys are probably minutes away from throwing me back into the cold cell and ordering my cooked breakfast and a mug of tea for the morning.

'Has my car been locked?' I ask, distracted by a sudden flashback.

'Officers have secured your vehicle. It was illegally parked on double yellow lines, so an officer has moved it to the free parking area opposite the church – no worries there.'

I nod my appreciation, looking from beneath my lowered brow.

'Miss Phillips, we're waiting.' His voice is becoming stern; a pulse below his left eye begins to dance.

My throat constricts. If I begin to explain I'll open a can of worms, it'll all come pouring out, and then what?

'Miss Phillips, are you prepared to co-operate?' asks the female officer.

I shrug.

'You've assaulted a police officer, I'm not going to accept a shrug of the shoulders as an answer, now am I?' he says, glancing at the solicitor, who continues to write.

He's right, fact was fact. Officer Stubble-chin had slapped the cuffs on me, bundled me into the rear of the patrol car and driven at high speed towards the police station. His patrol buddy Officer Excuse-Me-Madam had spent the entire journey doubled over in the front seat clutching his face and groaning.

Why hadn't I stayed with Lisa and Steph at the Pink Coconut? By now I would be plastered on Pinot Grigio, eating Marmite on toast in Lisa's kitchen while Steph pukes noisily in the tiny downstairs cloakroom. Instead I had the big idea to follow my gut reaction and go find myself. Correction, it wasn't that definitive – it was simply a case of flee and think later.

'Has he gone to hospital?' I ask sheepishly.

Both officers nod.

I need to come clean, tell the truth and face the consequences.

'*Firstly*, I never meant to break his nose. I'm not a violent or angry person, but he kept mentioning alcohol. I haven't touched a drop all night. I'd dropped something, we were both

14

looking and then... banged heads. Honestly, I never meant to hurt him.'

'OK... he'll make his statement once he returns from the hospital, then we'll compare details.'

'Did he hand anything in?' I ask, desperate to locate my treasured clipping.

They both shake their heads.

'Why here? Tonight?' he asks.

I hesitate. My shoulders droop beneath the warm blanket. *Here we go.*

'You're on a roll, don't stop now,' he urges, clearly bored with spending the early hours of Christmas Day in my presence.

'Tonight's visit was a spur of the moment thing. I was supposed to go dancing with my best friends but... I couldn't face another Christmas Eve Extravaganza party,' I say.

Arghhh, the thought of compulsory drinking purely to fit in with the crowd, forced to have a good time, endure the crammed dance floor, the crush at the bar... the queue for the ladies', strangers spilling their drinks down my new dress... the unwanted attention from drunken guys – all letching and leering over your boobs in the hope of a Christmas shag.

'We'd bought tickets but still we had to queue to enter, I ducked out at the last minute and drove here...' I continue in a whisper, as my voice cracks, 'where my mother abandoned me.'

Officer Stubble-chin leans across the desk, his hazel eyes scrutinising my features before he speaks.

'Say that again?'

'I was abandoned... on a doorstep.'

A comedy double-take glance occurs between the two officers.

'You're Baby Bede?' he asks.

I shrug.

'I'm not sure what I'm called... but I was definitely left on that doorstep.'

'Back in the eighties?' interrupts the female, an energy lifting into her bland expression. 'Everyone around these parts knows about you.'

Great.

'Sarge won't believe this...' he yelps, excitement bubbling in his voice.

'Neither will Joel,' squeals the female officer, hurriedly scrawling her notes.

Double great.

It takes the next twenty minutes to explain that I'd queued at the Pink Coconut while the burly doormen exercised their powers of slow security searches thereby forcing me to perform an aerobic workout of continual sidestepping to combat the cold. That was the moment when my mind overflowed with the dread of the evening routine.

'The Extravaganza party wouldn't be the answer to my dreams. Has anyone ever met Mr Right on Christmas Eve? Besides, I wouldn't choose a lipstick in the dim lighting of the Pink Coconut, let alone a life partner! So I might as well seek answers to long overdue questions.'

'And coming here would answer those?' asks Officer Stubble-chin, his manner softening somewhat.

'Possibly. I didn't really think it through, I just followed my instinct and drove. But now that I'm here, well not *here*, but back there – I did feel a connection.'

Silence descends. The two officers sit back and stare. The duty solicitor doesn't move, I'm unsure if he's kept up with the details as he appears to be asleep.

I can see their minds whirring. What do you say to the baby found by the newspaper boy on a cold foggy morning? Welcome to Pooley, please drive carefully and deposit your baby safely. There's no etiquette rules regarding *this* topic.

The silence continues.

'Are you thinking of staying?' he continues.

'*Maybe*. I thought about it earlier in my cell. I could ask around, maybe find some answers,' I mutter, my nerves having drifted away while a warmer feeling took root. 'Who knows, I might find who I really am?'

Officer Stubble-chin depresses the button on the recording.

'Well, that's the end of the interview, Miss Phillips. Officer Brown will take you back to your cell. I'll inform the custody sergeant and we'll have a chat regarding how we're going to proceed.'

Wow, the interview is over before I finish my tea.

'And the charges?' asks the solicitor, awakening hastily.

'We need to speak to the Sarge... she'll have to wait and see.'

I'm led back along the grim corridor and returned to cell number ten – the door clangs shut. I'm left alone to settle upon the blue plastic mattress with my comfort blanket.

Within minutes they deliver a plastic moulded tray piled with rice, a creamy mush and a proper mug of tea.

'Merry Christmas,' I mutter, balancing the tray on my lap. 'This certainly makes a change from previous years.'

I look at my cell: cold stone walls, a plastic mattress and a metal toilet with matching handbasin hidden behind a low-level wall for added privacy.

How am I going to explain *this* to my parents? Explain that my feisty temper and defensive nature has got me in trouble, *again*.

If I can find the missing jigsaw puzzle piece, know the truth about my birth, maybe I can relax into normality and create my own Jane Bloggs' existence. *Maybe*.

I ignore the plastic fork, lazily spooning and scooping at the rice and creamy sauce mountain. A couple of gulps of tea clears my palate.

There had been many times in my life when wanting to know the truth was far greater than anything else. Be it crying in the school playground because other children had their dad's chin.

Or my teenage years when I was convinced I was snogging my brother on every night out – highly unlikely given the two-hour drive separating Bushey and Pooley. Or the simplest questions: who is my birth mother? And why on a doorstep?

My abandonment is the default mechanism of my life: lost my job – everyone rejects me just like my mother did. Get dumped by a boyfriend – no surprise, that's due to my neediness and insecurity. Even a broken nail can trace a direct link back to the events of Friday, 10th October 1986.

I continue to spoon creamy rice into my mouth, swallowing without chewing.

If that is my actual birth date... she may have kept me for a day or so. Nursed me, wanted me and then found she couldn't keep me.

What if my birth date was the ninth or the eighth?

Shit! I've celebrated my birthday on the wrong day every year for thirty years! Worse still, I might have been hatched in early September and hidden away in disgust until being deposited on the doorstep. Six weeks with me and even my mother didn't want a relationship. No wonder previous boyfriends couldn't put up with me. What crime could I have committed to be deemed unkeepable?

'I'm staying,' I whisper, knowing I have a window of opportunity with my parents away.

My stomach flips. Instantly, I'm nervous with an uncontrollable urge to pee. I distastefully eye the metal en suite and know this is further punishment for having such a rotten beginning.

Joel

I stare at the cubicle of St Bede's hospital, taking in the array of medical equipment while the young nurse unpacks the swabbing. I've already had an X-ray plus a ninety-minute wait to reach this point.

'Some lager lout, was it?' she asks, peeling open the sterile packages.

'For once, no, a lone female.'

'Not the best start to Christmas, is it?' she adds, pushing spherical swabs up my nose. 'The drunks are the worst, loud and letchy – we're forever calling security for assistance.'

'She *wasn't* drunk. One minute I was asking her questions, the next we clashed heads as we both bent down to collect one of her possessions from the pavement. Bang! I doubled over as she caught the bridge of my nose.'

Who knows how much blood was spilt on the snowy pavement, but some poor bugger would be asked to it mop up. Eleven years of duty shifts to keep law and order, fighting crime and discouraging unlawful acts and all for what? *This*?

'Pitfall of the job, hey?' she laughs, plastering thick stripes of sticky tape along and across my nose.

'*Sadly.*'

It's happened many times: black eyes, a split lip, a couple of busted ribs and a broken collarbone, but never an injury caused by a woman.

'It had been a quiet night until then – dead almost... the local pubs were brimming with revellers and yet it's the lone female, who I thought was being sick in a gutter, who turns my shift upside down.'

'Did she get hauled in?'

'My duty partner came to my aid and quickly took control. I was no good to God nor man. She's probably giving him hell back at the station as we speak.'

'No doubt she'll have some sob story to tell.'

'Probably, though nine times out of ten it isn't worth hearing,' I mutter, climbing from the casualty bed. I touch my left breast pocket, feeling guilty that her folded clipping remains buttoned inside.

'You can expect the swelling to go within the week but the bruising could take up to a fortnight. Don't be tempted to blow your nose for a while, OK? You might end up causing more damage.'

'I won't.'

'Here, you'll need a couple of painkillers before the worst of it kicks in,' she offers me a plastic cup in which two tablets rattle about the bottom.

I raise it to my mouth and swallow.

'Don't you need water?' she enquires, her brow furrows.

I shake my head.

'The quicker I'm out of here the better.'

'Fair play to you. We're having a nightmare shift as well – we can hardly keep up thanks to the drink and drugs casualties.'

'Why do we do it?' I ask, knowing full well that all public-sector workers utter and mutter the same phrase but none of us would have it any other way.

'Your guess is as good as mine. See you now,' she laughs, adding, 'I believe an officer is waiting in reception to taxi you back.'

She swishes the cubicle curtain aside to reveal an A&E ward filled with the carnage of drunken revelry.

'Thank you and Merry Christmas,' I say, leaving the cubicle.

'Ho, ho, ho and all that!' she laughs, emptying the soiled swabs into a medical bin.

*

On returning to the reception area I find PC Gareth Wade waiting; I ready myself for his reaction.

'How funny is that?' he laughs, pointing at my face. 'Wadding *and* strapping, wait till the lads back at the station see you.'

'I'm predicting two cracking black eyes and a throbbing headache by the morning.'

'A traditional start to a good Christmas then!' crows my compassionate driver, digging his keys from his pocket.

'It shouldn't be when you've worked all night!'

The station banter had gone easy on me in recent months due to the break-up with Veronica but this, *this* was going to ignite the jibes.

The fresh morning air stung as we made our way across the snow-covered car park. There were several hours to go before a new dawn would illuminate the dark horizon.

'Merry Christmas, Joel!' laughs Gareth, unlocking the car. 'I should have been home hours ago.'

I settle into the passenger seat of his patrol car.

'You too. I appreciate you driving me, Wadey. Though it's cost you time with the family.'

Gareth shakes his head and proceeds to explain his plans for the day ahead centred around his wife, children and home.

'And yours?'

'I was supposed to be on duty tonight, but with this... I'm sure Sarge will send me home. So I'll probably gatecrash at my parents' and join the family gathering.'

Truth was, I wasn't too sure. I wasn't that keen this year.

Mum was doing the whole traditional get-together feast but I'd chosen to work. I didn't want it to be a Christmas of moping around or reflecting on last Christmas spent with Veronica.

Rolling on the floor with my two nephews would be fun until it ended in tears, but being scrutinised by Dana, my older sister, wasn't what I needed. Though Dana's interrogation may prove more fun than last Christmas, which was spent drinking amongst a huddle of strangers in the kitchen of a poncey stockbroker from Chippenham. My mind rewinds to a wasted day pretending to enjoy myself whilst engaging with folk who couldn't even remember my name – all in the name of relationships and compromise.

'You'll love them, they're *our* kind of people,' Veronica had said. Whatever 'our kind of people' *actually* were still baffles me. What Veronica had failed to mention was they were more her dream people, who she'd wanted me to morph into – forgetting to mention we'd be history if I didn't comply. I didn't, which explains the last four months. Personally, I couldn't see how they were *her* people, with their six-figure salaries, penthouse living and exotic au pairs. But that was Veronica all over: big ideas, no substance and wild claims, even at Christmas.

The passing streets are empty of life, the snow has settled and the early morning sky threatens more is to follow.

I can't remember the last white Christmas – every year seems sunny or wet now that the seasons have gone awry. Unlike that September day when Scotty had gained entry into my flat.

'We're finished,' I'd crooned to Scotty after three days of hibernation and whisky drinking.

'Sorry to say it, Joel, but I saw it coming... Veronica likes the cougar label and the associated attention but...' he'd snatched the whisky bottle from the coffee table, '...you've outlived your toy-boy thrill.'

'Oi!' I'd grabbed the half-empty bottle from his clutches and sloppily poured yet another drink. 'Nonsense!'

'That's your last, Joel. You've had enough.' Scotty wrestled the bottle from my clutches and took it into the kitchen. I heard the whisky glug down the sink and a crash as the bottle was slung into the recycling.

Veronica, wow! How quickly had those two years passed? She never promised a settled future of marriage and nappies, and at forty-five she was pretty much past the baby phase. One minute I was being given the come-on, next we were buying the flat together, two good years and now, four months down the line, I was yet to fill all the gaps where her absent possessions had created carpet dimples in the shagpile.

Gareth pulls up to the station gate, waiting for the sensors to react and drift open.

'Here goes, piss-takery galore,' I laugh, silently dreading the ambush of curt remarks.

'Pound to a penny Big Tony has a field day, that man's a laugh a minute,' adds Gareth, pulling through the gates and parking alongside the other patrol cars.

'He's probably mocked up my mugshot and glued it around the men's locker room,' I laugh.

'Or posted it on a down-and-dirty dating website with a false profile,' bellows Gareth, as we enter the station's back door.

'Oi, less of that, thanks.'

3

Flora

Above the doorway of The Peacock public house, the aged painting, in cobalt and emerald, swings back and forth. The leaded windows and Tudor fascia are confirmed as authentic in daylight.

I gingerly push the frosted-glass door as the church clock strikes eleven.

Surely it wouldn't be open at this time on Christmas Day?

A door chime announces my entrance. The door swings freely, revealing a welcoming sight of aged wooden beams, soft amber lighting and a real fire in the grate. Thick garlands of holly and gold baubles decorate a large lopsided Christmas tree standing beside the jukebox.

'Come in, lovey, Merry Christmas to ya,' beckons the plump woman lifting the hinged bar top and scurrying through the gap. 'They phoned to say you were on your way.'

I must look a right sight coming in from the snow, with my tartan blanket slung over my party frock, strappy heels and a silver clutch bag.

'Merry Christmas to you too. I'm after a room for a few nights,' I explain, as her chubby hand touches my forearm and guides me through the empty bar towards a back staircase positioned at the near end of the bar.

'They mentioned that too,' she laughs. 'I'm Annie by the way... and you're Flora?'

I smile and breathe. I like her motherly manner; her dyed mahogany hair reminds me of a friendly dinner lady from primary school.

'I understand your car is parked opposite the church?'

'The police mentioned *so* much in one call,' I murmur.

'The locals, even the police, don't hold back around these parts, lovey. It's free parking, so you won't get clamped. The room's thirty pounds a night which includes your breakfast... I don't charge much as we haven't the facilities of a posh hotel, but it's clean and comfy. Anything you need, just ask.'

Within minutes I am guided up the staircase and settled into room five, a decent-sized double with painted woodchip, Artex swirls covering the ceiling and a tufted bedspread. I push the aged voile aside and peer through the window overlooking the cobbled square, the church and St Bede's Mews.

Who'd have thought I'd injure a copper just across the way? Similarly, who'd have thought of leaving a newborn a few extra steps further along?

'Have a quick catlick and there'll be a fresh brew waiting for you downstairs... I hear police tea only just fits the bill as wet and warm, but hey, so does bathwater,' laughs Annie, placing my room key on the dresser and closing the door.

What the hell have I done? This time yesterday I'd have predicted a hangover for this time today, but instead I've got myself a police record, a mugshot, and crossed a night in a police cell off my bucket list.

'Flora, you naughty girl,' I mutter, flopping onto the bed.

It's a good job the injured copper confirmed we clashed heads by accident; that and my Baby Bede status, otherwise they'd have pressed charges for assault. I didn't much fancy a court appearance on Boxing Day.

I need to contact Lisa and Steph. With my parents away

enjoying themselves, they needn't be told, it would only ruin their cruise.

I grab my mobile from my clutch bag; seven missed calls and numerous text messages from the girls. I don't want to explain, but now I've decided to stay for a few days I'd best let them know. My fingers dance on the keypad, sending a brief text.

> Merry Christmas! I'm fine and dandy. Taking a few days away as a mini-break in a cute B&B. Love F x

I quickly press send as a wave of guilt flows from my innards.

My text to Mum and Dad needs careful consideration – how do I explain what I've done without worrying them silly? That text can wait. It's not that I'm keeping secrets from them, but they don't need to know, *just* yet. They won't truly understand, will they? It's my issue... although it's lingered deep within for years.

So, I might as well take advantage of my no job, no bloke and no home status and have a scout around while I'm here. I'd just left school the last time I had this low level of responsibility in life.

I look around room five: neat, tidy and spacious. Though at thirty pounds a night, can I afford to stay?

'Not bad for a place at the inn,' I chuckle. I probably won't be smiling when my bank account enters the red or when my credit card hits the maximum.

I collect my mobile, knowing their responses will be instant – it'll give me something to fill the time if I begin to feel awkward seated alone in the pub. I could even text my parents *if* a decent explanation comes to mind.

After a quick once-over in the mirror, I wipe a wet finger around my gums and tame my auburn hair with a quick ruffle; despite a desperate need for a change of clothes, I'm ready for a brew.

I bounce down the staircase, to find a tray of tea paraphernalia awaiting my arrival on the bar and Annie stacking the shelves with clean glasses from a wire rack.

'Hi.'

'Hi, lovey, help yourself,' she points to the tea tray, 'though mind the teapots, they dribble somewhat, so don't burn yourself. I won't join you – I need to restock before midday.'

I clamber onto the nearest bar stool and pour my tea amidst a backdrop of tinkering noises.

'Have you lived here long?' I ask, stirring my cup, looking over the bar at her busy frame.

'I was born and bred in this here pub,' she says, looking round as she speaks and standing up to grab a tea towel. 'I learnt to pull a pint before I could see over this countertop.'

'You know everyone who lives here then?'

She smiles and nods, wiping down the wooden bar a short distance from my tea tray.

'Every man and their dog...' Annie stops working and faces me.

'You already know why I'm here, don't you?'

'I told you, the locals don't hold back. You're the babe that was found over there...' she nods in the direction of the door, but I know she means St Bede's Mews. 'You'll see how nosey the villagers are come midday!'

'Surely not,' I scoff. 'It's only just gone half eleven, how could anyone know I'm even here?'

'Mark my words, I'm in for a busy lunchtime, Christmas Day or not,' she chuckles and continues to work. 'Is that why you've come back?'

'It was a spur of the moment thing,' I say, between sips.

'A moment of madness, hey?'

'*Maybe*.'

'Don't worry, I see plenty of those working in here,' she sweeps her hand over the empty bar. 'You'll be surprised what takes our fancy in an instant only to be regretted hours later.'

I sip my tea, watching Annie polish each pint lever and lay out the towelling beer mats at intervals along its length.

My phone vibrates, indicating a text.

I instantly snatch it open and view Julian's name.

Merry xmas. I'm so sorry. Need you x

Knobhead.

I delete his message and close the phone. I have no choice. If I don't, I'll probably reread it a million times and allow his sorry-ass apology to dissolve my armour.

That git can wallow; this time I'll call the shots.

'So, you're an only child, then?' asks Annie, busily straightening glasses.

'Yep, I think they'd have liked to adopt more but money was tight... and you know.'

'Hmmm,' mutters Annie, adding, 'yeah, we thought of adoption once but... *didn't.*'

I watch as her busy hands work quickly and her voice fades.

A silence lulls as I stare around the bar taking in the large stained glass window depicting another proud peacock, the stone fireplace, flashing fruit machines, plush upholstery, a silent jukebox and a swathe of Christmas decorations. Behind the bar the optics twinkle and shine amidst the large mirrors and wooden shelving, promotional posters offering 'mulled wine at £3.50 a glass' and virtual 'Dog racing – families welcome!' dominate the far wall.

'I can do you a turkey dinner for later, if you want,' says Annie. 'You can join me and our Mick through the back, or eat it in your room, if you prefer.'

'Thank you... I'd like that... some company would be good.'

What a bizarre day this was turning out to be – alone, away from home and reliant upon strangers.

I pour another cup of tea and stir.

'Anyway...' calls Annie, adding coal to the open fire, '... are they dropping the assault charges?'

4

Joel

'Hey, hey! Joel my son, how's it hanging?' calls Scotty, as I enter the police station. 'What a pair of beauties!'

'Knock it off, Scotty... they're not the first black eyes I've had and they won't be the last.'

I'd been home, slept, washed and changed before dropping by in my civvies. Despite my injuries, I couldn't lock myself away in the flat. People will stop staring soon enough.

A whistle lifts from Kylie, filling in paperwork at a nearby desk. I nod and acknowledge her appreciation of my darkening panda eyes.

'I'm doing an extra shift, so what's your excuse?' says Scotty. 'I thought you were heading to the Kennedy family feast?'

'I am later, just thought I'd drop by and see...'

'And have we got news for you,' jibes Scotty, stretching his legs by resting his feet on the nearest desk top. 'Guess who she is?'

'Seriously, you're playing games now?'

Scotty winks at Kylie.

'Don't squeal, make him guess, there'll be a pint resting on this one for sure.'

'Who?'

'Bloody guess, don't wreck my fun, you arse,' jokes Scotty, his head nodding in self-satisfaction.

'What's the point? It's obvious I'll never win... the pint is yours, I give in.'

'You... my son, got nutted by Baby Bede.'

His words didn't register at first. I look from Scotty to Kylie and back again before the penny drops.

'Are you joking?' I say, instantly remembering the folded newspaper buttoned inside my uniform breast pocket which hangs downstairs in the locker room.

His gloating look told me he wasn't.

'Does Sarge know?'

'Of course, I told him myself as soon as she blurted it out to us in the interview.'

'Why was she interviewing?' I say, pointing to Kylie.

'Hey!' shouts Kylie, throwing a pencil at me.

'Duh, because my duty partner got rushed to hospital as he couldn't handle a lone bird on Christmas Eve!'

'Is that the story you've put about?' I ask, looking to Kylie for confirmation of what the other guys had been fed. '*Seriously?*'

Scotty nods, enjoying his new-found status as hero.

'He put it across the police radio the minute Wadey walked you out the rear doors towards casualty,' grins Kylie. 'Though Big Tony's left a surprise in your locker.'

'*Really?*'

'The inflatable rubber doll left over from Reidy's stag do,' says Scotty.

'Be careful, she's a lone female,' giggles Kylie. 'She might accidently nut you as the locker opens.'

'Are you joking?'

'Nope,' laughs Scotty.

'I take it you helped?' I ask.

'Of course... I had to get my own back after you leaked it

round the station that I'd knobbed...' Scotty spins round to view Kylie's interested mush before stalling. 'Well... you know who?'

'All's fair in love and war, Scotty boy,' I retort.

Kylie's blank expression drifts between the two of us, trying to figure out the gaps in the conversation.

'Anyway, back to it. What are you up here for? Sarge has given you sick days so that face can recover, hasn't he?' asks Scotty, shuffling to stand and straightening his uniform.

'He has, but I thought I'd check in to see what was happening with her charge?'

'Ahhh, he dropped it... let her go after you confirmed it was a pure accident.'

'Wrong!' chips in Kylie. 'Sarge *actually* said you'd mentioned something similar when you crawled in with your nose splattered all over your face.'

'Thanks for that, I always want the *precise* details,' I add. 'So, she's gone?'

Scotty grimaces and nods.

'Don't look like that, Scotty. It *was* an accident, just bad timing...'

'All the same, mate, she assaulted an officer of the law... if we let them off it sends the wrong message out there – it's not acceptable.'

'It's not acceptable, but she didn't attack me on purpose, did she?'

'Ahhh see, from where I sat... I'd have said...'

'Bullshit, Scotty... for starters you couldn't hear what was said sitting in the patrol car. I'm glad he hasn't charged her... so where...?'

'Where she's gone?' Scotty hooks his right arm over my shoulders. 'I knew you'd ask. I phoned Annie at The Peacock... Baby Bede is staying put for a few days.'

'How much did you say?' I unfurl myself from his buddy grip.

'Not a lot.'

'But enough to let the locals know the news?'

'Annie won't say… she's as sound as a pound.'

'I know, but who else?'

'What?'

'Who else have you told?'

'Joel!'

'Scotty!'

'Don't you trust me?' Scotty's voice has dissolved into a whine.

'I've worked with you long enough to know you'd be bursting to share… so, who else?'

'Old Nancy might have been cleaning the office while I was on the phone.'

'Jesus, Scotty… nothing's secret with Old Nancy about – the whole village will know by now!' A sweeter old dear you couldn't wish to meet but, boy, is she nosey.

'Arrr well, no doubt Flora, that's her proper name by the way, she'll be asking questions soon enough, so there's no harm done.'

'There will be if Sarge finds out. You'll be sounding very different when he strings you up by your nads.'

Kylie falls about laughing.

'Sod off you. I bet you a pint Old Nancy hasn't said a word.'

'Bet you a pint she quit the cleaning early and nipped home to do just that!'

5

Flora

The church clock strikes midday as the door chime sounds simultaneously. Annie stands behind the bar waiting to serve, her fleece sleeves pulled up. I'm seated in the alcove beside the roaring fire enjoying a large glass of Pinot Grigio, on the house. A middle-aged bloke enters, surveys the pub and gives a nod in my direction, before heading to the bar.

I'm grateful I'm not still wearing my dress of shame accessorised by my tartan blanket. Instead a pair of black leggings and tasteful off-the-shoulder top, thanks to Annie's quick emergency phone call to a friend, owner of the local boutique, who swiftly opened her shop, delivering several changes of underwear and two acceptable outfits befitting a size 12 figure – on the tab for a few days until I can nip around and pay by credit card.

'Merry Christmas, Gene. The usual?' asks Annie, as he saunters to the bar, resting his right foot on the brass footrest like a cowboy.

'Ay, Merry Christmas, Annie – is our Mick about?' he asks, his greying hair slicked back and in need of a decent trim.

'He'll be through in a minute, he's changing the gas on the fizzy drinks,' says Annie, steadily pouring a Guinness.

I'd briefly met Annie's husband earlier. A giant of a man who'd wandered through from their living quarters, politely said a hello and disappeared into the cellar to organise the barrels. A tidier and cleaner version of his twin brother, but that was probably down to Annie's nagging skills.

'He's not out shooting clay pigeons, is he?'

'Phew, not likely, I've enough to do here to keep him busy...'

'Go on, woman, he's bloody useless with his dodgy back. He'll only get under your feet,' laughs Gene.

'He does, but he's not shooting on Christmas Day. This place is going to be rammed in no time – it'll be all hands on deck.'

The door swings wide and the chime sounds as two younger guys enter and head for the flashing fruit machine at the far end of the bar. Annie gives them a brief nod as she tenders the cash for the Guinness, and calls, 'Usual?' Both guys nod before continuing their conversation, the stouter one pumping a handful of cash into the machine. Neither youth looks in my direction.

I sip my wine, taking in the view.

It's a different world. Annie knows exactly what the regulars want the second they enter the pub; she doesn't even tell them the price, they simply hand over the money as the drink is delivered. I've never known how much a round of drinks will cost, let alone have 'a usual' known by the bar staff. I rarely enter pubs like this, pubs which Steph fondly calls 'spit and sawdust', though there's not a woodchip in sight. Is this the essence of the North/South divide? Or is life at a slower, more accessible pace, where neighbour knows neighbour and the landlady knows your order? I can't imagine walking into the Pink Coconut or the trendy One Plus wine bar to be served without asking for a specific drink. *Or* not spending ten minutes eyeing rows of slinky optics before knowing my choice, but it looks very appealing.

I look up, meeting the steely gaze of the leaner and smarter dressed of the fruit machine duo; his brown eyes don't flinch or waver as he gives me the once-over.

I'm suddenly aware of the mistletoe hanging above the bar.

As Fruit-machine guy completes his roving-eye routine, he gives a quick smile before turning his attention to his machine-playing buddy.

I avert my eyes and catch a quick wink from Annie as she carries their drinks the length of the bar, returning with the cash.

'Any food on today, Annie?' The stouter of the two youths asks as Annie delivers his change.

'Not really, it's Christmas Day. Why? What is it you're wanting?'

'A couple of ham cobs?'

'That's easy. I can rustle that up for you, two or four?'

I watch as the brief exchange conjures up an order for four cobs at a fair price.

'Flora?'

Hearing my name makes me jump.

'Could you eat a couple of ham cobs?' asks Annie, all three men turn and stare in my direction. I can feel myself blushing; my voice stalls under the spotlight. 'No worries, chick – I'll butter you a couple and see what you fancy.'

'Thank you,' is all I manage under the stare of the locals.

Cob? Does she mean a batch?

'You thinking of staying around here?' calls Gene, supping his pint and carefully returning it to the countertop, without looking up or at me.

'Me?' I point to my own chest, as if there's a row of us.

Gene fails to turn and face me.

'Yeah, he means you,' chuckles the leaner of the youths at the fruit machine.

'I don't really know... I haven't decided yet.'

He picks up his Guinness and sips.

'Don't mind him, he's harmless,' laughs the leaner guy, who strides across the floor, his hand outstretched. 'I'm Donnie, and this is Denny. That old git is Gene, Annie's brother-in-law – just say the word and she'll whip them into the middle of next week.'

'Thank you, Donnie. I'm...'

'Flora, yeah I heard,' he looks on apologetically.

I giggle and point towards the bar as Annie reappears.

'Oh no, not Annie... I met Old Nancy on her way home... she mentioned you were here.'

'Old Nancy?'

'Yeah, she cleans the cop shop.'

'That's quick.'

'That's how it is around here... news travels.'

'Be away with you, Donnie Dawson, the girl doesn't need no fussing from you,' Annie interrupts, putting a large plate down at my elbow. 'Here, lovey, two ham cobs, take it or leave it. Here's yours, Donnie, go share with Denny...' she thrusts a second plate towards Donnie who returns to his pitch beside the fruit machine. 'Shout if the locals bother you, sweet. I'll have a word with them, now eat up.'

I thank her and tuck in. Annie returns to her bar as a stream of customers pile through the door. I hadn't realised how many until I wipe my mouth having consumed both ham batches in a flash. I look up to be greeted by a series of nods and smiles from a hefty crowd filling The Peacock.

My worst nightmare is being the centre of attention. I've never been one to show off – I used to blush when asked to blow out the birthday cake candles at my childhood parties.

The majority of the customers are men, with a few females amidst the pint pots. Some stare openly, while others sneakily glance while I sip my wine and they slurp their pints.

It reminds me of last summer when I'd attended a wedding

as a plus-one favour for Lisa's brother – other family guests had stared, trying to suss out if I was a stand-in plus-one or his actual girlfriend. This felt similar; everyone in the bar knew my name and my story.

An idea hits me like a thunderbolt: someone in this bar could be a blood relation. I have *never* had a blood relation before.

With a renewed interest, I scour the females' features. Does anyone have my chin? My nose? My hair colour? Nothing, not a single woman present looks like me.

'You coping OK?' asks Annie, bringing over a fresh glass of wine and removing my empty plate. 'Take no notice. They're a warm crowd. They'll stare for a while and some might pluck up the courage to talk to you but most will disappear to discuss you elsewhere.'

'*Really*?'

'You should be flattered.'

'Thanks for the batches... cobs, can you add it to my bill?'

Annie smiles.

'On the house, it's the least we can do. Anyway, if this crowd continues, I may need you behind the bar serving pints, so you'll earn your crust that way.'

She scurries back to her domain and begins pulling pints. I watch her easy manner, her infectious smile – a woman comfortable in her own skin, a woman that knows her roots.

I could be like that one day, if I find some answers.

Behind my head, through the top section of unfrosted window, the snow has started to fall again in a heavy flurry.

I hope it settles, thick and fast, it'll give me a decent excuse for not returning to Bushey to house-sit. Yes, the houseplants may die, but what's a few poinsettias compared to knowing the truth about my birth mother?

The alcove feels comforting, its upholstered seating deep and wide enough for a gal to nestle in the corner, warm herself by the open fire and watch the natives sup their drinks. Sitting here, amongst the ivy garlands and twinkling lights, feels right. Strange. Of all the Christmas Days I can remember, and many have involved having my head down a toilet, this is by far the strangest. I'm a stranger amongst strangers, and yet, I'm not.

I look around at the warmth and conviviality surrounding my alcove... it has the potential to be one of my most enjoyable!

Joel

I stand back from the frosted door of The Peacock, allowing a small group of youths to exit onto The Square.

'You need to learn how to duck, mate,' jibes one lanky strip of wind, as he passes me. I laugh along in good spirit.

As soon as the doorway is clear I enter the pub, which is buzzing for a lunchtime, to a second round of wisecrack comments.

'Yeah, yeah, I've heard them all before,' I laugh, sidestepping through the crowd towards the bar.

'Merry Christmas,' says Annie, a gentle smile blooming as she eyes my swollen face and surgical strapping.

'Pint please.' I point to my usual tap.

I casually nod to a few regulars, acquaintances from both sides of my life: personal and career. The shifty ones don't like the local officers coming in whilst off duty and the older generation feel safe keeping in with us boys in blue. A tricky balancing act between private and public roles, so far, I'm managing to succeed.

I hand over my money as Annie places the pint on the bar.

'You'll find your sparring partner by the fire,' whispers Annie, nodding towards the far side. 'Looks like she did a decent job.'

I attempt to act surprised at learning she's here and turn as the crowd shifts and separates, providing a quick glimpse of the young woman seated in the alcove.

'I'll warn you now – you can take round two outside, you understand?' she chuckles.

'There'll be no rematch, Annie.'

I collect my change and make my way to the fireplace.

She looks out of place; wine glass in hand, auburn curls flowing over her shoulders and an anxious expression while watching the crowd swarm and chatter.

I'm mindful that I'm probably the last person she wants to see. If I'd accidently nutted a copper in the early hours of this morning, the last thing I'd want is to be faced with my handiwork.

Flora is looking the other way as I approach.

She looks different from last night; gone is the red dress in exchange for a more casual look, though it's not surprising given that my vision had blurred within minutes of speaking to her.

'Hello... can I join you?'

She jumps as I speak, her green eyes widen and a hand flies to her mouth on recognition. It is definitely the right woman.

'Oh. My. God. I am so very sorry!'

'Apparently, it looks worse from your side than it does mine,' I laugh, pulling up a stool and settling myself at her table.

'How shocking is that?' she peers from behind her hands.

'And better still, I believe you aren't being charged,' I laugh heartily, knowing the crowd are pretending not to watch us.

'*Apparently*, though I am *so* sorry... you mentioned alcohol and I wanted to prove that I hadn't touched a drop and then I realised I'd dropped something and... bang... we both moved and I... oh, what a mess I've made of your face.'

'Nose *actually*... but still,' the sentence dies as her eyes meet mine.

What makes green eyes so captivating and beautiful? Hazel brown are deep and smouldering, bright blue so entrancing, but green, huh.

'I'm Joel by the way, in case you were wondering who you'd damaged, and I hear that you are Flora.'

'News travels mighty fast around these parts,' she giggles, her cheeks lifting high, encasing her eyes.

'You could say that.' I lean forward across the table and whisper, 'Every person in this bar knows the details and probably knew before me that you weren't being charged with assault.'

Flora shakes her head, causing her locks to dance around her chin.

'In which case, they won't be shy in coming forward as regards details to solve the mystery of my birth, will they?'

I grimace.

Introduction over. Boy, that was a swift transgression onto business.

'*That* might be an issue.'

'*Really?*'

I nod slowly, supping my pint, before reaching into my inside pocket to retrieve her folded clipping.

'I believe this is *yours*.' I pass her the yellowed piece of newspaper retrieved from my uniform pocket, her eyes widen.

'Oh my God... I thought I'd lost it forever. Thank you so much.'

She carefully unfurls it, before reaching for her handbag and purse. The zipper action locks the clipping away from prying eyes.

Does she even suspect that I've read every word, several times over? I could recite it, if needs be. The newborn was found wrapped in a beige bath sheet on the steps of Doctor Fowler's home in St Bede's Mews by Darren Taylor, aged fifteen, whilst delivering the morning papers. 'I was shocked, really stunned, to find a baby on the doorstep of the middle house,' he beamed. Darren's cries for help were quickly answered by the doctor and his young wife, who contacted the police and local ambulance service. The baby girl had been named Angela by nursing staff at St Bede's hospital. Warwickshire police were eager to trace the mother as she may require medical assistance.

'Everyone knows everyone in this village, there's nothing they don't remember about each other, it's tight-knit, and yet, in all the time I've been here, I've never heard anyone suggest a name regarding Baby Bede, not one.'

'But someone must know... I didn't just appear. I wasn't delivered by a stork, you know.'

'True, but it won't be as easy as you think... they're a proud lot around these parts. Traditional too in many respects, so you digging up the past might not go down too well... so a word of caution from an outsider...'

'You're not local?'

'Local in that I live nearby, but I'll never be local... a lifetime won't make me a local as I wasn't born here.'

'I see,' she slowly looks around the pub. 'Which means I qualify.'

'Ackkk!' I pull a face and reach for my pint.

'I was definitely born *here*. It's the only detail I'm certain of. Whether *they* want to admit it or not!'

I was about to give another polite warning as regards the locals when the pub door burst open, sending the door chime into an airborne tither. A mountain of a guy dashes in, I recognise him from around the village. I know exactly *who* he is.

'Annie, is she here?' his voice silences the crowd as he lurches through the bodies towards the bar and then ploughs back through the crowd to land beside our fireside table.

His ginger curls frizz, his piggy eyes are filled with excitement while his enormous belly overspills his faded jeans. His inane teenage grin had greeted me earlier as I read the newspaper clipping in the locker room: two eyes staring from walrus-fat cheeks, as he cradled a bundle wrapped in a fluffy blanket, not the beige towel I've heard of.

'Flora?'

Her eyes grow wide and her startled expression doesn't subside as he drops to his knees, grabbing her slender shoulders and bear-hugging her roughly to his barrel chest. Her pretty face peers over his shoulder watching the silenced crowd.

'I'm Darren Taylor, the newspaper boy who found you,' he releases her for a split second, views her paling face and bear hugs her for the second time. 'You don't know how good this feels.'

'Darren, excuse me... she might need some air,' I interrupt, as Flora resembles a rag doll within his giant clutches.

'Oh yeah, sorry... I never thought this day would come, and yet, here I am looking at the baby I found!'

Once released, Flora straightens her top, runs a hand casually through her hair and sits back to stare at the man-mountain before her.

'Can I get you a drink, Darren?' I ask, feeling that someone needs to take charge.

'A pint of Cattle Prod, please,' he gasps, as he continues to stare at Flora. 'Isn't she beautiful?'

I disappear to the bar and collect another round of drinks. I shouldn't really have another after the medication I've swallowed.

Annie can't contain her smirking.

'Cut it out, Annie, I think she's had enough excitement for one day... what's this guy like? A crazy hothead or will his excitement die down in time?'

'Darren's like an overexcited Labrador... believe me, *this* is his dream come true,' she laughs, pouring my drinks. 'He'll calm down in no time and if he doesn't I'll give his wife a call to come and collect him.'

*

44

'You've grown,' he splutters, once the initial buzz of seeing Flora wears off.

'Just a touch,' she laughs, as a blush colours her cheeks.

'Aren't you the local copper?' he asks, starring at my blackened eyes and taped nose. 'Looks nasty, that.'

I nod.

'Fair play *but* this is a private conversation. I've waited a long time to talk to *this* lady.' He turns from me and continues, 'Seeing you takes me straight back to eighty-six – I was only fifteen, you know.'

'I know. I have the newspaper cutting that shows you holding me.'

'I've got that too... my mam framed it and it now hangs on our lounge wall at home, they'd called you Angela back then... so that's what we've always called you.'

'The nurses named me – it's cute in some respects but hardly fits my nature.'

'We named our eldest daughter Angela... after you,' he adds, 'I refused to consider any other name.'

Flora quickly apologises for the unplanned name change.

I want to belly-laugh, as rude as it would appear, but the situation is surreal.

'I carry the clipping with me everywhere,' she says, trying to fill the growing silence. 'I thought I'd lost it the other night, but Joel has kindly returned it to me. That's probably the longest I have been without it.'

'My wife keeps asking when I'm going to take down my framed clipping and I kept telling her "never", but this is amazing... seeing you... hearing you speak... it feels like I'm dreaming.'

I feel like a gooseberry. I sip my pint simply to give myself something to do. She doesn't look comfortable chatting to this guy, so I can't leave her.

'Would you like a new photo of the two of you, an updated version?' I ask, pleased with my initiative.

Darren's face beams at my suggestion. Within seconds, after a flurry of activity and repositioning of bodies and drinks, I produce my mobile phone. Darren puts a large consuming arm round her slender shoulders, squeezing her tightly, while I snap the new improved version: Flora and Darren.

Even I wish he'd had a shave this morning.

'My wife won't believe it when I show her, we'll need another photo frame for the lounge, that's for sure,' he announces, as we huddle and peer at the tiny screen.

'Scribble down your email address or mobile number and I'll send it to you,' I instruct, passing Darren a cardboard beer mat on which to write his details. 'Maybe your wife will prefer this version framed on the chimney breast.' Your arms tightly wrapped around the shoulders of an attractive younger woman, a true beauty. Or maybe not, depending whether she's the jealous sort.

'Darren, tell me what you remember?' asks Flora, sipping her wine.

'I remember it was foggy, so thick I could hardly see where I was going on my BMX bike, I'd stuck plastic cards into the wheel spokes so they'd make a cool clicking noise as I rode. It was all the rage back then.'

Flora smiles politely as he speaks.

'Anyway, I collected my papers from the newsagents, it's still there on the high street if you want to visit, then I started my deliveries. St Bede's Mews was fairly near the beginning of my route; I used to pedal along the high street, turn into The Square and up towards the church, deliver to the Mews before ducking through the archway, heading towards the big housing estate. *Well*, that morning I never got any further than the Mews... the paper shop had loads of complaints that day...' he pauses to sip his pint and looks at the silent crowd. 'Look... the whole damned pub is listening to my story, *again*.'

'Speak up, Darren,' calls Annie. 'We can't quite hear at the bar over the noise of the fruit machine.'

I cringe as Darren gives a glowing smile to the appreciative audience, Flora gives an embarrassed nod.

'When did everyone tune in?' Flora asks me, her neck and throat begin to redden.

'The minute you were arrested for accidently socking me one,' I laugh. 'But still, carry on, Darren.'

'Anyway, I always dropped my BMX bike on the kerb by the phone box, delivered to the first house – they always had the *Mirror*, the *Telegraph* went to the next house, but Doctor Fowler *always* had the *Guardian*. I did my usual three folds as I walked the length of the path but as soon as I reached the steps... there you were... wrapped in a towel.'

'And?' asks Flora, leaning forward, her hand trying to hide the glow creeping up her throat.

'I didn't know what to do. At first, I thought it was a joke... I knew the doctor and his wife didn't have any children so it wasn't a doll left out after playing the night before. Us kids used to leave our bikes, scooters and prams outside back then, when parents called us in for the night. It was nothing to see three or four bikes left out on a lawn – sometimes they weren't even yours but your friends from up the street, dropped down before running in. Kids couldn't do that nowadays, could they?'

The cheeky sod stares at me after his last remark, as if policing is solely my responsibility.

'I honestly didn't know what to do... I bent down, took my heavy delivery bag off my shoulders and touched your waving hand... to see if you were real and... yep, you were.'

As he speaks I can see that he's reliving that tiny arm free from the towelling waving in the morning mist, surrounded by grey concrete and those two ugly stone lions which guard Dr Fowler's front door.

A lump forms in my throat. I cough before sipping my pint.

'You were real!'

'Was I crying?'

'Oh no, just lying there totally silent – amazing, as you must have been cold.'

'Was there a note?' I ask instantly. That's more like it – never off duty.

'I didn't think of looking for one, I didn't know this sort of thing could happen. It was just you and the wrapped towel, nothing else.'

Flora hangs on his every word. Her green eyes dance around his unshaven features absorbing every detail.

'Sorry if you were told otherwise, but there wasn't a letter,' he adds.

'No, I only know what was written in the article, anything else is a bonus for me,' she assures him.

He continues to explain how he rang the doorbell, the surprise of Mrs Fowler and shock of Dr Fowler and their panic at calling an ambulance. Within no time their doorstep was flooded by police officers and newspaper reporters.

'It was front-page news, wasn't it?' she asks.

'For weeks...' he explains, 'but nothing came of it. Your mother never came forward, did she?'

I watch as Flora lowers her chin, a downcast look of rejection creeps into her posture.

'But hey, happy days could be just around the corner,' I add, trying to lift her spirit.

'Thanks, Joel, I appreciate the optimism,' says Flora, reaching forward and patting my forearm.

Shouldn't it be me reassuring her?

'What's the plan?' he asks, draining his pint in that lager-lout swallow-the-side-of-the-glass kind of manner.

Flora shrugs.

'Who knows. I rolled in last night on a whim, totally unprepared for this... and yet, this happens.' She looks round the sea of faces, some still riveted by the details, others losing interest and returning to their own chatter.

'May I suggest you sleep on it and think about what you want to do – hearing this from Darren might be enough for you... or it might not!' I say, standing to collect the three empty glasses. 'Either way, it's your choice. I think the locals will help you answer more questions if you choose to venture there, but whether you find the answer you want will be something else.'

'Thanks, I need to mull it over.'

'I'll leave my mobile number if you want... just call if you want to chat,' says Darren, abruptly standing and replacing his chair under the table. 'My wife's not going to believe this has happened. Boy, what a great start to Christmas!'

'You already know where to find me,' I laugh, taking the prompt to leave. 'The large building along the high street, panda cars parked in front.'

'Your phone number is easy to find too,' Flora laughs, her green eyes sparkle and dance.

Good girl, she can still laugh after everything she's been through, maybe this Christmas won't be as sombre after all.

6

Janet

'Flora, what do you mean you're not at home? You're supposed to be looking after the house while we're away.'

I listened in stunned silence as she explained.

'Surely, you're not staying there! There's no point, darling. Go home and when we're back from the cruise, we'll visit in a few weeks.'

'Honestly, Mum, I'm happy to stay on,' she'd said. 'What am I coming home to? A job? A partner? A house? Yes, there's Steph and Lisa but what else?' *Nothing, until we arrive back home.*

My stomach flipped.

I couldn't think of a single thing to say to convince her to travel back home. I know she was waiting for my weak attempt to talk her around; I would have, if I could have thought of one damned thing to say. Why had we chosen this week to book a cruise?

'If there's nothing else, Mum, I'll be going. Don't worry, I'm fine.'

I did the only thing I could: made arrangements to visit as soon as we arrived back in Bushey.

Thankfully she hasn't rejected our love and family just yet, but I've a nagging feeling that if a new mother comes on the scene this might be the last time I have my daughter before someone else claims her.

From the moment I saw her, I knew she'd be ours. She was tiny. Lying in the crib at the foster carer's house, dressed in a pink matinee coat with matching bonnet and booties.

They'd told us about her abandonment, of course they had. If anything, it made me love her more. To think, an innocent little baby could be left on a doorstep – who could do such a thing?

I couldn't.

I'd wanted to snatch her up and run. Instead, there were strict procedures and paperwork before she was declared ours. Our daughter. Even now, I can hardly believe it.

Whilst growing up, it never enters your head that adoption will be part of your life. From puberty, I always assumed I'd meet a man, fall in love, get married and have as many children as we wanted. The plan was spot on until the chapter about children.

I met David at seventeen. We met on the dance floor at Barbarella's, were married at twenty-one and made plans in the blink of an eye. We even had baby names, carefully selected and ready for the happy occasion. I had knitting needles, baby wool in pale pinks and blues, but sadly, not the patter of tiny feet.

At first I brushed it off as nothing, but as the months went by niggling doubts began to grow. It sounds crazy now, but we made such silly plans when we first got married. Like a school timetable laid out without complication. Married in January, we'd be pregnant by June, baby the following March, a second by the following August followed by a short gap of a year or so and then the third and final child the following April. Seriously, our plans were that specific month by month – we were so naive.

Our friends got married after us and yet they were having christenings within no time – honeymoon babies left, right and centre. After a couple more years of disappointment, I wouldn't have given a monkey's what month, what day or what gender – as long as I had a baby in my arms. *That's* when we turned to the adoption society.

They called her Angela.

David thought it fitting, but to me I needed, no *wanted*, to give her a fresh start from the one she'd had. I loved the name Flora – it represented everything she was: delicate, pretty and flower-like.

Flora was a dream. Such a good baby, she ate, drank and slept like clockwork, so different to my friends' babies who all seemed finicky and ratty. It was as if she was grateful so repaid us in the only way she could: pure enjoyment.

I'm biased, I know, but Flora was everything I'd ever dreamed of.

And *now*, I understand her search. From the day we told her the story of a baby on a doorstep her desire to know the truth began to grow. We knew this day would come, David's surprised it's taken this long. Maybe it's a fear of the unknown. We support her any way we can.

I've tried to prepare her for the worst, there must have been a serious issue or situation to force a woman to do such a thing.

I'll be honest, I wouldn't have come forward if it were me. I'd be too embarrassed to admit it. To think that friends, neighbours, maybe her husband and children would know the depth that she'd stooped to. Oh no, I couldn't show my face in public, but I couldn't have abandoned a baby in the first place. What kind of woman does that?

But then, who am I to judge?

I'm not jealous. I haven't got an issue with sharing Flora, if she finds out who her biological mother is and wants to build a solid relationship – great. We'll find a way to make it happen for both of them.

My concern will always be Flora's welfare and how she's

being treated. I'm not possessive or clingy... I never was. I've been lucky enough to share thirty years of her life, I wouldn't deny the *other* mother, it's the least we can do for the woman.

My only wish is that when Flora knows the truth it satisfies that urge; she can get on with her life... settle, be at peace with herself and do as she wishes rather than flitting from one thing to another. What will the future hold for my Flora? Happiness or hurt?

7

Joel

'I thought you were off to your mother's?' asks Scotty.

I scoot the office chair over to Scotty's desk, having dropped by for another visit after The Peacock.

'I am after this. I've left my car parked opposite the church, so ask patrol to keep an eye on it, will you?'

He smirks.

'Settled in has she?' he asks, looking up from the computer screen.

'Hmm, I think so... she seems nice, easy to talk to. The newspaper lad turned up... he actually said "you've grown!" as if.'

Scotty's fingers cease tapping the keyboard, his expression becomes serious and he stares.

'What?'

'Don't do it!'

'Do what?'

'What you're thinking... she's not one of us, in fact if anything she's trouble... I can feel it.'

'Not as much as I felt it,' I say, touching my swollen face.

'*Seriously*, Joel.'

'I don't know what you're talking about... all I said was she seems nice.'

'Precisely... phrases such as that get us lads into a whole heap of trouble.'

I shrug.

'What happened the last time you uttered such sentiment?'

I turn away.

'You hitched up with Veronica, that's what – so steer clear.'

I turn in the chair, pretending to examine the stapler from his desk drawer; Scotty's gaze remains fixed on my face.

Veronica. We'd been so good in the beginning. Yes, I was flattered – who wouldn't be? An attractive older woman showing interest in the likes of me. I thought all my birthdays had come at once: a mature relationship, decent conversations, travelling and, boy, the sex was amazing.

'Don't pretend the conversation is over... it's not and neither is the mess from... *her.*'

'Don't remind me, today of all days... it's supposed to be fresh beginnings and new starts and I look like this.' I point to my face again.

Scotty turns away and resumes his typing.

'Just be careful.' He gives me a concerned look from beneath his brow.

I replace the stapler on his desk and select the hole punch.

He's got a point; it wasn't as if I was in a position to consider getting to know anyone new, not when the previous woman was dragging her Kurt Geiger killer heels about resolving the last situation. I couldn't see what Veronica's problem was. She wanted out. We'd amicably agreed the finances and she had opted to be bought out of the property... why quibble and delay proceedings by not answering solicitor's letters?

'You know Uncle Scotty's right, so don't you go muddying the waters elsewhere... yeah?' adds Scotty. 'She'll only mess with your head.'

'Yeah,' I murmur, knowing he's looking out for me.

'Bloody hell, I called it right for once, woo hoo!' shouts

Scotty, whizzing about on his office chair. 'Put the date on the wall, Scotty Hamilton was right!'

'Just this once,' I mutter.

'Cheek... you're sat there looking like *that* and I'm the one being dissed? Man, you need a long hard look in the mirror... now make yourself useful and put the kettle on.'

This is why I love Scotty – in a bromance kind of way. He's fresh, funny and full of crap.

'Oh sorry.' I playfully elbow his temple as I stand up en route to the station kitchen.

Scotty's got a point. I have two black eyes, a busted nose, an ex that wants out but is hanging on for dear life... the last thing I need is another complication.

I enter the tiny kitchen and dance around Big Tony's bulging girth, an on-duty officer acting as tea-boy.

'I take it the other chap won?' he sniggers, admiring my injuries while spooning coffee into eight tea-stained mugs. 'Oh no, I remember now, the boys did say... it was a lone female! You're losing your touch, laddo!'

'*Really*? Hasn't anyone anything more interesting to talk about?'

'*Touchy*?' grins Big Tony, pouring boiling water into his mugs. 'If it's any consolation, we're only jealous – you received the only decent kiss on Christmas Eve, even if it was a Glaswegian one!'

I let him have his jibe, stir his coffees and then disappear to repeat our conversation in the top office.

*

I stroll back to the small office armed with two mugs slopping as I move.

'Big Tony's just said I'm losing my touch.'

'Did you give him the "your wife isn't complaining" line?' laughs Scotty, from behind his computer screen.

I shake my head at the schoolboy phrase, placing his coffee beside his keyboard, and resume my seat.

Scotty's face drops, his bottom lip protrudes forward.

'Seriously, I'm losing my touch, aren't I?' I mutter.

'With humour and snipes maybe, but given the last year... you've been under the weather.'

'Perhaps. Maybe this Christmas will be a chance to tidy the loose ends and start afresh.'

'Mmmm.'

'What?' Had I said something wrong? Why the sudden doleful expression? Shit! 'Sorry man, here's me moping while you and your dad come to terms with a Christmas without... sorry.'

Scotty shakes his head.

'Mum hated Christmas anyway... so it's not as though it was party-popper time in our house... but yeah, it gets dragged out into New Year too. The prospect of a year starting without her is pretty shite.'

Big Tony pokes his head through the office doorway.

'Hey Scotty-boy, what's it feel like to be the toughie of the partnership?' he asks, pointing at me.

'Ha, ha... and by the way, Tony, you reckon Joel's losing his touch... that isn't what I heard your wife gasping the other night! Bar-ba-boom!' Scotty punches his fists into the air.

So childish, so dangerous, yet so necessary when yanking Big Tony's chain.

'You cheeky little...'

I sip my coffee as Big Tony grabs Scotty in a headlock, and drops a few kidney punches in for good measure, with love from his missus.

8

Flora

The church clock striking woke me with a start – freezing cold, yet fully dressed on top of the tufted bedspread with a trail of dribble sliding down my right cheek.

It took a moment to figure out where I was.

I hadn't wanted to face the visiting in-laws downstairs in the pub; I'd spent all afternoon perched in the alcove while the locals politely smiled in my direction before daring to ask their questions. Thankfully Annie kept them at bay with her frosty looks and threats to send them home.

She invited me to share a Christmas dinner with her and Mick – which was kind of them. I helped her where I could by peeling sprouts and chopping parsnips but I was in the way most of the time. After closing the bar, Mick sat in their lounge watching a rerun of *The Wizard of Oz*.

At six o'clock the polite chatter began to wane.

'You're more than welcome to join us for the evening, we'll probably veg in front of the TV until Mick's family pop around for a drink later,' offered Annie, as we washed up the pots.

I chose to stay in my room instead; it had been a long day.

I'd felt guilty asking for a plate of cheese and biscuits and a couple of glasses of wine. If the truth were known, I needed peace and quiet. It wasn't as if *this* was a planned holiday, I'd simply upped sticks and dashed off, be it out of instinct or a morbid curiosity, but now I needed a plan.

'Sorry to cause such a fuss,' I'd said, when Annie arrived at room five laden with a tray.

'Nonsense, lovey, it's my pleasure, it's not as if I'm a busy mum running about after a couple of teenagers,' she replied, turning from the mirrored dresser, now my makeshift dining table. 'I brought you a bottle rather than two glasses, at least that way it survives my trudge up the stairs – I'd have knocked two glasses flying in the blink of an eye.'

I'd laughed. She'd laughed.

And then we'd stood in an uncomfortable 'what now?' moment. I'd filled the silence with another round of 'thank you's' for being so nice, for making my Christmas meal and for asking her friend to open up her local boutique. How the locals would have stared had I still been wearing last night's dress. Annie batted each comment aside like a Wimbledon pro on centre court.

I like her. I feel she likes me.

'You'll shout if there's anything else you need, won't you?' she'd said, promptly leaving me in peace to contemplate the events of the day.

Within minutes I had cleared my plate and began sheepishly answering my texts in a poor attempt to reassure my mother that I was still alive and not jumping from some ridiculously high bridge into a freezing river.

I'd repositioned the room's TV, enabling me to lie on the double bed, stare at the aged comedy and think, while supping my wine. My fingers instantly took comfort at plucking the tufted bedspread while downstairs the constant drone of muffled laughter suggested that Mick's family had arrived.

Somewhere within a radius of this pub was my biological mother. I found it hard to believe that this was the nearest I'd been to her since that October morning. Did she know I was

59

here? Had someone mentioned me to her whilst visiting family? What had been her reaction? Shock? Horror? Delight?

I presume the former, as Darren had been the only one to dash through the pub doors to embrace me. How amazing was that? Though how funny was him saying 'you've grown'?

Joel seemed the decent sort, and despite the busted nose, a tad good-looking for an officer of the law – though his duty partner wasn't bad either. Or was that fascination because he'd slapped cuffs on me and taken control of my freedom? Was the Stockholm effect purely for kidnappings? I shake my head and giggle.

I grab my mobile phone from the bed beside me: twelve thirty.

I have a text message from my parents:

Merry Christmas darling – wish you were here. Please stay safe. Call or text if you need us – we'll cut the cruise short and come straight home.

I reply with a row of kisses.

Bless her. Mum never fails to be a loving mum twenty-four hours a day.

Boy, it's quiet.

I suddenly become aware of the strange eeriness. I know Christmas Day is different, but do village pubs kick out early? Will it always be so quiet this time of night? On an ordinary night back home, the pub and club scene would still be buzzing. Many a night me and the girls hadn't left home much before midnight to head towards the action, this time of night the fun was starting and yet here, silence.

In seconds, I am pacing the floor.

I'm right to be doing this. I know I am. This might be my only chance to focus on me. No new man to distract my thoughts or time. No Julian to fawn over. This is my time to focus on me.

Lisa had her mad tattoo phase and crazy hair dye stage – we all accepted that. Steph had her gap year shag jolly round the globe – we all accepted her decision, after we'd plied her with an endless supply of condoms. *This* right here, right now, could be *my* phase. My I-want-the-truth-and-I-want-it-now phase – others will have to accept my decisions and be grateful for knowing where *they* came from.

I continue to walk in circles.

I need fresh air.

I scramble for my killer heels from party night, sensible replacements were not available in the local boutique and so I slip them onto my feet, before grabbing my room key.

My heels resound on the staircase as I fly down and emerge in a surprised fashion into the now low-lit, empty bar.

'Hi there, you OK?'

I'm startled to find Mick, Annie's husband, lying flat out on the floor behind the bar.

'Are *you* OK?' I ask, as I couldn't ignore his predicament.

'Don't mind me, my back's giving me jib... is there anything I can get you?'

'Nothing thanks. I wanted some fresh air,' I point toward the pub doors. 'Are they open or do I need a key?'

'Open, just push... will you be long?' he calls after me, as I head for the exit.

'Twenty minutes at the most,' I shout, as the door chime dances.

The Peacock's door swings closed behind me. The cold air hits me like a sledgehammer, I regret having left my blanket in my room.

The Square is silent, not a soul in sight, just me and an arrangement of orange neon lamplights illuminating a series of empty benches set round the community Christmas tree. The church spire punctures the inky black canopy glistening with diamonds.

I don't think. I simply walk towards the church. My ankles taking a battering upon the aged cobbles as my heels slip between the stones.

I'm not religious. I've never truly embraced the concept but likewise never consciously rejected the values taught at Sunday school. I suppose I cherry-pick the nice stories. I adore the Nativity scene each Christmas, repeat the 'Amen' in services and cheekily seek St Anthony's help when I've lost anything from car keys to a lottery ticket. I was christened. I have godparents. And given that I was once named after its angels, surely no one can complain if I seek solace inside. Right now, it's where I want to be. It might even be a place my mother once went.

I tiptoe along the pathway towards the arched doorway of St Bede's, beneath the glare of huge floodlights and silent angels.

My hand reaches for the large iron ring. Twist. Locked!

'For the love of God!' I spit. 'The only moment of my life when I've actively sought comfort inside a church and it's locked – thanks a bunch!' I traipse back along the pathway, disgruntled that even the church rejects me. Ironic, or what?

There's only one place to go.

I take a left turn as I step from God's path and head towards St Bede's Mews, the only other spot I can claim to know. The archway is before me, the ornate railings are highlighted by the lamplight and the pavement before the Mews has a huge pile of orange sand spread thickly to cover where a police officer was attacked.

The small row of houses replicates glossy images from *Homes and Gardens* magazine.

I tightly wrap my fingers around the wrought-iron gateposts and stare. The downstairs lights are doused but a homely glow exudes from the edges of bedroom curtains. I imagine the occupants snuggled up and warm issuing each other goodnights and blessing sweet dreams on anything that snores in a style similar to the Waltons' goodnight routine.

My phone vibrates in my handbag. After a rummage, I withdraw it to see one message from Julian.

Enough is enough – stop playing games and come back home. It's upsetting your mum!

I instantly delete it.

How would he know? Does he even know my parents are away on holiday? Who the hell does he think he is?

I return the mobile to my bag and focus on my own quest.

Why couldn't I have been born inside a house like this? Started life with a pink-painted nursery crammed with Disney characters? Instead I got a crappy bath towel and a bare arse.

My throat constricts as warm tears trickle down my cheeks.

Scott

'She's at it again,' I say, pointing out the obvious to Smiley Kylie, my duty partner in Joel's absence. 'I bet she's drunk.'

'*Apparently*, you said that last night and how wrong you were.'

'You listen to too much gossip at the cop shop.'

We continue to watch from the patrol car, parked alongside her Mini.

'Are you going, or shall I?' asks Kylie, as the figure leans against the railings and lingers outside the centre property.

'I'm not sure we need to do anything at the minute, she's hardly doing anything illegal, is she?' I mutter, as a feeling of déjà vu and role reversal sweeps over me.

'Is this what she did last night?'

'Pretty much, we watched her drive in, pull up, park on the double yellows and sit for ages in the driver's seat. We figured it looked dodgy given it was nearing midnight.'

'You can understand it though, can't you?'

'What, returning to the spot?'

We watch in silence; she remains statuesque at the railings.

'I remember being told about it as a kid... it was like a dirty secret that the older kids knew and no one else spoke about,' I recall.

'Until you realised that every man, woman and child in the village knew about Baby Bede's doorstep like the myths of the witch's woodland house and the headless highwayman haunting the dual carriageway,' utters Kylie, her gaze fixed on the lone female by the gatepost.

'True.'

'I remember asking my mum if I'd been found on a doorstep… I wanted proof that wasn't the norm for delivering babies. It took her an age to convince me that I didn't belong to the rich couple next door.'

'Did you really think that?'

'I needed serious reassurance.'

'Girls are weird!' I laugh, staring at Kylie's profile, imagining her pale blue eyes and freckled cheeks, readjusting my seating position to distance myself in case her weirdness is contagious. Funny how dubious I now am – earlier in the month at the staff Christmas party I hadn't been so wary. And afterwards back at hers I'd shown little resistance to any suggestions she had regarding handcuffs and nakedness.

'Seriously though, could you imagine leaving a baby on a doorstep?' Kylie stares at me, her eyes glisten. 'I can't drop a piece of litter without feeling guilty, yet a woman put her baby down and walked… she actually walked away.'

We both turn and stare at the lonesome figure.

'Whoever her birth mother is… she'll need to come up with some pretty good answers,' I say, adding. 'I think a giant can of worms is about to be upended.'

9

Flora

I woke late, which given my midnight stroll and emotional state, wasn't surprising. I dressed in my only other outfit, a combo of coloured jeans in a fetching red and an oversized granddad shirt, accessorised yet again by party heels.

I bounce down the staircase into the bar, finding Annie laying the bar tables with a selection of condiments ready for lunchtime.

'Morning, Annie,' I holler.

'Morning, lovey, did you sleep well?'

'Sound, did you?'

'Not great, our Mick's back is playing up again. He spent half the night groaning and moaning... he must have woken me up ten times,' she says, indicating I sit at the alcove table.

I offer to pull a few pints to help out, it's the least I can do.

'You can collect and load the glasswasher with the dirties once the punters start leaving, but don't get under my feet while I'm busy,' she laughs. 'Anyhow, what's it to be, cooked or continental? Tea or coffee?'

As soon as I order, Annie disappears; I help myself to fruit juice.

As I pour my juice, a feeling of familiarity sweeps over me. Haven't I always been here? Living in this village, in this pub, standing in this exact spot pouring juice into a glass tumbler, doing the same routine day in, day out, and yet, I only arrived yesterday.

It's only half eleven and already the bar has customers, mainly men in various stages of life: the lone drinkers enjoying their papers, the rowdy youths at the fruit machine and the husband pairings grateful for a quick half to escape the Boxing Day lunch preparation at home. Amongst the testosterone, there is only one female customer. She has tight frizzy hair, the kind of hair that can never be tamed, and is leaning beside Gene at the bar, dressed in a faded ruby top and jeans. I presume it's his wife.

Maybe it's never having had a brother, or simply that my dad never nipped to the pub unless accompanied by my mother, but the view seems fascinating. It feels surreal witnessing other people's downtime. Julian was the only guy I knew who insisted on having his drinking haunt and that was clearly off limits to me. We always drank in The Three Crowns on the high street. What was Julian doing right now? I glance at the clock. Sipping beer with his boys, as he frequently said. Or he could be rolling under the duvet with that slag from the chemist? Worse still, going out for a family Boxing Day lunch, of cold turkey and chips, to meet her parents. If that were true it would kill me.

I return to my alcove table and sip my juice.

Wow, I even have my own spot in the local pub!

I wonder if chemist girl has moved into the flat? Don't go there!

A tear comes to my eye.

What the hell is wrong with me? The emotional expectation of finding my answers? Or a deeper bond that comes from knowing *she's* here, somewhere nearby?

'There you go...' Annie breaks my train of thought by delivering a huge plate of eggs and bacon, accompanied by a round of hot buttered toast.

67

'How much do you think I eat?' I say, eyeing the portions. 'I'll be the size of a house staying here.'

'Start the day off right, that's what I say... do you mind if I join you?'

'Be my guest.' I could do with the company.

'Gene,' she shouts, dashing back to the kitchen. 'Shout if anyone needs serving.'

Gene gives her a nod, as the woman snuggles beneath his free arm.

Annie returns from the kitchen with her own humongous breakfast and seats herself in the alcove.

I'm liking her style, her motherly manner, her soothing ways. She's mumsy but not smothering – she's got the balance right, like Mum has.

'Any thoughts after yesterday?' she asks, cutting into her eggs.

'It's risky but I need answers to my questions... if I don't do it now I may never do it.'

Annie nods and chomps.

'Have you ever suspected anyone?' I ask gingerly, not wishing to pry but dying to know an insider's thoughts.

'Well, there's a question!' she smiles. 'It... sorry, I mean *you* were headline news around these parts, like never seen before... or since.'

I'm all ears; the smallest snippet of information could be the key to finding my birth mother.

'It was a Thursday or Friday... end of the week anyway... it was definitely a school day. The first thing we knew here in the pub was my dad shouting up the stairs telling my ma that an ambulance had arrived over at The Square. My ma was outside like a flash, she had to know everything... the locals nicknamed her News of the World Nell... they think I don't know, but hey, they weren't far wrong,' laughs Annie. 'The next thing, the police came knocking, asking if we'd seen or heard anything during the night?'

'You were how old?' I ask nonchalantly.

'I was fifteen, counting down my days at senior school...' Annie pauses, her fork and knife suspended – a wry smile spreading across her face. 'If you think for one minute that I'm your ma... you've got another thing coming... I'd have no more left that babe lying on a doorstep than fly in the air. I... I... I'd have fought hell and high water to keep a little 'un.'

I watch as her eyes gently glisten.

'Sorry, I wasn't suggesting... that was insensitive of me.'

'Don't apologise. I get it. Every female of childbearing age in eighty-six is potentially your ma.'

I nod.

'I get where you're coming from, lovey.'

'But without knowing the area... the families... the society... I haven't a clue where to start.'

'I'm no brainbox, but you need to start at the very beginning.'

'That's easy, me on a doorstep wrapped in a towel.'

'There's your starting point...' she points her knife across the table. 'You!'

'But how?'

Annie smiles, staring at the wall behind my head.

'I've got an idea but it'll take some organising... but I'm sure you'll be up for it.'

'What?' I ask, staring around behind me at the rustic brickwork of the alcove.

'Stop yapping, get those eggs down your neck and we'll make a start.'

'You've got a bar to run,' I say.

'I have, but, boy, can I multitask from behind that bar!' laughs Annie, adding, 'The question is, how are us girls going to ignite this neighbourhood and stir those memories?'

10

Veronica

My stomach flips as I number-punch the code into the entrance lock of the apartment block. My heels click-clack on the ceramic tiles, Italian handcrafted, may I add. I take the flight of stairs to the third-floor apartment as swiftly as I can, my hand tracing along the deep wooden banister.

It's hard to believe that I once lived here. Back then, I was so eager. I arranged a late-night viewing the same day that it came onto the market.

'Joel, the decoration is to die for and the bathroom – I can't begin to explain how amazing the design is.'

Joel hadn't time to change from his uniform but arrived straight from work – he'd looked strange wandering from room to room, as if seeking clues to a crime that hadn't yet been committed. Looking back, the true crime was the price we had paid for this poky two-bed property – financially *and* emotionally.

The apartment door key is clutched between my forefinger and thumb as I stand before the front door of apartment seven.

Wasn't number seven supposed to be lucky?

'Morning,' comes a sprightly voice from behind me.

I freeze, slowly turn around and view a young man dressed to impress leaving number six, the apartment opposite.

Breitling wristwatch and polished shoes. *Obviously*, a new resident at Acorn Ridge.

'Morning,' I reply as casually as my frantic heart rate will allow, hoping he's too busy or too late to chat. He smiles, strides to the top of the stairs and then darts down them two at a time, briefcase in hand, his blonde hair disappearing in no time.

I enter the apartment quickly and close the door firmly behind me.

That was a close call.

If the folks from number five had appeared they'd have definitely queried my actions – though given my rapid departure, I've questioned myself numerous times in recent months. Why shouldn't I visit? I still own this place.

The faint smell of Issey Miyake aftershave lingers in the cream-carpeted hallway.

I inhale deeply as I kick my shoes off; old habits die hard.

Was it really four months since those hairy-arsed removal men had bumped my belongings down the stairs? I'd felt awful that I'd left whilst he was on shift, but what was I supposed to do? Wait another two weeks for their next available slot? I explained that quite clearly in the 'Dear Joel' letter I left on the mantelpiece.

I enter the spacious lounge, with its deep wooden skirting boards and neutral tone decor. No Christmas decorations, not even a card from his parents. Obviously not celebrating here.

'It looks bare in here,' I mutter, viewing the expanse of cream carpet that was once filled with expensive furniture. It is tidy, much tidier than when I'd lived here. In fact, it looks like a show home ready for inspection.

'He's bought a bookcase!' I exclaim, zipping over to the new piece which dominates the far wall.

I finger the book spines neatly lined in size order – typical Joel-style.

Are these brand new or unpacked from his boxes of

belongings stashed in the spare room? He always said he liked literature. *And* poetry. He did show a flare for art whenever we visited museums.

I suppose he has time to kill now.

I instantly feel sorry for him.

Beneath the window sit his two acoustic guitars, both on black metal stands, their plectrums tucked beneath the strings.

These dust collectors weren't part of our lounge decor, instead he'd take himself off to the spare room for a guitar practice session.

Typical Joel, singular in nature and hobby.

I stare at the widescreen TV. I bet he's watching every football match that's on now I've gone. Lounging on the sofa, remote control in hand and shouting orders at the referee.

Stupid bleeding game, grown men kicking a bag of air around – where's the talent in that?

I can feel my irritation growing.

He's reverted straight back to his old ways: the single bloke with his music, his books and his Monday night football. Didn't he learn anything from me?

We did interesting things: dinner parties with other couples, weekend city breaks and learned culture. Although all he ever complained about was shopping for fabric swatches with pinking-shear edges and solid oak furnishings. The quality of which would last a lifetime, unlike our relationship.

I head for the kitchen, my choice of course, an array of chrome and dark marble surfaces – again it is spotless, not a cup ring or stray teaspoon in sight.

'Why couldn't he be this tidy when I lived here?'

He had driven me mental by leaving his belongings scattered on every surface: keys on the kitchen side, shoes in the lounge, wet towels slung over the toilet lid. Younger men had their uses, especially in the bedroom, but on more than one occasion I

72

suspected I was becoming a substitute mother: to cook, clean and bottle-wash – but *this*, this is spotless. *Just* how I like it.

I nosey in the Smeg fridge, the light illuminates a world of high-cholesterol, fatty foods and a stash of beer cans.

'Living on crap, I see.'

I nip out of the second kitchen door which leads back onto the hallway and towards the master bedroom, the aroma of his aftershave becomes stronger as I enter. I inhale deeply, sending a tingle along my spine.

So, you're definitely still wearing the Issey Miyake which I chose.

The bedroom is as I decorated; a combo of grey steel and feminine pink. The room is almost perfect, except for a dip to the duvet where I know he sat to pull on his socks before heading from the room.

How many times had I lay on the far side of this bed watching the muscles in his bare back ripple as he pulled on his trousers before standing to select a shirt? Not enough...

Was I too hasty in leaving? Was he on the verge of becoming the man I wanted and needed him to be? Or is he still the younger version of my ideal? I could say the opposite about Gordon Matthews. Is he really the older version of the mature man I desire or just a grumpy git that likes a younger woman on his arm?

What a mess! I'm neither here nor there.

I slump into the grey wicker chair beside the window and stare at the room. Memories of passionate nights flood my mind. The tenderness with which he held me tight, the frantic passion that enveloped us both, the dirty laughter and the silent intense moments replay in full technicolour as I stare around the room. We'd been good together, I hadn't been happier than when we were in that bed. And yet, I wasn't happy about that much: he wasn't financially secure, his shift patterns meant I had to go to invites alone, or defend his career choice amongst polite company. Who wants to constantly defend their other half's career choice? Not me.

I launch from the chair unwilling to revisit more memories and inspect the en-suite bathroom which I'd taken sole possession of. Joel had always used the main bathroom along the hallway. My mouth drops open at the tiny room filled with his toiletries. I expected empty shelves.

'Definitely moved on then, Joel?' I mutter, sitting down on top of the closed toilet seat.

I feel like crying.

I thought he'd still be hankering after me, unable to change his routines in case I came back, and yet, all I can gather is that he's slipped comfortably into the role of a single man.

I wonder if he's back on the scene yet, looking for a suitable younger woman? It wouldn't surprise me if Scott wasn't dragging him out every weekend to various drinking haunts, strip joints and single-men stomping grounds.

The idea rattles me.

He wasn't supposed to get over me *that* quickly.

My mobile rings, making my heart jump; Joel's name illuminates the tiny screen.

I answer the call whilst perched on his closed toilet seat.

'Veronica,' comes Joel's tinny voice.

'Yes.' I can hardly hear for the sound of my own heartbeat.

'Signatures, Veronica, I'm chasing yours regarding the flat.'

If only he knew.

'Where are you?' I ask.

'My sister's, why?'

And breathe. And calm. And answer.

'I'm not trying to be difficult, Joel... but you need to understand that I invested in the property too.'

'Surely you'd like your half of the investment back then?'

Would I hesitate?

Do I want my half back? Or am I stalling with the intention of getting him back?

'Joel... can we talk some other time?'

'It's been four months. I'd like this completed as soon as possible.'

'Couldn't we see how the market fares for the next few months. I'm certain there's going to be an upturn in property prices – it's a highly desirable location.'

'There's no point. You wanted to be bought out – that's what we agreed, now please, just sign!'

'Are you free tonight? We could talk properly.'

'How much more talking can we do?'

'Please, I can meet you at The Ivy House, any night at eight,' I say, knowing I'm pushing my luck.

His voice is gone in an instant.

I depress the red button and cradle the phone to my chest.

His annoyance is all I receive now, that and his bloody solicitor's letters.

The call may have ended but I can feel his warmth radiating from his sister's house a few miles away. If he caught me here, would he blow a fuse? Would he ask me to leave? Or drag me back to the bedroom?

I stand and nosey in the bathroom cabinet, sliding the mirrored doors aside, careful not to leave fingermarks, as I reveal its contents. I give a satisfied nod: no cotton wool, tampons or pink razors.

So why's he so eager to sign and complete the deal?

I return to the bedroom and resume my search. There has to be something that suggests his plans?

Opening Joel's wardrobe doors wide, I finger the right arms of his shirts neatly hung in a row like a monochrome rainbow. Joel never buys coloured shirts, just white or very dark navy or black. Whereas Gordon's tweeds are fusty with age, he calls it tradition – threadbare is my preferred term.

'That's new,' I mutter, pulling a navy jacket from the rail to inspect as if purchasing. 'And that... and that!' Other items jump from the rail for my inspection.

'Flashing your cash about, Joel?' I mock, whilst putting together his outfit in my mind. He's definitely smartening up his image.

I slam the wardrobe door shut.

That's when I spy it on his bedside cabinet. Between the lamp stand and his cufflinks, a beer mat – curled at the edges like a Christmas cracker fortune-telling fish. On snatching it up I read aloud the string of eleven numbers. There's no name.

A possible date?

A list of females comes to mind. I bet it's Kylie's number – I always said she had a soft spot for him.

'*Kylie*? She's only got eyes for Scotty,' he'd always say, if I challenged him. 'Though poor Kylie... he couldn't care less.'

'Sir doth protest too much, methinks,' I used to retort, certain I was right to be wary of the younger woman. She's probably happy she'd bade her time – New Year, new romp!

How many arguments had we had about her? You see it in the films all the time, patrol buddies cruising the quiet areas... what had they talked about for entire shifts? I was always happier when he was partnered with Scott. Less temptation than that strawberry blonde leggy piece.

I cringe.

Though why anyone would choose to wear their hair scraped back like that is beyond me – get a stylist, have it cut and make a statement.

I stare at the mobile number. Joel's handwriting smiles back at me, his digits have a cute slant due to his cack-handedness.

I miss him.

I stare round the bedroom, inhale his aftershave and sigh.

Do I replace the beer mat with the number or remove it?

11

Joel

I'm impressed. I've seen less effort go into a murder crime scene back at the station, but as I stand staring at the two-by-two-metre map of Pooley village, I have an instant respect for our newest resident.

'Did you do this?' I ask, as Flora proudly sips a large glass of rosé wine beneath her alcove display.

'I did... with Annie's help, though Mick wasn't chuffed at having to restock the bar on his tod.'

She was positively beaming, and I couldn't blame her.

The once brick walled alcove now resembled a true investigation. Central was the coloured map, obviously photocopied and enlarged, beside which was an enlarged photocopy of the news article depicting chubby-faced Darren proudly cuddling a scrunched-up baby.

'That's you then?' I say, pretending I hadn't studied the photograph on her clipping.

'Me... pictured on the morning of Friday, 10th October 1986.'

I step closer to read the black and white article again.

'Find it in the library, did you?'

'No... I've photocopied the clipping you returned. Don't you

77

remember, Darren said he has the same article framed on his lounge wall.'

'Jesus wept... I forgot he had *that* on his lounge wall!'

'You cheeky git!'

'Sorry I didn't mean you, of course I didn't, but that'll certainly keep the kids away from the coal fire or keep them awake at night!' I laugh, cringing at the very thought. 'Darren's face is one only a mother could love.'

Flora tries to hide her smile, but fails miserably.

'That's cruel.'

'Cruel but true!' I add.

I continue to read.

'Had you never seen it before?' she asks.

I shake my head, pretending I hadn't read it on Christmas morning. A white lie won't hurt.

'I'm not local as such... I grew up in the next village, I live between the two now... it's not the best idea to live so near,' I lower my voice, 'rubbing shoulders with the natives can go against you at times.'

Her green eyes scour the pub, notably the group of youths by the fruit machine.

'You won't have any memories or details to write in the comments book then?' She points to the large manuscript book complete with front cover label detailing the cause and purpose beneath the title: 10th October 1986 – where were you?

'I believe I spent the day playing with Plasticine and Stickle Bricks... followed by a lunchtime nap and a bedtime story,' I joke, trying to recall my interests, aged three.

'What's all this then?' interrupts Gene, wearing his tartan shirt, as always.

I step back, making room as he moves towards the display; Flora gleefully explains her handiwork. Around the bar several regulars have one ear cocked to hear her explanation whilst their gaze lingers on their pints as they pretend not to listen.

'If you can write down anything that you remember from that morning, then push a pin into the village map to show where you were living or even working – it'll help to build a picture from which I can work.'

'Ay, give me a pin and a tag then,' says Gene.

Flora reaches beneath the table and lifts numerous boxes from around her feet, rummages and hands over the necessary equipment for insertion of the first pin.

'Thank you,' she whispers, as the bulky man lingers, writes his tag and locates his parents' home of thirty years ago.

'Of course, being twins that applies to our Mick too.'

'Add his name if you would... I need to know as much as possible.'

I wander to the bar, order a pint and settle amongst the regulars to watch the attraction in the alcove.

This could prove interesting, if the right people co-operate, recall snippets and actively participate, she'll collect a huge amount of information, which if analysed correctly could suggest possibilities, even reveal an answer.

'Could you add your age to the label as well?' asks Flora. 'It'll give a fuller picture of the families living in the village.'

I watch as Gene eagerly complies, adding further details to his tag.

Let's hope everyone's as generous.

'She's doing OK, don't you think?' says Annie, serving my pint. 'It took her all morning, but she got it finished in time for opening... let's hope the regulars play ball.'

'She's doing very well considering...'

'And your black eyes are coming on a treat, did you renew the surgical tape yourself?' laughs Annie, handing over my change. 'Neat job.'

'Thanks for reminding me,' I utter, before returning my attention to the alcove, where a crowd of five gather eagerly to follow Gene's fine example.

Flora is handing pins and labels left, right and centre to all the compliant males. I look at the bar.

How many females are present? Three, including Annie and Flora.

And there lies the major hiccup in this investigation.

'Annie!' I call along the bar to grab her attention.

'You empty all ready? That's not your style.'

'No, I've a question – I know it's the lull between Christmas and the New Year rush but how quickly can you organise a ladies' night?'

'Joel Kennedy, that's not your style either... what are you up to?'

12

?

'Can I borrow your pen?' I ask the languid drunk seated at the bar.

One look at the stubby plastic pen indicates that he's stolen it from Argos or the local bookmakers. My money is on the latter.

'Here, keep it.' The nubbin of plastic lands on the alcove table, and I swiftly wipe it on a serviette before using it.

I select a fresh page, turn the book at an angle and write in a jaunty style:

> In 1986 Melanie Delaney was the biggest bike in this village. Every bloke in the village had a go. She'd do anything for half a Mars bar and a swig of your Irn-Bru. Girls in her family regularly disappeared for a long stay at aunty's house in the country – we all know what that was about. They never came back with their baby, did they?

I left the remark unsigned, it wasn't the messenger that was of interest – it was the content.

'Here's your pen back,' I drop it beside his near-empty pint glass as I walk out.

13

Flora

It didn't take Annie long to organise a ladies' night; she simply called in overdue favours from her friends on the high street. Within a few nights of my arrival, the Christmas decorations were boxed away and The Peacock pub was transformed into The Peahen beauty haven. Instead of males belching and grunting, svelte beauticians happily manned mobile nail stations performing mini manicures and pedicures, amidst a range of beautiful nail polishes. Another beautician was offering deep-cleanse facials and eyebrow shaping on a relaxing therapy table surrounded by a delicate silk screen. A trendy young artist seated on the opposite side of the alcove was adeptly applying delicate henna tattoos to hands. In the jukebox corner, an elderly tarot card reader dressed in her mystic finery was trying to be heard over the squawking noise of the local pretty-boy band prancing on a makeshift stage. I felt incredibly old in wanting to ask the baby-faced singer to pull his jeans up to cover his underwear – which was on full show whenever he shook his tush.

Was thirty too old to date such a young upcoming star?

I'd been retrained for the night from unemployed receptionist to barmaid. I looked around the busy bar at the array of ladies, while wiping a series of drips from the bar top.

Was my birth mother here right now? Was she eyeing me from her seat as I stand viewing the passing parade.

I quickly turn round to surprise anyone watching. No one meets my eye.

Ladies' night had seemed terribly sexist when Joel suggested the idea to Annie. I instantly thought of the Chippendales in their skimpy kecks strutting about with their baby-oiled bodies – a fitting parade for a pub called The Peacock, but maybe a tad near the mark for the ladies of Pooley. Annie soon corrected me, our token peacocks for the evening would be her Mick and the squeaky boy band prancing about on the mini-stage hastily constructed an hour ago.

The idea was to advertise a charity event in support of the local children's ward which settled my conscience and saved me from embarrassing myself by dashing to the chemist to empty the shelves of baby oil. The hum of female voices and laughter confirm the pamper/charity idea was spot on for enticing the local ladies to pour through the doors.

'New job?' asks an overly made-up blonde, as I struggle to uncap four bottles of tonic water.

'Just for tonight, it helps lighten the load,' I say, as one metal lid flies through the air, missing her shoulder by an inch. '*Sorry.* Ice?'

'Is it freshwater?' she asks, glancing at her three semi-cloned chums – all mature pouts and pucker.

I have no idea. My rapid bar-training session obviously wasn't as detailed or intense as required.

'I'll ask.' I quickly turn to ask Annie, a distance away, busy serving Martinis.

'Sorry, Veronica, but no, we ran out only this morning,' shouts Annie, giving the woman a sassy look, while I pour the tonic waters into four tall glasses of double gins.

'*Typical,*' mutters Veronica, rapping her false nails on the bar top. 'And they wonder why I don't frequent this hovel apart from charity events.'

I watch as Annie musters a strained smile but suspect she'd give anything to tip the drink over this woman's coiffed head.

This customer is just the kind of woman I can't stand. The ones that make me feel inferior in the bat of a false eyelash. Give me a vicious gossiper, even a super bitch any day over mealy-mouthed women who think every other woman is beneath them.

'She gets right on my tits!' spits Annie through gritted teeth as we both arrive beside the till to use the ice bucket. 'Her hair looks as brassy as Bet Lynch's.'

'Smile, my dear,' laughs Mick, his blue eyes glancing at who I'm serving. 'She thinks she's oh so high and mighty. Tell her she's taken the wrong turning... *this* is The Peacock not the bleedin' Ivy House.'

'I've got a bloody good mind to say I've found some fresh-water ice cubes in the cellar, then triple the price of her drinks order!' giggles Annie, plopping plain ice into my glasses. 'I'm surprised she's here, she refuses to acknowledge that she's a local!'

'Don't let her get to you, love – remember I know what she used do with our Gene for the price of a Hooch at the Wednesday night disco,' laughs Mick. 'She wouldn't want reminding, would she?'

'A can of Hooch or a strawberry Twenty Twenty, Veronica?' giggles Annie, releasing the ice tongs into the bucket. 'I bet her Botox brow would definitely see some movement if I mentioned that.'

I straighten my face and return to my customers.

'That'll be £16.80 please,' I say, delivering the drinks with a smile.

'I thought pub prices were supposed to be cheap,' whines Veronica, glaring amongst her cronies before fiddling in her purse and withdrawing a twenty. 'Drinks at the Shalimar cost only...'

'Cheers,' I say, removing the cash from her painted talons and returning to the till area.

They call us folk down south stuck-up and nobby, and yet, this woman, urghhh!

I shake off my coat of inferiority and remember the warmth that has been shown to me by Annie and Mick. Where else would a complete stranger receive such a warm welcome?

I glance up whilst punching in the transaction details, catching the reflection in the bar mirror – a heaving pub filled with women of all ages, sizes, features and fancies.

Who'd have thought that all *this* would have been organised to help me?

I return Veronica's change, her fingers snap at the coins like a Venus flytrap.

'Assaulted Officer Kennedy, didn't you?' she asks, her lip curling.

'Not intentionally but, sadly, I did cause his injuries – I was...'

'Nice try, take it from me, he's not the sort to fool around on duty,' she sneers, handing the drinks to her friends.

What's that supposed to mean?

'Could you fill in a label and pin it to the display board please,' I quickly add, as she turns about. 'There's a raffle prize for the lady whose pin I randomly select from the board later – first prize is a pampering facial at Skin 'n' Tonic on the high street.'

Veronica and her three chums smile politely at my request as they drift away from the bar, heading towards the boy band, in the opposite direction to my alcove display.

'You're welcome,' I smile, before moving to my next customer.

Please don't let that awful bitch be the supplier of my genetics, because she'll expect me to start getting up mighty early each morning to practise my bitch moves.

I giggle to myself on glancing my own reflection in the bar mirror as I pour the requested martini for my next customer – ninety minutes as a 'barmaid' and I'm as happy as a pig in muck.

Having served the martini, I stand and admire the growing queue of women waiting to pin their details onto my village map. A second queue snakes along the floor to write in the comments book. There's been a few numpty comments earlier in the week, such as 'was busy sleeping' and 'was out shooting a stork!' but I'd laughed and took it on the chin – Annie said it was best to.

I have a thicker skin than most, given my start in life.

'Annie!'

I step back as the woman I'm about to serve, with her frizz of curls, leans across the bar and screams along its length.

'What'll it be?' shouts Annie, having given a wave.

'Something different, I'm sick of white wine, I don't know...'

'How about going retro with a Taboo and lemonade?' calls Annie, busy serving her own customer. 'Or there's a vat of mulled wine going begging.'

'I can't tell you the last time I drank Taboo,' she shouts, turning to me to add, 'Bloody longer than I care to remember. I'm Melanie by the way, married to Gene.'

I recognise her from the other day.

I am about to introduce myself when she says, 'Flora... I know.'

I smile. Everyone knows.

'Taboo and lemonade?' I ask, grabbing a clean glass.

'Make it a double – though my legs will be drunk before my brain is.'

She gives a little laugh as if it were the height of naughtiness. Instantly, I like her.

'Your Gene staying in tonight?' calls Annie.

'He's on babysitting duty,' shouts Melanie, over the noise of the boy band squawking.

'Aren't the kids old enough to look after themselves?' asks Annie frowning, nipping over between customers.

'Not the kids, with the dog! She's not well. She's got poorly ears thanks to canker... horrible brown stuff which literally cakes them.'

'A night out with your sister then?' adds Annie, glancing up at the lookalike standing behind her, with matching frizzy hair.

'Two Taboos?' I ask.

'Yeah, course... she's under the weather. She hates Christmas and New Year, as you can imagine, Annie.'

'Heart attack,' mouths Annie, in my direction.

I pour another large drink and add ice.

'Did she ever get a settlement on his insurance payment?' asks Annie, waving a just-coming hand to a woman waiting along the bar.

'In a fashion... it wasn't what she'd thought, but it paid the mortgage off.'

I add lemonade and place the two glasses on the bar.

Annie gently touches my hand as I was going to tell Melanie the price.

'On the house.'

Melanie blushes and baulks at the freebie.

'It's nothing less than your Gene's had over the years,' laughs Annie, disappearing back up her own end of the bar to serve.

'Bless ya, Annie,' says Melanie, putting her purse away. 'You've managed to get a good turnout at such short notice.'

'So few women come in nowadays... it makes a change to have a decent run on the wine, Prosecco and speciality gin... I might crack out the cocktail shaker in the next hour!' shouts Annie, serving her customer.

'Woo-hoo ark at you, Annie – it'll be like our teenage years all over again,' laughs Melanie, collecting her drinks and moving backwards to her sister. 'Thanks, Flora.'

*

During my short break, I stand looking around the pub. What a mixed bunch for such a small village. I expected to see the same features repeated on numerous women, but it doesn't seem to be the case. I thought everyone would be related by birth or marriage.

'Your birth mother could be in this *very* room,' whispers Annie, joining me as we rest before another flood of customers need serving.

'Strange, isn't it?' I add, giving a small nod. 'She could be any one of them.'

'I've known them all my life and never in a million years could I suspect any of them, but stranger things have happened in this village,' whispers Annie, crossing her arms and surveying the crowd. 'Like the year Old Bert, the school lollipop man, married a woman a third of his age, or the New Year that Melanie's older sister jumped in front of the Crewe to Euston train. Or in more recent times… like two and a bit years ago, when that nice young copper was snared by the crafty cougar Veronica.'

My gaze travels to the mealy-mouthed bitch guffawing with her girlfriends at a nearby table – her head tilted back, mouth wide open showing a full set of veneers.

'*Really*? Her with Joel?'

'And now, she's hooked up with the local gentry sort,' adds Annie. 'The poor old git hasn't the sense to refuse her sexual advances – mind you, he won't fall for her tricks, Major Matthews will cast her aside when she pushes him too far.'

'A Major?'

'Oh yeah, we've got the gentry up here too, you know. The family used to breed polo ponies for the folks down South, but it went downhill when they lost a bucketload of cash on the stock market.'

I watch as Veronica waves her hands about while talking, as if to cut in and shut the others up whilst in mid flow.

What on earth did Joel ever see in her?

'If he's got any sense he'll take notice of someone nearer his own age,' says Annie, interrupting my thoughts.

'Who, the Major?'

'No,' she laughs, walking off to serve a new customer. 'Joel.'

*

Four hours later, Annie secures the latch on the pub doors, kicks her shoes off and walks stockinged foot back to the fireplace where I sit in the alcove cradling a glass of Chardonnay.

'So, my lovely, how was that for you?' she asks, sitting down and staring up at my display in awe of the numerous tiny flags waving from the village map.

'I'm amazed that so many people remember where they were on the day I was found. Seriously... look at how many names have been added tonight.'

'And all females... who you weren't getting before, were you?'

'Precisely! I can't thank you enough for tonight, if there's any cost implications please just say...'

'Zero, zilch and naught, my sweetie... like I said, I called in a few favours that were long overdue from the ladies about town.'

'Melanie was utterly shocked when she won the pampering session,' I say, remembering her alcohol-fuelled 'whoop whoop!' that filled the bar at the prize draw.

'She certainly was – she doesn't get out much does our Mel.'

'And as for using your favours on me... I'm touched, I really am, Annie. I couldn't have asked for anything better.'

Before I know it I'm up on my aching feet, embracing her in a bear hug.

As soon as my door closes, I flop onto the double bed.

'That was amazing!' I mutter to myself, grabbing my handbag, I delve inside for my discarded mobile: one text.

> We're worried. If you need us – we'll come straight home to be with you. Please text and let us know, love Mum x

Bless her. My mum, a true mum that worried when I sneezed, heated milk as dawn broke and would walk round the earth to make me happy. But sadly, not the woman that gave birth to me, who shares the same genetics as me or possibly has the same smile as me.

I answer Mum's text purely to reassure her, that no, I don't need her to dash anywhere. I am perfectly fine.

Though I'll phone tomorrow simply to ease her fretting.

I clamber to the window and draw back the tinted voile, staring out across The Square – the neon lamplight gives the cobbled square a romantic aura.

It has been a busy few days. I've organised the display for the alcove wall, paid the boutique lady for my delivery of new clothing and pulled my first pint under the strict tuition of Mick.

I might have met my mother tonight. Was she proud? Annoyed? Or more determined than ever to conceal her identity?

My mind swam with ideas and questions.

Had every woman of the right age put a location flag onto the map? I hoped so, though doubted it. I know marketing people claim that only ten per cent of people answer and return completed questionnaires. Could I hope for any more than ten per cent interest in my display board?

I view the four routes leading into The Square. One narrow street going down each side of The Peacock leading away onto the high street, the way I drove in via the country lane and the final option via the stone archway leading to a housing estate.

The light in the telephone box flickers constantly. Was it there in 1986? Had she considered leaving me inside, protected from the weather? Or had she hidden and watched from inside the phone box as a spotty-faced newspaper boy rode along on his BMX? Had she mingled with the growing crowd like Annie's ma had, or nipped off quickly without being spotted?

So many questions, yet not a single answer.

I close the curtains and prepare for bed.

Tomorrow, as they say, is another day, but am I any nearer to finding my birth mother?

14

Flora

'Morning,' calls the florist, heaving a water-filled bucket into place amongst the gladioli and gypsophila, as I enter her shop. Her dark hair, flecked with grey, is tied into a messy bun and her brown apron flaps around her boots. She knows who I am; everyone's been talking about me for days.

'Good morning,' I say meekly, staring at the flower displays. I haven't a clue what their botanical names are but am drawn by the array of colours and delicate fragrances.

She busies herself at the cash till as I browse the selection of ready-to-go cellophane-wrapped bouquets by the window.

I've never received a bouquet. Julian never came home with florist or garage forecourt flowers even when he was in the dog house.

I touch the shiny cellophane wrap and imagine the delight of opening the front door and seeing a bouquet delivery addressed to me.

'Is there anything in particular that you're looking for?'

I shake my head as my fingers touch the delicate rose petals.

'Shout if I can help,' she says, adding, 'I'm Kathy, by the way.'

'Thanks, I'm Flora.' Or Baby Bede to the folks here.

'I saw you last night at ladies' night... you served me a vodka and cranberry.'

She dashes through to the back room, collects a large book and swiftly returns, her messy bun bouncing with each stride.

'Order book, I'll lose it one of these days – I've got three deliveries and a complaint to the wholesalers to deal with, so no time for slacking.'

On returning to the shop floor, she finds me admiring the trailing spools of ribbons and satin bows used to decorate the deliveries.

'Are you interested in flowers?' she asks, settling at a workbench and brushing aside broken clumps of oasis foam onto the floor.

'I used to be. I thought about training as a florist when I was leaving school,' I say, adding, 'I didn't get the grades so I couldn't start the course without retaking two exams and then...'

She smiles. Her crow's feet stretch into her greying hairline.

'No doubt you've heard that story many times.'

'I have. We lose track of what we wish for, don't we? The dreams of a child wasted by an adult.'

'And yet, deep down they remain with us,' I laugh.

'So what did you become?'

'A receptionist,' I giggle, slightly embarrassed by my lack of aspiration. 'But only because my ex-boyfriend was the boss's son... I fell into the job, as I wasn't qualified for anything else. Which explains why I hated it beyond belief.'

'The reception work or the ex?' she laughs heartily.

'Both eventually.'

Kathy shakes her head, whilst flipping to reread a page of her order book.

'As a youngster, I'd always loved being creative – so why I didn't carry on creating and designing... but I didn't. I answered a phone all day and signed for deliveries – hardly creative, is it?'

'That's what I love. I can do anything with flowers, be it a simple buttonhole or an elaborate archway... as long as there's a solid idea, I can create it in flowers.'

'How long have you been here?'

She shakes her head.

'It's not me, sugar – if that's what you're thinking. I haven't any children.'

She gives a weak smile before mouthing 'sorry'.

I turn towards the nearest potted fern and trace my finger along the length of its delicate fronds.

'No worries.'

I know she is watching my every move; everyone else in the village has been.

'I suppose every female twenty years older than you is up for questioning?'

I nod and purse my lips.

'Worth a try if it gains you an answer,' she says, filling the silence. 'The closest I've got to children... is my nephew. I hear that you've met.'

'*Joel*?'

'Scott.'

'Oh.' My voice conveys my feeling.

Kathy laughs.

'He arrested you, didn't he?'

'Yeah, slammed those cuffs on good and proper,' I say, rubbing my wrists.

'That's typical of our Scott... he's got an eye for the ladies but doesn't really know how to treat them right.'

Silence descends as I watch Kathy's hands work.

'How's Joel's nose coming on?'

'The swellings gone down but the bruising has turned purple and black – not even a hint of blue any more,' I say, cringing.

'On the mend then, that's good to hear,' says Kathy. 'Annie looking after you, is she?'

'She's a sweetie, so warm and motherly... though she's not my mother *either*.'

Kathy laughs.

'That's how I've seen you most days, dragging the flower tubs in, morning and night.'

'They break my back most days, it's the weight of the water in the tubs, but hey, needs must,' she says, crossing the shop floor to another messy workbench and grabbing a handful of tools from amongst the floristry wire and blocks of oasis.

'It looks like hard work, which isn't what you'd imagine working with flowers.'

'Believe me, there's more to this than selecting pretty blooms and tying bows.'

'Do you work here alone?'

She gives a nod and returns to the original bench.

'Yep, alone and for too long, some might say, but it suits me – I'm never lonely surrounded by these beauties,' she says, waving a hand towards the array of flowers in every shade of the rainbow. 'In a village this size there's only enough business to keep me in a wage.'

'There must be times when you need an extra pair of hands?'

I watch as her fingers nimbly wrap tiny silver wires with green tape.

'Occasionally... Mother's Day, Valentine's Day... the rest of the time I can manage... this time of year is dead. Are you looking for work?'

I lean upon the countertop, resting my chin on my hands.

'I am... *if* I stay.'

'Like that, is it?'

'Yep.'

'Can't Annie find you some hours in the bar?'

'Perhaps, though it feels a little like the receptionist job I fell into last time... I need to choose a career... something that I can enjoy.'

I need her to feel sorry for me. My flickering light of hope seems to be fading behind my sea-green eyes. I just want a chance. Nothing grand. Nothing but the opportunity to prove to myself that I can do something. Anything other than mess it up and run away from a bad situation.

'I remember the very first day I opened for trade, I turned the little door sign to "Open"… my heart leapt from my chest with the anticipation of serving my very first customer.'

'Queuing at the door, were they?'

'Nah! It took two hours before anyone crossed the threshold.'

'That's how I feel right now, on the verge of something great but needing a nudge in the right direction. I'm all hope and energy and waiting to apply both to something amazing.'

Her hands still from wrapping wire.

'Can you make coffee?'

I frown.

'Of course.'

'Without instruction or supervision?'

'Yes.' I stand upright, a wry smile addressing my lips.

'Welcome to The Posy Pot – if you make a decent coffee, I'll talk you through the basics as I work.'

'You'd do that?'

'I might.'

'You *might*?'

'After I've tasted your coffee.'

I whip off my coat and head into the back kitchen while Kathy continues to wrap tiny wires in floristry tape.

How hard can it be to make a home made frappé crème-caramel from Nescafé and skimmed milk?

15

?

Why leave a baby on Doctor Fowler's doorstep? The apple never falls far from the tree!

I scribble the comment in the corner of an almost completed page.

As I leave the pub, I throw the biro into the nearest litter bin.

16

Flora

'Big smiles,' orders the photographer from The *Pooley Post*, as he bends and bobs to capture the right angle of Darren the newspaper boy and I posing in front of my wall display. My cheeks hurt from the constant fake grin, and my politeness levels are slipping rapidly. His camera whirs annoyingly with each snapshot.

'So this... is an eighties Retro Rave?' asks the half-soaked journalist from the sidelines, surveying the transformed interior of The Peacock. For the last fifteen minutes his main job has been to wave his dictaphone around, recording our answers, and mumble a few details of his own about my search. I've spent half my time shouting over the thump of the jukebox as it warbles hits from Whitney Houston, The Pet Shop Boys and Wham! On the tiny dance floor, the masses have attempted to perform the MC Hammer dance, the Moonwalk and walking like an Egyptian in a poor rendition of eighties coolness.

'Annie's put on a fine spread,' I say, trying to hold my pose and answer. 'Totally eighties, from the prawn cocktail vol-au-vents, Black Forest gateau, chocolate cracknel and mint custard to the frozen Jubblys and Tip Tops on ice behind the bar.'

'My favourite is the popping stuff on your tongue,' mutters the photographer. 'Have you any of that?'

'*Space Dust* is being sold in bags by the fruit machine, alongside Mojos, cola cubes and sherbet flying saucers,' I add, having forgotten the sweet counter manned by Donnie and Denny.

'So, Miss Phillips, what are you hoping to achieve?' asks the journalist, holding the tiny dictaphone beneath my chin.

Isn't it obvious? Annie's usual New Year's Eve celebration had been hijacked and upgraded with a retro-eighties theme. Three days of planning and the daft prat asks such a question!

Civil, be civil.

'Like a police reconstruction, we are attempting to take those that are old enough to remember the era back in time and hopefully a memory or a snippet of information may surface which will help to locate my biological mother.'

The journalist nods.

'I wasn't born then,' he announces, before smirking at the few locals gathered in the alcove.

Someone help me, I must be a magnet for imbeciles.

'Flora!' calls Joel, holding aloft a flute of sparkling Buck's Fizz. 'You look like you need it.'

A wave of guilt fills my chest. He's still wearing surgical strapping from cheek to cheek, probably as a precaution, but his blackened eyes look comical like a superhero mask.

'I do,' I smile, my cheeks plumping like apples. 'If I swig it quickly will you get me another?'

'Sure, but take it easy – you've got the whole night ahead.'

I down it and pass the empty glass back for a refill.

'Buck's Fizz, Babycham or Cherry B?' asks Joel.

'Surprise me!'

'That's enough.' Finally, the press photographer has all he needs. 'Anyone mind if I help myself to the buffet?'

'Perk of the job,' laughs the journalist, stuffing his dictaphone away.

I snatch an extra two seconds of his time to reinforce that

we need this in the local paper as soon as humanly possible for the desired impact.

'No worries, two days max,' is his final remark before emptying a cocktail stick of cheese and pineapple into his widening chops.

Darren grabs my arm as soon as I finish talking and leads me towards the bar stools.

'And this is my lovely wife, Denise... sister to Melanie, who's sister-in-law to Annie,' explains Darren, proudly pushing me towards a tiny woman with more frizzy hair, dressed in a pink ra-ra skirt and wearing silver deely boppers. 'Denise, this is Flora.'

Denise's deely boppers bounce, scattering glitter everywhere, as she shakes my hand.

'So nice to finally meet you... though I've seen your face every day of our married life above our mantelpiece,' she giggles, her blue mascara fluttering up and down.

I feel like a let-down, Darren's had me on a pedestal for all these years and yet here I stand, just an ordinary girl, no glamour, no extra pizzazz, and definitely no star qualities to justify my status on their lounge wall.

'Yeah, sorry about that, Darren did mention it,' I jibber. 'Let's hope my story gets resolved and you can take it down pretty soon.'

Denise smiles politely, like that thought had *never* crossed her mind.

I look for Joel, as the awkward silence lingers.

'Here,' he says, handing me another Buck's Fizz and rescuing me from the frustration of yet another person who clearly isn't on my wavelength.

'Thank you... how's Annie coping at the bar?'

'She's OK. Melanie and Gene are helping out where they can... how long is Mick laid up for with his back?'

'Lord knows, it's a recurring issue, I believe – though what does he expect lifting beer barrels like he does.'

'Oh well, we'll chip in where we can for tonight.'

'Thanks for saving me – they don't get it, do they?' sipping my fresh drink, eyeing Denise's retreating figure.

'Nope, but why should they? Most folk around here were raised like me in a family with the national average statistic of two point four kids… but forget them, look at all this!'

I follow his sweeping hand indicating the crammed pub, the bustle of busy bodies coming and going – everyone who is anyone in the village has turned out in support. Thankfully not everyone is wearing a pastel-coloured ra-ra skirt, luminous towelling head and wrist sweatbands and a 'Relax' T-shirt. I wear the only dress I have, my red chiffon.

The synthesised music drifts from the jukebox, I instinctively hold my breath on recognising the tune's intro, the melody which makes Janet, my mum, cry at *every* family occasion.

'Oh no!' I moan, instantly turning away from the crowd to face the display wall. My eyes well up as Stevie Wonder sings 'I just called to say I love you', his voice drifts above the crowd, encouraging them to warble along.

'Flora?' asks Joel, his body ducking around mine to view my lowered chin. 'You're crying.'

'It's nothing.'

'It's touching but a dire rendition – I suppose the crowd are here to enjoy themselves too.'

'It's not that… it's…' I wave my hands about my ears. 'The music.'

'Sorry, but it's all authentic eighties,' he laughs, before realising I wasn't laughing. 'Flora, do you want me to go and switch tunes?'

'No, don't. It'll cause a scene and the crowd are enjoying it.'

The bodies round us sway in unison, as their voices raise the roof, reciting every word. I dab at my eyes, avoiding the curious stares.

'Just breathe, it'll be over in a minute… it's not a lengthy song,' whispers Joel, his arm gently snaking around my shoulders as I try desperately to control the flow of tears. 'It's strange how music has the power to evoke such emotions.'

'Turns me into a gibbering mess – yet, all he's doing is singing a bloody calendar!' I laugh, trying to hide my embarrassment.

Ten minutes earlier they'd played Madonna's 'Papa Don't Preach', I'd listened to every lyric while my head was consumed with one idea: did my birth mother relive her summer of doubt every time she heard it? Would her papa preach if he'd known about me? The lyrics spun in my head and heart with as much passion as I could muster for a woman I've never known.

Eventually, Stevie sings his final lyric, I wipe my mascara from my chin as Joel's arm squeezes tighter around my shoulders before releasing me.

'Thank you, you're so kind,' I whisper, between undignified sniffs.

'My pleasure,' he whispers. 'But before we turn to face the crowd let's check what's playing next?'

We stand apart, heads tilted and listen. Joel pulls a comic face as the jukebox churns out another disc.

'Excellent, you're safe… it's the Spitting Image Chicken Song.'

I crumble into fits of laughter, as the crowd simultaneously raise their volume and hold aloft an imaginary rubber chicken.

'I doubt if that line has *ever* been said before?'

'Plenty of times in our house, believe me,' he splutters between laughing. 'Come on, I'll race you to the bar.'

He grabs my hand.

I stand firm, wrenching him back.

'Joel, thank you – I do appreciate your support since Christmas.'

'The pleasure's all mine.'

'My mum seemed very taken with you the other day when I mentioned you, she thinks you're verging on superhero status by forgiving me the headbutt and then assisting my search.'

'What's a guy to do? Leave a damsel in distress?' he laughs.

My eyes search his face, unable to resist his gaze.

I just need one moment of clarity. I like him, he *seems* to like me and my parents would be smitten from the word 'go' with this one, and yet, nothing is moving forward. Is the search for my birth mother the only interest he has in me?

'Seriously, I mean it – you've been a star!'

'I know,' he says, giving an embarrassed smile. 'But for now, we need a drink… what's it to be, a pina colada or SodaStream?'

'SodaStream cola flavour, please,' I say quickly, adding, 'Though, I hope it doesn't come out like the ones my mum used to make.'

'Did you ever try it with milk?'

I grimace at the suggestion.

'Precisely. It tasted weird and it wrecked our SodaStream.'

*

'Where is she?' booms a voice barging through the crowd. 'The Bede gal from down south – where is she?'

I look up to see Annie directing a portly gent with a large red nose and dressed in heavy tweeds in my direction.

'Evening!' his voice sounds like a drum, he indicates to the nearest seat. 'May I?'

'Hi, of course.' Given his girth, I wouldn't dream of refusing.

He pulls a small upholstered bar stool towards him and balances his portly frame on the tiny seat.

'I'll cut to the chase, young lady, I've heard a fair bit about your search over the past few days and wondered if there was anything that I could do to assist?' He peers from beneath bushy grey eyebrows which overhang his face.

'Can I ask, who... you... are?'

'Height of ignorance me, yes, sorry, my dear... Major Gordon Matthews from the manor house... Veronica... you know her?'

'I know *of* her,' I say.

'My lady friend,' he says, tapping his chest. 'She mentioned your plight the other evening... I was wondering if there was anything that I could assist with or offer – a bit of charity never hurts, does it?'

I blush. Veronica of all people to be on Team Me – wonders never cease.

'I don't know... I've put the display wall together and the usual interviews for local papers, but I haven't any other plans – I'm waiting for information really.'

'Has anyone suggested DNA testing?'

My heart leaps. I'm not a science enthusiast but even I know the importance and capability of such testing.

'As a way to prove a match?'

He nods eagerly, his throaty excess wobbling.

'But surely I need to identify a person first?'

'Not necessarily. If you'd allow me to assist I could arrange and fund a mass screening programme... for the whole village, if necessary.'

I'm all ears as Major Matthews explains that he's spent decades listening to the locals debating the mystery of my birth.

Funny, no one seems to have a theory when I ask!

'Now's their chance to prove how generous they really are and together we could bring a bit of community spirit to this tired village – let's ask them to volunteer for a mass DNA screening.'

'What if someone objects?'

'Phah! There's always the kind that object, that's their role in life. Object to a new zebra crossing, longer opening hours of the library and even taking a quick swab sample for your benefit, but I think there's enough folk around these parts that would wish to help. Don't quote me... but I think we only need one person from each family to agree for a test for you to gain an overall picture *and* it won't cost them a penny.'

'But who's...?'

'Footing the bill? Me, of course, sorry, silly me – did I not say that first? Call it what you will, a community project, human interest story or other such poncey terms... I'm happy to help, my dear.'

I'm stunned.

'So... that's my offer and we'll get an answer once and for all.'

How generous can strangers be?

I want to bawl my eyes out. I can't speak, so stare at his round bloated face with wide eyes.

'Is that a yes?'

I frantically nod.

I wouldn't know where to begin arranging such a test. The local hospital? Doctor's surgery? Village newsletter?

I know on tacky TV they have a daily dollop of DNA results and shenanigans, but never in my life did I think such a test could find a person before I knew their name.

'Spare me the TV cameras, a cheeseball host and a loud-mouthed audience please,' I mutter, as my stomach flips.

What if the locals refuse to comply? What if their goodwill has dried up and they consider this a step too far, an invasion of their privacy?

'I thought testing was expensive?'

'Leave that to me, my dear,' he says, in a double-handed Michael Winner manner.

He instantly stands, his hand outstretched and energetically shaking mine before my brain gets into gear.

'Thank you,' I stutter, as he departs the alcove.

'My pleasure... I'll be in touch with a specific date, good evening.'

'Are you not staying to enjoy the party?'

'No, my family lost thousands of pounds on Black Monday so the eighties were bad enough to live through without revisiting them, thank you,' he grunts. I watch as his retreating frame barges back through the crowd and swiftly exits the pub.

The crowd turn around and stare like a bunch of meerkats at the zoo.

'He's offered to pay for the entire village to be DNA tested to see if any biological connections come to light,' I announce to the bevy of dumbstruck faces.

*

Within a few hours the buffet is bare, the *Jubblys* and *Tip Tops* have been sucked to death, removing all the flavouring and colouring, but the comments book has a constant flow of merry revellers entering their memories.

I watch as the locals pass the biros between themselves, eager to add their snippet of village life. Darren drunkenly elbows his way to the front, playing his status card, as always. What else could he possibly write? I'm sure I've heard every detail ten times over. His ruddy cheeks beam, as his hand frantically dashes across the page, for which a circle of hands reach and snatch to read.

'Ten, nine, eight, seven...' shout the crowd, as Annie dongs the bar bell in time to the countdown.

'Six, five, four...' I shout, steadying myself at the bar, as loved ones strategically reposition themselves for celebratory hugs and kisses.

'Three, two, one, Happy New Year!' screams the crowd, as party popper streamers shoot above our heads, Annie's bar bell rings frantically and music from the jukebox fills the pub. I stand alone, momentarily watching the crowd of bodies grab, hug and kiss each other before moving to the next person.

'Come here, you,' shouts Annie, pulling me into a bear hug before releasing me, before Gene, Melanie, Denny and Donnie repeat the very same bear hug in quick succession with varying degrees of force.

How lovely to be able to include a stranger in such a short space of time. I don't want to be anywhere else? A wave of guilt fills my chest. *Besides* with Mum and Dad, of course. Next year, I promise to spend New Year with them at home watching Jools' Hootenanny.

'Happy New Year, Flora!' Joel approaches, complete with facial injuries, his arms open wide, he steps forward, leans in close... and then stalls. A subtle withdrawal from the potential hug before he fumbles about snatching up my right hand and raising it to his lips.

Awkward.

I stare as he kisses the back of my hand, his bruised eyes lift to look at me as his soft lips touch my pale skin.

'Happy New Year!' I chorus, trying to detract from my profuse blush.

He smiles, before moving to the next woman, who he hugs and then backslaps her male companion.

He kissed *my* hand. Why withdraw from the planned hug? I try to follow his path through the crowd tallying how many hugs he delivers, but I am spun round as two strangers grab my hands across my body and a boisterous circle is formed thanks to 'Auld Lang Syne'. I scan the group for Joel's face as my neighbours energetically pump both my arms in opposite directions and mime the unknown words. I have no idea what this song means but have learnt the order of the sounds much like I did French in secondary school, where I could recite from the practice audios without understanding a single verb.

Where was Joel? Enjoying himself in a darkened corner having found a desirable bear hug which included tongues? Or had he dashed out before the taxi drivers hoicked their prices up?

*

What if my birth mother is here? Watching me, watching the dwindling crowd.

I slowly turn and view the entire bar, no one appears to be standing out, cautious and anxious, but maybe she's learnt to cover her guilt. She wouldn't have got to this point without being as cunning as a fox.

I stare at each female in turn: Annie, Melanie, Kathy, Denise and Veronica and countless other women drinking, dancing and laughing – is she amongst them? Is she determined not to blow her cover or is she desperate to be found? Exhausted by her own secret? Or eager and curious to witness the passing parade that every other villager is intrigued by?

A shriek from the end of the bar draws my attention to Melanie and Gene, as they play-fight over a bottle of Vimto complete with a paper straw. He holds the bottle aloft and she swings on his arm, trying to retrieve it, but she's far too short. They're a good match – every pot has its lid, as my mum says. Though I don't ever recall her saying that about me and Julian. I watch as Gene kisses the top of Mel's frizzy head and returns the drink, she snuggles into the crook of his arm.

How would I feel if I was theirs? Or just hers?

She's kind, friendly enough, but everyone keeps mentioning her reputation as a teenager for 'putting it about'. It's likely that the stakes are high, otherwise I wouldn't have been abandoned, would I?

'Cheer up, it might never happen,' laughs Denny, passing by me on his way to the fruit machine.

'Yeah thanks, but it already did back in October eighty-six.' My heart feels heavy, standing alone and watching the antics of the revellers.

How would her neighbours react after three decades? Shun her? Empathise? Or make her pay for her actions?

I hope I have the chance to find out, because if I don't find this woman it means I'm likely to spend the rest of my days wondering and wishing life was different. I don't think I can go through what I've been through for the last three decades.

My mood is sinking and my anxiety building as the jukebox throws me another stab to the heart as de Burgh's intro fills the pub.

'The Lady in Red' – I love this song.

I lean against the wall, drink in hand, and absently nod along to the beat as couples push past me, surging towards the tiny dance floor. Someone flicks a switch and the main lights dim further, providing the perfect backdrop for the night's smoochie number.

'Would you like to dance?'

Joel's smiling face is before me, his hand extending towards mine. *Ironic*, given de Burgh's praise for his lady in red and me wearing the *only* dress I currently have and which I wore at our chance meeting on Christmas Eve.

I give the smallest nod and peel myself from the wall. How long has it been since a man asked me to dance? Julian never danced with me, despite my asking.

I'm grateful that Joel's hand wraps round my fingers as he leads the way through the dwindling crowd, my eyes fixed on his broad shoulders. In seconds, we're at the centre of the swaying couples, his arms wrapped around my waist, holding me close. I drape my hands around his neck and inhale the citrus freshness of his aftershave as his surgically strapped face hangs low above mine.

How many times have I ended an evening watching the couples embrace and sway? Wishing that I could be one of them, lost in the final dance before the lights come on and taxis are called.

De Burgh's voice hits a note and within two verses my face is buried into Joel's jacket lapel and my tears flow as we gently sway, our feet almost static, amongst the crowd.

*

'Flora?' whispers Annie, approaching my alcove after the party guests have gone home. 'Are you OK?'

I nod. My emotions are somersaulting, I feel overwhelmed by their generosity and yet I am drowning in self-pity.

'What happens if I never find her?' I say, as the tears cascade.

Annie's arms wrap around my shoulders as she settles beside me on the upholstered bench.

'Shhh, there, there,' she soothes, '…it'll do no good thinking like that.'

'But, Annie… I've spent thirty years not knowing. I *need* to know.'

'And if you don't, you'll carry on as before… you'll live – breathe in and out without thinking.'

'I won't.'

'You will, it'll smart for a while, the pain will be as raw as ever, but in time you'll cope.'

'I won't.' I sound like a petulant child unwilling to listen to wisdom.

She gently rocks me back and forth.

'We all have such thoughts about different issues or problems but somehow day turns to night and night comes around to day – and we realise that we made it through another twenty-four hours.'

I lift my head as a wet blob lands on my crown.

'Annie, you're crying!'

'We've each a different story to tell – I vowed I'd never survive, but hey, I'm still here... *somehow*.'

I watch as she quickly wipes her tears away and sniffs.

''Ark at me, sitting here snivelling. We should be celebrating a decent start to the new year – I reckon half the village dropped by.'

She's right. I have many things to be grateful for – a loving family, caring friends and... I pause, suddenly unable to name a third thing. What a miserable, pathetic wretch I am!

I give myself a kick up the ass, before Annie offers. I should be buzzing, it's a new year, I had a smoochie dance with a handsome copper and my story will be all over the local paper in a matter of days.

'Would a sherbet and Vimto challenge cheer you up?' she asks, releasing her tight hold.

'Never heard of it,' I sniff.

'Come on, on your feet... I challenge you or double dare you – whichever you prefer.' She races to the bar and begins gathering sherbet powders from the nearly emptied sweet counter. I settle on a bar stool as she snaps the caps off two bottles of Vimto.

'Right, no cheating. Empty a full packet of sherbet into your mouth, swig the pop – the first to grimace loses... got it?'

I nod, taking the sherbet packet offered.

'You ready, steady, go!'

I follow her lead. A cloud of lemon sherbet fills the air before I swig from the Vimto bottle. I choke and splutter as the bubbles of sherbet rapidly expand on my tongue, the froth fills the back of my throat before descending unceremoniously via my nostrils.

My face twists in agony thanks to the citric flavourings.

'You lose!' shouts Annie, her mouth frothing like a rabid dog. '*Again*?'

17

Flora

I love libraries but this is the pokiest library I have ever entered. My heels clip on the polished tiles as I wander to the main desk. A tiny enquiries desk is being run by 'Betty' or so her name badge says, and she also seems to man the ticket desk and answer the ringing phone whilst hastily speeding back and forth between the first customers of the new year.

I complete the request card and stand waiting while Betty, with her grey set hairdo, disappears into the depths of beyond.

I stare at the desk computer and wonder if my mother's name is on their system? Does she come here on a weekly basis to borrow the latest Jo Thomas or Katie Fforde novel?

The keyboard beckons me.

If Betty was in the back of beyond for a while I could take a cheeky peek at the database, couldn't I? I could do my own research. But who would I search for? A Karen, a Denise or a Jennifer? Without a name, I am stuffed from the start. I could hardly type in 'abandoning mother' and hope the search details find a match.

A lump lifts to my throat.

Why must I torture myself? Others can live and let live, but me, I have to keep beating myself up by navel-gazing.

I turn to view the library: a small arrangement of brightly coloured seats strategically arranged around tables and large potted cheese plants break the repetitive pattern of giant bookcases.

'Here we are,' announces Betty, bustling through the connecting doorway. 'I didn't think they'd take quite so long to find, but hey ho... the job's done.'

I seat myself at the nearest table to the counter, in case I require her help during my search.

'Anything in particular, you're searching for?'

I'm taken aback that she doesn't already know. I had the impression that every man and his dog knew about my unexpected arrival on Christmas Eve.

My brief explanation takes seconds. I stop when her mouth drops wide.

'Oh I... well, I...'

'Yes, it sounds like that date won't ever be forgotten here... Ta-da! All grown up and searching. My... hasn't time flown. I'd just started working here when all that business occurred... quite a shock for the village, you know.'

'Quite a shock for me too,' I add, laughing.

'Sorry, how insensitive of me.' Betty's mature skin blushes.

'No worries, I think I've upset a fair few in the village... some seem to wish I'd disappear and not exist.'

She gives a sensitive head tilt, the sympathy oozes from her.

'How are these labelled?' I indicate to the large bound book positioned on the table.

'Date order. This book contains the *Pooley Posts* for the entire year.'

'Tenth of October then.'

'Actually no, the earliest news report would be the Friday issue of that week.'

'The tenth was a Friday.'

'*So*, the following week… sounds so antiquated, doesn't it?'

A weekly paper printed on a Friday collating all the news from the local area – how quaint. I suspect I'd have featured on the hour every hour on Sky news had I been abandoned nowadays.

'Do I need white gloves?' I ask cautiously, having watched too many antiques and genealogy programmes.

Betty shakes her head, her melancholy look not having dissolved.

'It's the *Pooley Post* not the Magna Carta.'

I heave open the front cover to reveal yellowed pages of the *Pooley Post* circa 1986.

'You'll need to flip through to October first before looking for the right date.'

'I take it was headline news?'

'Yes, for a few weeks,' her tone is apologetic.

The wodge of paper weighs a tonne, but I'm soon staring at myself squashed in the arms of a spotty teenager with curls – headline news on Friday, 17th October 1986.

'It certainly brings back memories,' says Betty, lingering at my shoulder.

'I hope so, if there's anything you can add or tell me I'd much appreciate it.'

I spend a few minutes telling her about the display board and comments book at The Peacock which the locals had been kind enough to pin flags to.

'Though, there's nothing of interest yet.'

I flick past the article that I've read a thousand times in search of other details or images previously unknown.

'Were there any other big stories or village news of the same time that may be linked?' I ask, as my eyes devour the yellowing pages.

'Not that I know of, though to be fair the village was much smaller back then, just a pub, a police station and a postbox.

I was new to the village and not knowing many people...' she mumbles, adding '...still don't.'

Amidst the forecasts of a hard winter, the allotment association's annual pumpkin prize and the autumn school bazaar, little of village life is mentioned. The black and white photos show crazy gelled haircuts, thick gloopy eyeliners and a flamboyant dress style of either wide shoulder pads or flouncy highwayman ruffles.

I spend an hour leafing through the newspaper reports but each is a rehash of the original details.

An air of despondency gathers like a low fog.

'Nothing new,' I sigh, closing the file.

'It was worth looking though, maybe something will come to light from your comments book,' says Betty, before her face lights up in surprise. 'Have you been to the doctor's surgery?'

I shake my head.

'Now, there's a profession that knows everyone's intimate business – there's only one, so everyone here uses the same surgery. Maybe one of the receptionists remembers a positive pregnancy test... or a young woman seeking assistance – it's worth a try.'

It feels like an information relay with Betty passing me the baton and within minutes I've forgotten the *Pooley Post*, thanked her and bade her goodbye and am heading for the doctor's surgery on the high street.

*

The receptionist slides the frosted glass across, her inquisitive stare peers from beyond the hatch opening. She's about Mum's age, wearing a lambswool jumper, no make-up and has unplucked eyebrows.

I pause, expecting her to speak or greet me, but she doesn't.

'Can I book an appointment to see Dr Fowler, please?'

'Older or younger?'

I shrug.

'We have Fowler senior and his nephew both practising here,' she adds curtly.

'Older, please.'

The frosted glass shoots across on the runners and bangs closed.

How can one tiny action convey such irritation?

I want to laugh, but stop myself.

Through the frosted glass, I can see her fuzzy outline moving around a few yards to the right, her hands look as though they are flipping through the pages of a large book. She eventually returns to the window.

'Two weeks on Tuesday, will be the earliest...'

'I can't wait till then,' I interrupt, leaning nearer the window hatch to whisper. 'It's personal.'

'Most things are in here, dear,' she gives a weak smile.

'No, I mean... really personal. Private in fact.'

She merely raises her eyebrows and stares.

'I was found on his doorstep back in the eighties,' I say, whilst contemplating the possibility of creating business cards printed with this exact phrase.

'Oh, the Bede Baby lady?' says the receptionist, glancing over her shoulder at another rotund woman seated at a desk, who swiftly ceases working and glances up at me.

Both possible candidates – right age, right era. Could I be the secret love child of doctor and receptionist – given my life experiences, nothing would surprise me.

On confirmation, I half expect a smile or some compassion – I receive neither.

'Doctor *may* see you after surgery, you'll have to take a seat and wait,' she nods towards the waiting room, where others are seated.

'I do appreciate it,' I add, eager to stay in her good books.

The sliding window crashes against the wooden hatch frame in the same manner as before. Where do they train receptionists to slam a sliding hatch window with such attitude?

I take a seat on the back row of the waiting room. A smattering of patients occupy the other rows: a broken-legged man, a runny-nosed child with a sea-lion cough leaning on her mum and an elderly lady coughing for England, who doesn't raise her hand to her mouth when necessary – such a small gathering for the post-New Year surgery.

In the far corner, bracketed high upon the wall is a plasma TV screen showing the latest episode of Slang Match TV where DNA and lie detectors are guaranteed to rile the audience. The volume is muted, but given the close-up camera shots of women screeching and randomly pointing their index finger towards a slouching youth in a bucket seat – I get the gist of their story.

Why do folk do it? Surely there's a more civilised way to access a paternity test? The cost must have dropped substantially given the recent demands from society.

I read the caption beneath the ranting woman's face 'Seven years denying he's the father' – surely in that time you'd find the money from somewhere, anywhere, rather than put up with the constant issue hanging over a child's head?

I cringe.

'Ark at me! Awaiting the memory recall of a perfect stranger to inform me of my own story whilst picking fault with another's.

A buzzer sounds, the snotty-nosed girl and her mother go through the end door.

My phone vibrates in my pocket. I snatch it and open it hoping to distract myself with a message from my mother or my girlfriends. Instead, a text from Julian.

Sorry x

I don't reply – he isn't worth it.

Within minutes my phone comes alive with a series of texts begging forgiveness and demanding I return home and return to work. As if no one had noticed that I hadn't answered the phones in two months, emptied the shredder bag or even watered the large display of potted greenery positioned in the foyer. A mental image of my old reception desk forms, the main switchboard lights are glowing brighter than the Blackpool illuminations, a mountain of shredded paper cascades over every surface and the potted greenery is now crispy, bedraggled and brown.

Are the bosses not asking when I'll be back from lunch?

Give me a break, Julian. You made the choice; you chose to cheat.

My fingers dance upon the tiny buttons as I angrily punch a reply and send.

No, you're not!

He replies: Believe me, pleeeeease.
I reply: No.
He replies: Come home!!!!!!!
I don't reply. There's no point, he isn't listening to me. What does it matter to him if I am in Pooley or Bushey? It wasn't him I'd be going home to but my parents' musty back bedroom with its Laura Ashley limited edition quilt cover set and matching wallpaper.

His demanding texts continue several more times.

I shouldn't have answered. I vow not to answer any more.

I snatch my phone, flick to contacts and rename Julian Wright's number as 'cheating bastard'. There, now a mini reminder should a moment of weakness occur if he should call or text again.

119

I sit back content with my new contact and select a dog-eared magazine from the nearest table: October 2013.

How old?

I flick through the tatty pages – a variety of celebrity articles but nothing on which to focus my mind.

I return the tatty magazine to the table.

I fiddle with the zip on my clutch bag, as I look round the waiting room.

The broken-legged man continues to stare avidly at the muted plasma screen as an on-set fight breaks out and studio furniture is toppled over – such nonsense played out for the cameras and jeering audience.

How come my world is never as dynamic?

In real life things aren't said, lies aren't uncovered and families don't address the issues they should. Instead they ignore the sensitive subjects, swallow the lies and look past the secrets, promising to deal with them one day. Trouble is, for most folk one day never comes.

Is this my one day? My chance to discover my truth?

I stare at the nameplates alongside the green bulb buzzer system: Dr Fowler (senior), Dr Fowler (Junior) and Dr Vaughan – the lower three buzzer lights have remained silent during my wait.

Dr Fowler – a name I've known all my life thanks to the newspaper article. I am about to meet another significant person from *that* day. How great if he could give me the snippet of information that answers all my prayers.

I have butterflies in my stomach at the very thought.

Why was it his doorstep? Did my mother think it best, due to his profession? Or did she think there was something wrong with me that needed medical attention?

I glance at the muted screen. The family continue to fight over the paternity results.

Or could he be my father?'

The frosted window of reception suddenly opens wide.

'Doctor will see you now,' calls the sour-faced woman.

I look around the waiting room; I am the only one left.

I hadn't heard the buzzer call the other two inside or see them walk across the waiting room.

Breathe, breathe.

My heels clip-clop on the white tiles as I cross the empty waiting room, behind which is a long sterile corridor with a neat row of doors, each dominated by a large nameplate. Dr Fowler (Senior) is the last room on the sterile corridor.

I softly rap the door.

'Come in,' calls the male voice.

I enter to find an elderly man, bespectacled and dressed in a tweed suit, seated behind a messy desk.

'Dr Fowler?' I remain standing in the doorway, scrutinizing his features for anything that resembles mine. Nothing.

'How can I help?' he indicates the nearest chair.

'Are you the doctor that had a baby left on his doorstep?'

His hooded eyes widen and his bottom lip protrudes on hearing my question.

'Well, well... this *is* a surprise,' he says, removing his glasses to stare at me intently, before giving a sharp nod. 'We've been expecting you for all these years and now, when we'd all thought you'd never show, you take us by surprise!'

I seat myself and thank him for the warm welcome.

'Sorry to interrupt your surgery, but I wanted to make an appointment to discuss *that* morning.'

After scratching his head, he stares at his watch and then back at me.

'Surgery doesn't finish for another hour so I'll have patients till then, so...' he explains, moving an array of medical paraphernalia to gain access to a small diary. 'Could we say six o'clock?'

'Sure. I'm staying at The Peacock.'

He writes 'Peacock six p.m.' into his diary.

'Most people do,' he mumbles, adding, 'Annie's warm hospitality is hard to beat around these parts.'

18

Joel

She bursts from the doctor's surgery, like a greyhound from a trap, slamming straight into me.

'Whoa there, what's the rush?' I say, before realising that it isn't a young scoundrel inconsiderately dashing into unsuspecting passers-by.

'Sorry. I... hello again,' she smiles, her green eyes included in the warm greeting. 'I was in a world of my own.'

I instantly change tack, grateful that I'd gone against medical advice and removed the stupid-looking surgical tape from my nose, despite the remaining bruising having gained a tinge of green. I can only look a prat for so long.

'Never mind, no harm done.'

'No more broken noses,' she laughs, instantly blushing. 'Sorry, that slipped out.'

'Fair play, I can laugh about it too, you know.'

Her blush deepens to crimson.

Idiot! She was being light-hearted and you've switched it to a reprimand.

'What's the rush?' I repeat, quickly changing the subject.

It takes her all of a minute to explain about the newspaper records and the lack of information and another minute to explain her conversation with Doc Fowler.

'How about coffee beforehand?' I ask nonchalantly, trying to erase my earlier sternness.

'That would be nice.'

I ditch the idea of a haircut; I'll go another day.

'The best coffee is at The Corner Café, this way,' I say heading towards The Square.

She falls in step alongside me, tottering on her high heels – a good job the deep snow has finally subsided into dry, bright but chilly days.

'The librarian's right, it might be the tiniest remark that has lingered as a suspicion which unlocks the whole mystery... it's worth a go.'

I don't answer, but continue to stare straight ahead.

'Don't you agree?'

'Not quite, with such a privileged position in the village... he's sworn to secrecy. I couldn't blab about details of my police work.'

Flora stops dead in her tracks.

I look back having walked on.

'Seriously, even in such circumstances? An abandoned baby – surely that's a criminal act... is it not child abuse? Neglect?'

I shrug.

I hate the look of disappointment that furrows her brow before she catches up and we walk on.

'You don't want hearsay and gossip regarding suspicious details. We waste no end of time following up on false leads due to people's idea of acting suspiciously. You want cold hard facts – that's how you'll get your answers. I'll be surprised if the doctor tells you anything you don't already know, he can't divulge private and personal information.'

'I'm prepared to give it a go,' she says, adding, 'There may be personal information about himself that he needs to divulge.'

'Such as?'

'You never know... doctors have secrets too.'

'I doubt if Doc Fowler has *any* secrets – not with old Hinge and Bracket watching him like a hawk from the reception desk,' I laugh. 'Did she slam the reception window on you?'

'Yeah!' she giggles.

'Wow, you're almost a local.'

'That's my problem, I almost am!'

Our laughter dies as we approach the emerald awnings of the café, I crane my neck to see over the lace curtain and establish how busy they are: packed.

'It's not too cold for a table outside, is it?' noting the flimsy jacket that she is wearing.

'That's fine.'

It isn't quite so fine with me, it is the last place I wish to be perched, slap bang opposite the estate agents.

'This was my shout, so I'll pay. What are you having?'

I ignore my inner voice that suggests we go two minutes up the road to the other café, slightly pokey but still serving hot coffee and where we'll definitely get a table inside.

'Hot chocolate, please.'

Flora drags a couple of chairs to the nearest chrome table, I disappear inside.

A sea of green and white gingham covers The Corner Café: tablecloths, plastic menu covers and Alexandro's serving pinny all co-ordinate.

The second I enter; I want to leave. I recognise the back of her head in an instant, as she turns I try to duck out of sight.

'Joel! What a nice surprise… and with such *fetching* bruising,' says Veronica.

'Veronica, good to see you.' I notice the curl of her lip.

'Day off?'

'On the sick due to my injuries.' I point to my face purely to reinforce the details.

'Full pay? That's good, it ensures you can cope financially.'

I smile. Is she trying to start an argument?

'Cope? I'm coping just fine thanks... which reminds me, can I ask what the delay is regarding you signing over the flat?'

She squirms as I ask for the umpteenth time, her harsh lip-lined mouth twitches and tweaks but nothing audible emerges.

'I thought I'd crossed all the 'T's and dotted all those 'I's and yet still you remain... unsigned,' I say, adding, 'I can't think why?'

'Joel, you simply don't understand the property market.'

'Correction. I understand the property market very well thanks to you and your expert tuition. I have a sneaking suspicion that you may be watching the market and hoping for an extra slice of the pie should the market value increase...' I allow my sentence to fade.

'Are you seriously implying that?'

The rotund figure of Alexandro offers a welcoming distraction at the counter. I quickly sidestep my ex-girlfriend, ignoring her flimsy plea of innocence as she clutches her skinny latte with extra sprinkles.

'Yes, two hot chocolates, please.'

'I don't want a hot chocolate!' squeals Veronica, holding up her cartoned drink.

'Hold your horses – it's not *for* you!' I retort, amused that she'd even entertain the idea.

The steam shoots through the jug of milk much like the surprise on Veronica's face.

'Well who?'

I smile, and dig into my pockets for change.

'Who?' she repeats impatiently.

'Sorry?'

'I said... I asked... who?'

Her manner becomes snippy as her power slips away, much like mine had in our relationship.

I'll admit I was flattered at the beginning, an attractive

woman taking an interest in me. Her age didn't come into it. I soon realised that maybe the compliment was reversed and it should be her flattered by a man twelve years her junior taking an interest. That is until she discovered that sugar daddies flatter her more financially.

'I said... and I know you heard me correctly... who?'

'A friend,' I say, turning my attention to Alexandro who has produced two perfect hot chocolates complete with whipped cream and marshmallows.

'Thank you, put the change in the charity box,' I add, taking my leave. As I walk to the exit carrying the drinks tray, I'm aware of the totter of heels following my strides.

What now?

Once outside I slide the tray in front of Flora and settle opposite.

'Well, I never,' jibes Veronica. 'Little orphan Bede?'

'Hello,' beams Flora, not sensing the tension.

'Flora, meet Veronica...'

'Nice to meet you again... we met at the ladies' night.'

My eyebrows lift in surprise.

'Veronica, you actually went to The Peacock – you always said it was a dive of a pub. Did you enjoy yourself at ladies' night?'

'Give it a bloody rest, won't you!' snaps Veronica, before stomping across the road towards the estate agents.

'What's rattled her cage?' asks Flora, as I unload the tray of drinks.

'Long story...'

Flora nods and politely smiles – the penny drops.

Had I found her attractive? Was it my own insecurities that had drawn me towards her flattery and attention? I was never a Casanova where the ladies were concerned but I'd had my share of girlfriends.

'Anyway, less of Veronica… let's focus on your search.'

We spend the next thirty minutes sipping and chatting about her quest.

Flora's so animated; her hands wave about as she discusses the people she's met. Her eyes sparkle as the excitement overflows like a child at Christmas.

'Had you given much thought to your father being found?' I ask, cradling my half-spent drink.

The look of surprise is clear.

'I hadn't given him much thought… until today. There's got to be a reason why I was left on Dr Fowler's doorstep. What happens if he knows but has never said?'

I don't know what to say to her.

'Joel?'

'There will be a reason, but you're not going to confront him, are you?'

'No, but it's a possibility.'

'Maybe.'

'*Maybe*?'

'There's a fair chance that whoever your father is… he might not know about a pregnancy.'

I watch as she pauses, sips her drink and turns away.

'You have to cover all angles – as painful as that could be. There might be many reasons why she did what she did.'

'Perhaps… but maybe the doctor will enlighten me on one.'

'Anything is a possibility at this stage, don't rule anything out until proven… that's how we work on an investigation – anything is feasible within a given set of circumstances.'

Veronica

Since when has he ever drunk hot chocolate? Never, that's when. Yet look at him now, with her, the whole works: cream, marshmallows and a frigging long-handled spoon!

I bet he wanted a latte. He always wanted a latte when ordering with me.

The times we spent in The Corner Café on a Sunday morning sipping hazelnut lattes and poring over the morning papers – and now, he's drinking hot chocolate with *her*.

'Bitch!'

I duck behind the advertising board; as they turn to look in this direction my breath catches in my throat, surely he's just helping her answer a few questions on police matters and suchlike? Yes, that's more like it.

'What are you doing?'

I spin round to find my young assistant Donnie watching me from the door of the kitchenette, his skintight trousers giving him a Max Wall style outline.

'Nothing,' I lie, resuming my task.

He joins me behind the hoarding and peers over at the café.

'You still mooning over him?'

'I can assure you, I am not! I've moved on from that one... my belongings are out of his cramped apartment and unpacked in my lavish new home with Major Matthews.'

'Your home?' he scoffs.

'Yes, *my* home. You young kids know nothing about relationships... it's give and take in every respect.'

'Mmmm,' he says, eyeing me in a comical fashion.

'It is *my* place. I've replaced the kitchen cupboard handles to fashionable knobs, chosen the colour scheme for the downstairs cloakroom and ordered a tonne of luxurious scatter cushions, so that proves I've truly moved on and moved *in*!'

'Proves nothing if you're still moping over Joel,' he says, adding, 'Anyway, changing knobs doesn't mean anything and you know it, Veronica.'

Is he making fun of me, or was that an unfortunate turn of phrase? I glance at his profile. He doesn't appear to be sniggering.

'Brushed chrome?' he continues.

'No, coloured ceramic actually...'

'*Nice*.'

'Co-ordinated to complement the Aga.'

'Very swish, but even so... you're still moping.'

'I'm not. Joel's too immature for my liking, too intense and, what do you call it?'

'Young?'

'You cheeky swine... that makes me sound ancient,' I say, sucking in my stomach.

'Inexperienced?'

'No!'

'Youthful?'

'Donnie, you're not helping... commitment-phobic!'

'*Really*?'

'Wouldn't fully commit despite the property purchase... always on the lookout for a way out, to distance himself and slow the relationship down.'

'He never came across like that. I thought he was truly, madly, deeply into you. I imagined that it was you that didn't want to settle down and define the relationship.'

Donnie isn't as naive as I'd imagined.

'Strange how relationships come across, isn't it?' I mutter, unsure who I am trying to convince.

Silence descends as we watch them sip their drinks.

'So that's why you slept with the old guy then... to force Joel's hand towards making a commitment?'

Donnie's words hit a bullseye in my chest.

'Haven't you got a viewing to attend to?' I snap, surprised that Donnie knows so much about my private life. 'If not, take a break and nip along to The Peacock to chat with your brother about madam over there.'

'Phhh, I won't get any info from our Denny, his only contact in life is with that damned fruit machine.'

Joel

We sit in silence, sipping our drinks, before I feel the need to fill the gap.

'I don't think you look like the Doc,' I add, wanting to be honest with her.

She smiles, turning to face me.

'Nor me, but even so.'

'What a twisted web we weave in life.'

Her green eyes stare directly at me, her pupils enlarge.

'I'm truly sorry about your nose.'

'Mmmm,' I say, breaking off my analysis of her eye colour.

'Seriously I am, I've never hit or hurt anyone in my life and to think that the first person was...'

You. Go on say it. Let the word slip from your lips. I dare you to. I promise I'll fill the silence or embarrassment that may follow.

She says nothing. I can hear her breathing. I can see a twinkle in her widening eyes. It's as if I can see her thought process. A slight smile dawns upon her lips as she breaks the spell, shifts her seating position and sips her hot chocolate.

'*So...* tell me when are you back at work having been assaulted by a crazy woman?'

The atmosphere changes.

'A few more days until my rota starts again, by which time I'm hoping this...' I point to my bruise, '...will have gone.'

Missed it. Chance gone. Big Tony's right, I'm losing my

touch. I thought my gallant kissing her hand gesture at New Year might have worked, obviously not.

'Anything interesting planned?'

'I was planning to support a private investigation but I don't know if the crazy wench needs a...' I pause.

Shit, I was about to say partner... but that'll sound too forward or will it sound coy? Do it. Say it.

'Partner.'

'Oh really, so *this* crazy wench needs a partner, does she?'

'I think so.'

'Don't you think she's doing OK as she is?' asks Flora.

Shit is she talking partner or *partner*?

'Maybe, but in some respects... no.'

'No?'

'Yep, no.'

'Explain?' her brows crease.

Her head tilt suggests impatience.

'Isn't everything easier when there are two of you?'

'Like you and what's his face?'

'Scotty?'

'Yep him, my arresting officer...'

'*Exactly*, we're a duo. On the job, we make up for each other's weaknesses.'

Mine being I'm losing my touch and being assaulted by lone females.

'And his?'

'His?' I mouth, not sure what she's asking.

'Weaknesses?'

I shrug, trying to act nonchalant.

I didn't see that one coming. Dare I be brutally honest? Love him as a mate, but announcing he's a player will surely put her off him, won't it?

I shift in my chair.

133

Though maybe Scotty is more her type, younger, energetic, good-looking and a dab hand with the cuffs.

'I'll tell you his weaknesses... being too rough whilst putting those cuffs on... plus he manhandles you when he bobs your head into the patrol car,' she says.

Phew... for one minute there I thought she was interested.

'I'll have a word, don't worry.'

She drains her mug.

'Anyway, thanks for the drink and the chat – I owe you one. I must dash, but if you're around later, I'll catch you in The Peacock.'

'*Absolutely*. Take care.'

She collects her belongings and hastily departs.

I smile as she bounds across the road towards The Square. I drain the dregs from my mug before standing and pushing my chair under the table – a sudden movement from the window of the estate agents catches my eye.

'Seriously, Veronica, you're stooping to new depths here.' I pretend not to have seen and walk straight past the estate agent's window, heading back to my car.

19

Dr Fowler

I'm early, it's only quarter to six.

Despite living across The Square, it's been a while since I visited The Peacock. I nod and acknowledge a few recognisable faces and make my way to the bar. Nothing has changed. The atmosphere remains warm and traditional, a smattering of drinkers and a group of youths congregate around the flashing fruit machine – a different generation but the same mentality.

'Hello Jeffery... what'll it be?' asks Annie cheerfully from behind her bar.

'A Scotch and water, no ice, please?'

I watch as Annie moves rhythmically around the optics.

Pleasant woman, I've known her since childhood, though sadly I wasn't able to assist her and her husband as I'd have hoped; options regards fertility were limited back then. Science doesn't always work as we'd wish, regardless of attempts or effort.

'On the house,' murmurs Annie, placing the drink on a bar mat.

'*Annie.*'

She shakes her head firmly.

'I'm sure.'

'Thank you, good health to you both.'

'Nice one,' she laughs, drifting off to serve another customer.

When was the last time I came in here? It must have been when me and Nina were still married… I'm going back almost thirty years. It hasn't been that long, surely?

I turn to view the roaring coal fire, the adjoining alcove looks intriguing as it's filled with a large map and multicoloured pinned flags. I near the display as the recognition hits me… my house!

Drink in hand, I peer at the array of photos. A series of snapshots, taken from various angles of The Square, have been pinned round the edge and linked with string at various points, into which the tiny flags are stabbed like an abstract finger-buffet positioned on the wall.

I sit down in the alcove and absorb the many details.

Boy oh boy, some work has gone into this.

A manuscript book on the table requests that I browse and add comments.

I sip my drink while flicking through and reading the chunks of handwriting in various ink colours. It's like a trip down memory lane seeing some of the names and remembering them – all grown with families of their own, I suppose. It takes me back to those days.

I hadn't expected her to cry that much. From the moment Nina answered the door, she didn't stop crying. A torrent of tears stained her face for weeks, nothing I said gave her any comfort.

I'd wondered what the racket was while I was in the bathroom, but to come downstairs with a shaving foam beard and razor in hand to be greeted by my young wife, the paperboy *and* a baby was some shock.

Did I run back upstairs or wipe my face on a dishcloth from the kitchen? Who knows, I can't remember, but coming down the stairs and seeing that lad standing in our hallway while Nina sobbed was an image that I've replayed many times.

'Jeffery, it's a baby!' Nina's smile was from ear to ear, as she cradled the newborn, as though the stork had delivered her wildest dream.

'I can see that, but what's it doing here?' I'd said, pausing halfway down the staircase in my trousers and a vest.

'She was on your doorstep, Mister,' said the paper lad, peering up at me.

I called the police. And then an ambulance. Nina never forgave me for doing that.

The baby girl looked healthy even in that manky towel. And all the time, Nina stood on the sidelines, sobbing and begging. What was I supposed to say? She wasn't ours to keep, was she? And the lad knew that, he'd found her. How could we pretend otherwise? Even a doctor's wife can't hide a pregnancy *that* well and then step out into The Square and parade a Silver Cross pram.

I take a swig of my drink.

I knew it would hit Nina hard, but I never fully appreciated her instinct or reaction until it was too late for us. Was that morning truly the beginning of our end?

The image as I ran down the stairs to behold the three of them clustered in our hallway fills my memory.

Oh Nina, what could I do?

After her tears dried, the harsh accusations began. The niggling doubt that played upon her mind for every minute of every hour. How many times had she accused me of having an affair? Why would I want to be a father without her being the mother? But it was too late; the catalyst for such insinuations had arrived on *our* doorstep. Who'd have imagined that five years of marriage would unravel from that day onwards? Not me.

Before *that* morning, the focus had always been us having a child, but once the police and ambulance had taken away her dream, she'd called me selfish. Was I? Could we have concealed her? Could the newspaper lad have kept such a secret for three decades?

I sip my drink.

And yet, someone had!

I eyed the bar, watched Annie laugh with a young couple before disappearing along the bar to tidy glasses.

Maybe we could have concealed her with some planning. Nina said the young are so naïve... *surely* not that naïve? Could Nina have gone into hiding, started to drip-feed the happy news before 'hey presto' the arrival of a baby girl.

I shudder at such ideas.

Don't refine the perfect plan now, Jeffery – it's thirty years too late, old chap.

Guilt rises in my throat; I wash it down with whisky.

How could I not understand how broody she was? But how could I be dishonest within our new community? What would old Dr Bird have said if the deceit came to light? My old medical mentor would have run me out of the surgery had I followed Nina's thinking. Why couldn't she be patient and give science a chance. It was early days regarding test-tube babies but it had worked for some couples – it might have worked for us. If not, adoption remained an option, but no, Nina could think of nothing else but the baby I sent from our doorstep.

I wonder how Nina is? Did she ever believe me about the baby? After all these years, she must do. Maybe I should give her a call someday, go for a drink and catch up... though maybe Steve... was it Steve she married? Yeah Steve, he might not appreciate that. Would I want a wife catching up with her ex-husband? Mmmm, maybe not.

The church clock strikes six. Flora arrives at the bottom of the staircase dressed in red jeans and a large shirt.

Come on, old man, what's there to worry about – a simple conversation recalling and remembering – how difficult can that be?

20

Mick

I found her crying in the cellar. Standing amongst the metal barrels with plastic pump tubing trailing up and over her bowed head. I knew, as soon as I laid eyes on her, I knew.

'Come here, Annie,' I whisper, as I put my arms around her. She sinks into my chest and we stand in silence, as silent as it can be in a working cellar, as her tears flow.

'Is that better?'

She nods, wipes her eyes on her sleeve, looks up with her smile secured in place.

'That's my girl.'

'I couldn't help it, he came in, and I served him and it all came flooding back. I gave him a drink on the house but... I know it wasn't his fault... I know that but...'

'Buts... Ifs... what have we said over the years – it wasn't meant to be, my darling, and if we hadn't met, and you'd married someone else, and I'd won the pools, and if you'd left the village to travel across America... there are too many ifs and buts and whys to try and make sense of it all, aren't there?'

She nods. She calms, as always.

'Do you think Flora being here has brought it to the forefront for you?'

'Maybe, though I love her being here, Mick. I know she's

extended her stay longer than the original few days, but she's lovely to have around… and I do want to help her as much as possible…' she says, as a second wave of tears erupts. 'Because if we feel like this at not having a baby can you imagine being her and not knowing who her parents are but knowing… they didn't want her!'

I gulp down my own emotion and pull her close for round two of tears.

'Poor gal.'

*

I don't know how it started. One minute I was serving behind the bar while Annie cleared a table of empty dessert dishes. The next thing, Marie Salter was on her arse in the middle of the bar with our Gene's wife, Melanie, screaming blue murder in her face.

'Hey, hey, hey, we'll have none of that, ladies!' I charge round the bar, as quick as my bad back would allow. Separating the two women as groups of men turn to stare at tonight's entertainment.

'She started it,' shouts out Melanie, looking for Gene, who is standing further along the bar and pretending not to have noticed the carry-on. 'A dirty little tramp like that accusing me of stuff… who the bloody hell do you think you are, Marie Salter?'

'Gene, take your Melanie home,' I shout, putting myself between the two women and extending a hand to help Marie up from the carpet.

'I don't know who you're calling a tramp! You shagged every lad in the sixth form behind those bike sheds… so you can drop the act of being all high and mighty.'

I instantly let go of Marie's hand; she falls backwards onto the carpet in a heap.

'Oi, you frigging oaf,' she snarls at me.

'I tried to help, tried to intervene to keep it peaceful, but you couldn't leave it,' I mutter, lifting her under the arms and walking her towards the door. 'Out!'

'You can wipe that frigging smirk off your face Melanie O'Neill... you might have married into this family but you'll always be a lowlife Delaney... shagging your way round the estate one bloke at a time.'

I close the door on her foul comments.

'Gene, take her home please... we don't have that sort of behaviour from the men in here let alone the women.'

Gene drains his pint glass and nods, leading his bedraggled wife out. Slowly the crowd resume their drinking and chatting. I glance along the bar at Annie and shake my head.

'I thought her teenage jollies had been long forgotten,' giggles Annie, returning change to her customer.

I know my sister-in-law wasn't raised in the best of manners but is it necessary to drag up the dirt on our neighbours?

'Marie Salter was no angel though, was she?' I add.

'Not according to Billy McKenzie, he was always bragging about their Sunday drives out to the countryside,' adds Annie, wiping the bar top.

'It's stuff like that that's being raked up. It's not Flora's fault, but everyone's turned detective,' shouts Denny, from the far end of the bar.

I couldn't agree more, as much as I like the young woman... this village is having its clock turned back and who knows what memories people are going to start dragging up.

21

Joel

I put my coffee mug down and stare at Scotty's side profile as he completes paperwork at his desk.

'Would you want to know if you'd fathered a child?'

I wait while he stares at me and thinks.

'Too long, mate, I could answer that question in a nanosecond.'

'Of course,' mutters Scotty, his stare intensifying. 'Are you trying to tell me something? Is one of the WPC claiming that I'm…?'

'Sod off – you can relax.'

'Phew! Don't joke like that, man,' says Scotty, acting astonished.

'But you'd *want* to know if there was a little Scotty running about somewhere, wouldn't you?'

I watch his blank face.

'Scotty, it's your flesh and blood and… well, yours!'

Scotty nods slowly.

'He couldn't have known, could he?'

'Who?'

'Flora's father.'

'I wondered when we'd get back round to her?' He checks his watch, adding, 'Bingo, all of ten minutes.'

'Look, the chances of two people knowing about such a plan and pulling it off with them both consenting and never telling anyone else in thirty years would be some pact, wouldn't it?'

Scotty leans back and grimaces.

'Haven't you got anything better to do whilst on sick leave... you're not even supposed to be here. Go home!'

I ignore him.

'People make pacts all the time, and instantly go back on them when the reality of the situation hits home. Look at me and Veronica... planning a life together... she's gone back on her word in a matter of years, let alone thirty!'

'*And*?'

'My point is... the guy doesn't know that baby was his!'

'He wouldn't be the first.'

'No, and I'm not saying that makes it all right... so the mother must have acted alone and simply lived with the secret.'

'So, your theory is someone else would have dobbed her in? *Perhaps*.'

My instincts are calling the shots on this one.

'Think about this village and the families around here... they would have crucified her if they'd found out... can you imagine it?' I say, adding, 'They'd have disowned her if they'd even suspected.'

Scotty shrugs.

'*So* not even her family knew she was pregnant... so surely it couldn't have been a married woman... you'd notice if your partner showed any signs of a full-term pregnancy.'

Scotty shrugs again.

'What! You're saying you wouldn't notice a pregnancy belly? Be serious for once in your life!' I say in disgust.

'How would I know?'

'Pregnancy hasn't happened to me either, mate, but I've got eyes in my head – I'd definitely notice.'

'OK, I'd notice too,' says Scotty.

'Don't say it just to shut me up.'

'Bloody hell, you're right touchy since she blackened your face, you know that?'

I ignore him and continue.

'So, what situations or circumstances would a couple have to be in for her not to tell him she's pregnant and for him not to notice and never find out?'

'An affair?'

'Possible.'

'Especially if he's older or married... or a break-up when the pregnancy was pretty early on so the mother might not have known at the time but later discovers she is.'

'*Now* you're thinking, Scotty.'

'Rape.'

'Let's hope not... but sadly, a feasible suggestion.'

'Especially if she didn't report it in the first place...'

'*OK*, I'd dearly like to rule that theory out. Next.'

'Or, the chap was away a lot,' adds Scotty.

'The armed forces?'

We both give knowing nods.

'Some army tours can be pretty lengthy,' adds Scotty. 'Young lad, home on leave, a few pints and some fun with a young lady before rejoining his squaddies on tour.'

'Maybe the mother didn't know how to contact him, so she felt under pressure and faced raising the child alone.'

'Or a housewife left at home with a couple of kids discovers she's expecting and knows she can't cope with another baby while her husband's on a tour of duty.'

I shake my head.

'I can't see a woman who has raised children doing *that*... putting her down and walking away – I can't see it.'

'You never know, Joel... it's a possibility.'

'So, who in the village has links to the services?'

'Well not now... but back in eighty-five or eighty-six there could have been a family in the armed forces... you don't know everything about this village, you know. I grew up here, you didn't!'

'Yeah, but even so, how old are you? Oh yeah, I forgot you weren't even born... you're only twenty bloody six!'

'A number, mate, just a number.'

'You don't know everything either,' I jibe, pulling a face for good measure, though it wasn't the best idea, given my bruised features.

'You know I've got work to do and my coffee has gone cold... so if you're thinking of hanging around here yet again... go make yourself useful and brew up, tea boy!'

He's got a point. I was supposed to be on sick leave but being alone at home didn't appeal.

I prise myself from the office chair, collect his cold coffee and head for the staff kitchen, my mind buzzing with feasible scenarios.

22

?

Not all the Pooley girls stayed around this dump. Who left and never returned? You'll be surprised by the secrets some people keep.

23

Flora

'Morning, Gene,' I say, coming down for breakfast, surprised to see him seated at the bar.

'Morning,' he answers but instantly stands up, taking his half-eaten breakfast into the private living quarters of the pub.

I stare along the bar at Annie, querying what I said wrong?

'Don't worry, lovey, a bad night in their house, so he's kipped here, but don't you worry about that pair... fiery relationship if you ask me. Here's your morning tea – do you want a cooked breakfast?'

I nod, as I settle in my alcove.

'Has Melanie kicked him out?'

'Nah, nothing like that, just another stupid row... it'll blow over,' she produces a fake smile. 'But have you seen your display board?'

I stare up at the alcove wall, taking in the multitude of new pins and flags.

'It's coming along, isn't it?' she adds.

'It is, but there doesn't seem to be many connections – it's great knowing where people lived, but it's the relationships, the fallouts, the drama and gossip that I need.'

Annie's face drops.

'Is it not helping?'

'Yes and no. I spoke to Doctor Fowler yesterday, but it was all very factual and precise about me being found. I know the basics – I've read the article a million times. What I need is a gossipy old lady who hasn't got Alzheimer's or dementia, who I can take to tea for a good old chinwag about the olden days.'

'Less of the olden days, thank you!' laughs Annie.

Mick comes from their living quarters through into the bar.

'Morning Flora... the young officer left you a note last night, here,' says Mick, handing over a slip of paper.

I quickly unfold the paper and read aloud.

Flora,

Sorry I couldn't make it for a drink last night, but if you're free today maybe we could take a tour of the village and I'll talk through a couple of ideas that we've had.

Joel.

I look up to see Annie and Mick grinning at each other.

'What?' I ask bashfully, folding the note.

'*What*? she says... like she hasn't got a bloody clue,' says Annie, snuggling up to Mick.

'Bloody women, us guys make it as obvious as we can and you still give us the runaround.'

'Hey, Mick, do you remember that programme *Runaround* with Mike Reid... I used to love the way he shouted it,' says Annie, dipping from beneath his arm.

'*Runaround*!' bellows Mick, before darting into the gap made by the open hinged bar and holding onto the bar edges. Annie runs about and yet goes nowhere. I haven't a clue what programme they're on about but both are laughing and acting like big kids.

'See what you've started – everyone's drifting back to the eighties since you arrived.'

Yes, but not too many are linked to my birth mum.

The pub door bursts open, sending the chime swinging on its tiny hook. Mick and Annie's laughter ceases as Melanie storms into the bar, her face like thunder.

'Where's Gene?'

'In the back enjoying a quiet breakfast,' answers Mick, thumbing towards the living quarters. 'So please don't...'

'I don't give a shit what you lot think!' she shouts, pointing at Mick. 'I'm not the mother of *that* baby... and if I have to keep defending myself till my dying day, I will!'

'*Excuse* me?' I call from the alcove.

Annie shakes her head slowly.

'Sorry... no offence, but you aren't looking for me – despite what folk say,' shouts Melanie. 'One day this village will apologise for the hurtful things they've all said about me. I'll be gracious and accept their piteous attempts, but I'll never forgive them for the damage they've caused.'

I watch as the heat of her anger subsides into tears.

'Melanie,' says Mick, starting to walk towards the quivering form.

'Don't!' she yells, refusing Mick's hug. 'And now Gene's gone on another of his sulks.'

'It's what blokes do when it suits 'em,' adds Annie. 'Get used to it, Mel.'

Is this what my search is costing the local community? I want the ground to open and swallow me whole.

Melanie turns on her heels and flees from the pub, leaving three stunned faces exchanging silent glances. Gone was the *Runaround* laughter, the joviality of the morning dashed as the door chime swung back and forth.

*

I wolf down my breakfast in record time, as the day had suddenly gained importance thanks to Joel's note. I dash back to room five, apply a dab of make-up, not much because I haven't that much to hand.

I reread his note, there isn't a stipulated time but surely any reasonable person would know or at least assume that I'd be up, dressed, breakfasted and waiting by nine o'clock. Surely?

No.

I sit for a short time in the bar impatiently, Annie craftily involves me in glass cleaning and polishing, so when the church clock strikes eleven and the door chime sounds I am quite absorbed.

'Hi,' smiles Joel, crossing the bar in a sprightly manner.

His bruising looks horrendous: a double blob of deep purple and green, like a tainted superhero mask.

A chorus of 'Hi' rises from Annie and myself, though I notice she quickly disappears into the back, leaving us alone – as subtle as a brick, Annie.

As he waits for me to collect my belongings, my phone vibrates on the table.

I smile as the screen illuminates: 'cheating bastard'.

'Nice, have all your contacts such descriptive names?' asks Joel, nodding towards the vibrating phone.

I blush at such a juvenile stunt.

'No, but he deserves it.'

Joel gives a nod.

'Could I request "decent chap" or even "Friday night date" as my name?'

I'm taken aback, being so brazen didn't appear to be his style.

'*You're* not in my phone.'

'Maybe I should be.'

My cheeks are burning; I'm not used to this flirting.

I simply stare and watch his eyes search mine.

'Either name will do, alphabetically it'll place me after him,' Joel grins at his own smartness.

I can't think of a clever answer, so fumble with the phone before quickly putting it away.

Within minutes we've shouted our goodbyes, left the bar and are striding across the yellow slush piles of The Square towards St Bede's Mews.

'How are we?' he asks, zipping his jacket against the cold.

'I'm fine, the display board has exploded with new information but nothing that connects or suggests a name.'

I pull my coat collar up, having gratefully borrowed yet another item of clothing from Annie.

Joel smiles.

'That's where I come in... my Grandpop has lived in Pooley all his life, he's got a memory like an elephant and can talk for England.'

'Just what I need!' I can hear the excitement in my own voice.

'*Exactly*, so I figured he was an invaluable source.'

'Are we meeting up?'

'No, he doesn't walk too well and doesn't like visitors either, so...' Joel pulls a notebook from his inner pocket. 'I called round last night, which was why I didn't pop down to The Peacock, and took notes, so we have plenty to work from.'

I choke back a wave of gratitude before I can even begin to look at him, let alone thank him.

'Thank you so much... this is exactly what I need,' my voice trails as his dark brown eyes bore into mine. Stop staring and finish your sentence. 'I owe you one, big time!'

A broad smile crinkles the sides of his bruised eyes and a vigorous nod confirms it.

'And I'll hold you to that, come on let's start at the church.' He strides off, I remain in situ. 'Come on, don't lag... and change your face, I know your story isn't linked except by nickname – but *you* need to know what was once the heart of *this* community. Now, hurry up.'

I trot behind him, my feet squelching in a pair of borrowed

boots. I must purchase some of my own tomorrow; I can't keep switching between party shoes and Annie's generous nature.

In minutes, we are treading the pathway that I'd tried a few nights before.

'It'll be locked up. I came over the other night.'

I watch as Joel confidently twists the iron ring on the oak door: open sesame.

'Depends who you know, doesn't it?'

He pushes the door wide open and stands aside, allowing me to enter first.

'But... but...'

'Father Maguire is waiting for you, go through,' he whispers, nodding towards the depths of the church.

Annie's boots resound on the mosaic floor, as my eyes take in the rainbow of colour in the stained glass.

'It's beautiful,' I gasp.

'I know.' Is his only comment, before he nods towards the large crucifix and crosses himself before striding the length of the aisle between the dark wooden pews towards the altar.

Am I supposed to do that?

I perform an awkward nod but nothing more, then stumble along the carpeted aisle in pursuit of Joel.

At the altar, Joel takes a right turn, cutting across the front pew, which is empty but for a pile of fabric-covered hymn books, and heads towards an arched doorway.

'Joel, wait!'

He doesn't answer me, I simply follow.

The door opens into a huge changing area where various coloured robes hang on individual hooks set into the stone walls. An array of boots and black shoes are slung beneath the long benches on the far side. On the black and white tiled floor there are open boxes of candles in various shapes and sizes, some red, some blue.

'The floor tiling is amazing.'

Joel scrunches up his brow and peers at me.

'What?' I point at the geometric mosaic of tiles. 'I've never seen this area of a church before.'

He ignores me.

'Father?' calls Joel, beckoning me through another doorway. 'Father Maguire?'

'Is this where he lives?'

'Shush, please!'

Cheek. I was only asking.

I pout.

Joel turns his back to me; repeating his call towards the connecting oak door.

'Joel, my boy...' the second door swings wide revealing a rotund man in his later years, wearing dark robes, his outstretched hands clasp Joel's hand warmly and shake it before pointing to his bruised face. 'Ouch, that looks nasty.'

Great, even the church knows about the accidental headbutt.

'Hello, Father Maguire, nice to see you looking so well.'

'The pleasure is mine, my lad. And who is this?'

'Father, this is Flora... the lady I called about earlier.'

'My, oh my... the very lady herself. We've heard a lot about you this last week.'

Really?

'Hello.'

'You've got everyone's tongues wagging, hasn't she, Joel?' says Father Maguire. 'Anyway, come through, I've arranged for a tea tray in my study.'

He turns, leading us through the second doorway, Joel waves me past and falls in line at the back of the procession.

My eyes grow wide as I'm led through a network of stone corridors: high ceilings, flagstone floors and decorative windows before we reach another impressive carved door through which we arrive into a carpeted hallway.

Father Maguire enters, changing his shoes into slippers

waiting beside the door. I glance at Joel – that's the sort of thing my dad would do.

'Is this where he lives?' I silently mouth.

'Yes, the presbytery!' mutters Joel in the same mouthing manner, though I could tell his tone of voice would have been snappy had it been louder.

It's not my fault, I don't know what I don't know. Obviously, he's been brought up with all these traditions and routines, especially as he's been called 'my boy' and 'my lad'.

'Joel was one of our finest choirboys when he was a young-ster, weren't you?' says Father Maguire, as his slippers flip-flop along the hallway. 'One of the best we've had here.'

'Joel hasn't mentioned that little detail,' I say, beaming a sneaky smile in Joel's direction. He slowly shakes his head.

'Not quite, Father. I can sing, but I'm sure there are plenty of good choirboys in this village.'

'Name me one better than you, Joel?' teases Father Maguire, his blue eyes shining.

I watch as a slight flush comes to Joel's cheeks.

'As I thought, you can't,' continues Father Maguire. 'He's a decent sort, young lady, so mind you tread carefully... I wouldn't want to see him hurt again.'

'*Father*,' appeals Joel in haste.

Father Maguire smiles before leading us into his study.

'Come through, take a seat.'

The roar of the coal fire warms my cheeks as I enter.

Within seconds I'm sitting in a comfortable fireside chair, Joel sits opposite me, Father Maguire is on the adjacent couch besides which awaits the tea tray and a huge plate of biscuits on a side table.

'Shall I?' asks Joel, indicating the tray.

'Please, I can get to know this young lady and maybe help in her quest.'

Joel busies himself pouring tea.

'What is it you'd like to know?'

I remove my coat and drape it across the arm of the chair.

'Absolutely anything to be honest, Father... I know nothing apart from my discovery on the doorstep,' I explain. I venture further, mentioning that Darren has been in touch, that Betty at the library showed me pieces from subsequent newspapers and that the display at The Peacock grows by the hour but so much seems to be missing or unconnected.

'I see, and me being the old goat that I am could hold a vital piece that starts you on the right track?'

'Something like that, or at least your confessional box could,' says Joel, handing me a quivering china teacup, before handing Father Maguire one.

'Thank you... I would prefer a large mug, but I bet she hasn't laid one out, has she?' he mutters.

'No, just biscuits,' laughs Joel, returning for the plate of goodies and his china cup.

'More's the pity,' he mutters. 'You understand that I can't break the faith of the confessional?'

'Of course, she wouldn't want you to, but maybe you remember something of that time to point her in the right direction,' says Joel, settling himself after offering the biscuits around. 'For instance, I remember when I was at school, Rosie Bradshaw stood on an art room table to announce that she was expecting a baby with Steve Hopkins... it wasn't true but it showed they'd played about and I've never forgotten the look on his face as he stood staring up at her – the teacher was furious, but the damage was done. I haven't seen Steve for years, and yet, I remember *that* moment.'

'I see.'

Father Maguire pauses, eats two bourbons and slurps his tea.

Joel smiles in my direction as the silence stretches. I sip my tea and nibble at a custard cream.

'Eighty-six you say?'

'Correct,' confirms Joel, watching his wizened features.

'We were raising money for the new roof back then,' he mutters. 'It took so long it became a community joke – St Editha's in the next village beat us in no time.'

I screw my face up at Joel.

This bloke seemed great, but on second thoughts.

'Shhh,' mouths Joel in my direction. 'What was that, Father?'

'Eighty-five was a bad winter for us here at St Bede's... you won't remember, Joel – you were just a babe in arms, but the roof leaked terribly. We had plastic buckets all over the place catching the dripping rainwater. Enough was enough when it poured through the ceiling on the McNally wedding – shame that... a beautiful service totally ruined. Anyway, the church council finally agreed we needed to raise funds, so we had one of those ghastly fundraising boards pitched out the front beside the trees. Each week the W.I. ladies wanted to update it... they drove me potty adding a millimetre of red paint to show the week's new total... foolish really but they insisted that it would boost donations. I let them do it, but really, I despise such carbuncles in front of my church. Ridiculous really given that by the following December some bugger had stripped the new lead from the roof and we had to ask the church council for financial support. But maybe...'

I stare intently at Joel.

What the hell?

Joel bares his teeth at me.

'And how might that be important, Father?' I ask, not sure that I want to hear more W.I. fairy tales.

'I have long thought that the charity fundraising for a new lead roof might have played a part...'

'Why?' asks Joel, before I could utter my confusion.

'The teenagers... they used to... you know... behind it.'

I wait for him to finish his sentence, nodding encouragement.

'You know... copulate behind it.'

Joel spits his tea down his shirt and into his lap.

'Father!'

My face goes into a spasm of shock, my mouth gapes and I flush deep crimson.

'Fear not, young man... we had to take it down because it was becoming quite an issue for us.'

'Father Maguire! Flora, are you OK?' asks Joel, mopping his lap with a paper serviette.

'The ladies of the W.I. put up a great fight, but we couldn't ignore the situation any longer. The young folk showed such little respect back then, and once the hoarding was erected, well...' he peers over at me. 'I have always wondered if your dear self was a result of...'

'That's quite a revelation,' laughs Joel.

'You were born in October, yes?'

I nod; words were currently not my strong point.

Father turns to Joel, as though man's talk was about to occur.

'New Year joviality and then...' he waves a hand in my direction.

'I see.' Joel gives a nod.

'Great, so you're suggesting I was conceived behind your "raise the roof" hoarding!' I gasp.

'Flora, you're missing the point... it's not the billboard hoarding but maybe the New Year revellers, including youngsters enjoying... teenage kicks.'

'Great, it gets better... I was the result of a teenage fumble... a drunken one at that... oh, isn't it great that she deposited, sorry abandoned me in sight of the church *and* my conception spot. Am I supposed to be thrilled about this or deeply ashamed that the beginning of my sodding existence is such a mess and is getting decidedly tacky and dirty as the days go by?'

The flood of tears stops my rant as my voice subsides to miming and mouthing. I crumple in the armchair.

A pair of arms are around my shoulders in an instant, I look up to view a blurred vision of Joel kneeling before me.

'My dear, your beginning isn't what defines you... believe me. Our Lord was born in a stable.'

'The teenagers gather where they can for some laughs and teenage kicks,' adds Joel, stroking my hair.

'The youth club used to be located on the far side of the archway, so the drunken antics of the young spilled into The Square,' adds Father Maguire.

'Where many an adult fumble has occurred after a few too many in The Peacock,' adds Joel, conjuring a white tissue from his pocket to wipe a tear from my cheek and stroking his thumb gently along my jawline to collect the line of dripping tears.

'Thank you,' I hiccup, as he stands and resettles in the chair opposite. 'I don't think anyone understands how upsetting this is. My birth mother is out there, somewhere close by, and all I want is to meet her, speak to her and get answers... if she doesn't want to see me again after that, fine. I'll respect her wishes. I've come this far without her and... although my life is a mess, I've done OK for myself. I'll cope whatever her reaction, but at least I'll know her name. I'll have seen her face... even if she refuses to see me afterwards.'

'And will that be enough?' asks Joel, his gaze fixed upon me.

'Honestly, I'm not asking anything more of her than to answer some basic questions. The rest is up to her... I'll leave here and go back to Bushey.'

'I hope not,' mutters Joel.

What did he say? I look up, his expression looks hurt.

'What?' I ask, unsure that I heard correctly.

Joel wets his lips but remains silent.

'He said, "I hope not..." make of that what you will!' says Father Maguire.

A million words pass between us in a few seconds of silence before Father Maguire interrupts.

'Anyone for more tea?'

24

Flora

'I'm sorry, Joel, that obviously didn't go as you'd expected,' I say, as he closes the church door and we head back towards The Square.

'I get it, don't worry. If anyone knows and understands human instinct and emotion, it's Father Maguire, OK?'

I feel reassured, though deep down I wish I could replay and delete the last thirty minutes of sobbing.

'Our whistle-stop tour, based on my Grandpop's memory, takes in certain houses and streets – I've got a snippet to read for each...' he says, stopping at the bottom of the church pathway. 'Flora, are you listening?'

'Sorry, I was checking out where that charity hoarding was placed.' I point to a spot on the grassy frontage a short distance away, directly by the pavement and adjacent with St Bede's Mews. '*Classy.*'

Joel cracks a smile.

'Please say if you think this is too much for you. I don't want you to feel obliged to continue – we can do this some other time.'

'I'm fine, honest I am. Ready for anything.' I take his arm in a jokey manner and skip playfully past the invisible wooden hoarding of 1986 towards the stone archway. 'Anywhere away from here.'

'*Deal*!' laughs Joel, unlinking our arms to turn pages of his notebook. 'Our first stop is through the archway... unless you need another view of the doctor's doorstep?'

'Nah.'

'Run,' shouts Joel, taking the lead with his long legs; I dart after him, slipping and twisting my ankle on the yellowing slush covering the aged cobblestones. I cringe as we pass the faint bloodstained splatter still visible under the snow-covered pavement despite the Highway Agency team's best efforts.

He's easy to be with, so likeable, so... me.

Don't even go there – haven't you enough on your plate right now?

'What?' he asks, as I reach him at the entrance to the archway.

'Sorry?'

'I thought you said something.'

'Nope!'

I quickly avert my gaze. Had I said it aloud? Or had he heard my thoughts?

'Let me begin the guided tour of Pooley village... according to records, a popular dwelling place due to the local river since 945AD when the first settlements came to the area having travelled east from the neighbouring village of Kordan.'

'Why?'

'Why what?'

'Why come from the east?'

'There was a massive flooding of the river which wiped out the original Kordan dwellings, so they were forced to seek refuge elsewhere. Is that enough history for you?'

I smile.

He's funny and yet sincere.

'Are you reading notes or have you memorised this stuff?'

'I knew that anyway before you arrived, though I've made a shedload of notes from Grandpop – I'd hate to get it wrong and set you off on the wrong path.'

I'm impressed.

'Always the police officer, hey?'

'Something like that.'

Silence settles as we walk through the brick archway built between two imposing buildings.

'What are these?' pointing to the right-hand side.

'They're flats now, but once this one was the old doctor's surgery,' he points right. 'And this one...' he points to the left, 'is simply the side of the first house in St Bede's Mews.'

'Do we know who lived there?'

In seconds Joel runs through the occupants of St Bede's Mews – all strangers to me apart from Dr Fowler.

'No one of significance?'

'Everyone is significant till proven otherwise – when you don't know what you're looking for.'

He's got a point.

'This end house was home to the Duggan family – mum, dad and a couple of teenagers, a typical working-class family is what Grandpop calls them *but* they lived in one of the nicest houses in the village.'

'Obviously worked hard... do we know the father's occupation?'

Joel consults his notes.

'Plasterer by trade but turned his hand to anything, I've written here... worked seven days a week apparently.'

'Goes without saying,' I murmur.

'Now, as we leave The Square behind us we have the spread of the working-class sprawl before us – Grandpop's words not mine.'

'Oi, there's nothing wrong with working class.'

'It wasn't a knock, honest.'

I view the buildings around us: typical three-bedroomed family houses of modest stature.

'Are you suggesting she walked this way?'

He nods.

'Yep, now think logically about this. There are four roads leading into and from The Square. One leads out of the village, on a long dark country lane – the one you drove along which brought you here… I can't see a woman nipping along there to deposit a baby.'

I agree.

'The two other roads run either side of The Peacock, both leading into the high street, where surely there is more chance of meeting people at any time of day, even early morning.'

'Which leaves this route, possibly the quietest.'

Joel nods.

'Afraid so, in which case she must have lived on or passed through this estate.'

'What's on the far side of the estate?'

'Now there's a huge housing development but back in the day it was scrubland, cattle grazing and meadows – the local kids used to play football there. The only feasible route to take was towards The Square as there was nothing the other side. Apart from the industrial estate a mile down the road.'

'Certainly, nowhere to guarantee a baby being found safe and well.'

'Exactly.'

My birth mother walked this way. The detail suddenly becomes fact in my head. Whether she was old, young, married, single, lower or middle class, she walked along this footpath carrying me in a towel and nipped through the brick archway.

'Flora, are you OK?'

His tender voice brings me round.

I nod.

'It seems so sad. When she came this way, she must have known what she was about to do,' I whisper.

'I wonder if she knew what she was doing or was she perhaps in shock after the birth.'

'Do you think so?' I ask, hoping he's right.

'*Maybe*?'

'Why didn't she come forward after all the weeks of news coverage... they gave her plenty of chances, didn't they?'

He shrugs, his brown eyes portray a gentle warmth, despite the bruises.

'Let's go, I don't like standing here,' I mumble, striding across the road into the middle. 'Now which direction?'

'Grandpop said that this was a T-junction not the crossroads that we see today, Sycamore Road ahead didn't exist – it was either North Street on the left or Rowan Rise on the right... which is it to be?'

I turn on the spot, looking left, then right.

Does my DNA recognise the place or the topography of the streets? Nothing comes to mind, so I select left.

'North Street it is, come on.'

I traipse behind as he strides the pavement.

'On the left here is the house where Mrs Delaney lived, she was renowned for her large sprawling family... a noisy lot according to Grandpop.'

'I've heard that name before.'

'Melanie, Annie's sister-in-law, is one of the Delaney family,' says Joel. 'Loads of teenage girls in *that* house.'

'Yep, I've met her – married to Gene.'

'Not the best of reputations... that's all I'll say.'

'Gene spent the night at the pub because they had a bust-up over a comment made last night – Mick stepped in but it was too late and the two women came to blows.'

'You should include her and all her sisters... there's a chance...' his sentence fades.

'Oi you! I don't sodding care as long as she's my birth mother – though she's claiming not to be.'

My protective shield lifts like the Thames barrier – it would be enough to find out her real name and get to ask her questions. I could deal with anything else if I managed to get the confirmation I need.

'Sorry, I'm not judging, seriously I'm not.'

We walk in silence for a few houses. I can see the style has changed, the brickwork has given way to painted pebble-dash and overhanging porches.

'Is this estate a private one?'

'Nope, mainly council houses, some have been purchased but back in eighty-six it was virtually all council still. Big families squeezed into three bedrooms,' he says, referring to his notebook.

'Working class, then.'

'You don't know that for certain,' he murmurs.

'Joel, don't kid yourself, what upper-class girl has to give up her baby by leaving her on a doorstep?' I say, turning round to take in the full extent of the area. 'I get a feeling that *this*… is me.'

'Salt of the earth my Grandpop would say.'

'I bet he does, along with many other things,' I joke, feeling the apology rising in his voice. 'Come on, tour guide, your spiel has dried up somewhat.'

'Sorry, you're a difficult punter to please… anyway, along here we also had the O'Neill twins: Mick and Eugene at number forty-three, the Kelly twins at number fifty-six and over there on the far corner lived an elderly couple by the name of Sable who had just one daughter, *Veronica*.'

Veronica? I stare at the end house – not the roots I'd expected given her superior attitude.

'Any other teenagers?'

'Grandpop seems to think that there was a lorry driver who had a couple of teenage girls and the local butcher who had a daughter along here too… so a fair few females all within an age range of sixteen to twenty-two.'

'All at school together?'

'Possibly. The nearest secondary school is off the high street so they'd have visited The Square each day on the way to school.'

'Walking?'

'Oh yeah... none of this school-run nonsense – the catchment area is so tight-knit I bet no one travelled into the area by bus or taxi.'

'And where does this road lead?'

'Two left turnings: Windmill Road and Florence Way a little further up... but look, this is what I wanted to show you,' he says, crossing the road towards a large building in darkness. 'The Pooley Community Centre... the weekly youth club used to be held here.'

'Right on the corner.'

'And look, if you turn round... what's the only thing to see?'

I swing round to view the stone archway from which we'd just walked.

'The Square,' I murmur, more to myself than to Joel. 'This feels right, doesn't it?'

'We don't know for sure, but it fits with teenagers getting their kicks... down there and afterwards meeting at the youth club – all living in this close area, everyone knowing each other, everyone living the same life, in the same street.'

'How many pupils attend the local school?'

'Two thousand or more now but back in the eighties the number was nearer a thousand.'

'Phew, still loads... even if we discard the lower years that hadn't yet discovered boys,' I say, adding, 'Is that where you went?'

'I did, though I was driven in by my father each day. But as you were saying, it still leaves a couple of hundred adolescents with raging hormones and immature attitudes towards contraception... I mean, how old were you when you started dating?'

'Sixteen.'

'And having sex?'

I stare at him.

'You're getting a tad personal, aren't you?'

'I'm just saying... the older generation imagine we're all twenty-five-year-old virgins but I remember many kids experimenting at school.'

I nod, he's right.

'The reality is she could have been as young as thirteen!' he says, giving a whistle.

'I hope not, but it's a possibility.'

Suddenly I feel pretty low, my mood has dropped.

'Joel, can we continue this another day. I feel a bit...' I pull a face.

'Yeah, of course, is it back to the pub for a quick half or not?'

'I'd like that.'

'My shout, given that you've given up your spare time to my quest and you bought the hot chocolates last time.'

*

'Any luck?' asks Annie, wiping down the bar.

'Not sure, though I've met Father Maguire... he's a card, hey?'

'Certainly is, not the usual sort... he'll knock you for six with some of his comments,' laughs Annie. 'And he swears like a trooper!'

'He kindly informed me that I was probably conceived behind the church roof fundraising hoarding.'

'Ah, I remember... I think my Mick's mentioned that one,' says Annie, turning to call along the bar. 'Mick... you remember the church roof billboard, don't you?'

Mick puts his thumb up and gives a gleeful grin.

'So romantic, aren't you?' jibes Annie, shaking her head.

'Apparently, half the village teenagers had a fumble behind it,' confirms Joel, as Annie's expression turns to disgust.

'I never did but how disrespectful amongst the graves!' she mutters. 'Mick, it had better have been a teenage fumble and not the full works!'

'What did you say, love?' calls Mick, frowning as three expectant faces stare intently.

'Has Gene gone home?' I ask.

Annie shakes her head.

'But you said... you said that it would blow over – now, look what I've caused.'

'I know. Apparently, he's staying here for another night. I don't know why... he knew she had a history and a reputation amongst the local lads before he married her... phew, it's beyond me. Blokes... they want their bloody cake and eat it!'

'Then complain when other guys remember nibbling the crumbs beforehand,' I laugh.

'Exactly!' laughs Annie, folding her tea towel.

'Excuse me, I am still standing here, you know?' interrupts Joel. 'You're hardly making us lads sound great!'

'Current company excused from the general tarring and feathering,' I laugh.

'I'm glad to hear it... anyway, back to business. Annie, do you know of any girls or women who moved away from the area after eighty-six?' asks Joel, picking his notepad from his top pocket.

'Tommy Duggan's sister moved to Sheffield at about that time, we'd only just left school and yet she upped and offed,' explains Annie. 'What was her name?'

We hang on every word, Joel with his pen poised, me simply willing her to remember.

'Mick!' shouts Annie, along the bar again. 'What was Duggan's sister called?'

'Emma!' a huge grin spreads across Mick's face. 'She was a beauty.'

'I bet she bloody was!' mumbles Annie, focusing back on us.

'Any news of her since?' I ask.

Annie shakes her head.

'Not from what I know... actually, there's Tommy – go ask him yourself,' says Annie, pointing over our shoulders.

We turn in unison to view a whippet of a man, seated beside the dart board: alone.

'Excuse me,' I ask, walking across. His doleful eyes lift and a brief smile appears. 'I understand that you have a sister that moved away from the area back in the early eighties... could I ask if you are still in touch?'

His expression deepens, the ridges of his mouth flicker.

'Our Emma... course I am, she's my sister.'

'I wanted to know some details – I'm searching for anyone who might know anything about my birth mother who lived in this area.'

'I know who you are, lass, you've got half the village talking,' he says, adding sternly, 'Our Emma didn't move until eighty-eight and, believe me, she didn't have any bairn before going either.'

'I just thought I'd ask...'

'I'm glad you did, but don't you go spreading rumours about my sister... she moved out of this godforsaken village, I wish I'd followed her... away from this dump!'

I back away; his voice is suddenly thick with drink.

'Sorry, I... sorry to disturb you.'

I return to the bar in two strides.

'Miserable git,' I answer, to Joel's inquisitive stare.

'He wasn't rude, was he?'

'Obviously drunk and...'

'Bitter,' adds Annie, serving a young couple drinks.

I nod.

'I can't think of anyone else who moved away during that era but...' Annie's face suddenly drops and she leans across the bar to whisper to Joel. 'Veronica's just walked in.'

'Great!'

'Afternoon, Veronica,' chirps Annie, sashaying along the bar, 'you're becoming quite a regular, which is what we like to see.'

I watch as the woman sidles in, alone, and parks herself at the bar beside Joel's back. He doesn't turn round.

'Any law against that?' returns her steely voice.

'No, just saying,' chirps Annie. 'What can I get you?'

'A large Pinot Grigio,' she says, adding, 'Oops, Joel, didn't see you there. How's the nose? Has the bruising cleared up yet?'

'Cut it out, Veronica.'

'*Touchy*!' she says to me, leaning around Joel's frame. 'Can't a girl enquire after your health nowadays?'

'With pleasure, but I'm unlikely to accept your concern at face value, am I? My ex... if you hadn't realised.'

'I know,' I say, staring at her thickened eyeliner and red lips. She's attractive in a mature manner, but a little less make-up would be flattering to her skin.

'Desperately trying to separate our lives, but someone keeps refusing to sign over the papers on the property... isn't that how my solicitor termed it?' says Joel, talking over his shoulder.

'Maybe it's not quite over, Joel?' adds Annie, smirking between the pair.

'Believe me, it definitely is... I've moved on,' snarls Veronica.

'Maybe your financial interests need to follow suit,' retorts Joel.

'Or is Joel the safety net in case the current beau doesn't work out?' adds Annie.

'And people wonder why I don't use this pub more often,'

snorts Veronica, collecting her drink from the bar and walking across the room.

'You've only started coming in since Flora arrived?' mutters Annie.

'For a landlady... you're *so* very rude,' retorts Veronica.

'For a cougar... you didn't recognise a decent catch when you had one and now he's free you can't keep away!' retorts Annie, placing her hands on her hips.

'Annie!' calls Mick, from along the bar.

Veronica sneers, and continues towards the nearest table.

'Stuck-up bitch... Flora, do you remember the mean girls at your school?'

'Utter cows.'

'There's one from my day.'

'*Ladies...*' interrupts Joel. 'Haven't we more important things to focus on?'

'I hate that mare,' mutters Annie, with a false smile dressing her lips.

We exchange a glance.

'*Really*? I couldn't tell,' I laugh.

25

Veronica

I didn't expect him to show up at The Ivy House. Now, I wished I'd taken time to redo my hair rather than just reapply my make-up. I feel the flush of embarrassment as his bruised eyes stare at my large glass of red wine sitting upon the pristine white tablecloth.

'Hi, Joel, sorry... I ordered.'

'No problem... have you been here long?'

I confirm no; I'm trying my hardest to be polite.

'It's fading.' I indicate to his face.

'I know, it'll be gone in a few more days,' he says, settling himself opposite.

He's wearing the blue Ralph Lauren shirt that complements his eye colour – a birthday present I purchased whilst in Milan.

How many times have I told him not to button the collar – he looks strangled.

As the waitress takes his drinks order, I watch his gentle smile creep across and crease his five o'clock shadow.

Has he not shaved? Joel always shaved before going out.

'What is it you'd like to discuss?' he asks, fiddling with the cutlery place setting.

This was a new Joel, not my Joel from The Peacock. He was never usually offhand, nor as direct and straightforward when we were together. He'd always been a slow burn, an around the houses type of guy in any conversation before getting to his actual point. I had expected his polite conversation, the usual waffle about work, weather or well-being. But no, he's gone straight in.

'When are you signing over the flat?' he asks.

'I think it's time we talked…'

'We've spoken each time I've seen you, I have never ignored you, but it's made no difference regarding you signing over the flat.'

'Talked properly?'

'Veronica, we've gone through the talking properly period. You outlined what you wanted, I eventually agreed and we contacted the necessary people. I don't see… thank you,' he says to the waitress as she interrupts his flow to deliver the pint. 'I don't see what more there is to discuss.'

Another waitress approaches and Joel shakes his head at the leather-bound menus she's clutching.

'Purely drinks,' he says, politely.

'Joel.'

He sips his pint and sits back, his dark eyes never leaving my face.

I fiddle with the cloth napkin, before sipping my red wine.

He's waiting. He has no intention of speaking or being distracted by polite waffle – here goes.

'I wondered if we'd… you know?' I wave my hand, linking the two of us.

He stares, blinks and stares some more.

That had been his cue to speak but he doesn't… he simply stares and waits.

'Do you miss me?' I quickly change tack.

He inclines his head and sighs before reaching for his drink.

What's that supposed to mean?

'Well?' I urge impatiently.

'Veronica, we've been over this. *You* made a decision. *You* chose to leave. To move out of our flat and move on with your life.'

'Yes but...'

'When I asked you to reconsider, you hadn't time to discuss or listen to what I had to say, and now, months later... *now* you want to talk.'

I bite my lower lip.

He's not buying this. Maybe I was hasty? But surely...

'Cut to the chase, Veronica – what is it you're after?'

'Joel!'

'No, seriously, you've made all the decisions and I've gone along with them.'

'Is there no possibility... of us?'

Without a moment's hesitation, he shakes his head.

'You didn't even think about it.'

He sighs.

'Veronica, I did nothing *but* think of it those first few months, but now, sorry but no.'

'Are you with someone?'

'That's none of your business.'

'It is!' I knew it wasn't, but it was worth a shot. I knew that Scott wouldn't waste any time dragging him out and showing him the ropes again. The boys' weekends away, the hottest clubs, the ladies... I bet he's got his eye on someone. Poor lovesick Kylie, no doubt, or even that Bede girl.

'No, it's not. You chose to leave – I dealt with the situation, and now, my life has regained a normality.'

I cringe, he wasn't supposed to say that. Had he discovered that the beer mat was missing? For several days, I've repeatedly played this moment in my head – he was supposed to jump up, take me in his arms, kiss me, hold me and we'd start afresh. I could pack my essentials into a few bags and canvas holdalls and move straight back in. We could have returned to our nights of passion and...

'Is there anything else you'd like to discuss?'

'What?' I say. I can hear the narkiness in my tone.

'Signing the papers, for instance... though now I understand why it's probably taken so long, given that you seem unsure of your decision.'

'Phhh!' I snatch at my wine glass. 'Unsure of my decision... phhh! Me and Gordon are great, I'll have you know... we've made plans for the Maldives, Fiji and Goa.'

I glug at my wine to drown the truth.

'I understand, I'm not trying to be difficult, but for me... this,' his hand waves back and forth between us. 'This is finished, I've moved on.'

I stare at him over the top of the wine glass.

How did I let this happen? We had plenty of good times, had a rosy future in fact and yet... Gordon *really* hadn't been worth it. Yes, he was an older gent with an affluent lifestyle, a considerable amount of property and nice interests. Everything was calculated in relation to his pleasure and his gain, no thought of mine. And now, Joel sits as brazen as you like, rejects my suggestion and gives such a straight answer.

I glance around the restaurant at numerous couples enjoying their meals and intimate conversations beneath mellow candle-light. Was anyone else struggling to connect or was it just us?

Now, where am I to go with this discussion? I want to linger on the subject of a rematch, but how can I when it would appear needy.

'What would you say to putting the apartment on the market to test the interest of a buyer?'

'Instead of me buying you out?'

I nod eagerly – where did that idea come from?

'Are you serious?'

Was I? I hadn't thought about it until now, when he'd rejected my other offer. I'd arrived and delivered my practised lines only to have him refuse me.

Time seems to be suspended as we both stare at each other.

What's he thinking? Planning? Is that what he wanted me to say? *Or* have I walked into a trap to buy him out of the property or lengthen and secure our ties for another few months?

'Yes,' I whisper, unsure of the plan.

'No thanks... you agreed on the price, the valuation was a fair one and I was able to find the funds to buy you out. Why change it now?'

'Wouldn't you prefer somewhere new for a fresh start?'

I'd pondered that idea on my fleeting visit a few days ago. Why hadn't he purchased additional furniture to fill the gaps – the place seemed so sparse.

'Not really, I like the flat.'

'It's an apartment actually,' I correct him.

When will he ever learn?

'Whatever... its location is pretty decent – as you said when we viewed it, "location, location, location" – I thought you said that was the most important aspect of property.'

'But surely there's too many reminders of me?'

My annoyance flares as he pauses to think about it.

'I've switched things around, made a few changes and *now* it feels like home.'

A few guitars and a bookcase? Shoot me down, why don't you!

He gently nods, purses his lips and picks up his drink.

'That's good to hear,' I mutter, before sipping my drink. What the hell is he playing at? I thought he'd fall over himself to have me back. I've even waxed my legs and told Gordon I won't be home for supper.

26

Flora

It took a second day for Joel to walk me around the village pointing out the scenery and history as of eighty-six. We re-visited The Corner Café where the teenagers of the day had sipped hot chocolate, minus any toppings of whipped cream or marshmallows. The local Memorial Hall car park where BMX ramps were constructed from bricks and wooden planks, and even the local park which had proudly boasted a huge dome-shaped climbing frame, complete with a gleaming metal arc shelter under which the youths smoked and swore.

Every new scene convinced me that my mother was one of those teenagers – I could virtually see her cheering as the BMX bike boys popped wheelies, or huddled under the climbing frame shelter to share a pack of Park Drive, and yet there was no face, whether she be thirteen or eighteen she remained a featureless body amongst the crowd.

This morning, straight after breakfast, I want to get my thoughts written down. I drag two tables alongside each other creating a larger desk. With my new understanding of the area, views of the local scenery and a whole jumble of stories about the local folk, I need to start ordering my thoughts. I flick to the rear of the comments book and begin dashing down the details.

- The Delaney family had a daughter commit suicide whilst studying for her 'A' levels at the local comprehensive.
- Tommy Duggan had a sister who moved away to Sheffield.
- 1986 village carnival (highlight of the village year) was postponed due to thunderstorms and lightning which covered most of the country.
- The school lollipop man retired after thirty years.

I look up to call Annie from behind her neat and tidy bar.

'Annie, do you remember the wife-switching incident of eighty-six?' I shout across the bar.

The row of male heads seated at the bar turn around and stare in my direction.

Annie bustles over, wiping her hands on a tea towel, mouthing a definite 'shhhh!'

'You silly bugger,' she mutters, settling in beside me at my makeshift desk.

'*Sorry.*'

'Yeah, we all do. The Smiths and the Jones family switched partners – it was the talk of the village for months. They started as best friends, couples having couples over for dinner parties... Fondue was all the rage back then, but within no time one of the kids let it slip they'd seen mummy kissing Uncle Tony and daddy snogging Auntie Barbara!'

'You are joking me?'

Annie shakes her head.

'So they...?' my hands move back and forth rapidly.

'Switched partners,' says Annie, her head still bobbing, a flush appearing at her neck. She leans in closer to whisper. 'But don't 'ark on about it, you see young Denny at the fruit machine?'

I nod, my eyes travelling to the chubby youth who still needs to pull his trouser waistband over his ass.

'They're his grandparents, so shhhh,' says Annie, shuffling back to her bar and waiting customers.

I cringe, but can't help but stare some more at Denny, before adding an entry.

- Wife-swapping incident
- The Johnson family were burgled but the jewellery was later retrieved stuffed down a drain at the back of the Blue Lion pub.
- Royals visited the church of St Bede – every child was given the day off school.

'Annie!' I leap up and cross to the bar. 'Do you remember the Royals visiting?'

Annie stops pulling a pint and stares between me and the row of men seated at the bar supping their drinks.

'That wasn't eighty-six, Flora... whoever's told you that is out on their dates,' she says.

'Eighty-five, for sure, I was working down the pit on night shift,' pipes up an old boy, cradling a pint glass. 'My missus took the kids down to watch from the crowd, boy was she mardy about me not getting out of bed to view the toffs pop by to cut a ribbon.'

'The whole village was repainted for a thirty-minute visit,' adds a second old boy, to a chorus of nods.

'There, old Stan's put you right, I knew eighty-six wasn't correct,' says Annie.

'*Great.* If that's wrong how much of the other stuff from Joel's grandpop is wrong?' I ask, heaving myself onto a bar stool alongside old Stan.

'Best part of it, by my reckoning,' he mutters, before taking a sip of his drink. 'Folks likes to say they remember, but they don't... not accurately.'

'But *that's* exactly what I need.'

'Here.' Annie pops a glass of mulled wine before me. 'Take a break.'

'Cheers, I need it.' Surely the mulled wine vat must be nearly dry by now?

I spend the next thirty minutes listening to the older blokes talk about their pit days and the goings-on at the Legion on a Friday night. Nothing is of great importance but amongst the banter and their forgotten tears they paint a picture of a quiet village where nothing extraordinary or unresolved ever happened until a foggy morning one October.

*

I resettle at my makeshift desk, abandon my task of writing notes and turn to the front of the comments book for a reread.

I flip through the pages rereading the various comments, ignoring the churlish and crude entries until one scribble catches my eye.

Foggy morning, silent walk to work with Dad, saw a girl enter Windmill Road.

How long has that been there? I only read the comments book a few days ago. I search for the accompanying name and cannot read the scrawl beneath.

'Annie! Annie!' I shout, drawing her from the back kitchen. 'Look, what does that say?'

Annie leans across the bar, peering at the page and my index finger.

'Isn't that a "T"?' she says.

'I don't know, that's why I'm asking.' My patience has upped and offed with my discovery.

Annie traces the line of ink.

'Yep, I'd say that's a T...'

'So, who's been in?'

'Tommy Duggan?'

'Yeah Tommy! Given his rudeness the other day, I'm surprised he bothered writing anything,' I say.

'He's a strange one, all right... always has been.'

'Joel's Grandpop said something about him living in one of the nicest houses yet coming from a working-class family or something.'

'His pa worked seven days a week though, he earned his crust.'

'Why would Tommy be going to work... he'd be at school surely?'

'The Duggans have always worked... I bet he was probably doing a bit before school started.'

Windmill Road – Joel mentioned that the other day after we went through the archway towards the council estate.

'Annie, do you remember any girls that lived in Windmill Road?'

'Plenty... our mate Veronica for one, she lived on the corner of North and Windmill.'

I grab a piece of paper and title it: potentials. I quickly write Veronica Sable.

'Before this week, was she a regular in the pub?

Annie shakes her head as she begins refilling the fruit juice bottles.

'Are you joking? She came in on high day and holidays – our dislike of each other dates back from school – nothing has changed.'

'What about when she was dating Joel?'

'It made no difference, he came in as always but she didn't…
until recently.'

Annie turns round and pulls a face.

Interesting.

I'm out of the door before Annie can say another word.

*

I dash towards St Bede's Mews, not even glancing ahead
towards Dr Fowler's stone step but instead my eyes are fixed
on the end house, number five. I swing open the gate and I'm
down the pathway in three strides, hammering on the door like
there's no tomorrow.

'Hold on, hold on!' comes the craggy voice from within.

I listen as several bolts are pulled across and the door eases
open to reveal Tommy in work overalls.

'Which girl did you see entering Windmill Road?'

'Eh?'

'In my comments book you've written "foggy morning,
silent walk to work with Dad, saw a girl enter Windmill Road"
– that was you, wasn't it?'

'Yeah, the other night.'

'Who?'

'Did you see I wrote it was bloody foggy?' he croaks.

'I know but…' this isn't getting me anywhere fast. 'Look,
Tommy, this is important; you seem to be the only person that
saw anyone that morning… this could be *my* birth mother… I
need to know. Please think.'

He stares at me, wipes his stubbled chin.

'Do you want tea?'

I exhale, and a plume of breath clouds before me.

'I might as well, the rest of my day is relying on what you
tell me next.'

Within minutes I'm seated in his lounge, staring around

a room decorated with nicotine stain swirls on the walls and ceiling.

'So...' he mutters, handing me a milky tea. 'I was supposed to be in bed... my mother thought I was, but my dad, well he would go to work dead early in the morning in those days. He walked everywhere did my dad, Shanks's pony he called it. Anyway, it was my birthday the week before and I'd had a new BMX bike... it was dad's idea. What my mother didn't know was that each morning I was dressing with my dad and biking alongside him as he walked to work. I was there and back before her alarm clock went off.'

I nod, listening intently.

'Anyway, he walked and I cycled through the archway, across to the T-junction that was there, though now...'

'Yes, I know it's a crossroads now,' I snap impatiently.

'...We turned left into North Street then continued to the end. The fog was a proper pea-souper, it really was... for a kid of my age it was funny to be out so early in such strange weather – it's only as we neared the corner of Windmill Road that the silhouette appeared in the fog, she turned into Windmill and we went straight on.'

'Didn't she see you?'

'We weren't talking or anything, me and my dad didn't talk.'

'How close were you?'

'From here to where that chair is...'

I look at the short distance indicated.

'That's less than twelve foot.'

'Yeah I know.'

'So, who was it?'

I watch as he shakes his head.

'I don't know.'

'But you must know?'

'I have no idea... we didn't speak to her, we were behind her, almost caught her up but then she went her way, we carried on.'

I sip my tea, whilst biting my tongue.

'How do you know it was a girl?'

'Because of the parka coat.'

My eyebrows lift.

'Those fur-trimmed coats with orange lining – they were supposed to be for boys but back then girls had made it a fashion thing... us boys wouldn't give you a thank you for one during *that* stint – when it was over, us lads went back to wearing them.'

'Are you sure?'

Tommy pushes his bottom lip forward.

'Don't believe me then...' he sips his tea and sulks.

I want to believe him, seriously I do, but I'm not that lucky, am I?

27

Annie

Bless her, Flora was out of that door before I could speak.

'I hope the miserable git's at least kind to her, otherwise she'll have yet another day sat staring out of the window,' I say to Gene. 'All she needs is a break, a helping hand to start the ball rolling.'

'I've got a funny feeling when this ball starts rolling it may well answer more than just her questions – it'll ignite the gossips once more,' he chunters, shaking his head.

The pub door chime sounds, I look up and watch as Old Nancy, a spindly woman with a paisley headscarf and a large shopping bag on her arm, enters the pub.

'Is this where the orphan girl is staying?'

'Yes, it is... can I help you, Nancy.'

'Watch yourself,' mutters Gene, eyeballing me. 'Talk of the devil.' He sits shaking his head; Nancy's reputation precedes her.

'I wasn't after a drink, not at this time of the morning. I was looking for the young woman,' she says, pulling a crumpled note from her pocket. 'Flora Phillips.'

'She's out at the moment but she's expected back any time soon... would you like to wait?'

'Could I?' she says, tottering away from the door, unsteady on her swollen feet.

I come from around the bar to help settle her in Flora's alcove, make her a pot of tea and show her the display boards.

'Are you still cleaning at the police station?' I ask, knowing she's long past her seventy-fifth birthday.

'Yes always, the boys look after me, they do,' she beams, her wrinkled cheeks lighting up.

'That's good to hear, I bet you look after them too.'

'Five thirty start, seven days a week, is what I've done for forty-seven years.'

I nod politely. I can't imagine her yellow duster and Mr Sheen collects much dirt or takes much out of her, but it's probably what keeps her going in life. I'd guess she's finished and off home by seven o'clock when the proper cleaning team arrive.

I show her the alcove display. She's interested, she reads the comments book and views the pinned flags and even smiles at the numerous photographs that have created quite an intricate display.

'She's been very busy then?' says Old Nancy, sipping her tea.

'She has. She's trying her best to find details about her birth mother... I promise she won't be much longer.'

'I'll wait. I only want a moment of her time.'

*

I breathe a sigh of relief when the door chime finally sounds.

'Annie, you'll never guess.' Flora's face is flushed.

'Old Nancy's waiting for you,' I point towards the alcove. 'I'll bring you a fresh brew over.'

As I disappear into the kitchen, I hear Flora introduce herself before the noise of the boiling kettle drowns everything out. I keep dancing from the kitchen to the bar entrance in hope of catching a comment or remark but to no avail.

'Here we go, ladies, a fresh cuppa.' I deposit the tray and stand back to witness the wide eyes and anticipation on Flora's face.

'Annie... guess what Nancy used to do?'

I shake my head, not wishing to be rude by guessing incorrectly.

'She used to clean the wards at the maternity hospital,' says Flora.

Old Nancy beams with pride.

'Did she now?' I mutter, not convinced I'd heard that mentioned before.

'I've thought about her many times as if she were my own. And now, to think she's all grown up,' adds Nancy, slyly slipping sugar sachets into her large shopping bag.

'But look at this, Annie!' Flora's hands dive into a plastic bag on her lap, revealing a ragged beige bath towel – by anyone's standards it has seen better days. Personally, I wouldn't use it as a dust rag on the bar floor.

'Nice?'

'It's what I was wrapped in!' beams Flora.

I cringe.

'Someone actually wrapped a newborn baby in that?'

Annie, change your face because Flora wants a good response here.

'I saved it, I did,' boasts Old Nancy, looking up at me. 'The ward sister threw it out but I took it out of the bin.'

'You've kept *that* for thirty years?' I mutter, not sure whether to trust her word.

'I get it... it's faded tat to you.' Flora's smile is eclipsed.

'No... not at all,' I stutter apologetically, knowing I've ruined her moment.

'It might look like a rag to others but this means the world to me,' she explains. 'My birth mother wrapped me in *this*... she and I have held and touched *this*!'

I watch as Flora pulls it into her chest and inhales the scent, though I imagine it doesn't smell too great, given her wrinkled forehead.

'Nancy, I can't thank you enough for taking the time to visit and bring me this... such a precious item.'

I get it, honestly, I do. But the truth still remains: a woman wrapped her and left her on a doorstep in a tatty beige towel. What woman does that to a newborn? I'd have wrapped my baby in soft woollen blankets, lovingly stitched by hand, crocheted or woven by me... not some smelly remnant of an avocado bathroom suite.

'They fought over naming you... but the ward sister won in the end, so she called you Angela – I'm pleased your parents changed it, it didn't suit you.'

'I'll leave you to it,' I murmur, plodding back to the bar. I shouldn't admit it, but seeing Flora chatting so freely to the village gossip, clutching that tatty rag, makes my blood boil.

That could be any ragged towel picked up in a charity shop. Flora's not mine and never will be. It's not fair, some folk don't appreciate what they have in life. I'd have given anything to have a daughter like her.

I collect a tray of steamed glasses from the dishwasher and begin polishing them.

'If you'd have been mine I'd have kept you forever.'

28

Joel

'You spend more time here whilst off duty than you do when you're on duty,' laughs Big Tony, causing everyone in the large open office to lift their heads. 'Are you still playing Poirot?'

'Ha, bloody ha, Tony... haven't you got enough to keep you busy?' I retort, dashing through the office heading for the Chief's room. 'I'm sure a stint helping with community service will fill your day.'

'Frig off!' moans Big Tony, returning to his paperwork.

I stand in front of the Chief's door reciting my lines, before I rap on the glass section. Inside, I can see he's on the phone, his head lifts and he beckons me inside, indicating the nearest office chair. I settle and politely pretend to be deaf to his conversation.

'Seriously, how much are we talking?' the Chief growls into the phone, his jowly features topped with a silver-grey short back and sides.

I stare at the framed certificates on his wall, photographs of his wife and daughters – though I avert my eyes in case he thinks I'm being too nosey. I inspect the skirting boards, the double plug sockets and the computer cabling all before he signs off and replaces the handset whilst grumbling about the caller.

'Joel, how can I help you?'

'Sir... I was wondering if I may have permission to read the file relating to Baby Bede?'

A quizzical look crosses his jowly features.

'And the reason being?'

I pause.

His eyes scrutinise me.

'I see... like that is it?'

'Sir, it's purely professional... I know I'm on sick leave but I'm hardly ill, so for the short time that she's here I want to help as much as I can. I'm sure there must be something in the files, some small detail that may have been overlooked, which might assist her search.'

'The files have been read a hundred times... so what if I say no?'

I pause again, hoping this isn't his final answer.

'I shall accept your decision...'

'Bollocks will you! You'll sneak down there with young Scott, wheedle your way past Old Browning and have a mooch.'

'Honestly, Sir...'

'You might as well go and take a look... though should you wish to discuss the matter with the first officer on the scene... I'll be waiting to answer your questions!'

'You?'

'Yes me! Back in the good old days of street patrol when I used to walk mile upon mile round this village – those were the days. I can't believe it's taken her thirty years to find her way back.'

'And no one ever came forward?'

'Not a thing... I don't believe we suspected anyone – though no doubt the locals have pointed a finger or two over the years.'

'Sir, I can't thank you enough... I...'

'Sod off, Joel, you're making me feel old and I have work to do,' says the Chief, lifting the phone handset and punching in a new number, mouthing for me to leave.

I can't wait to tell Flora.

I dash from his office, ducking past Big Tony's desk to avoid further insults.

*

Across his counter, Brian Browning glares from behind bottle-bottom glasses at me as I complete the docket to officially retrieve the file. I carefully print my name, ensuring he doesn't question my actions and I have to waste time fetching written authorisation from the Chief.

I take a seat in his squalid archive room and wait. He shuffles off into his domain of shelving and locked cabinets, he's not the fastest mover, much like his namesake Brian-the-snail, who is sprightly in comparison.

My nerves jingle; this could be it, the moment when I find what she needs.

How brilliant would that be?

'Joel,' shouts Browning, handing me the box of files. 'Don't lose anything, will you?'

I give him a hard stare. Like I need telling.

I pull my mobile from my jacket pocket and speed-dial for help.

'Scotty, my man, what are you up to on your free day, anything?'

'No, why?'

'No Xbox marathon or gym sessions planned?'

'Nothing, why?'

'How do you fancy rereading and digging through a police file with me?'

'Sod off, it's my day off!'

'I'll owe you one.'

'You're supposed to be on the sick – the Chief will go mad.'

'Nope, I've cleared it with him.'

A long pause follows, in which I hope my silent pleas are telepathically communicated.

'Where are you?' he asks.

'At the station, with the file in my hand and I'm about to start... get down here quick and I'll buy you lunch at The Peacock.'

I end the call, knowing full well he'll be down within ten minutes.

*

We find an empty office on the third floor of the station, away from the prying eyes of Big Tony and his cronies.

'Here goes,' I say, emptying the file contents onto the tabletop.

Opening the box file reveals several brown folders, each of them dog-eared and stained. I spread out the contents: lots of written statements, a pencilled map, a yellowed bus ticket in an evidence bag and a tiny silver ring of a twisted rope design between two plain hoops, squashed like a deformed Hula Hoop.

I hold up the evidence bag and peer at the ring.

'I bet there's no inscription,' mumbles Scotty. 'This ring belongs to...'

'And what fun would that be, having all the answers fall into our hands?'

I replace the evidence bag in the box file to avoid losing anything and look through the accompanying documents to see where it was found.

'Silver ring (damaged): found in the gutter by the archway of St. Bede's Mews,' I read aloud from the docket. 'No definite fingerprints recorded on item and no inscription.'

'There must have been thousands of those sold in the eighties... every girl I went to school with had something similar worn on her right hand and purchased from Argos,' says Scotty, turning his nose up at the plastic evidence bag.

'It was the same in our year too, though they wore it on their left hand, pretending it was an engagement ring.'

'Exactly. *Every* teenage girl has countless cheap silver rings... that means nothing.'

I snatch up the plastic bag containing the ring, the blood pumping through my veins.

'But it could be *hers*!'

*

For three hours, we read every word on every statement: from Darren the newspaper boy to milkman Fred, who delivered two gold top and a bottle of Stera milk during the commotion.

'Nothing jumps out at me,' murmurs Scotty, as we walk the short distance to the pub.

'Me neither, though the squashed silver ring annoyed the hell out of me... and I'm not keen on the statement from the PE teacher of the local school.'

'Sounds like a right witch to me.'

'They usually are,' I add, thinking of the file safely locked in Scotty's desk drawer. 'Surely they should have a moral duty of care to teenage girls?'

Within minutes we're ordering a couple of pints and two bar meals from the lunchtime menu.

'Are you both off duty?' asks Annie, taking our order.

'Yep, sick day today but I'm back on normal shifts soon,' I say, adding, 'How come Flora's with Old Nancy?' Spying her engrossed in a conversation with the elderly lady.

Annie raises her eyebrows.

'Apparently, she used to clean up at the hospital, so go figure.'

'When did she turn up?' I ask.

'First thing this morning along with...' Annie places the first pint on the bar. 'A dirty rag, saying it was the towel Flora was found in – that is what it looked like to me.'

'Annie?' calls Mick, from along the bar.

'Stop listening to my conversations, will you!' she shouts, her brow furrowing.

'Are you OK?' I ask, retrieving cash from my wallet.

'Phhh, there's something, I can't put my finger on... something's brewing and I hope that Flora doesn't come a cropper. All she wants is to know the truth.'

'Isn't that what we all want for her?' I ask, passing Scotty his pint.

'Yes. No. I mean... I don't know what I mean any more... she's been here a few weeks and this place has been turned upside down. Someone, out there,' she points to the customers seated at the bar, 'knows something and they are not letting on, and yet, they contentedly watch that young woman make her displays, read the comments book and be greeted by uncle Tom, Dick and bloody Harry!' Annie slams the second pint onto the countertop, spilling beer across her hand.

'Easy... you're upsetting yourself,' I whisper, as the other customers turn round and stare.

'I can't help it.'

I offer her a twenty-pound note, Annie waves it away.

'On us... just help her find out who her birth mum is, OK?'

'I'm trying, I promise.'

Annie gives me a wry smile and tilts her head, as Scotty takes his pint and walks to a vacant table.

'*What*?'

'I'm pleased you're helping her, Joel.'

'All part of the job.' The phrase rolls from my tongue whenever the public praise me for my efforts.

'Something tells me it's more than public duty,' she winks, a tear in her eye.

'*Really?*'

'Believe me, she's interested, Joel... but right now, finding her mother is the biggest thing in her life. If you can step back and allow her to satisfy that... that need... she'll be putty in your hands.' Annie gently pats my forearm before dashing into the back room.

I settle myself opposite Scotty at the nearest table, I'm guessing Annie will be a while before she returns to serve another pint.

*

I can't help but watch her chatting to the Old Nancy. I ignore that Scotty is watching me watching Flora whilst eating his lasagne.

'Fairy dust for afters?' says Scotty.

I simply nod, chomp and stare.

'Poor git, you've got it bad,' he laughs.

'What?'

'Earth calling, Joel. I'm chatting bubbles and you haven't a clue what I'm saying, because you're not even listening, are you?'

'Sorry, mate... I am.'

'No, you're not... you're trying to follow their conversation.' He gives a nod towards the alcove seats.

'I can't get this case out of my head. She's here, staying amongst us, and yet no one's owned up, suggested a name or even hinted at who they think it is... Annie's right, someone knows.'

'Pretty sick, eh?' adds Scotty, looking at the bar. 'But so is leaving a baby on a doorstep... if you can do one – surely it's easy to do the other?'

I shrug.

'How many times have we worked on cases where we're disgusted by the initial crime, we make an arrest and then can't believe that individual actually acted in that way?'

'Loads… it's mind-boggling what people can do.'

'And think they'll get away with.'

I wipe my mouth and push my empty plate away. I look up to find Scotty scrutinising my face.

'But that isn't the real reason, is it?'

'What are you getting at?' I ask.

'You…' he nods towards the alcove. '…and her. That's what you're thinking, yeah?'

'I don't know – I really don't.'

Scotty sits back from his empty plate, takes his final swig of beer and stares, a knowing smile on his face.

'Don't.'

'Don't what? If you like her go for it… she's not my sort, a bit too feisty, but hey.'

'Your sort? That's charming given your recent…' I falter searching for the phrase.

'*Conquest*?'

'Exactly! I think it proves you haven't got a sort!'

'Love 'em and leave 'em wanting more,' laughs Scotty, standing up and pointing to my empty glass. 'Another?'

'Make it a Coke for me.' I watch as he goes to the bar and orders. He's my buddy but sometimes I envy his relaxed mannerisms, his crafty smirks and never too distant laughter. Why couldn't I be as easy-going as him? Nothing fazes him, he couldn't care less if he's in a relationship or chasing the latest recruit at the station. Yet me? Everything is calculated, everything planned, details and forward planning even when it comes to chancing my hand and getting to know someone new. Big Tony's right, I'm definitely losing my touch.

Scotty returns minutes later with two pints of Coke and ice.

'Do you think I'm losing my touch like Big Tony says?'

'*Seriously*?' he says, pulling a face. 'You're worrying about remarks made by the big fella?'

'No, but life hasn't been great lately, has it?'

196

'No but that's because...' says Scotty, faltering.

'Go on.'

'You've lost your confidence since shacking up with Veronica... you need to get out there... live a little.'

I cringe at his 'shacking up' term.

Had I? Or had I matured? Obviously not in Scotty's eyes, and he should know – he's known me long enough.

'Maybe,' I mutter, reaching for my drink.

Flora

'Annie, I can't believe my luck. Firstly, Nancy had smuggled the towel away all those years ago and this morning Tommy Duggan admits that he *did* see a girl,' I recall, excited about my morning's work.

'Joel's waiting for you over there... he's got some exciting news too,' she interrupts my flow.

'Oh!'

I turn around and receive a polite wave from Joel, and a stare from Scott.

'Annie, I was thinking...' I turn back but she has gone.

Bloody hell, what's got into people today?

'How are things?' I ask, settling on a stool at their table.

Joel pulls his mobile from his pocket and begins to flick at the screens.

I frown.

This is why I dislike technology, it interrupts every aspect of life or conversation.

'*Joel*?'

'Sorry, I forgot earlier, this won't take a minute.' He places the phone to his ear.

Great. I bet it's another appointment with Veronica about their bloody flat. When's he going to wake up and smell the coffee?

In my handbag my phone shrieks into life; I rummage and retrieve it.

'Decent guy' is illuminated across the tiny screen.

Joel leans forward, blatantly nosey.

He snaps his phone shut, ending his call.

'Just checking,' he laughs. 'I'd hate to be labelled as the saddo git.'

'*Joel*!' I give an embarrassed laugh.

'That was a class act, my son,' laughs Scott, raising his pint of Coke. 'Big Tony will laugh himself silly when I tell him.'

I blush and drop the mobile into my handbag.

'Sorry, Flora, that was childish. You asked about our day, we...' his finger points between the two of them, 'have had the most exciting discovery.'

'*Really?*'

'We've reread your file and in an evidence bag we found this...' Joel offers me his mobile phone, showing a photo.

'A ring?' I say, peering at the mangled silver pictured on his screen.

'Correction, a squashed ring,' adds Scott.

'Never!'

Joel nods.

'He's right. Pure chance, but it has been overlooked – it was found on the pavement.'

'From my case?'

They nod in unison.

'No one has ever mentioned a silver ring... ever.'

'Nope. I'm suggesting we hold this back and use it when we need to. The evidence docket says there aren't any decent fingerprints on it, so it was a dead end. It was then forgotten about in the file,' explains Joel.

'Can I see it?'

'You'll need to come down to the station, but yeah, you are more than welcome to see it,' adds Joel.

'Can we go now?'

'Excuse me, we're having our bloody lunch!' gripes Scott, eyeing me with annoyance.

'Sorry, but I've had a pretty amazing day myself and it seems everything is picking up speed,' I say excitedly, relaying my news in a breathless rush.

29

?

Why did Julie Delaney kill herself in 1987?

Guilt – that's why! It had nothing to do with her sitting her 'A' levels – how difficult can media studies, drama and sociology be?

That family has only ever produced a bunch of village bikes.

30

Flora

The Peacock Pub
The Square,
Pooley,
Warwickshire.

Dear Ms Phillips,

You don't know me but last Friday I saw your appeal and photograph in the local newspaper, The *Pooley Post*.

I used to live in the village and can provide some details regards your birth and parentage – if you would care to meet I'll happily share the details.

Kind regards,
Christine Hawthorne
0774009----

I finish reading the letter aloud to find Annie and Mick staring at me from the bar.

'Who?' asks Mick, hobbling through the bar hatch towards the alcove.

'Christine Hawthorne… do you remember her?'

Mick and Annie exchange a glance.

'It sounds familiar, but I can't put a face to her,' says Annie, leaning against the bar pumps. 'Can you, Mick?'

Mick reaches for the letter and scans the few simple lines.

'Christine Hawthorne? Wasn't she the girl who left our primary school when we all went to the big school?' he asks Annie on completion.

'Lord knows, I can't remember what I had for breakfast let alone who attended our primary school.'

'You do... she had a thick frizz of blonde hair, cut short like a boy's style... she wore navy blue socks.'

'Christ, Mick, such detail... I bet you can't recall what I wore on our wedding day and you can remember blue socks on an eleven-year-old classmate!' laughs Annie, coming over to join us in the alcove. 'Are you going to call her, Flora?'

'Yeah, like I'd waste a chance like this... she might know all I need to know,' I say, eager for our conversation to be over so I can dial Christine's number.

'Christina! Yes, Christina... I knew Christine didn't sound right,' mutters Mick, handing me the letter. 'Annie, you do remember.'

Annie pulls a quizzical face, reinforcing her knowledge.

'You do. Think back to Pooley first school... the climbing frame, the coloured hoops and ladders painted on the playground...'

'Yes, I remember. I'm right back there playing games of kiss-chase, stuck-in-the-mud and leapfrog... yes, I remember – I see it all.'

Mick smiles proudly, missing her sarcasm.

'What I don't see is a little girl with frizzy boy hair wearing navy blue socks...' Annie returns to her domain and begins wiping down the bar. 'And I don't see her running for the break bell, nor the lunch queue or the gate at home time.'

Mick shakes his head, tapping ferociously at his temple.

'Well I do. They lived on the high street above the butcher's at the far end…' he hobbles through the bar hatch, disappearing into their private quarters.

'What's up with him?' I ask.

Annie gives a shrug.

'Maybe she stole his dinner money and he's now developed post-traumatic stress from primary school.'

'No, *seriously*, what's wrong with him?' I ask. Mick was becoming grouchy. I was uneasy that it related to my stay.

'His back's giving him jib again… reckons the pain is off the scale. Fingers crossed the doctor can organise a scan pretty soon.'

I punch Christine's number into my phone – suddenly eager to arrange to drink coffee and chat.

*

'Joel, it feels like that telly programme where missing family members meet up having found each other after years apart,' I say shakily, as The Moat House hotel looms ahead of us at the end of a wide driveway.

He'd been good enough to drive me into the next town whilst off work. I'd felt cheeky asking but knew he'd be perturbed if I asked Mick to drop me in, having assumed the role of chief investigator for this reopened case, second to me of course.

'In that case, I'll leave you here to walk the remainder,' he laughs, gently patting me on the shoulder.

'Don't you dare… I want you to come in.'

'I will, but I'll sit elsewhere to give you some privacy.'

My eyes trace the outline against the cloudy skyline.

'It's got a strange look about it, don't you think?' I say, pointing towards the great building.

'Ey, it has… in the olden days it used to be the local asylum for women.'

'Seriously?' I shudder.

'The Victorians were big on asylums and locking folk up – this place has a huge history.'

'Stop it, you're scaring me,' I squeal, as my imagination suddenly imprints tortured faces at each tiny window.

'Think positive then… in under ten minutes you might have your answers about your birth mother,' he says, leading me through the impressive doorway.

'Oh,' I exclaim, seeing the interior's modern decor. 'How different is this from the outside?'

'See, not so scary after all,' laughs Joel, leading me by the arm towards the bar. 'And that… could be your lady?'

He points in the direction of a tiny woman, seated by a roaring fire in a wing-backed chair of modern check, a pot of tea on the table beside her. Her bird-like features peer from behind a frizzy fringe of silver grey.

I smile, more in acknowledgement that I have the right person in a busy bar than out of politeness. Her smile lights up her tiny features – this must be Christine.

'Go settle yourself, while I order you a pot of tea… I'll be over there if you need me,' says Joel, pointing to the far end of the bar where a pile of newspapers are stashed.

My stomach gives a jolt as I step towards this stranger. Could she be a blood relative? How could she be in the same year as Annie and Mick – she looks much older.

'Hi, I'm Flora,' I say, offering my hand.

Her delicate fingers wrap round mine in a gentle handshake. I need to relax.

'Christine.' Her voice fits her appearance, it is tinny like a small chirp. 'Please take a seat.'

I glance at the bar to see Joel watching us, my pot of tea is being organised by the staff.

I sit down in my coat, but the bulk of the collar lifts about my ears. Fool. I stand, remove and sit down again.

'Nice to meet you, Christine, have you been waiting long?'

'Twenty minutes or so, I wanted to be early... didn't want to miss you.'

I scrutinise her face as she speaks. Thin painted lips, darkened eyebrows and rouged cheeks sit upon transparent skin. Is there any resemblance?

'Of course. Anyway...' the words hang like lead. I want to dive straight in, ask a heap of questions, hear what she knows, but that would be rude, surely? 'Thank you for the letter, it's nice to know that the article in The *Pooley Post* has been noticed.'

'I wrote straight away... I wanted to talk to you as soon as I could.'

Joel approaches, delivering a small tea tray.

'Thank you,' I say, grateful for his support.

'Hi, would you fancy a fresh pot?' he asks Christine, who shakes her head.

Joel indicates he'll be just over the way and leaves us.

Begin again.

'So...' I want to hear the details, I'm pussyfooting about with politeness when I simply want the raw hard facts, the secret revealed, the names, addresses and postcodes.

'*Well...*' her voice lingers as long as my 'so' did a few second ago. I wait, hanging on her every word, hoping it is soon followed by a torrent of others. It's not.

'Christine?'

Her gaze lingers on my face, not quite meeting my eyes but taking in every inch of my face. My heartbeat increases. I want to know what she knows. What's going on?

'Christine... was there something in particular you wanted to share?' I sound like I'm begging.

She picks up her teacup and takes a small sip. Her skin is so frail I can almost watch the sip of tea travel down her throat. Slowly she returns the cup to the table and leans forward.

'How much do you know?'

'I know what was printed in the paper last Friday, that's it.'

She gives a nod, her eyes not leaving my face.

'So, you don't know about Simon?'

My heart leaps.

'Who is Simon?'

She gives a knowing nod and sits back in her chair.

'Christine... who is Simon?' I feel like a child wheedling for information.

'Simon Hawthorne... is my brother.'

*

'How did it go?' calls Annie, as we enter The Peacock.

'Don't ask...' I mutter, removing my coat and settling in the alcove. 'A total waste of time.'

Joel heads to the bar to collect coffees. I continue to shout across the pub as though it were a private lounge without a smattering of early-evening customers lining the bar stools. My business has become their business in recent weeks.

'Mick was right... Christine Hawthorne from the high street.'

'Bloody hell, we'll never hear the end of it. *And*?' laughs Annie, pouring our coffee.

'You won't believe what she said.'

I quickly set the scene and retell the conversation.

'*Your* brother?' I'd said to Christine, shocked to hear her news.

'Yep, my brother Simon returned to Pooley once he'd turned eighteen – got up to some how's-your-father with a young girl in the village... my ma never liked her anyhow.'

'And I was the result?' I asked, unsettled by my own ability to speak so casually about my beginnings.

I'd watched as Christine's frizzy head bounced up and down.

207

'Like I said, my Ma didn't like the girl, she made things difficult for them, so our Simon knew it would be a no-goer...'

A no-goer? Wow, that was a new one for my list: abandoned, dumped and a no-goer.

'So, they abandoned me on a doorstep?'

'Best choice they had... her being underage and all that.'

'And *they* told you all these details?'

'Oh yes, years later... that's why I've come forward after reading the paper.'

'And my mother's name?'

'Sally West.'

'Sally West.' I'd repeated the name to see how it sat on my tongue. It felt awkward. 'And Sally and Simon... are they still around this area?'

Christine shifted in her seat.

'Well Susan is, our Simon moved away a while back but...'

'*Susan*?'

'I mean Sally. Sally's still in touch and our Simon visits when he can from up North but...'

'They're not together?'

'Oh, Lord no... Ma wouldn't have let that happen, as I said she didn't like the girl.'

'Are they aware that you've arranged to meet me?' A tingling excitement grew in my stomach.

I'd watched as Christine shifted in her seat, again.

'Christine, they do know?'

'See it's like this... life hasn't been easy for me...'

It hasn't been bloody easy for me either, I thought.

'I'm between jobs at the moment so haven't got a regular income coming in. The bills have stacked up and my overdraft is... well, it's huge. I was wondering if there was a reward or anything for information.'

'What?' screams Annie. 'The cheeky cow!'

'Seriously, straight out, she just asked.'

'How much did she want?'

'Three thousand.'

Annie pulls a face as she finishes the coffees and returns to serving a pint of bitter.

'Three grand – for a couple of addresses?' Annie is as stunned as I'd been. 'You are joking me?'

'I kid you not, as blatant as the nose on her face. She didn't even hesitate or stammer, said it straight out as if she was asking me to pass her a teaspoon.'

'Tell me that's not so?' asks Annie, turning to Joel.

'Sadly, it is... though Flora played a blinder when she'd recovered from the shock and called me over.'

'Christine didn't know where to put herself, did she?' I add. 'Tried to make out that I was lying when I repeated her request to Joel.'

'She quickly said how she was joking, how she'd felt so sorry to read the article about Baby Bede and just wanted to help,' says Joel. 'When I mentioned I was a police officer she got ready to leave, didn't she?'

'Some people have a bloody nerve,' tuts Annie. 'Does she actually know Simon and Sally?'

I shrug.

'I doubt it, given that Sally's name kept changing to Susan every two minutes,' adds Joel, bringing the coffees over from the bar.

'Now what? Are you going to report her?' asks Annie, wiping down the bar top.

'I'll mention it at the station, get her details and mobile logged,' says Joel, settling beside me.

'I want to follow up on Simon Hawthorne and Sally West,' I add, quickly slurping my coffee.

'Don't trust her, Flora – I bet they don't exist,' says Annie, shaking her head. She turns to the line of customers stood near the bar. 'Do any of you remember a Simon Hawthorne living above the butcher's?'

The line of customers shake their heads and pull quizzical faces.

'See.'

'How could someone be so heartless?' I ask, fighting the emotion snagging at my throat. 'Waste of an afternoon then, wasn't it?'

'Any news?' asks Mick, coming through from the rear living quarters.

'News! She's got news. Your little Christina Hawthorne is a crank. She's tried to swizz Flora out of cash for information – so no more feeling sorry for the little darling, OK?'

'We get it all the time in investigations – we have people fessing up to all sorts of crimes, *sometimes* murder, purely for the thrill – they want a slice of the drama,' explains Joel. 'Or maybe she's a bigger piece of the jigsaw, we just don't realise it yet!'

31

Janet

It brought a tear to my eye; seeing her sat by the pub's roaring fire. Her smile is bright and her eyes glisten on seeing us enter.

How can someone so beautiful and intelligent be my daughter?

'My darling, how are you?'

'Mum!' squeals Flora, jumping up from her seat and charging across the bar. Her arms wrap around my neck like the three-year-old she used to be. 'I've got so much to tell you.'

'Hello, can I get anyone a cuppa?' asks the cheery lady behind the bar.

'Mum, this is Annie… she's looked after me so well since Christmas Eve… Annie, these are my parents, Janet and David. Annie's husband, Mick, works the bar too, but he's laid up in bed with a bad back.'

'Doctor's orders and all that,' says Annie, shaking her head, 'though it never seems to get any better.'

I let out a sigh of relief, I'd been dreading the moment of introduction in case she'd changed her outlook. What if she'd said these are my adoptive parents, Janet and David? Seriously, I've had nightmares for the past week in case her feelings had changed towards us, despite the years of love we have shown her. Part of me was preparing for it. I should have known better, we brought her up to have manners and respect.

A round of hellos and thank yous follow before we peel off our coats and settle beside the coal fire. I can see why Flora feels so at home here, who wouldn't with such friendly people? It sounds ungrateful, but I don't think an overnight stay is going to be long enough for us to see everything Flora has to show us.

'I can't believe how tanned you both are,' says Flora.

'It was beautiful, simply beautiful... I just wish you'd been with us. Don't ask how much weight I've put on with all that luxurious food, urgh!' I laugh, adding, 'A whole dress size, would you believe it?'

We covered the necessary topics such as her health and happiness, David kept nudging nearer to the question of finances: did she need a little extra from us to tide her over? I knew better than to ask, Flora has always been so self-reliant. Maybe that's down to her start in life, not relying on anyone else might provide a sense of security, I suppose.

'And *this*,' says Flora, pointing to a huge wall display above our heads, 'is the local residents' information about where they were on the morning I was discovered...' I didn't hear any more that Flora said. I kept repeating her 'discovered' over and over in my head. Discovered? All her life, she'd always said *abandoned*. For years that was her phrase, yet here she is saying *discovered*. This has been a life-changing few weeks for her.

'Mum?'

I jump as she gently touches my arm.

'Are you OK?'

I find three faces staring at me.

'You've done so much, Flora.'

'This is nothing – I've found out loads.'

'But first, let me get a fresh tray of teas,' offers Annie, leaving us to chat.

The next thirty minutes are spent catching my breath back as my daughter talks non-stop about a silver ring, an old bath towel, a parka coat and a near-miss charge of assaulting a police officer.

*

'And that... is where I was found,' says Flora, pointing at a set of stone steps overlooked by two ugly lions.

I want to cry. Flora and David stand as proud as punch staring at the stone step, but I can't... that poor woman having to walk along that pathway and then...

'Oh don't! I can't glorify that day, Flora... her hurt led to our gain, but still... I can't pay homage to *that* doorstep.'

'Mum, come here,' her arms wrap around my shoulders, as my head sinks into the crook of her neck. She holds me tight and yet continues to explain her feelings.

I inhale the precious smell of my daughter, the smell I craved so badly and for thirty years have had the pleasure of knowing.

I frantically dab at my eyes with a crumpled tissue.

'Your mother's finding this hard, Flora,' offers David, looking smart in a new M&S sweater. 'She's going to need some time to get her head around the prospect of... sharing you.'

How selfish am I? What have I to fear from this mystery woman? She hasn't had what I've had? She won't ever have her first steps, her first words, every first event of this beautiful young woman's life. A wave of peace flows through me and I release the child I've raised.

'Oh, Mum, please don't... I don't know if we'll even find her let alone have a relationship... she might slam the door in my face.'

'Don't say that!' retorts David. 'She'd be a fool to refuse you for a second time.'

'Seriously, I just need to know who she is. Where I was actually born? And how it happened? Afterwards she can slam that door on me if she wants, Dad.'

How could anyone refuse that beautiful smile?

In the next twenty-four hours if she asks me to do a door-to-door police-style enquiry, smile inanely for local or national newspapers or simply retrace a feasible story about this village – I will. Anything to bring my girl her answers.

'More fool her if she does!' I say, wiping my eyes.

'Honestly, I have no idea what she'll want should we ever meet... but I know I have to do this, Mum, really I do.'

'We know... I didn't think this day would come, that's all,' offers David, swallowing hard and turning his head away.

'If it's any consolation, neither did I,' I add.

'Come on, we can't stand here all day – let's go back to The Peacock... there's someone I'd like you to meet,' says Flora.

32

Joel

I sit in the waiting room, staring at my freshly polished shoes, avoiding the staring blue eyes sat opposite.

I didn't want another meeting with Veronica, but what choice do I have after her suggestion the other night? If she thinks she can continue to drag her feet by refusing to sign, I'll show her otherwise. This has gone on for long enough. We're finished, there's no chance of a reconciliation, she made her bed and now she can lie in it. The privilege of making that clear has cost me another fifty-pound letter on embossed cream paper and yet another expensive appointment at Wick, Wick and Wick solicitors.

How much more will this cost me?

Veronica sits opposite, fiddling with her handbag toggle, wearing the smoky blue dress I bought for her when we visited London last spring. Or was it the year before? She's now avoiding eye contact, unlike ten minutes ago when she was staring at me in horror-film fashion.

I pretend to look at the framed watercolours decorating each wall but remain focused on her twitching fingers.

Why can't those twitchy fingers sign one loopy signature and all this aggro would be over with?

I straighten my white cuffs. I like this shirt. My style has changed greatly from the 'Before Veronica' days. Was that her biggest influence on my life? B.V. I'd been a smart dresser but nothing in my wardrobe cost the earth, no investment pieces. Duty days were uniform days and off duty I was happy with jeans, shirt and pumps – the casual laid-back approach. It might not have been 'the look' she was after, but with some gentle persuasion she'd opened my eyes to a sleeker design and gone was the morning routine: shower, shave and shove off look. Now, it was shower, shave, face scrub, moisturise and brow tidy.

I sigh. The aged receptionist glances over but Veronica doesn't.

Those were our early days, when we were eager to please each other, willing to embrace joint experiences and we got along fine.

What happened? What changed? What had I missed that changed her? Who knows, but now we sit in silence waiting for her solicitor to arrive at my solicitor's office.

Veronica

'Sorry, the traffic is snarled up on the main road – how are we?' announces my solicitor, when he arrives some ten minutes later than arranged.

Joel looks up and smiles.

'I'm well thanks, and you?' I ask as he forcibly pumps my hand up and down, in a clammy handshake.

'Can't complain, can't complain.'

I bet you can't given the hourly charge.

'Can we?' he indicates to the receptionist, who agrees we can venture up to the appointment, and we three, Joel included, take the stairs up to his solicitor's office.

A quick rap on the door, an old boys' greeting and we're down to business: the apartment.

Seated in a row of three along the same side of desk facing his solicitor feels awkward, surely Joel should have been seated on the other side facing us? That's how it would be in a Hollywood film.

'Is there a reason for the delay in signing?' asks Mr Wick, his pen poised, jowls hanging.

'My client wishes to revalue the property in light of the current housing market...'

'Is that likely to be advantageous or not to my client?' asks Mr Wick.

'Fair's fair.'

'No.'

'But...'

'My client wished for a swift resolution after your client decided to move from the said property and Mr Kennedy has agreed to every request made by Ms Sable. The arrangement has been fair and still the papers remain unsigned... why?'

I look at each solicitor and then scrutinise the burgundy leather-topped desk. The silence lingers as I fail to think of an adequate response. Joel stares at my profile, waiting.

What can I say? I can hardly say, I've noticed how you look at that new woman, can I? I can hardly say let's stop all this nonsense. Let's forget I moved out, forget the papers, the apartment valuation, the disruption, the upset, the arguing – or can I?

I shrug. I can't think of a reply.

His solicitor coughs.

Joel exhales a deep breath.

I never asked for *this* meeting, though it's costing me an arm and a leg to sit in silence thinking of something, anything to say. I could have done this elsewhere for free.

'Ms Sable, is there anything you'd like to add?' asks his solicitor, drumming his pen on the table.

Joel turns away and looks out of the window.

'I feel that given my expertise within the property market I have a hunch that the...'

'A hunch? My client doesn't deal with hunches, Ms Sable... he'd like a clean break and a resolution... with no hunches attached,' he says, opening the file to select a legal paper before sliding it across the desk. 'A signature is all he is requesting.'

I stare at the dotted line laid before me.

If I sign it's over. Done. Sorted.

Joel remains staring out of the window at the blue sky.

His solicitor gently nudges a pen in my direction.

I gulp.

Is this what I want? Do I want this man out of my life permanently?

'I need time to think,' I mutter.

Joel's head snaps back to face the table, his eyes don't meet mine.

His solicitor looks at him and the briefest of headshakes occurs.

'Well, there's nothing more for my client to discuss... please inform us of any requests or signatures as necessary,' says his solicitor abruptly, pushing his chair back from beneath the table and extending his plump hand for a concluding handshake.

'Joel?' His name slips from my lips without thought.

He raises a palm to silence me and bids his solicitor good day.

'Why does this have to be so difficult? I'm only thinking of what's best for us both,' I screech, as Joel strides from the solicitor's office.

*

I totter from the solicitor's office, knowing I can't be more than a few steps behind him.

I dodge a few old-age pensioners with their tartan trollies and can see him striding along the pavement a distance ahead.

'Joel!' I shout, ignoring the strangers that turn and stare. 'Joel!'

I scurry along the pavement, my heels catching in the crevices as I try to trot in a ladylike fashion.

He's heading for the car park. I follow, knowing he'll remove his suit jacket and hang it on the tiny hook in the rear of the vehicle before climbing in and pulling away. That'll give me a few extra seconds to catch him up.

What should I say? Be honest, be fair... or follow through with the original plan?

I reach the car park; Joel performs his jacket-hanging routine.

'Joel!' I stand in the open doorway, my hand on the car roof. 'Can I have a word?'

'You can have two, sod off.'

'Now, now.'

He puts the key in the ignition.

'Don't try that line, Veronica – you wanted out, you wanted *me* to buy you out, you wanted it all official with solicitors involved and now... *now*, you decide you aren't signing. What's that about?' He licks his bottom lip and stares at me, waiting.

I shrug. My mind hasn't found a reasonable line to excuse the current situation.

'Another shrug! Do you know how much these shrugs are costing?'

'Look, I'm sorry... I'm just not ready to...'

'To cut ties? Am I the safety net in case you and what's-his-face don't work out?'

'Joel!'

'Do me a favour, Veronica, sign the bloody papers and let me get on with my life!'

He pulls at the door handle forcefully. I sidestep to prevent damage to my hips. He slams the car door and reverses out of the space without a goodbye or a wave.

Typical. Bloody immature men, just what I hate.

33

Flora

'Come in,' says the elderly guy, opening the front door, his cigarette hanging from the corner of his lip, wiggling up and down as he spoke – yet not a drop of ash has fallen to the banana-leaf patterned carpet.

I stare at the bungalow's dingy hallway.

'Take a seat, she'll call when she's ready,' he mutters, before disappearing through a doorway.

I take a seat at the delicate telephone table and stare ahead at the painted chipboard. The door to my left is closed. I can hear the TV in the room where the old man waddled off to.

I should have told Annie where I was going, but it's not as if I'm answerable to her and Mick. I'm a grown adult. I can make decisions for myself, *sometimes*. I felt mean not telling them, but sometimes I want to do what I want to do, when I want to.

This reading was one such occasion.

How Annie had laughed about the tarot card reader on ladies' night. Hadn't she mocked those who'd queued to have a reading? I was prepared to take a gamble on anything if it brought me information.

'*Jessica*?' The door to my left opens and an elderly woman in a bejewelled headscarf appears, staring at me.

I blush.

I'm certain she knows I've given a false name.

'Yes, hi… nice to meet you.' I straighten my coat, extend a hand, but it's ignored as she leads me into her coven.

The room is dimly lit by a Pixar-style lamp with a turquoise voile draped over it. I stare around the room as she seats herself. Every inch of every wall is covered in masks, fairies, crosses, angels, cherubs, painted skulls and crystals, like Aladdin's cave. My eyes circle the walls before returning to the woman. Her kaftan gown billows from the yoke and her headscarf coins twinkle as she watches me.

'Take a seat,' she says, adding proudly, 'it's a lifetime's work is all that.'

I'm sceptical. An hour on eBay and I reckon I could purchase all this for delivery in three days.

I sit as her hands swiftly unwrap a red silk scarf, revealing a set of tarot cards. She places the cards face down on the small painted table, a colourful sun and moon design decorates the surface between us.

'Three cards for twenty, five for thirty,' she says, wringing her gnarled hands in her kaftan lap.

I don't understand, so hesitate. Didn't she charge ten pounds per reading at ladies' night?

'Three please.'

'Take the pile and shuffle, keep shuffling until you feel the cards want you to stop – then choose your three, place them face down on the table – I'll take the remaining cards.'

I follow her instructions. The cards feel awkward in my hands, I wish I could shuffle but I can't. My hands stumble through each movement as I struggle not to scatter the pile across the painted table. After an embarrassing few shuffles, and not when the cards tell me but my dignity does – I choose three cards, placing them face down as requested.

She takes the remaining pile from my clutches, probably for the best, given my handling skills. She slowly turns the first card over, showing a colourful picture depicting a woman surrounded by hearts and vines.

'The Empress... an interesting card,' she says, adding, 'she's associated with fertility, birth and rebirth. Can you see how the healthy vines bloom around her body? Maybe you'll receive news about a pregnancy, or find yourself expecting.' She glances at my ringless fingers. I move my hands from the table into my lap.

'Oh.' Was all I could say. The birth and fertility could link to my search or maybe I'll experience a rebirth once Major Matthews organises the DNA testing and the results are known. Or if my search proves futile maybe I'll experience a rebirth by accepting that I'll never know the answer but at least I can move on.

'Not the answer you were seeking, Jessica?'

I smile. I don't want to answer. I don't want to feed her any information. I want to know what she can see or feel from the psychic world, if such a talent exists.

'The Empress has strong connections with good times and contentment in the future. Maybe you're looking to settle down, enjoy a time of certainty, create strong foundations on which to build a new life.'

I nod politely, hoping that's a true prediction.

'I can see you enjoying a lot of contentment in the coming months, Jessica... things have been a bit rough lately, but these issues will disappear with time, they always do.'

Her fingers flip card two over to show a plainer one depicting a solitary man walking with a stick.

'The Hermit – he represents a time of solitary thinking, a time to withdraw from the crowd and focus on yourself, find yourself and discover the real you.'

I nod. It sounds about right, I suppose I have become a hermit of late. Leaving my life in Bushey, going it alone in Pooley amongst the villagers, thinking about my past life and the possible outcomes.

'Any nearer to what you're experiencing, Jessica?'

'Yes, I can relate to that card – I feel like a hermit at the moment, but will it always be like this?'

'It's not all doom and gloom for the hermit, you know. Self-reflection is good for the soul, helps it to breathe – which is never a bad thing. And finally…' She flips the last card to reveal a brightly painted boy stepping off the edge of a cliff, a cheery smile addresses his face. 'The Fool!'

I smile, surely the clue is in the title.

'He's a welcome card because he represents unlimited potential in human nature despite our flaws and fortunes. Can you see he's stepping off the edge into the unknown – frightening, scary, but it allows you to begin a new chapter of your life.'

'That's me… I feel like that!' I say, unable to hold my tongue. I didn't give too much away about the first card, The Empress, but she got the connection almost right.

I'm overwhelmed with excitement, though I try to hide my reaction.

'From this card, I see you're having unsettled times, but take heart, Jessica, time passes and this will pass too and then a brand-new chapter of your life will begin,' she says, shuffling the three cards back into her pile. 'Be brave and dare to go where angels fear to tread.'

Excellent, what else?

'I don't take cards or cheques.'

Her final sentence snaps me straight back to reality. Is that it – the end? How long have I been here, five minutes or an hour? I really couldn't say.

'Cash then,' I stammer, my question is met by her cool eyes. Not another word is said, she has literally ceased to communicate after saying the word cheques. Wasn't there a summary to finish? Nothing, she sits and waits for her payment.

I collect my handbag, dig out my purse and give her a crisp twenty.

'Cheers, Jessica, if you'll be wanting a follow-up reading please just give me a ring.' I watch as she pops my crisp note down her neckline and performs a tucking-in action.

I stand and make for the door.

'Jessica...'

'Yes,' I say, eager for any additional information.

'Will you say "hi" to Annie for me... I keep meaning to drop by and ask how Mick's back is.'

My heart sinks. Not so psychic after all.

*

'You silly mare!' laughs Annie. 'Why didn't you say?'

'I didn't think it necessary,' I mutter, like a chastised kid.

'Everyone knows everyone around here – I'd have saved you twenty quid by telling you Dippy Doris is Old Nancy's bloody sister. Psychic, my foot. Bloody gossip queen more like.'

'So how did she get me to select those particular cards then?'

'Lord knows... but Old Nancy will have told her your story – so she knew what to aim for.'

'Maybe she'd have linked my search regardless of the cards I chose.'

'Mmmm, does Joel know?'

'Why would I tell Joel?'

'Why not? He'd have warned you too.'

'I don't have to run everything I do past Joel, you know?'

'Really? You could have fooled me! Here, get a glass of wine down your neck and next time don't be so naive.

34

Joel

My first day back on duty was pretty quiet. A long stint driving the patrol car on a bright and breezy day was interrupted only by a petty theft committed by a lanky streak of a teenager. Hardly a big crime day for us boys in blue. I quickly change from my uniform as soon as the shift ends. I grab a coffee and head back to the small unheated office to restart my search through the original file.

Maybe Scotty missed something.

A wave of guilt creeps through my mind as I nip between the offices without being noticed by the duty officers. It doesn't feel like police business but a private matter that I'm squirrelling away, unwilling to share or discuss.

I'd welcomed Scotty's previous help, but in recent days his lack of enthusiasm and narky remarks were beginning to grate on my nerves. It was clear that he wasn't interested, but why should he be? His only involvement was slapping the cuffs on tight and bobbing her head into the rear seat of a patrol car.

If I'd have known that night how this case would mushroom, I'd have acted differently. A little more compassion on seeing her crouched in front of the wrought-iron gate, more patience when asking for her details, but hey, how was I to know?

How had *this* happened? Plodding along, minding my own business and then bingo, Christmas Eve! And now, I'm giving up my free time to wade through a thirty-year-old file.

I flick through the paperwork, looking for the statement made by young Darren. As I reread his words I can hear the immature voice of a teenager lift from the page. Had he seen the mother leaving The Square? Or was he a typical teenager oblivious to everything? Had she hidden in the phone box? Timed her delivery with his? Only to nip out and leave as he rang the doorbell and the commotion began? Why was the bus ticket even collected? A lazy copper hoping to please his sergeant or an overactive imagination amongst the original squad?

I finger the evidence bag in which the torn bus ticket lies.

It only complicates the situation by suggesting she'd travelled from further afield. Or had she?

I peer at the aged ticket stub.

The orange ticket hasn't a complete date – the tear occurs through the digits.

Is that curve part of a zero or a nine? A tiny spot of ink part way up suggests a nine. It wasn't even the right date, so why had some useless git bagged it? Had they fingerprinted it? My fingers nimbly flip through the file searching for the answer: no. We know that the baby wasn't on the doorstep all night, don't we? Hadn't the nurses aged her at hours old on her arrival at the hospital?

Note: bus ticket eliminated.

*

Within the hour, I had finished with Darren and moved on to list the names of every witness that had given a statement. The names on the list jump to life as I visualise the people I know from The Peacock alongside other faceless unknowns I haven't ever heard of.

Where are these people now? Guilty or not guilty – only time would tell.

I close the file, pushing it away having finished for the day. My mind buzzes with details and yet nothing.

Darren, Tommy, Nina, Doc Fowler, Fred, Flora, Old Nancy, Veronica, Melanie, Donnie – the names circle my mind as I stand, collect my belongings and straighten the office to hide my presence.

Duggan – where's his statement?

I flip open the file – my fingers skitter through. I know the answer before I've reached the back cover – it isn't here.

I grab my mobile and speed-dial.

'Flora?'

'Joel?' Her voice is tinny and small.

'You mentioned that Tommy Duggan saw a girl wearing a parka coat?' I pace the empty office as I speak.

'Yep.'

'Did he say he'd told the police?'

'Yes, him and his dad both gave a statement.'

Silence.

'Joel... what's happening?'

'The statements aren't in your file.'

'No way! He said him and his dad saw a girl walking into Windmill Road as they walked in the fog... have you still got the file?'

'Yes, right in front of me... I've reread the whole thing in case Scotty had missed a trick. I've listed the statements and his isn't here.'

'Now what?'

'I need to speak to the Chief – we *need* his statement.'

'You're the best, Joel.'

I pretend she hasn't made my day with such flattery.

Am I? Isn't this what every copper in this station would do given the chance of finding the answer to a thirty-year-old mystery? Or have I an ulterior motive?

35

Flora

I have butterflies in my stomach as a sea of faces greet my entrance into the bar. I feel sick. I could faint at any moment but I have to go through with the process. The wheels are turning and I must go with the flow.

Major Matthews had swiftly arranged for a private company to attend and perform the swab collection.

It must be costing an arm and a leg. How am I ever going to repay his generosity?

The bright lights of the local TV crew glare above my head, a cluster of camera operators and techies fiddle about with equipment while the news reporter, Beth Copper, tidies her hair. I've never been on TV before so the very thought fills me with dread, but as Annie keeps saying, 'it's vital to get the story out there.'

The crowd stand and stare.

All these people have given up their evening for me and my cause, the least I can do is be polite and sociable.

'Flora?' calls Annie from the bar, holding aloft a glass of rosé wine.

'In a minute, I need to do this first,' I say, grateful that she's always one step ahead of me. She knows me so well in such a short time.

Hours ago, I thought what will I do if no one turns up? Step one: I'll die of embarrassment. Step two: dash home to Bushey never to be seen again. *That* fear has been suppressed by this wonderful crowd that now stand by the bar.

My journey is in the lap of the gods, but I am turning to cold hard science to do the detection work for me.

'Flora!' calls Beth, the newshound. 'How are we feeling?'

'Very nervous,' I mutter, twirling a long strand of hair round my index finger.

'There's no need, just be yourself.' Beth spends a few minutes explaining that the camera crew would like to film my oral swab being taken, they'd like general footage of others having theirs taken and, afterwards, once I've calmed down, they'd take me aside for a few questions, whilst in the background the others continue with the task. They'd already interviewed Major Matthews about his grand gesture and generosity.

It all sounds fine to me.

'And when will this be used?' I ask, unsure if I'd be on the ten o'clock local news.

'We could feature midday tomorrow, if all goes well... a feel-good feature at lunchtime lifts everyone, then there'll be a rerun on the early evening news as well.'

I'm stunned, I'll be on the telly twice in one day. Wow!

'So, are we fit and ready?' she asks, giving the camera crew the immediate thumbs up.

*

'Who's first?' asks the nurse eagerly, scanning the crowd for sample number one.

The sea of faces turn towards me.

'I suppose that's me!' I laugh, stepping through the crowd and standing before the makeshift testing station. Nothing high-tech or laboratory-like, but a testing area consisting of a couple of bar tables and hard-backed chairs, plus two sterile nurses.

Not the usual Tuesday night karaoke do at The Peacock, ironically 'I will Survive' is looping through my mind, as the camera crew stand a little way back from the action.

'If you could take a seat,' asks Nurse One, opening a plastic bag containing the paraphernalia for DNA testing. 'Could you open wide, please?'

I never imagined how embarrassing it would be to sit before a crowd and camera crew with my mouth open wide. Seriously, I blushed like a nun passing Ann Summers and yet all she did was insert a large cotton bud and swipe about my inner cheek. I've shown less embarrassment at smear tests. The nurse carefully places the swab inside a clear tube before writing my details on the tiny label and ushering me and my sample sideways towards the second nurse and her paperwork station.

'Next,' calls the swabbing nurse.

I watch Joel step to the front of the queue. No one in the bar queries his actions – they simply gather round and stare.

Have mercy if I have committed some deadly sin by unknowingly headbutting my older brother. I quickly do the maths in my head. Could we have the same mother?

Joel sits down and follows Nurse One's instructions just as I had – the camera crew continue to film.

Please let his be an unrelated result. That would be my silver lining to counterbalance any disappointing result from tonight's mass testing.

I look amongst the crowd, Denny and Donnie grin inanely from beside the fruit machine.

Could I cope with the fruit machine loons being my younger brothers? Or wife-swappers being my grandparents?

A wave of panic crashes over me.

What if this testing doesn't work? A big fat zero result comes back after I've badgered everyone to attend and be swabbed.

I'll definitely die of embarrassment and crawl back to Bushey if I'm not related to anyone – that will be a sure sign. Maybe that fictional stork did fly by and deliver a baby just once.

'Collect a free drink once you've had your swab taken,' shouts Annie, filling the bar with a selection of lager and wine glasses. 'And no, you can't queue for a second and third swab to get another drink!' A ripple of laughter lifts from the waiting crowd.

Suddenly the crowd surge into an orderly queue in front of Nurse One, as I leave paperwork nurse and collect my wine.

'Well done, darling... that couldn't have been easy in front of everyone,' says Annie.

'How red did I go?' I say, gratefully lifting the rosé to my lips. 'Cheers and thank you, Annie, this wouldn't have happened without you.'

'It's nothing... maybe you should publicly thank Major Matthews.'

'I will once everyone's been swabbed, there's no way I could have forked out for all these tests... it'll cost a pretty penny and people wouldn't have paid for their own.'

Annie nods in agreement.

'Are you pleased with the turnout, Flora?' asks Joel, sidling up to the bar and collecting a pint glass.

'Absolutely delighted. I had a wobble earlier imagining that no one would attend... how stupid was I?'

Joel scans the busy bar.

'By the looks of it virtually every family in the village is represented, even those who we've lost contact with... surely someone here must have some genetic connection to you.'

'I hope so.'

We stand in silence as a mass of Delaney females gather at the front of the queue.

'Even if you end up being one of the...?' Joel nods his head towards the gaggle of women.

'Yep, even if...' I playfully slap his shoulder.

'Brave girl,' he adds, supping his pint.

'I wonder if there'll be people who refuse to attend?'

'Such as?'

I shrug.

'I couldn't say, but there must be someone in the village that's not prepared to give a swab.'

'I can't imagine there's many, they all know your story and the issues it has thrown up for you... though there's always someone who'll complain that testing goes against their basic human rights.'

'Exactly, how would I find out who they were?'

'You can't unless you're going to tick off the residents' names from the electoral roll.'

'But they could use that as an excuse for hiding... the truth.'

'I doubt it'll happen... if there's a woman in this village trying to avoid *this*... most will be uncovered because their children are here offering to be tested.'

He's right. There can't be anyone in the village who could hide – the bar is heaving with bodies; the door keeps opening, welcoming people of all ages.

?

36

'Have you got a pen I can borrow?' I ask Denny, as he pumps another load of change into the fruit machine.

'Yeah,' he says, digging about in his back pocket, his waistband launches up and down revealing greying underwear as he furtles about. 'Here.'

'Thanks,' I mutter, taking the offered pen, unsure if I should accept, having seen how grubby he actually is.

I flick the comments book to any page; I'm looking for a small area in which to add a comment.

Annie O'Neill has lived in The Square all of her life – she wouldn't have had too far to run, hide and watch.

I finish my sentence, leave it unsigned and continue to flick through the pages, feigning an interest in the other comments before handing his pen back.

37

Lisa

'This feels like old times,' I laugh, trying desperately to hang onto the edge of the double bed while the other two sprawl across it.

The three of us squished on a bed, doing our make-up while drinking large glasses of wine and deciding on which clothes to wear or share. Flora has pinched my heated rollers to tame her auburn locks, while me and Steph had fought over the straighteners – which we'd duly shared.

'We haven't done this for ages,' I say, watching the others peer into tiny compact mirrors.

'Since we were about twenty-two...' adds Steph, grabbing her glass and glugging her drink.

'And that was probably the time you half-stripped on a table in Manhattan's demanding that Nigel Calder ravish you senseless in the back of his Golf cabriolet,' laughs Flora, rolling onto her back.

'Nigel Calder, now there's a blast from the past – he's married now with five kids,' I add.

'Never!' they chorus, before grimacing.

'That could have been me!' cries Steph, sitting bolt upright.

'No way – you couldn't get past first base with him,' squeals Flora.

'He left you half-naked parading on that table after you scared him to death… you'd have never have got to five babies!'

'I was passionate, that's all,' corrects Steph, primping her blonde locks.

'Powerless, more like. Didn't we have to carry her home that night?' I ask Flora, whose memory is much better than mine.

'If you've got it, flaunt it!' cries Steph, returning her glass to the floor and pouting in her compact mirror.

I can almost imagine that we're in Flora's teenage bedroom, but we're not – we're camped in room five of Flora's hideout, The Peacock pub. As youngsters, I'd loved going around to her house, it was less cramped than ours, her being an only child. Her mum was never shouting, whereas my mum did nothing but bawl and scream. In our house, if my friends ever came round to play records in my room we'd be constantly hijacked or jumped on by three younger kids, all with dodgy home haircuts and faded hand-me-downs. Flora always had brand new clothes selected from the rail in British Home Stores and Adams' – nothing in her life was hand-me-down, except her birth. At Flora's house everything was neat and tidy, with bottles of Ribena in the cupboard; our house was flat cola with a dodgy corner-shop label. I never had to be asked twice to dinner at Flora's house; I never offered in return.

Always 'my special friend', as my mum called her, the girl that had 'you-know' mouthed above her head as we spilt from primary school like a broken dam. Everyone knew, though I never mentioned it. It rattled about some kids' mouths like an unpleasant skipping song kept from the adults, 'My mum says that your mum's not your real mum!' I was desperate to be friends with the special girl, the chosen one. She had stuck by me ever since.

'When are you coming home?' Steph asks for the umpteenth time since our arrival. 'We're missing you and your mum is beside herself.'

'I keep telling you. I'm not, not *yet* anyway.'

'Flora, look at this place, the wallpaper dates from the Ark, the tufted bedspread is bald in places and matted in others... and don't get me started on that corner sink unit!' continues Steph, our eyes following her pointing finger to each offending item in room five. 'Need I say more?'

Flora shrugs, closing the lid on her lippy.

'I get that *you* don't get it, but I *need* to do this.'

'Now that you've done it for a few weeks... come home!' laughs Steph.

I linger, watching from the sidelines, unsure if this is going well. We'd followed Flora's instruction and brought with us a suitcase of her own clothes from home. A careful selection of outfits that were definitely post-winter and pre-spring wear. It seemed an unnecessary request if she was coming home with us on Sunday night.

Flora's chin wobbles.

'Steph... leave it,' I mouth, trying to be invisible, but clearly not, as Flora answers.

'Lisa's right, please leave it... can't we go out and enjoy your weekend visit?'

'I'd enjoy it better if I knew you were coming home with us on Sunday night.'

Flora launches herself from the bed, breaking the trio pose.

'I'm staying put, Steph. I'll wait for the DNA results and see what's what and *then* decide,' she says, repositioning her make-up products along the edge of the offending sink unit. 'I shouldn't have to apologise for wanting what I want.'

'Decide?' Steph looks horrified. 'Lisa, talk some sense into her.'

'No.'

'Lisa!'

'I can't, I'm with Flora.'

They both stare at me. I can't please them both. How many

years has Flora fought this crap? Twenty-three years of not knowing, ever since Jan and Dave told her, aged seven, how special she was. Special enough to be chosen on a weekend visit to view a helpless newborn crying in a Mothercare carrycot in a foster carer's lounge. Flora *is* special, and I need to repay all my friend's specialness in the best way I can, by standing by her.

'We've watched Flora take the crap dealt by others right on the chin. I've held my breath every time she's found some happiness, only to pick her up when the bubble bursts, and now... she's here and *she's* decided to be here, and you want *me* to talk her round?'

'Err, yes please!'

'No!'

'Lisa!'

I shake my head.

'Right now, I want to get glammed up and paint this town... village... red!' I spring from the tufted bedspread to stand beside my special mate in the middle of the floor. 'And, Steph... I'm not dragging her home come Sunday night.'

Flora's arms wrap around my shoulders and squeeze.

'I get it, I really do,' I tell her, my voice muffled by her bear hug.

*

We start in the bar downstairs. Apparently, our pub crawl is going to be the world's shortest, given there's only a few pubs and a wine bar in the local vicinity. Even so, it feels like a novelty, as it is the closest any one of us had lived to the free flow of alcohol.

The sight of us three cavorting down the staircase in killer heels, slinky dresses and a tsunami of lip gloss appears slightly out of place amongst the corduroy and cardigans, but we don't care – you don't tend to when you've shared a bottle of vanilla vodka while drying your hair.

'Raises your glasses, ladies,' instructs Flora. 'I propose a toast!'

'To us!' we chant, before gulping back our shots and instantly ordering another round from the jolly landlady. The jukebox is firing out hits, but in the split-second silence of a changing disc a bitch comment fills the air. I hate it when that happens. Steph loves it.

''Ark at them, three little girls playing at Barbie!'

We turn in unison towards the surprised announcer, a mature woman with scarlet lipstick and a mauve suit, clutching a double G&T.

'*Sorry*, you were saying?' asks Steph. Flora's hand lifts to touch Steph's forearm, a gesture of caution and care. The woman turns her head and continues to chat to her friends. 'Oi lady, would you care to explain?'

Here we go!

'Moi?' She spins round to answer. 'I *never* explain!'

'Steph meet Veronica Sable, Pooley's local estate agent,' Flora says, changing to a whisper and adding, 'careful... she's a bitch and a half.'

In a blink, Steph is across the bar, her glass leisurely swinging from her raised hand as she looms over the offending one.

'I shouldn't have said that, should I?' mumbles Flora, blushing. 'Annie will kill me if Steph kicks off in here.'

'Too late now,' I add, as Flora blushes at the scene about to unfold.

'*Steph*!' Flora hastily follows Steph, trying to hold her back.

'Stephanie Johnson, nice to meet you... sorry to interrupt but I heard your vile remark as you were unfortunate enough to be loud and vulgar whilst in public. My breeding doesn't allow me to ignore such remarks... so would you care to explain or shall I presume that this is your usual style.'

I wince.

I've seen Stephanie do her pull-you-up-in-public stunt many times before – the ending is never pretty. I'm pretty certain that landlady Annie will not be amused, and Flora knows it.

Veronica gives Steph the head-to-toe-and-back-up-again stare, which doesn't quite cut it when you're seated on a tiny bar stool and the opponent is looming tall in Kurt Geiger killer heels.

The bar falls silent, even the jukebox remains mute.

'Congratulations, you've even perfected the bitch overlook, more's the pity,' continues Steph, casually sipping her drink mid-sentence. 'A word of advice... you need to tone down your foundation by two shades for the mature skin type, scrap the red lipstick – it screams desperation, a feathered-cut fringe would flatter your face shape and get your roots touched up!'

A chuckle ripples through the bar.

'Steph?' whines Flora, trying to turn Steph away from Veronica.

'Sorry, how rude of me, what I actually meant to say was... if your intention is the killer cougar look you do need to keep on top of your maintenance regime, otherwise you look like mutton dressed as lamb! Ciao!'

Veronica's jaw drops wide.

The other customers snort and splutter into their beer, Veronica and her two gal pals stare after Steph's shapely wiggle as she strides towards us – we neck our drinks in a unanimous decision to move bars.

'*Flora*!' shouts Mick, across the beer pumps, his brow puckered and his hand pointing to the door.

'Come on, let's get out of here before she starts a catfight with a yokel,' I whisper, linking arms and half dragging a triumphant Steph through the bar's exit.

*

'You're so morbid!' sings Steph, swinging round the lamp post with her arms outstretched.

'I'm not, I'm interested,' I quickly correct her, knowing full well that Flora was dying for one of us to be interested. She's repeated her story at every milestone occasion and birthday celebration and now, tonight, that mini-drama that was once far away has become a reality and we stand in the actual place. '*And* I want to see *the* doorstep, so hush up.'

Steph joins us and we totter, arms linked in a Dorothy and Co., Yellow Brick Road style, beneath a clear night sky, heading over the cobblestones towards the neat row of houses. A sense of solemnity descends as Flora leads us along the railings towards the middle house.

'Ka-ching!' snorts Steph, viewing the house. 'You're a posh bird!'

'Ignore her,' I say. 'Who lives here now?'

'The same doctor that I've mentioned – him and his wife divorced, so he lives alone… seems my arrival highlighted their marital differences and they split soon afterwards.'

'Ughhh!' moans Steph, leaning against the railings and allowing the spikes to dig into her bare forearms. 'I think I'm going to be sick.'

We should have called it a night several rounds ago but Steph's gregarious nature had demanded more shots in the other pubs. She staggers a short distance towards the phone box and doubles over in the gutter.

'Seems I'm bad luck for everyone,' mutters Flora, her gaze fixed on the stone step.

'You're not!'

'I am.'

In Flora's world, her birth must feel like an omen. How does anyone get through life if your mother gives you away on day one? Given away before you've dirtied your first nappy, crashed the family car during a crazy girl weekend, dated the most unsuitable men in the local area and returned home aged thirty with no job to kip on their couch. I had to admit, Flora hadn't the luckiest track record in life.

'If I was going to have a baby left on my doorstep, I'd have wanted it to be you!' I announce, squeezing her tight.

'You say the sweetest things, Lisa,' coos Flora, petting my cheek.

'Oh *shucks*,' I blush, happy to please.

'And *over* there is the spot where I accidently nutted the copper on Christmas Eve,' says Flora, pointing to a spot a few feet away by the corner, where Steph is hacking up her last three rounds.

'Are we going to meet lover boy?' asks Steph, looking up from gagging to inspect the policeman's pavement stain.

'He's *not* lover boy!' snaps Flora, jumping back from the railings. 'He's *just* a friend.'

'Your mum seems to think he is,' I add, knowing Flora hates others gossiping behind her back. 'Given that you introduced him during their visit.'

'Well, she's wrong. Joel's helping me sort the fact from the village fiction, that's all.'

'*Jackanory... Jackanory*,' sings Steph, staggering from side to side as she rejoins us at the railings.

'I'm not. This is about me finding my birth mum. Nothing more.'

'But if he made a move?'

Flora gives a brief smile.

'Perhaps... but he's still tangled up with his previous woman... the cougar, Veronica.'

'Phew! She's history,' calls Steph.

'But if he asks for a date, you'll say yes, won't you?' I push, knowing she's playing it coy.

'*Maybe.*'

'We believe you, but thousands wouldn't,' mocks Steph, walking back towards the corner. 'Your mother for one.'

'Ignore her, honey, she's only jealous.'

'Of me?' asks Flora, shaking her curled locks.

'Oh yeah, because I've always wanted the love of a cheating ex… begging for my hand in marriage…'

I gasp.

'*What?*' asks Flora.

'Nothing,' I snap, sending a dagger stare towards Steph, who sobers up in seconds, yet pretends to vomit some more over the pavement.

'Has Julian been in touch?'

'No,' I say, a tad too quickly.

I can't lie, seriously I'm crap at it.

'He has, hasn't he?'

'No,' adds Steph, even less convincing than my poor attempt.

'Julian wants me back?'

'No!' we say in unison.

'Lisa… tell me.'

I stall. I breathe. I'm going to have to tell her.

Like the time that Steph accidently snogged Flora's first boyfriend at the school disco while 'I Believe I Can Fly' by R Kelly played in the background – I had the job of telling her the truth, while Steph hid in the toilets crying. Like then, Flora deserves to know the truth, even if Julian remains the pig-headed git that broke her heart by knobbing another woman.

'He came round after Christmas, asking if I'd seen you… I said yes, I lied of course, but hey, he didn't need to know. Anyway, he said that he'd jacked the blonde and…'

'The bastard!' spits Flora, shaking her head in disgust.

'And wanted to have a chat about you guys getting back together and starting afresh… he hinted that he might even consider…' I couldn't bring myself to say it.

244

'Wedding bells,' interrupts Steph, adding a giggle to her impression of church bells.

Flora is stony-faced and staring at Steph.

'Flora?' I touch her arm and break her trance.

'You didn't tell him I was here, did you?' gasps Flora.

'Dooh!' adds Steph, wiping her mouth and leaning against the telephone box.

'Give it a rest, Steph – it's wearing thin... no, Flora, I didn't.'

'Please don't... he's the last person I want to see milling about the village. Veronica's bad enough in the wrong light, let alone Julian.'

'I did the right thing?' I ask, relieved by her response.

'Sure you did, say the same if he comes knocking again, Lisa.'

'Deal!'

'Can we go back to The Peacock so I can knock ten bells out of old Veronica the Harmonica?' laughs Steph, opening and closing the telephone box door.

I give Flora a hug, she looks crestfallen.

'Ignore Steph – you know what she's like.'

38

Voluntary Police Statement: Mr Thomas Duggan

I, Thomas Duggan, of No. 5, St. Bede's Mews, Pooley, Warwickshire, for claim number: PB101084B. The facts in this statement come from my personal knowledge. We did see a girl that morning back in 1986. We didn't think it was any of our business to grass on others. Live and let live was my dad's motto, so it might as well be mine. The morning that baby was found, my dad and I left the house just after seven o'clock. I'd had a new BMX bike for my birthday so wanted to ride alongside my dad as he walked to work. A plasterer by trade but he was doing shift work at the hatting factory. Times were tight for my parents; in fact, the eighties were tight for most folk around here. We lived in a decent-sized house compared to those over at North Street. Dad found himself in a spot of trouble with debt collectors and one thing led to another – he had to make ends meet. He never *shat* on his own doorstep, never. And folks around here respected him for it. He had a sharp eye and a light finger, but it got him through the trouble. He chose well, a couple of local businesses that could afford a claim on their insurance. Anyway, we left the house later than he'd wanted, he was annoyed that I'd wasted time getting my bike from the shed. We set off under the archway. She entered Windmill Road from North Street, wearing a parka coat, the ones with the fur hood. I doubt she saw us; it being foggy that morning, which was why dad was eager to get going. I didn't see her face. We never spoke to her. That's it. There's nothing more to add. Which is why my dad didn't want to get involved at the time. We couldn't identify her, so why waste police time? I believe the details in this statement are true.

Signed: T Duggan
Date: 08/02/2017

39

Flora

My centre a heart that beats with pace,
Left or right defines her grace.
Hedging my bets that you'll know where I am.
Waiting for you to succeed where you can.

'What's this?' I ask, thrusting the piece of paper towards Annie as she peers over the bar, her bemused expression collapsing into a fit of giggles.

'Don't shoot the messenger, *please*,' she splutters. 'Joel came in, asked if you were about and left that envelope for when you surfaced. That's it, otherwise no comprende.'

I read it aloud, *again*.

'Is it some poetic prank?' I ask, waving the poem about. 'Something else to make me look like a gibbering idiot at the expense of others?'

'I *think* it's called romance... he's trying to show some interest.'

I cut Annie short.

'Get stuffed! Joel's not interested in me! He's only interested in solving a case and closing a police file,' I scowl. The weeks were passing with hardly any developments about my birth mother or Joel. 'Has he asked me on a date?'

Annie shakes her head, and slopes off along the bar.

'*Annie*?'

'You're obviously in a mardy... got out of bed on the wrong side, did we?'

'What's the note supposed to mean?' I deflect her comment and attempt to backpedal.

'Go figure.'

'*Annie*, look...'

She waves a hand in defeat and continues her bar cleaning as far away as possible from me.

I've never been any good at poetry. Throughout school my English teachers were asking me to feel the emotion, depict the imagery and decipher the poet's language – nothing made sense because it was never in plain English. And now, at the ripe old age of thirty, when school days are a distant memory, my humiliation about hidden meanings finally forgotten – I'm supposed to take delight in delivery of a poem before the clock has struck ten in the morning. *Seriously*?

I ignore Annie blatantly staring from the far end of the bar and continue to scoff my breakfast of egg on toast as a niggling headache brews above my right eye. A dull headache that I'd had since my friends went back home after their weekend visit.

Why couldn't I enjoy a simple breakfast? Begin the day like a normal person? No chance. I've got to be bright and sodding breezy while others laugh at me. Proving yet again, that I'm some nitwit when it comes to anything cultured.

As I chew, I stare angrily at the torn envelope and discarded poem.

'What the hell is it supposed to mean anyway? Since when has Joel been into poetry?' I mutter. 'How am I supposed to know unless he asks me for a date?'

'Read it again?' The male voice startles me.

I look up to find Mick seated behind me reading his newspaper by the window.

'Bloody hell, Mick, you made me jump. Is your bad back better?' I hadn't seen him for near on a week.

'Better than it was... read it again.'

He listens intently as I reread each line.

'I'll take you if you want?'

'Where?'

Mick taps the side of his nose and winks in an exaggerated fashion.

'I wouldn't bother, Mick, she's in a devil of a mood and she'll snipe at you instead of thanking you,' shouts Annie, polishing the beer pumps.

'*Well?*'

'Well, what?'

'What's the answer?' I snort, as the reflection of Medusa looms in the bar mirror.

'See what I mean?' calls Annie, shaking her head. 'Good luck, Joel – she's got her arse in her hand today, that's for sure.'

*

In no time, Mick and I are seated in his red minivan charging out of The Square via the stone archway, cases of fizzy pop from the budget Cash 'n' Carry rattling in the back.

'It's been a hell of a long time, but I still think I'm right,' shouts Mick, over the noise of the spluttering engine.

'Where will he be?'

'At the manor house...'

'Yes but why?'

'Their maze.'

'A maze?'

Mick nods.

'We used to play in it as kids... many a time we got lost within those hedges... it was such a scream.'

'A maze?'

'Yes, left and right turns and a huge space in the centre with benches and birdbaths and...'

'A beating heart,' I murmur, more to myself than Mick.

'Joel.'

'Thanks for that, Mick, even *I* got that metaphor,' I add sarcastically.

'*Just* saying.'

We drive in silence, out of the village and along narrow country lanes with hedgerows and aged bare-limbed trees whizzing by my window. It seems like the snow has long gone, maybe spring was around the next corner.

Had I ever mentioned wanting to see a maze to Joel? Had I ever said I'd seen one previously? No and no, but anyway I'll go along with his game.

'Here we are,' announces Mick, indicating and turning right into a grand entrance complete with ornate gates and a quaint stone lodge beyond.

'Isn't this private property?'

'Yep, Major Matthews' place, but he allows the public to use the open space and visit the maze which is along the driveway... it's away from the manor house so they retain their privacy.'

'Wow! Veronica's living here?' I gasp.

'Yep, though I can't imagine Major Matthews being the typical sugar-daddy type – so I wouldn't feel too jealous.'

'Jealous of Veronica? Nah!' I retort. 'Though I'm grateful that he coughed up the funds for the DNA testing – I could never have paid for a mass testing.'

'He's generous when he chooses to be. The local news clip where you named and thanked him is *his* kind of publicity – a good deed but he'll ensure everyone knows about it.'

'But still, he didn't have to offer,' I add, feeling guilty for any criticism being aimed at him.

The windscreen frames a vast open space dotted with ancient trees standing at obscure angles.

'This is amazing… why has no one mentioned it before?'

'I can't imagine that many village folk still visit.'

How true is that? Back home, I live within a short walk of a museum and art gallery but have only ever visited them during trips from primary school. Funny that.

'So, he doesn't mind?'

'As long as you don't do any damage.'

The driveway eventually forks; we take the right-hand road leading to a gravelled car park. I presume the left is to the house, though I can't see a thing through the mass of mature trees through which the left-hand road disappears.

We park alongside a solitary silver Audi: Joel's.

Across a stretch of grassland, a bank of emerald hedging rises skywards.

'Ha-ha, I'm not as daft as I make out,' laughs Mick.

'Thank you, I would never have guessed,' I unbuckle my seatbelt. 'Aren't you getting out?'

'No, here's where I'll leave you. I don't remember a "plus-one" being attached to your invite. No doubt he'll drop you back to the pub later. Enjoy.'

'Thanks, Mick, bye.'

I climb from the minivan, wave as Mick reverses and is gone within seconds.

'To the maze.'

I pull my jacket on and head towards the tall hedging.

As I get nearer, a tiny wooden arrow nailed to a stake kindly points me round the corner to the 'entrance'. From here the sheer size of the maze can be seen as the hedging stretches forever across the manicured grass.

'Here goes,' I say, stepping inside.

The sunlight is instantly muted but it's not as dark and drab as I had feared. I expected the hedging to be overgrown and hanging like forgotten ruins, but like the outside every hedge wall is straight and pristine, a red gravel pathway crunches beneath my pumps.

I plod along the pathways, deciding left or right as I meander through the corridors.

The coolness prickles at my skin but it's not unpleasant. Being surrounded by vibrant green is quite soothing, a definite improvement on the recent snowdrifts. It's refreshing to have nothing to think about except left or right? Gone is the search for my birth mother, gone is my decreasing bank balance, the nagging regret about Julian's cheating, Annie's suggestions regarding Joel… everything is focused on left or right?

I have all the time in the world. Is this what's meant by living in the moment?

I imagine that Joel is seated at the centre with a cheesy grin of self-assurance that I would find him, and then what? A drink? A quick drive to have lunch? A relationship?

I stop dead.

'Get a grip, Flora, keep it simple – left or right?'

A dark cloud moves overhead, casting a lingering shadow on the gravel pathway.

'Left,' I murmur, vocalising my decisions. 'Right.'

I could do this all day.

I might have to if I don't find the centre by nightfall.

I stop and listen. Nothing. No music, no drunken conversations, no glasses clinking. Nothing.

I listen harder. Birdsong, the movement of tree branches, a distant hum of faraway traffic, but nothing unpleasant. Even the constant nagging voice in my head which spends half its time correcting me and the rest of the time trampling on my positive nature has gone.

Just… silence.

I arrive at a hedging T-junction.

'Bloody hell,' I say aloud, as a giggle escapes from my chest.

Left or right? I survey each and decide to do alternate sides: right, then left, then right. Would that work?

Five minutes later, I'm recognising corners or, to be precise, specific twigs jutting from the hedging or random stones on the gravel pathway.

Didn't I pass this way earlier? Is this section new or revisited?

I have the worst sense of direction in the world, confirmed as I go back and forth along the pathways, a sense of déjà vu greets me at each turning.

My mouth becomes dry. My palms begin to sweat. My heart rate increases.

I jog towards the end of the hedging corridor. I turn round and run back.

I have no idea what I'm doing or where I am heading.

What had seemed like a sense of adventure and delight suddenly turns to panic.

I'm lost.

Joel

'Joel! Joel!'

I hear her shouting my name across the hedging. Her cries sound childlike with panic.

I put down my book, which I'd been absorbed in for near on an hour, and stand up from the tartan picnic blanket.

'Flora, I can hear you,' I call, in reply.

'This isn't funny, I'm stuck. I've no sense of direction and I feel ill.'

Which direction is her voice coming from? I turn around to try to locate a sense of her whereabouts.

'Keep going... you'll find a way through to the centre... I've got a whole load of goodies laid out for a picnic.'

Silence.

I move around the centre space, decorated with delicate wrought-iron benches and a stone birdbath mottled with lichen.

I pace back and forth listening for her cries – an age drifts by but nothing.

Has she given up and gone home? Sat down along the pathway to sulk?

'Flora?'

'Joel?'

Her voice is nearer, yet on the far side, which is the correct pathway given the numerous twists and turns.

'Keep going you're nearly here.'

'I hate you, I hate this and there had better be a reason

why I've been dragged out on a chilly day to play such childish games and oh... there you are!'

I whip round to see her standing in the gap that signifies the exit. She's breathless and grouchy.

'Hi,' I whisper, striding across the centre to greet her and then dragging her, two-handed, towards the picnic spread. 'Surprise!'

She pouts.

'Oh dear, not impressed?'

'I don't get it.'

'What's there to get? I wanted to surprise you with a picnic brunch in the sunshine.'

'Inside a maze?'

'Why not? It's quiet, it's secluded and never busy.'

'It's February!'

'Rubbish – a picnic's what you make it.'

'Well, it's a hell of a traipse for a glass of orange juice and some croissants,' she moans, striding across to the picnic blanket. 'Next time make it a fairy-tale picnic if you're lost for a theme.'

'Ah, you must have taken the scenic route...' I stop, her face flashes its annoyance, a sure signal for me to give up with the polite chatter.

'And this...' she spreads her hands at the spread before her '...is it?'

'Yep, I thought you'd be pleased, obviously... I was wrong.'

She shrugs.

'What's wrong?'

'I love picnics but...' she mutters. 'I like posh boozy picnics with bubbles and...' her disappointment trails to silence. 'Nothing is going right, is it? I've been here for weeks and yet...'

This wasn't part of my plans. I'd expected smiles, laughter and a decent off-duty day. Her scowling face tells me I have much to learn about Flora Phillips.

'Ever been in a maze before?'

She shakes her head, staring at the blanket.

'Ah, the silent treatment... such fun,' I joke, reaching for a plate.

Her gaze follows my hand, dipping and diving from plate to plate: bagels, muffins, pain au chocolat.

'Are you joining me or sulking?'

She snatches at the other plate and begins to select from the picnic.

'Next time place your hand on either wall and walk where it leads you – it takes longer but you'll probably arrive sooner than you did.'

'There won't be a next time. I've walked about three miles.'

'Three miles! Half of one, more like.'

'You might have walked less... I've walked three!' she snaps, tucking into a cream cheese bagel.

All I wanted was some chill-out time, a nice picnic and some chat to get to know her. Instead I get frowning, huffing and the silent treatment – what's a guy got to do?

I sit back and eat, ignoring her current mood: crumpled brow, pursed lips, snatching and swiping at her food.

Who does she remind me of? Helen, my first girlfriend. What a nightmare she turned out to be, though woe betide the times I tried to ignore her bad moods. Just sixteen years of age and I'd be sentenced to the silent treatment for days on end. That relationship didn't last long...

Please tell me this isn't Flora's usual style. I'd planned for the smiling, happy and jolly woman, not the feisty bugger I'd first met on Christmas Eve.

When she finally sits down, Flora curls her legs beneath her body, chomps the bagel and gingerly lifts the lid on the nearest container.

'Smoked salmon, nice,' she splutters, looking pleased with herself.

'Wow, that was nearly a smile – excellent.'

I kneel alongside and begin conjuring drinks from the wicker basket.

'Grape or pineapple juice?' I ask, offering both bottles like a wine waiter.

'Grape please,' she mutters, picking up my upturned book and reading the back blurb. 'I didn't have you down as a reader.'

'Why not?'

She shakes her head, and flips to page one.

'Don't know, I suppose I thought you'd be too busy, all action with crime-fighting, to sit still and read... just not my image of you.'

'And this?'

'Nope, nor the poetry,' she says, attempting to hide the surprised tone.

'This is me... I love nothing better on a decent day than to come out here with a book and lounge.'

'You know this is Veronica's fella's maze, don't you?'

'I do... *thanks* for reminding me,' I add, offering Flora a glass of juice.

Flora takes the glass, flips the book over and down onto the blanket.

'Cheers,' I say, raising my glass towards hers.

'Cheers.' I watch as her pale throat rhythmically moves as she drinks. 'Thanks.'

'And you, on typical days off what do you do?'

She bursts out laughing and blushes.

Her mood has instantly changed.

'Come on, I've been honest. I love this place, a good book and hours to chill out – and you?'

Flora lengthens her legs from beneath and rests back on one elbow.

'Nothing... how embarrassing is that?'

I sip my drink and frown.

'Seriously, I do... did bugger all outside of work... yeah, I shopped, saw the girls, did housework in the flat, but that's it. I don't do fitness classes, I don't study or improve myself, I don't have a hobby,' she nudges the book as she speaks. 'I don't read. I literally do nothing... just breathe in and out.'

Not what I'd expected to hear. I'd been captivated by her humour, her wit, her energy, and yet, she does nothing.

'Are you happy with that?'

'With breathing in and out? Yeah, pretty much.'

I raise an eyebrow as I select another bite from the picnic.

'I suppose I was... but the last few weeks it's dawned on me... what have I got to show for my life?'

'That's a bit harsh.'

'Not really,' she says, tucking into a pain au chocolat. 'You have a flat, a career – before coming here I was living at my parents'. The reception work wasn't a career choice – I fell into that role by dating Julian.'

'And before Julian?'

'There *wasn't* anything before Julian... that's how I ended up being a receptionist for his parents.'

'So, do something about it.'

'That's easier said than done!'

Was I being too hard on her? If she discovered her biological mother would the rest of her world miraculously fall into place?

She continues.

'I'm in limbo, aren't I?' she says, adding, 'And it's not a nice feeling, every aspect of my life is temporary.'

I reach for my flat keys and begin removing the spare one.

'Here... this might alleviate the limbo feeling – if you need some alone time away from The Peacock you can use the flat – you know my shift pattern, make the most of an empty space and chill.'

'I can't,' she says, reaching out her fingers then snatching them back empty.

'Take it, I'm trying to be kind and assist the new you.'

'I fear it may take more than a spare door key,' she blushes deeply, removing the key from my fingers. Her chin drops, a coy smile dresses her lips. 'That means a lot to me though, thanks.'

Flora pushes the key into her purse, while I peel lids off containers and dish up slices of smoked salmon, cured ham and cheese.

'What hobbies did you do when you were young?'

'Plasticine, play dough and skipping.'

'Excellent choices for a woman of thirty years,' I laugh, offering her the plate. 'Maybe you could take those up again.'

Flora rolls onto her back, straightens her neckline to protect her modesty and continues to chomp on the pain au chocolat.

'I enjoy the floristry at The Posy Pot – Kathy's been so generous with her time.'

'There you go – something to pursue.'

'I've never wanted to do anything, if you get me,' she continues, adding, 'Lisa was always dance crazy – tap, ballet and modern stuff. Every weekend she did classes and travelled to competitions wearing sparkly outfits covered in sequins which took hours to sew on and she'd come home having won trophies and awards. Steph was into horses until her parents split, after which they couldn't afford the stable so her horse was sold, but still she rode at weekends with friends, but me... I was hanging around the house, waiting.'

'Waiting for what?' I say, tucking into my plate of food.

Flora stops chewing, looks straight at me and pauses.

'*This*.'

'This?' I hold up my plastic plate. 'My food is pretty decent but it's not worth waiting years for.'

'No, *this*. This section of my life, looking for my birth mother and finding the answers to my questions.'

I nod.

I get it.

She suddenly breaks from her trance, smiles and blushes deeply.

'How sad is that? Wasting a lifetime searching for someone who abandoned you.'

'I don't think you're sad at all, I think you're courageous and brave doing what you're doing… plenty of folks would have run away after Christmas Eve but you've stayed to face the music. And who knows, this might be your time to find the answers you've been searching for.'

She continues to stare; I continue to eat.

'And if I don't?'

I stop chewing and lick my fingers.

'If you don't, you'll find a way to something new.'

'Where? What? How?'

I shrug.

'Who knows what any of us will find in our future, look at me… who'd have thought I'd still be wrangling with an ex-partner to sign over the flat, but I am. I've no idea how and when that will be resolved.'

'Won't she buy it from you?'

'Nah, she doesn't truly want it, never did. She jumped at the chance for me to buy her out… but now she's dragging her feet.'

'Does that mean she has to wait for her money?'

'Of course, she's not getting a penny until the flat is in my name.' I take a bite of a bagel.

'Maybe it's not the flat she wants.'

I nearly choke on my mouthful of food.

'*Seriously*, it's not me… she made that quite clear when we broke up – her cougar days were behind her, she'd switched her interests and got herself a proper sugar daddy. She's hinted we could try again, but I'm not interested. Honestly, I think there's more to it… she seems unsettled.'

'Would you want it to be about you?'

I shake my head.

'Not now.'

She nods, and stares up at the blue sky.

'This isn't a date, right?' she asks, her hand blindly reaching for more smoked salmon.

'Nope... just two friends,' I pause, watching her reaction, '... having an enjoyable brunch.'

'Cool.' She giggles, folding the slithers of salmon onto her tongue. 'If this *was* a date I'd have preferred to be asked before attending, that's all.'

I like her honesty. She's spunky, alive and very honest, unlike Veronica. *This* is refreshing.

'You've heard the term trophy wife?' I ask, following suit and selecting a forkful of smoked salmon.

Flora nods, as she chews.

'Veronica made that claim once... "I am a trophy wife", she actually said those words – do you know how clichéd that sounds?'

'Arrogant to say the least, I'd use that term in relation to the elite,' she adds.

'Exactly. Nah, Veronica used it to describe herself,' I say, adding, 'You know it's over when comments like that make you cringe inside.'

'I had the same with Julian. He was such a lazy arse, working for his parents. He took liberties where the other guys wouldn't and couldn't, just because he was the boss's only son; I used to feel sorry for his parents.'

'Something inside slowly dies, doesn't it?'

Flora nods.

'It sure does. Then one day, out of the blue, they pull the rug from under your feet.'

'I always knew she would.' A tiny voice lingers in my head daring me to ask if she would ever pull the rug from beneath anyone's feet? Maybe, I'll ask her another day.

40

Veronica

I withdraw my sleek fountain pen from my handbag, flick open the comments book to reveal a clean page. I adore my refined script that follows in purple ink.

Memories of 1986. I was chosen as carnival queen. The parade of decorated floats around the village was postponed due to poor weather. I was awarded straight 'A' grades in my school exams. I won a scholarship so left the village in the September to live in Cheltenham. I returned having gained my degree at university and started work at the local estate agency, before starting my own agency, Sable's.

I sign with a flourishing signature, known and recognised by every home-owning resident in the village.

I glance towards the bar; Gene is lounging against it, talking to his brother Mick. If I hadn't left this village when I did I wonder if I'd have been married to the likes of that? My potential lost due to poor choices and a beer-swilling husband. I'd be another Annie or Melanie, slumming each day with little joy or pleasure – how's that a life?

I inspect my long red nails. I bet Annie O'Neill's never had a manicure in her life. With all the scrubbing she does behind that bar, I bet she's never had a decent set of nails either.

I nudge my empty gin and tonic glass away; the used ice lingers alone at the bottom.

41

Flora

The smell of fresh flowers hangs in the air, as I help Kathy strip the thorns from eight hundred long-stemmed roses.

'Ouch!' I cry, for the umpteenth time.

'Be careful, you don't need to rush we're ahead of time,' she says, peering from beneath her dark yet greying fringe.

'I know, I want to do it right for you and your customers.'

'Bless you, you're doing fine.'

Since our visit to the maze, I'd volunteered every morning at The Posy Pot – I wanted to be helpful, was striving to master the skills I saw Kathy perform with such ease and finesse. I knew that if I could apply myself to one thing and it be a success, I'd be building a future.

'I'm not doing fine, believe me.'

Kathy stops and watches me. I continue to work.

'Last weekend, my friends delivered a bundle of post, which has sat staring at me from the dressing table every day since.'

From the corner of my downcast eyes I can see she's still watching me.

'You can guess the contents of each envelope – overdraft demands and notifications of missed credit card payments. Each envelope will just depress me.'

'Did you open them?' Her voice has acquired a mellow and motherly tone.

I shake my head, without looking up.

'This is a one-off chance to find my birth mother – yet, they want to focus on my cash flow crisis by giving me penalty charges I can't pay.'

'Flora…'

'If I can survive a few more weeks until the DNA results are back, then who knows, I could happily move back to Bushey, find a decent job and start to deal with my overdraft.'

Kathy steps around her workbench and gently takes the flower stems from my hands. I freeze, fighting back the tears clogging my throat.

'Look, it will all work out in the end – it always does. But you can't afford to ignore the basics in life and we all have to deal with money matters. How about later this afternoon, you fetch the envelopes and then we'll sit and go through them together and get you organised?' Her warmth flows round my shoulders like a blanket of kindness.

'Nah. I can't.'

'You can, we can… we'll divide the statements into piles and organise the payments.'

I raise my chin to thank her, just as tears spill over my lashes.

'Hey, don't get upset… we'll sort it.'

'Thank you, you're so lovely, but seriously, I can't… I threw the bundle of envelopes onto the fire first thing this morning.'

Kathy tuts and shakes her head, bouncing her messy bun, left then right.

'That was silly, you can't run away from certain things.'

'You. Want. A. Bet…' I sniff, wiping my eyes. 'I've run away from most things in this world.'

Kathy waves a stray hair away from my tear-stained face.

'Maybe now's the time to stop running and start facing reality?'

'When I've got proper answers, I promise to sort it out, until then I'll focus on my mission here and if the worst comes to the worst, I'll sell my Mini to pay for my stay.'

The shop door swings wide and Joel strides in dressed in his uniform. The police car fills our view of the street through the window, Scott's silhouette is visible in the driving seat. Kathy raises a hand to wave to her nephew, and he eagerly waves back.

'Morning, ladies,' calls Joel, casually flipping through his notebook.

'Morning,' we chorus, as he joins us at the workbench, I frantically wipe away my tears.

'Valentine's Day by any chance?' he scans the bundles of red roses.

'In three days... so remind the station guys I'm doing a bargain delivery price for a dozen long-stemmed, will you?' says Kathy. 'They are charging twice that price in town.'

'Decent offer,' laughs Joel, before nodding at me. 'Could I have a word?'

'Sure, be my guest.'

I step aside from the workbench; Joel checks his notebook before speaking.

'An update to keep you in the loop – we've arranged a home visit to speak to Melanie O'Neill later this morning and a possibly a second chat with Duggan about his sight- ing... is there anything else that's come to light from the comments book?'

I shake my head. I dearly wished there was.

'You already know the comment about Dr Fowler and the accusation about Annie,' I remind him.

'Those are sorted, nothing more than malicious gossip that pushes us off track, but still, we need to know who wrote them – it's hardly a laughing matter, the world and his wife have read the comments book so have seen the accusations.'

'Dirt sticks.'

'It certainly does. So, nothing else?'

I shake my head.

Joel looks so tall in his uniform. How did we clash heads all those weeks ago?

'The last time you spoke to me dressed in your uniform was...'

'Yep, I know. Believe me, Scotty's on full alert in case you pounce for a second time.'

I turn to view Scotty seated in the police car. I give a small wave, he stares and gives nothing in return. *Great*, his buddy still dislikes me.

'OK, I'll leave you good ladies to your roses, catch you later.'

Within seconds Joel has gone.

'How's it going with him?' Kathy nods towards the shop door.

Her question snaps me from my thoughts. My mouth is agape.

'Oh, don't come that with me. I see how you two are with each other.'

'There's nothing going on between us, if that's what you're implying.'

'*Really?*'

'Yes, really.'

'Was your picnic in the maze nice?' she laughs.

I slowly shake my head.

'Is nothing private in this village?'

'Nope, folks around here know everything.'

Silence lingers, giving me chance to replay the maze picnic in my mind. He was lovely, he was kind, he was perfect but...

'Would you like there to be?' Kathy interrupts my thoughts.

'Kathy... I broke his nose.'

'*So*, I smashed my car into my husband's on our first date... we've now been married for twenty-five years.'

I didn't say anything, but watched my hands strip at the thorns.

'Am I barking up the wrong tree?'

'Kathy!'

'Am I?'

I blush.

'Like that, is it?' she says. 'Veronica's off the scene, you know – he won't go back to her, if that's what you're thinking.'

'Phew! *Veronica.*'

'She's not that bad actually.'

I roll my eyes dramatically.

'Seriously, she's not all bad… if anything, learn from her mistake – she's regretted her decision, hasn't she?'

I look up and outstare my friend.

'I can't imagine Major Matthews being as agile in the bedroom as a toy boy,' she says, blushing to her roots.

'She's just *so*… annoying.'

'She's got a good heart really, she *means* well.'

Silence lingers, as I replay this conversation in my head before continuing.

'If I were here under different circumstances, then yeah, maybe… but I came here to find my birth mum and…'

'How could he not fall for you?'

I lift my head and see her wry smile.

'Oh, stop it! You're playing with me.'

Kathy shrugs.

'What's the harm in a little additional project while you're here? Think of it as a distraction, some downtime from your main focus.'

'Kathy!'

'I'm being honest. There's something there… and you *know* it!'

She jumps down from her work seat and heads to the flower displays, plunging the trimmed rose stems into water buckets.

269

Can't a girl have any secrets around here?

*

'Hello!' I call, dashing into the pub during a busy lunchtime session, rubbing my hands together for warmth. 'It's turned chilly out there.'

'It sure is, the forecast says we might have snow, and yet, you are in such a good mood,' chuckles Annie. 'Who or what's put the spring back into your step – another picnic with Joel?'

I pull a childish face.

'Flowers.' I make my way to the bar, peel off my borrowed coat and join Annie. 'Need a hand?'

'I never say no,' she answers, pointing to an empty glass collection cage. 'A glass collection and a load in the washer would be good.'

'OK.'

'*Flowers?*'

'I've spent the morning with Kathy at The Posy Pot – she's being talking me through her morning's orders.'

I make my way around the pub floor, collecting from each table and bringing the dirties back to the bar edge to place in the wire cage.

'*And?*'

'And I've enjoyed myself... it felt good to be doing something productive rather than waiting for something to happen... which is why I thought I'd start helping out more behind the bar, if you don't mind?'

'Phah! Do I look as if I'd complain about an extra pair of hands?' says Annie, waving at the customers stood along the bar. 'Fill your boots, girl!'

I will. I was being honest. It may be hours of listening and watching with Kathy, it may be emptying lager slops here in the bar, but the feeling of being useful rather than standing around

270

waiting for something to happen feels good. I'd had weeks of sitting about, virtually years of waiting, and yet what I needed was to be busy. Maybe that's why reception work hadn't truly suited me; waiting for the next phone call, the next delivery guy, the next instruction – simply wasn't me. I am a doer.

Why had I never realised that before? Thirty years of age and finally, I recognise a trait in myself.

'Annie – did you always want to run a pub?' I say, heaving the filled glass cage from the bar top towards the back room.

She shakes her head.

'I fell into the job because my father had been the landlord when I was growing up. Why?'

'Nothing, I wondered if you were happy doing it when you could be doing other things.'

'Not at my time of life I couldn't, but there's no stopping you – you're in your prime.'

That's what I wanted her to say.

'How would I get a job in something I have no qualifications for?' I call from the back room while loading the dirty glasses into the dishwasher and pressing the operation buttons.

'Depends what you're thinking of...'

'That's it... I'm not certain.'

Annie stops pulling the pint she's halfway through.

'Flora, that's a biggie if you're changing direction.'

I blush as her male customer raises his eyebrows at my stupid conversation. Annie continues with his pint, her head shaking at my ideas.

I join her at the bar.

'Seriously though, if I could do something I loved as a job – I know there would be happiness attached to it. I could be proud of working each day rather than going home and complaining about some lousy paperwork or grumpy colleagues.'

'You could, but there's always a pain-in-the-arse task with every job and that's what we all moan about, Flora.'

'True. If you weren't here what would you be doing?'

Having served all the waiting customers, Annie begins wiping the bar down.

'I dreamt of being a nursery nurse at one time.'

'I can see you doing that... would your father not let you?'

'No, I went to college and passed my certificates by which time me and Mick were thinking of getting married and...' her voice falters before she continues. 'I didn't think I'd be cut out for it after that.'

That didn't make sense. Why would getting married make any difference to her being a nursery nurse?

'Why?'

'What?'

'I said why? I think you'd be ideal... you're the mothering type, a practical person, good with the old advice...' I stop talking as I see her eyes glisten. 'Annie, have I said something wrong?'

'You couldn't if you tried.'

A weak smile crosses her face and her hand reaches for my forearm, giving it a reassuring pat.

42

Voluntary Interview Statement: Mrs Melanie O'Neil

I, Melanie O'Neill, of No. 19, Windmill Road, Pooley, Warwickshire, for claim number: PB101084B. The facts in this statement come from my personal knowledge.

People are accusing me of being the mother of the baby dumped back in October 1986 – I have volunteered to attend the police station to discuss the claims. I know nothing regarding that baby. I am not her mother and to the best of my knowledge neither is any of my four sisters. At the time, I lived on the estate with my parents, but so did lots of teenage girls. That day was like any other school day. Mum woke us at seven o'clock. We had breakfast around the kitchen table, probably Ready-Brek given the time of year. We walked to school at quarter past eight and I knew nothing about the baby incident in The Square till I arrived home at three thirty when mum explained. Darren Taylor, he was the newspaper boy, had been absent from lessons, but no one mentioned it at school. Afterwards, while Mum was cooking tea, me and my sisters went to The Square to see what was happening. We stood with a small crowd watching the row of houses – there was nothing going on or to be seen, just one uniformed policeman stood by the gate. The next day at school Darren was the centre of attention on the playground, he kept repeating how he'd found her on the doorstep. I didn't see any of the girl pupils get upset and no one was absent from school that day. In morning assembly, the headmistress, Mrs Huggins, said a prayer for the new baby and the safe return of her mum, but nothing else was said. I didn't have a baby at fifteen. I don't know anyone that did. I don't know any other details apart from those learnt from newspaper articles or discussions that others have had. The comments book in The Peacock points at me because my family were different – our house was loud in a quiet street on the estate, lots of kids, fallings-out and arguments. People say my parents didn't take great care of us. Our family may not have had much money, but as a family we were tight. Us Delaneys look after our own. That baby would have stayed in our family if she'd belonged to us – my mum, Sylvia Delaney, would have found a way to keep her.

I believe the details in this statement are true.

Signed: Melanie O'Neill
Date: 11/02/2017

43

Joel

I hadn't entered Sable's estate agents for a while, but nothing had changed – Donnie was busy securing property photographs to the board and Veronica was on the phone.

'She's...' he pointed at Veronica, 'busy.'

'Thanks, I'll wait.'

Veronica eyed me as I stood a short distance from her desk, her conversation about the dimensions of a conservatory took ages.

'That's fine, absolutely fine... call me back should you wish to place an offer, Mr Jones.'

Finally.

'Well, well this *is* a surprise,' she beams, returning the handset to its cradle. 'An off-duty day, I presume.'

I look down at my casual attire and nod.

'Can I have a word?'

The room temperature drops a degree or so, much like the big freeze predicted for the coming days.

Veronica stares at me, as though she can read the unexpected event of today on my forehead.

'Of course, how can I help?'

I smile.

'Shall we?' She indicates to the rear of the shop.

'Not really, I'm not staying and...'

'Don't be smart, Joel... it never suited you,' she snipes. 'Isn't this about our apartment?'

'No. This is about you writing additional comments in Flora's book.'

The hesitation before she speaks says everything I needed to know.

'*What*?' her brow creases as she feigns bewilderment.

'I recognise your handwriting in the comments book... despite you trying to change it – I suggest you stop playing games with other people's lives.'

It had been a chance find discovered just ten minutes ago. I'd dropped by The Peacock to invite Flora out for a bite to eat at lunchtime only to find she was still working at The Posy Pot. I'd settled in the alcove with a quick half-pint and flipped open the comments book to view for myself the malicious remarks. Veronica's handwriting greeted me. Yes, she'd tried to disguise her natural handwriting, larger loops, longer tails, a diagonal slant, but it didn't fool me.

'I would never do such a thing.'

'You would. You forget that I know you ... I mean it, stop adding remarks and red herrings otherwise I shall be reporting you.'

'Joel?'

'Don't try to squirm out of it – you changed pen numerous times and even tried to change your handwriting, but I can still see that certain letters match yours exactly.'

'You're not on duty, you can't come in here throwing your weight about,' she snaps.

'I'm not throwing my weight about. I'm letting you know that I know. And in about five minutes time Flora will also know.'

'Just listen for once in your damned life,' she screams. 'Why do you have to be such an arse? I once thought you were a great guy, a guy I could love and live with, but now, phhh... you've turned into an obnoxious, arrogant, immature boy that makes me feel like his friggin' mother. I can't stand needy schoolboys who should grow a backbone!'

I furrow my brow, turn around and walk.

Donnie jumps, pretending he wasn't earwigging.

'I'm definitely not signing now,' she shouts, as I near the door.

I turn to see her flushed features.

'Fine, you can buy me out instead if the place means *that* much to you.'

'Joel! How dare you walk away when I'm talking to you!'

How the hell did I date and live with that woman?

'Are you listening to me?'

As I reach the door, I stop and turn.

'Veronica... I'll remind you again not to speak to me like that. We aren't in a relationship, so I expect some respect and civility when we communicate... is that too much to ask?'

'I wanted to...'

'Veronica...'

'I just wanted...'

'Veronica... stop! How I ever thought that you and I had a future together – I must have been delusional!' I turn on my heels and walk from the estate agents, heading for The Peacock.

'Joel! Come back!' she screams, as the door closes slowly. 'How dare you ignore me... how dare you!'

I dare.

44

Flora

I glance at his profile as we drive through the dark evening: fine features, clear skin, a shadow lingers on his jawline... doesn't he shave on off-duty days?

'What?' he says, without turning his head.

'Nothing.'

'Seriously, *what*?'

I shrug. Should I ask if this is a Valentine's date given that it's one night early or just presume that if tonight goes well he might surprise me again tomorrow? Though isn't he on a night shift tomorrow?

'So, you're staring for no reason?'

'Shut up,' I joke, feeling my face flush.

I need to change the conversation. I can't admit to watching him, taking note of every little detail, so I stare out of the window at the passing hedgerow and the countryside covered in a thick blanket of fresh snow. Snow has fallen for most of the day.

He smiles. He knows.

The silence continues for a few minutes.

We'd had to drop by his flat once he'd collected me from The Peacock, a slight diversion as he'd forgotten something in his hurry to be on time. I'd happily sat in the car park as he ran inside to collect a box of matches.

'You look beautiful in that dress,' he says, staring ahead.

'Thank you. I scrub up all right, don't I?' I tease, hiding my sudden embarrassment.

'Seriously, the colour red suits you.'

'You've seen it before.'

'I know, the night you rearranged my nose.'

'And at New Year,' I giggle.

That night seemed so long ago and still I haven't cleared the dress from my credit card bill. I don't want to think about the mountain of unopened post and bills waiting back in Bushey – I'd already disposed of one pile of mail.

'Isn't this the way to the maze?' I ask, quickly changing topic. 'Are we going back?'

'Not quite and nope, I turned off that road a little while back.'

'So where are we going?' I murmur, like an impatient child to a parent.

'You'll see...'

'I don't like surprises... you should know that about me.'

'Nor me.' He glances sideways and winks.

What's *that* supposed to mean? Is he suggesting something? *Or* am I reading too much into a weird wink?

I focus on the passing scenery and dwell on the previous surprises I have encountered, the ones that taught me surprises usually equal disappointment on a grand scale. The surprise of finding Julian butt naked with another woman. My surprise in the schoolyard when I learnt that the latest whisper and unkind skipping songs were about my adoption. The surprise of hearing my adoptive parents describing a pink bundle collected from a foster carer's home and not from a maternity ward, and the ugliest surprise of all, seeing a bare doorstep guarded by stone lions.

My mood is faltering.

'Whisking a girl off into the countryside at night, without a hint of the destination – is this your normal behaviour whilst off duty?'

'Sometimes... only recently have I returned to doing things like this, but I rarely take young ladies with me, I tend to go alone.'

My bare shoulders are covered in goosebumps. Why hadn't I brought a coat?

'Don't worry, you're quite safe,' he adds quickly, as if sensing my response.

I shrug, pretending I wasn't intrigued.

'You seem to do everything on your own.'

'Is there something wrong with that?'

'No, but others might think it strange.'

'Let them think what they want... not everyone needs others to rely upon, some of us can manage without the constant crowd.'

'A loner?'

'*Independent.*'

'A loner then... people only say independent to make it sound positive, but what's so positive about being a solo act?'

'What's so great about needing to be surrounded by others every hour of every day? I don't get that, so who's right and who's wrong?'

'I'm a people person. I love having people around me... love sharing and telling... that's not wrong, surely?'

'No, but what about the moments for yourself... the thoughts, feelings, the self-satisfaction of knowing that you have your own mind, can make your own choices and rely upon yourself when others let you down?'

I shrug, his voice sounds serious.

'*If.*'

'If what?'

'*If* others let you down… you said *when* others let you down,' I say, correcting him.

'Everyone lets you down at some point,' says Joel.

I shake my head.

'Not everyone…' I mutter, listing in my head those who'd never failed me.

'You're lucky then.'

'You've been a cop for too long, you've seen too much.'

'Maybe… so have you ever been completely alone?' he asks.

I tut and roll my eyes, as if that were a suitable answer.

'Spent a weekend by yourself enjoying the solitude of nature, time without anyone interrupting. Have you?'

'No, should I?' a lump has formed in my throats as the car pulls from the secluded country lane onto a large spacious area surrounded by woodland and snowy fields.

He kills the engine.

'You should try it – it'll do you the world of good!'

So, being alone for six weeks away from my family, surrounded by a whole host of strangers, wasn't enough? I need more solitude, *great*.

I watch as he opens the car door wide, takes the tartan blanket from the rear seat. 'Now, out you hop… I want to show you something beautiful.'

I hear what he's saying. Maybe some alone time could benefit my soul, but surely as an abandoned baby I need all the social interaction I can get? Wouldn't the psychologists say that 'if your own mother doesn't want you, surely the temptation is to shy away from others'? In which case, I've done well to be as social as I am, haven't I?

Through the windscreen, I watch as he places the tartan blanket on the car bonnet, before coming to open my passenger door like the perfect gent.

'Madame…' His right hand waves an arc, indicating my path, like a bowing royal courtier.

I undo the seatbelt.

There's a chill in the evening air as I step from his car into a remote landscape covered in crisp, glistening snow overlooking the village. It looks like a picture postcard.

'It's beautiful,' I whisper, scared of breaking the magical hush.

Joel smiles, his eyes crinkle deeply at the sides as he views the distant twinkle of village lights.

What is this all about? I can't be in danger, not with Joel about, but he's driven me to a lonely spot, a mile or so outside the busy village.

'Flora... you're quite safe,' he whispers, as his hand touches mine. 'I promise.'

I laugh, unsure of what I'm actually laughing at.

'Young women are warned about dates like this.'

'Is this a date?' he laughs, his mouth opening wide to show his rear fillings. 'Are we calling it a date?'

Shit, I didn't mean to say that. He'd invited me, he'd suggested the evening, he'd collected me from the pub and I'd spent an age getting ready and curling my hair – so yeah, in my mind it was.

'No, I... just... thought... oh sod off, Joel – you know what I mean.'

'I know exactly what you mean and if it were any other guy bringing you up here for any other reason than to share a winter picnic with you... I, too, would warn any young lady against attending, but it is me. I promise, you're quite safe.'

'A winter picnic! A posh picnic,' I scream excitedly, before adding, 'You promise a lot, don't you?'

'Sadly, I do. And yes, it might even have bubbles. Now please, can you hurry up?'

My feet slip and slide on the fresh snowfall. I wish I hadn't worn going-out shoes, wellies would have been preferable.

'Can I ask where we are?'

'Pooley Point... the local beauty spot, happy now? Convinced that I'm not some savage beast?'

'I was only joking.'

'You've already proven that you can look after yourself where blokes are concerned.'

Within seconds, Joel has emptied the car boot and is lugging a large wicker picnic basket with giant buckles. I totter behind, the picnic blanket in hand, as snow forces me to walk in a fairy-step style like the page of St Stephen.

*

In no time Joel has selected the spot where he lays a sheet of thick plastic on the ground and the blanket on top, making a cushion of snow, and unpacks the wicker basket.

'Please sit down,' he says, reaching for food boxes and glasses.

I gingerly take my place on the corner of the woollen tartan, the surrounding snow twinkles as if I am sitting amongst diamonds.

'So, do you picnic in the snow often?'

'Fairly often... I like this spot.'

'Why?'

His brow crinkles at the question. I gaze at the expanse of open countryside for miles around, every field, tree and hedgerow frosted like a chocolate box Christmas scene.

'You can see for miles and miles,' his hands swing wide, showing the obvious. 'I like the serenity of the place... it gives me a feeling of renewed energy and...' He stops and shakes his head.

'Please, tell me,' I urge, seeing a softer expression veil his features.

His face changes; a seriousness creeps along with the slight blush to the cheeks.

'...Being here makes me grateful. You're a wealthy man when you can enjoy the simple things in life.'

'*Oh.*' Not what I was expecting.

How deep is he? I'll run if he expects me to follow suit with my inner thoughts. Or he'll run if he forces me to expose my deepest delights or, worse still, fears.

Joel laughs, unpacking jars of candles which he pushes deep into the snow around the blanket edge and lights, creating a flickering mellow arc.

'Unexpected?'

'Perhaps,' I chuckle, removing the cling film from a plate of smoked salmon.

He gives a nonchalant shrug.

'Oh well, that's me... take it or leave it.'

I focus on my busy hand, while my mind whirls at the thrill of being spoilt by a rather handsome, single and deep-thinking man.

'Are you blushing?' he asks, dropping to his knees beside me upon the blanket.

'No.'

He gives a cheeky smile.

'Seriously, I'm not,' I lie.

I shiver.

'Are you cold?' he asks, reaching inside the basket. 'I've brought another blanket if you are.'

I nod eagerly. What was it with this dress? Despite the boutique mannequin having displayed it attractively, I seemed destined to always accessorise it with a blanket.

He opens the blanket, thankfully not a standard police-issue one, and swings it around my shoulders, holding the corners beneath my chin. He offers me the grasped ends and our fingers touch during the handover. A sudden spark nips at my skin and tingles along my spine.

I watch as his brown eyes bore into mine, the twinkle is back and it's beckoning me nearer. We both freeze and stare into each other's faces, his breath touches my cheekbone. My breath must be doing likewise on his jaw.

I can feel every goosebump along my spine tingle.

OMG, he's going to kiss me. Get ready, this is it. He's going to kiss me.

Time pauses. I glance at him. He continues to stare into my eyes.

'Is this goat's cheese?' I say awkwardly, breaking eye contact and holding aloft a plate of puff-pastry tartlets and ruining the moment.

His mouth breaks into a weak smile before he looks at the offered plate.

'Yep... with caramelised red onion.'

'Great, I'm starving.' I preoccupy myself with the food. I know he's still watching me.

The silence lengthens before he interrupts it.

'*Good* because I've brought enough to feed a small army and then some.'

I break off a piece of cheese, popping it into my mouth as my mind whirls with the what-could-have-been moment that I'd just trampled on.

He was about to kiss me. Why did I speak? Why did a warm tartlet suddenly become so important in my life? Do I not want a gorgeous man to kiss me under the moonlight? Does he know I panicked?

Joel's hand returns to conjuring delights from his wicker basket like a culinary Mary Poppins. I watch as he retrieves and arranges plastic boxes, plates and glasses in a buffet style – I'm expecting a wooden hatstand and a gilt-edged mirror at any moment.

'Champagne?'

'You think of everything.'

He holds the bottle aloft as if requiring an answer.

'Isn't it always *yes* where champagne is concerned?' I say.

'It should be – could you hold these, please?' He offers me two glass flutes, then struggles to open the bottle. I look away, knowing every guy wants his champagne-opening moment to go smoothly and not be a frantic struggle between man and cork. Finally, it gives way. Pop!

I hold the glasses as he pours carefully, not spilling a drop.

'To brighter futures,' he says, holding his glass aloft, clinking on the side of mine.

I repeat his words. I'd have preferred 'To us', though that sounds very presumptuous given the moment I just ruined.

Joel sips, I sip.

The bubbles dance on my tongue.

When was the last time I savoured a glass of bubbly? Too long ago... this really should be repeated more often in my life.

'Flora?'

I'm startled back from my thoughts as Joel offers me a china plate and a serving spoon.

'Sorry, I was away with the fairies, thank you.'

'Dig in, don't stand on ceremony.'

The next twenty minutes there is silence as we sip and nibble at crayfish cocktails, Waldorf salad, stilton scones and warm medallions of beef with horseradish sauce.

'I feel like a queen,' I say, having completed my second plate and second glass. 'A snow queen dining in the prettiest, most magical landscape ever.'

'Good... that was my intention.'

He refills my champagne flute again but not his own.

'Are you not joining me?' I nod towards the bottle.

'I can't, one is more than enough when I'm driving.'

Of course, someone needs to drive back. I couldn't walk that distance in these shoes.

'I can't believe you've created this picnic and you're still single?'

'Mmmm.'

I want to kick myself as soon as the words leave my lips.

'Sorry.'

'It's OK, but yes, I cooked all this and I am *still* single, though that was Veronica's choice, not mine... though now, I am happier with her decision.'

'You weren't at the time?'

'No way – I was gutted.'

I watch as he lies back on the blanket, the base of his champagne flute resting in the middle of his chest, his eyes skywards.

'When I found out...'

'She didn't tell you?' I interrupt.

Joel looks sideways at me.

'Did what's-his-face tell *you*?'

'No,' I whisper.

Joel returns his gaze skywards.

'Anyway, she let me find out the hard way from everyone else... that's her style, or rather the only way she knows how to communicate. She's got a reputation for it. She'll always skip out, apparently with no regard or respect for the other person.'

'Did you love her?' What's with me tonight? I'm not in control of my mind or mouth.

He pauses – the silence lasts for an eternity. I'm not sure he's heard the question until he chooses to answer.

'I think I did... I honestly thought she was the one I'd stay with, but now I realise that she behaves differently to what I saw. I saw *my* version of Veronica, not the real version... does that make sense?'

I nod. I know exactly what he means. Julian was always *my* Julian when we were alone. He could be caring, generous and at times very loving, but once he was with his mates, his family, even strangers, he morphed into a different Julian who spoke and joked in a laddish way. At home, I got Julian on his best behaviour, until my back was turned.

'And you?'

I purse my lips; I try not to think back to that day.

'I knew things were rocky... they had been for a while, but I never dreamt he'd cheat on me.'

'Did he tell you?'

I snort.

'Did he heck! I walked in one Saturday afternoon, back early from a ladies' day of shopping, to find her legs wrapped round his naked rear.'

Joel sits up in surprise.

'No?'

'I thought I'd told you that. The full graphic image etched upon my mind, forever. Worse still, he didn't know whether to stop or carry on once I'd entered the room, but hey-ho – you live and learn.'

Joel lies back again, shaking his head and stifling a chuckle.

'You can laugh, I won't be offended – he was a waste of space!'

'But to walk in and find...'

'Yep, not a pretty picture.'

'So you left?'

'There and then... I landed back at my mum's and a few days later she went to the flat to pack my belongings. I took the week off work by calling in sick, but I had to consider what to do... so bang went my job too. A double whammy!'

'Sorry,' says Joel.

'At least I was the first to know – I take it you were the last to hear?'

Joel laughs.

'OK.'

'OK? Like you don't believe me.'

'I believe you, but *you* kissed me,' I say, trying to repin my hair.

'Yeah, I did, but you kissed me back and...'

'And what?'

'Forget it.'

'No.'

'Yes.'

'No! If you've got something to say, say it.'

'What's a guy to do when you do *that* to him?'

'Ah, so it's all my fault?'

'You undid *my* trousers.'

'You undid my dress first,' I shout, as if the villagers of Pooley need to hear.

'No, I didn't.'

'Yes, you did.'

'I didn't,' says Joel, tucking his shirt tails into his waistband.

'You did!'

'For the love of man, you want it all your own way!'

'Phhh!'

'Don't phhh me,' he growls.

'I'll phhh as much as I bloody well like, thank you.'

I'm confused. A minute ago we were in the throes of making love and now he's acting weird. Typical bloody men, get their own sodding way and afterwards act as if they don't understand and are from another planet. Just like Julian.

A cuddle might have been nice, another passionate kiss perhaps, but oh no, Joel offers me an apology, then mimics and repeats my words like a child when I try to cover his embarrassment. Cheers!

I collect my shoes from each side of the blanket, prising my numb feet into each. My hair has come undone from the pins and trails unattractively about my face.

I stride towards the car, sinking and stumbling on the blanket of snow.

'Where are you going?' he asks, collecting the debris from our picnic.

'*Home*!'

Joel

'Flora, wait!' I shout repeatedly at her receding image, but she's gone.

'What the hell was that?' I gasp, falling backwards onto the blanket. 'One minute you're chatting nicely, enjoying the conversation, the next I'm kissing her and it leads to *that*...'

I rake a hand through my hair as I stare at the ghost of a cloud above me.

Was that love or lust? It felt like love, we were good together, made for each other. I thought she'd slap me for taking a kiss without asking, but bloody hell, when she kissed me back – we lost it!

I hear her voice repeat, 'It was what it was'.

Was it?

Why did she ruin it with such a cheap line? Maybe that was Flora's idea of meaningless sex but not mine. I'm not like Scotty. I've never been one for the laddish behaviour of the one-night stand – I certainly didn't expect that reaction from her.

I stare up at the ceiling of stars.

What had I expected from a winter picnic? Champagne, conversation and a gentle drive home? Yes. A peck on the cheek? Maybe. A gallant gesture of a kiss on her hand? Perhaps. Actually yes, that *had* been my plan.

I scan the array of debris: boxes, plates, two flute glasses and an empty champagne bottle.

I've messed that one up – for sure!

I scramble to my feet, bundle the plastic sheeting and tartan blanket into a giant ball with dirty plates and cutlery inside and march back to the car.

I dump the tartan remains in the boot before scanning the area for any sign of Flora's outline against the blackened night. I half expect her to be leaning against the car waiting for me, having cooled down.

Nothing.

*

As I leave the car parking area I expect to see her silhouette walking along the side of the lane but, search as I might, I can't see her.

What if something has happened to her walking between the picnic blanket and my car?

What the hell have I done?

My foot presses the accelerator. I'm not certain if I should be racing like a bat out of hell towards the village to raise the alarm and gather a search party or crawling the lane's hedgerows peering into snow-covered ditches.

I opt for the former. I race along the lanes, full beam on, my heart in my mouth, praying that any minute she'll appear around the next corner. And *that's* what she eventually does. It's amazing how far a woman can walk in a short time, even in uncomfortable heels.

I pull alongside her stomping frame and automatically lower the passenger window, the car rolling at a minimum speed.

'Flora!' I call, leaning over the passenger seat as best I can whilst steering. No reply. 'Flora – get in!' I stop alongside her. She carries on walking, clutching the blanket beneath her chin. I catch up and shout again. You'd think she was deaf by the lack of response.

I swerve around her and park a short distance in front, jump out and run back to her.

'Don't be like this. I'd planned a nice treat. I wanted to spoil you, show you the sights of Pooley Point and deliver you home. I never imagined that...' my words falter as I near her and she walks past me as if I were a ghost. I turn around in the road, her wiggling hips striding towards the village.

'Flora!' I shout.

She stops.

Finally.

I begin to run after her, but all she does is bend down, remove her shoes and hook them over her fingers before continuing to walk in the snow.

'Flora, wait!'

It's no use. By this time she has reached my parked car with its hazards flashing and walks around it.

'What the hell am I supposed to do now?' I mutter, chasing after her. Is it gallant to walk with her or stupid to drive alongside calling her name and insisting that she climbs into the car? What the hell? From nowhere, Big Tony's belly laugh fills my ears, 'You've lost it, laddo, you've definitely lost it.'

45

Flora

I barge into The Peacock, sending the wooden door reeling backwards on its hinges and the door chime spinning. The row of startled customers turn and stare.

'What's up with you?' asks Annie, laughing from behind the bar. 'You've got a face like a slapped arse.'

'My hair's come undone and my feet are sodding freezing!' I lie in response, knowing the truth is harder to explain.

'I thought you went out with Joel?'

'I did, but it ended badly... so I've walked home.'

'Are you kidding me?' she laughs.

I spread my hands, indicating the state of my clothes and snow-damaged shoes.

'And he let you walk? Did you argue?'

'No and no, but I still walked back. I fancied some fresh air. He drove up to the door to make sure I arrived safely,' I add, acknowledging his gallantry.

'Like *that* is it... here, come and sit near the fire. I'll get you a brandy.'

I settle myself in the alcove as Annie pumps a double brandy and dashes over to deliver it.

'Here, can I get you anything else?'

I shake my head. What I need is a long, hot shower and a damned good think.

'I'll go up for a shower after I've drunk this.'

Annie returns to the bar. The customers return to their conversations.

I breathe a sigh of relief every time the door chime sounds. I don't want Joel coming in here causing a scene.

As the brandy warms my innards, I watch the open fire as the flames flicker and dance.

Great evening that was! Was it even a proper date? Yes, he'd asked me specifically if I'd like to go out with him, made arrangements to pick me up, and yes, he'd gone to loads of effort with the food and the champagne.

I cringe. Why did things always go wrong for me? Other women can enjoy male company and arrive home after an enjoyable night. With me, it starts off nicely, full of potential, and then rapidly descends into a soap opera. Why did I storm off? Couldn't I have listened to what he had to say? No, I have to get all defensive and stroppy then hike it home.

The questions continue to buzz around in my mind.

What the hell do I say when he walks through that door?

*

It takes fifteen minutes for the brandy to disappear, which is bad news as it settles upon the champagne; working its own magic in seconds.

Joel doesn't appear.

As I stand up, the cosy bar spins several times before I get my bearings. I concentrate on every step taken towards the staircase leading to room five.

'Shout if you need anything,' calls Annie, as I clutch the bannister rail and leave the bar behind me.

297

Once in my room, I kick off my shoes, loosen my hair and peel off my red dress.

This dress is jinxed. I wish I'd never bought it.

I traipse towards the en suite, letting the shower run while I collect my things. The steam quickly fills the small room. After collecting and depositing fresh towels on the loo seat, I free myself of underwear and step into the shower.

I stand for ages letting the hot water burst onto my face and cleanse my body as I recap the evening with Joel.

How had I gone from wary of being alone with him in a secluded wood to making out al-fresco style? We hadn't even bothered with protection – how stupid was that?

A kinder inner voice tries to talk me down – 'these things happen – it's passion, it's natural. Everyone would get defensive if they'd had your start in life – you've had to fight your own corner from day one.'

Was that his plan all along?

No, he wasn't the sort. He'd have chanced his luck with me before now if he'd been a player. He was trying to get to know me. Show me the things he's interested in, how he spends his time. Well great, he knows me a whole lot more than I was expecting. I bet he wishes he'd gone alone.

I shake the voices from my head.

I reach beyond the shower curtain for my towel: *nothing*.

Shit, it must have slid onto the floor from the toilet lid.

I bend down, lowering my reach and feel for it. *Nothing*.

Did I bring it in? I'm sure I did. Wiping the water from my face, I whip the shower curtain aside and peer through the mist.

That's when I see him holding my towel.

A guttural scream fills the wet room.

'Julian!'

My naked appearance suddenly becomes an issue, as my hands try to cover my body by a rapid assortment of positions and hand holds.

'Flora – *looking good*.' Julian smirks, holding my towel at arm's length.

I cringe. Did he really say that?

'Give me my towel.'

As I reach for it, he snatches it back.

'Can't we have some fun first? I've missed you, Flora.'

'Oh feck off, Julian, it's been months and you got your fun from your other girl!'

I drop my hands. I can't cover what he's seen many times before, so what the hell – I'm not in the mood for games. I step from the shower and stride into the bedroom.

'Who let you in anyway?' I say, grabbing the tufted bedspread and wrapping it round my wet body.

'I sneaked up the stairs while the landlady's back was turned... hardly a difficult manoeuvre.'

'What do you want, Julian?' I snap.

He puckers his brow, tilts his head giving me *the* look. The look that used to get me into bed, the look that used to get him a pass stamp for weekends away with his boys and the look that once smouldered my defences and tore down my barriers. The look now hardens my heart; reminding me that this is the bastard that took away my life when he stripped naked for someone else.

'You've got five minutes to get the hell out of here before I start screaming and a herd of blokes charge up that staircase... now, I suggest you be quick. What do you want?'

'You, Flora. I want you to come back home for Valentine's Day.'

I stand and stare at the man I once loved. Once adored. The giant hands that had once held me safe are now tainted by another.

'Home? Home for now is here... so please don't flatter yourself that I even think of that pokey, squalid little flat as home.'

'Cut the crap, Flora... you sound like Steph!' His voice

hardens. 'We both know *this* isn't you. Carry on spouting much longer and you'll be snivelling in two minutes, so do me a favour and save us both the time. Do you want me to pack or are you leaving this shit here for the wench downstairs to send on?'

Wench downstairs? What an arrogant bastard.

'You haven't changed a bit, have you?'

'I've changed loads, thanks to you.'

I shake my head. Why now?

'Can I ask you something?' I say.

'Sure, but make it quick though because this room is bugging me.'

'Did you know I loved you?'

'*What*?' he says, screwing his face up, making his beautiful face ugly.

'I said, did you know that I loved you?'

'Course I did!' he says, puffing his chest out.

I nod as his answer painfully registers.

'Why ask?' he says.

I take in his full stance, cocky, self-assured and oozing arrogance.

'So, why did you do it? If I knew someone loved me *that* much I'd never hurt them for the world.'

He shrugs.

'It just happened.'

I lower my head, knowing full well what can just happen.

'I nipped into the chemist's for a can of deodorant and... she served me and was finishing her shift... I invited her around for a beer and...'

'You bought a can of deodorant from her... and then?'

He shrugs apologetically.

'Julian?'

'What, babe?'

'Firstly, don't call me babe... and coming back to you would be the biggest mistake of my life... please leave!'

'Flora?' he steps forward, arms outstretched. 'Flora baby...'

His fingers touch my naked shoulders.

'Don't you Flora-baby me... get your dirty hands off.'

The crack from his open hand across my left cheek sends me reeling backwards and down onto the floor beside the double bed.

His body looms above me, his blue eyes flare and bulge.

'You friggin' bitch, now look what you've made me do!' he rants, his hands reach for the crumple of bedspread I'm clutching at the base of my neck. 'How dare you blame me for your inadequacies... you bitch!'

I scuttle backwards. Cowering on the floor to escape his anger.

'Get your fecking hands off of her!'

I watch as Julian's looming body is yanked back and up, lifted off his feet by Mick, who burst through the door at a vital moment. 'Who the hell do you think you are?'

My mouth is wide and speechless as Mick bundles Julian from my room. I can hear the scuffle of clambering feet and grappling hands being forced down the staircase and the chime above the door signals his undignified exit.

A rumbling of hurried feet brings Annie to my doorway, as I prise myself from the carpet.

'Oh, my darling, I'm so sorry. I never saw him come up... young Denny just mentioned that a bloke had nipped up the staircase.'

'Annie, please don't apologise – you weren't to know.'

Annie sits me down upon the edge of the bed, I clutch her bedspread to my body.

'Annie, I'm OK.'

'Is she OK?' Mick appears in the doorway, he is breathless and his round face is flushed.

'I'm fine thank you. He surprised me that's all... can I have a minute to get dressed and I'll come downstairs.'

In a chorus of 'of course' and 'sure' the two disappear, giving me a moment to reflect how close I'd come to seeing far more of Julian's temper than I'd ever seen before.

*

I sit in the bar's alcove for the remainder of the evening, with my comfort blanket slung around my shoulders. Mick keeps stretching his back as if he's pulled it again, whilst Annie keeps a cautious eye on me amidst a stream of reassuring comments. 'Plenty more fish in the sea' and the occasional 'you're better off without him, lovey', all of which I know, but to see him for the first time since we'd split had been a shock. Even the girls' message that he wanted me back hadn't prepared me for seeing him in the flesh.

Was that really the guy I had once loved? The 'one' I'd once imagined marrying – where had he disappeared to? A once decent bloke replaced by a heavy-handed, cheating thug. Had he driven straight home or checked into a B&B for a few days? No doubt the locals would know by tomorrow morning.

I'm shocked when Mick puts the beer towels over the pumps at closing time. I'd spent the entire time gazing into the fire and thinking, my mind jumping from one memory and thought to another. Apparently, I'd cradled the same glass of Coke for the last two hours.

Annie and Mick tidy and upturn the bar chairs before bidding me a goodnight.

'I'll leave this back light on for you,' whispers Annie, as she gives me a peck on the cheek. 'Call if you need me.'

'Thank you, I really do appreciate everything you have done for me,' I reply, pulling the blanket corners tight beneath my chin.

I watch as they disappear into their living quarters, leaving the bar still and silent with a warm orange glow from the coal fire.

I curl my legs up, resting my chin on my knees, and watch the dark night outside through the top section of unfrosted glass window.

The hours pass by, the coal fire smoulders to embers and the darkness begins to wane.

A new dawn, a new day and a new plan would emerge with the light, wasn't that right?

But what do I want?

I wrap the blanket tighter around my shoulders and begin being honest with myself.

'I don't want Julian. He'd proven he couldn't be trusted and as for tonight's behaviour – boy, is he history,' I mumble to myself.

So, *what* do I want?

I want answers from my birth mother. I want to be happy. I want security. I want a job that I love. And… I want Joel.

The thought pulls me up sharp.

Do I? Or is this a knee-jerk reaction to Julian's heavy-handedness?

I *do*, I want Joel. I want his kind gentle looks, his half-joking banter, his methodical fact-noting, his chivalrous manners, even his deep conversations about stuff I haven't a clue about.

My stomach flips.

How could I have been so stupid?

Not simply in a date-wise, picnic-fumble-wise, helping-me-find-my-birth-mother manner but… OMG!

Words fail me. I can't define exactly what I mean, but I know what it is. I *want* Joel.

I dash up the staircase heading for room five before I can change my mind. After another quick shower and a change of clothes, I look presentable, although the startled rabbit look still lingers in my eyes.

I sneak from the pub like a thief in the night. I haven't a plan of action, I just know that I need to talk to Joel. Now.

I nip across The Square heading for the car park opposite the church. The snow has frosted over, providing a firmer icy crunch beneath my feet. A plume of breath billows in front of my nose.

Given that my car hasn't been driven for just over six weeks, I feel a bit nervous as I approach the car park and wonder if the engine will start.

The Mini's bodywork looks perfect under my fleeting inspection. It takes seconds to hastily scrape the glistening layer of frost from each window.

Once inside, the smell of perfume hits me. I used to spray it every day of my life, half choking on the vapour cloud, a flavour of my old life, the one I haven't inhabited since Christmas Eve.

The engine punctuates my maudlin thoughts.

The Mini jolts and splutters as I pull away, I check the petrol gauge: half a tank.

With a quick rev of the engine, I'm out of there.

In seconds I pass the church, through the stone archway, saying goodbye to The Square, and trundle to the crossroads beyond. My excitement grows as the snow-flurried country lanes surround me, it feels good to see the frosted emerald-green hedgerows whizzing past my side window. I head for the snowy lanes of Kordon and beyond, where Joel will be at home, quietly reflecting on tonight's awkward situation. I imagine he'll let me in, we'll chat over coffee and hopefully laugh about my strop and then he'll listen, with that intent look on his face, and nod in agreement at the end.

But what happens if he doesn't? What if he refuses to see me? Refuses to talk because he's totally regretting the picnic and wants nothing more to do with me, or my search? I'll have blown my chances with him and lost his support in finding my birth mum.

What was I thinking the very last time I drove this car from

Bushey? I wanted answers. I wanted to find my birth mother. I wanted security. So much has changed.

I know where I am heading. The route is easy to remember, though whether it is a sound decision at just after six o'clock in the morning is debatable.

Recent events have taught me to respond and react, not to sit back and wait. I have learnt my lesson in life, from now I will *always* react.

Within minutes, I pull into his quiet cul-de-sac of apartment blocks and community car parking. Instantly, I want to cry, given the sight before me. In the two parking spaces allocated to Joel's flat number seven are his silver Audi, beside which is *her* black BMW – the windows of both cars are thick with snow and frost.

'Caught you!'

My dashboard clock reads six twenty.

I park opposite, switch off the engine and slump in my seat, a boiling rage rumbling deep inside; my stare fixed ahead.

'So you think I'm stupid, do you? Thought I wouldn't find out?'

My defences begin to lift like the Thames barrier.

'Thought you could have your cake and eat it?'

There could be a reasonable explanation, I suppose. Veronica could be visiting a friend in a neighbouring complex and parked here out of habit?

But I need to know for sure.

I calmly step from my car and walk towards the entrance to his complex. The elongated glaze of blue glass twinkles in the neon lamplight, inside I can see the staircase twisting and turning for each landing.

The brushed metal intercom button beckons but, dare I?

This wasn't plan A, but how dare they fool me into thinking they had separated when all the time they were together. Does she know he'd taken me out?

I bite my lip and imagine the scene if I push the button.

'Hello?' the female's croaky voice would be thick with sleep, but I would recognise it as Veronica's.

I'd freeze, unsure what to say.

'Hello? Who is it?' she'd repeat, impatiently.

I'd then have the chance to walk away; I'd know all I needed to know.

I pause. I have a better idea. I retrieve his spare door keys from my purse.

*

My hand jitters on the wooden stair rail, my eyes staring upwards as I climb steadily to the third floor.

I can't believe I have the nerve to use his key.

I'm prepared for what I'll see: strewn bedclothes, naked bodies, the smell of passion lingering in a darkened room – it'll be no worse than walking in on Julian and his chemist girl.

I reach flat number seven. My fingers raise the key to the lock, insert and turn.

The door springs wide.

A pristine cream carpet stretches before me, inviting me to step over the threshold. This is not how I'd imagined I'd enter his flat. He'd lent me the key to use it as a place of solace, I'd expected to enter clutching a romcom DVD and a bag of popcorn goodies for an afternoon of chilling. Stealing in like a burglar wasn't the plan.

I stand alone on the doormat, preparing myself to witness a second round of cheating. Would it be cheating? I feel cheated, lied to, misled, so yeah, in my book it's cheating. He hadn't said he was still seeing Veronica. He'd clearly led me to believe he wasn't.

The carpet springs beneath my feet: expensive taste.

I tiptoe along the hallway, passing one door which is ajar

306

revealing kitchen worktops, whilst ahead a closed white door beckons. My hand gingerly touches the handle; this too springs wide open, revealing a minimalistic lounge in tones of mellow mocha. Large sofas dominate the room, along with a TV screen, guitars and a huge bookcase. I creep through towards a series of doorways that lead from the lounge. The first is the second entrance into the kitchen. The second door is firmly closed. The third is ajar.

I stop before the open door, take a deep breath and slowly exhale. A gentle push is all that is needed as the hinges swing freely and the darkness opens before me.

My mouth dries, sticking my top lip to my teeth.

I step across the gold carpet runner.

I can hear breathing.

I'm in Joel's bedroom. The blinds are firmly closed, but a whisper of light intrudes from the edge.

The double bed is centrally positioned, the billowing duvet cascades over the edge of the bed onto the floor.

I can't bring myself to look but know I have to.

Beneath the skewed duvet lies Veronica, her tousled blonde hair spread over the pillow, her right arm placed above her head, her naked right breast revealed by the fall of the duvet. Beside her the bed is empty.

I catch my breath. Joel *isn't* here.

His pillow is plump – no dent. The revealed bed sheet is smooth and unrumpled. At the end of the bed, the ottoman guards one set of yesterday's clothing: hers.

What the hell is *she* doing here? Any second now, she'll wake up, and there's not a chance in hell that she'll miss me standing here watching her.

My rage begins to bubble.

I watch as her make-up-smudged face dribbles and her lips sleep-slap in the most unattractive manner.

Had she her own key? His key? Their key? And, *where* is Joel?

I don't think before I act. I grab the edge of the duvet and yank it from her body, revealing her full nakedness. She wakes with a start, instinctively staring towards the empty doorway before looking at me.

The seconds last for an age as her panda eyes take in my presence, her hands whip up to cover her flesh and her mouth and eyes widen.

'Surprise! And can I ask why you're here?' I ask, unsure that it's really my place to ask.

'Flora!'

'Yes.'

'What are you doing here?'

'Funny, that's exactly what I was wondering, Veronica.'

'Is Joel with you?' she asks, scrambling from the bed and grabbing her clothes from the ottoman. Her naked flesh wobbles as she dances about on one leg, tugging and pulling at her jeans.

I don't answer. I have the upper hand, am fully dressed and know that Joel isn't with me.

So, what am I waiting for?

She calls my name several times as I run along the hallway, down the spiral staircase and out into the communal car park. I don't stop, *can't* stop, to answer Veronica.

I unlock the Mini and start the engine. I swiftly do a nifty three-point turn in the car park. As I straighten up ready to accelerate away, a figure in my rear-view mirror catches my eye. I slam on the brakes and watch Veronica run from the main entrance heading to her parked BMW.

Good luck explaining this to Joel, I think as I drive away.

46

Flora

The large-faced clock behind the station's front desk reads a quarter to seven.

'Where is he?' I demand, impatiently tapping the wooden countertop.

'How should I know?' answers Scott, dressed in his uniform, from behind the perspex screen. 'I haven't seen him since last night. I'm not his keeper, you know.'

A second officer turns round and watches our exchange.

'Last night?' I echo.

'He turned up in a taxi for a few bevvies at ours,' he said, adding, 'What's it to you anyway?'

'It's his day off, right?'

'That's the pattern before a night shift.'

I wave a finger up and down, questioning his presence at this time of day.

'I'm doing an extra shift... hey, I don't need to explain myself to you!' he spouts.

I'd wasted enough time being polite to this guy. He'd been brewing for an argument since the night of my arrest, but now wasn't the time.

'*Goodbye.*' I smile sweetly at the second officer, ignore Scott and take my leave.

'Boy, she hates you,' whispers the second officer as I march away from the front desk.

'Only because I arrested her – she'd fancy me otherwise.'

'No, I wouldn't!' I shout over my shoulder as the glass doors gently close.

I climb into my Mini, parked between two police cars, and switch off the radio so I can think.

Where would he be? The weather is dismal, there's a promise of more snow, yet he's out and about with the larks.

I call his mobile: no answer, so I leave a message.

'Joel, it's Flora, call me as *soon* as you get this.' I throw my mobile onto the passenger seat.

Where the hell is he?

*

Her black BMW shoots past the police station frontage, its windows scraped in mini arcs, it doesn't hesitate to pull into the car park but darts past in a blur.

Veronica knows where he is!

Instantly, I know where Joel is too: the maze.

I fasten my seatbelt, turn on the ignition and put the pedal to the metal.

It takes less than a few minutes for me to catch up with and start to tail Veronica.

We zip through the narrow country lanes and the snowy hedgerows flash by as my Mini races towards the maze behind the sleek BMW.

Please let him be there otherwise I'll look like a raving nutter charging after Veronica as she drives home to Major Matthews.

My Mini sweeps into the gated driveway of the manor house and at the forked road I eagerly take the right-hand turn towards the maze in Veronica's speeding wake. She hasn't turned left towards the manor house.

The maze stands proud against a backdrop of lilac sky and snow as daybreak begins. The car park is empty. Has a taxi dropped him off here?

I park, then leap from the car, slam the driver's door and charge towards the maze, which has a thick frosting of snow. Veronica does the same. I enter the maze in a galloping fashion. Not my favourite puzzle, but now it has new meaning, there is a purpose in getting to the middle. I have to speak to Joel, tell him how I feel.

My feet eagerly crunch along the snow-covered gravel as I practise my lines in my head.

'Veronica's been sneaking into your flat!' Or, 'I wasn't snooping, but Veronica's been sneaking into your flat!'

Nothing sounds right, everything that I say makes me sound like a seven-year-old snitching on a classmate in a maths lesson.

I hear the steady crunch of feet alongside me on another unseen pathway: Veronica.

'Shit!'

Where am I? I haven't been concentrating and now for the second time I am passing the spiky branch that forced me to duck my head – I am lost, *again*.

I jump up and down in a poor attempt to see over the tall hedging. Not a chance. I don't want to resort to the damsel in distress routine like last time, but hey, if it means I get to him before she does...

'Joel!' I holler, hands cupped to my mouth as though I'm shouting through a mountain pass in the Alps.

'Flora?'

'Joel, I need to speak to you urgently!'

'Joel!' shouts Veronica, unseen but a short distance to my right. 'I need to speak to you!'

'Say that again,' shouts Joel, sounding confused.

'Veronica is here too,' I shout, as I change direction in a panic. 'Joel – I'm stuck again but I need to talk to you – it's urgent.'

'Flora, do the hand on the wall routine – it'll work, I promise.'

'Will it work part way in?' I know the answer before he replies.

'No!'

'How do I go back?' Duh, stupid question.

'I can't direct you without knowing where you are?'

'Joel?' shouts Veronica's voice.

'Veronica – sod off!' I shout in annoyance. 'Joel, she was asleep in your bed – she's been there all night!'

'*Veronica*?' calls Joel.

'It's not how it seems… I can explain,' she calls.

'How, Veronica?' I shout, turning in a circle to cover all directions.

'What's it to you?' calls Veronica, from behind me, nearer than she was a moment ago.

'You're playing games, that's what it is to me!' I shout defiantly at the green hedging.

'Flora, keep heading towards my voice, you'll get to the middle,' shouts Joel. 'And Veronica, you have no right to enter that flat without my permission.'

'How dare you!' she shouts.

'Who me?' I ask.

'No, me,' shouts Joel, somewhere to my left.

'Both of you, you've got a nerve suggesting that I'd steal anything from that apartment, and you, you need to grow a backbone where she's concerned – she's walking all over you!' Her voice now sounds as if it is in front of my position.

'Look who's talking!' I retort.

'Hold your horses, Veronica… you've got a nerve calling the shots,' laughs Joel.

'It doesn't have to be like this, Joel, we could have done this amicably, made sure that both of us were looked after, but no, she pokes her oar in and now you don't even return my phone calls.'

'Bloody cheek!' I shout, for good measure.

'We were over long before Flora showed up and I've given you plenty of chances to sit down and talk... but you said no. Fair's fair.'

'That's not true... you said...'

'Veronica, you wanted out and you decided we were over and now... you seem to be forgetting that.'

I pause and turn as the two voices appear to be switching sides, left, right, behind and in front of my static position.

'Will everyone stop moving,' I yell. 'This is giving me motion sickness.'

'If you can't handle the heat stay out of the kitchen,' sneers Veronica, somewhere to my left.

'Frig off, Veronica! You're only interested now because I'm on the scene, so sod off and get your claws into someone your own age.

'Flora!'

'But, Joel, she...'

'*But, Joel...*' mimics Veronica, in a slushy tone.

I turn a corner and there she is. Veronica Sable in all her cougar glory blocking my path like the Ice Queen of Narnia.

How has she got ahead of me or was I going backwards?

'Not as clever as we thought, hey?' she sneers, her bright red lips contorting.

'Ditto. You lost your man and now...' I retort with venom.

'Ladies, as lovely as this is – I'd prefer to discuss this face to face rather than shouting over the top of hedges.'

'Joel, stop playing games – send this one packing and we can pick up where we left off,' calls Veronica, thrusting her breasts forward.

'You think!' I say, looking her up and down.

'Believe me, sweetheart, I *know*,' she purrs.

I fix my gaze at her and stare. I was world champion of this as a kid. She knows nothing. She doesn't know how to get to the middle, she doesn't know what Joel truly likes, she doesn't even know that he's well and truly over her. She. Knows. Nothing!

So why is my faith waning?

'Are you going to move out of my way, or am I going to have to move you?' growls Veronica, her voice low and husky.

'Make me.'

Where the hell did that come from? Am I eight years old at primary school?

Veronica's right eyebrow lifts in response.

'Or else you'll headbutt me, is that it?' she snarls.

Shit, she means it. I've never been physical in my life, apart from headbutting Joel – there's never been a fight or a cat scrap in my history, but now, is this the answer?

Her shoulders straighten, her breasts lift and her stance widens. I copy; not knowing what to expect or what to do. Do I punch first or wait and punch back harder?

Without warning she charges at me, hands outstretched and features twisted. As she nears, I close my eyes. She doesn't hit me, as expected, but barges me aside. I fall sideways into the prickly hedging, causing a flurry of snow to cascade down.

'Oi!' But she's gone, the pathway is empty and I can hear her feet crunching rapidly on another pathway.

'Flora?' shouts Joel. 'Are you OK?'

'She's ahead of me, she barged past...'

'Sod off and go home, little girl,' shouts a breathless voice.

Little girl? Go home? Who the hell does she think she's talking to? The fire in my belly ignites. That's it, she's asking for it!

I start running along the pathways, following her noisy footsteps, every now and then I turn a section quickly enough to see her backside flying round a corner.

My chest is on fire. This is the most exercise I have ever done in my life. If I catch her will I have the energy to barge past her or wrangle her to the ground?

I can't outrun her.

I stop running.

I look around for a plan B. I stare despondently at the tops of the hedges looming way above my head.

Could I climb over? Go under? Go through?

My heart skips a beat. I could barge through the hedging in the sparser areas of growth. My arms and legs are sufficiently covered with clothes; I could protect my face with my hands.

Let's try.

I crash through the hedging, scattering the snow frosting in all directions, into the next pathway with relative ease and very little pain. Result!

'Now, keep going,' I tell myself.

After six hedge bursts, I fall into the centre section, joining Joel and a breathless Veronica, who is doubled over, panting like a marathon runner.

'Joel!' I screech in delight, trying to pick bits of broken twigs and snow smatterings from my hair, whilst kneeling in the snow.

I stare at Veronica. She stares back – taking in the glorious mess before her. Why couldn't I have been the one that arrived panting and breathless but with my hairstyle still intact. No, my style is *literally* dragged through a hedge, my cheeks decorated by a million tiny scratches and I'm picking debris from my hairline.

Joel stands between us like an adult version of piggy in the middle.

'Joel!' demands Veronica, her throat straining.

'Flora, you made it!'

'Joel!' repeats Veronica, twice as loud and twice as stern as before.

A moment of silence lingers as he looks between us.

He's in front of me in two strides, much to her horrified expression.

He grabs my upper arms and lifts me to my feet.

'Joel, we can start over… how it once was, just you and me… we were happy Joel, remember?'

Joel pulls me up to my full height and looks at my scratched face.

'I got lost, again… and I'm sorry about last night… what I said sounded so wrong.'

'Me too… I never meant for that to happen and then you walked home, refusing to listen to me. I needed to straighten my head.'

'I'm sorry too. Scott said you went to his.'

'I just needed somewhere to chill… I took a cab to his house, had a few beers and then hailed a taxi here,' he mutters, gently stroking my thorn-snagged face. 'Happy Valentine's Day, Flora.'

'Happy Valentine's, Joel,' I say, as my previous accusations melt guiltily away.

'You've left the pub far too early for Kathy's delivery schedule,' he whispers, lifting his hands up into my hair. 'So, you've ruined your flower delivery.'

Our faces move nearer; my next sentence is stifled by his lips finding mine. His arms wrap around my shoulders and pull me into his body. I kiss him as forcefully as he kisses me.

Veronica coughs.

'Do you mind?' she snorts.

Joel breaks his lips away first, his broad smile greeting me.

'Actually, I do,' he says, turning to view her snarling features.

Panting for breath, I drop my head forward to rest on his chest.

'I do mind, Veronica, very much so. I mind that you *think* you call the shots around here, that *you* think you can say whatever *you* choose to Flora, and yet have failed to get the message – we're over! You made your bed – so go and lie in it.'

A giggle lifts to my throat, I gulp to suppress it – gloating would be too unkind.

'She *was* in your bed!'

'Caught red-handed!' he says. 'You took everything when you left – so what could you possibly be doing there?'

Veronica shakes her head, her mouth keeps opening to speak but stalls before a word is uttered.

'You were there too!' shouts Veronica.

'He gave me a key, and yes, I used it as I was desperate to speak to him.'

'At half six in the morning?' she snorts, flicking her blonde hair.

'You wanted to speak to me?' mutters Joel, turning back to face me, a smile crossing his lips.

'I wanted to talk about last night, and then Julian turned up.'

'*Julian?*'

'He arrived at the pub, causing a whole load of drama.'

Veronica sidles alongside us, tapping her foot.

'Are you actually choosing *that* over me?' she blurts, pointing at me.

Subtle, Veronica, not a hint of desperation.

Joel looks deeply into my face, his dark eyes flicking back and forth across my scratched features.

'As strange as this may sound to you, Veronica – yes, I am.'

'You *arse*!' she shouts, before storming out of the maze.

47

Joel

Annie phones me as soon as the envelope arrives.

'Flora needs you to come to The Peacock, Joel – be quick.'

I don't need asking twice. In the week that had elapsed since our early morning kiss in the maze we'd become closer. There was no need to rush, it felt right to be taking our time and enjoying each other's company. A natural routine had developed, Flora helped out behind the bar on certain days and at The Posy Pot on others – we met up for quiet evenings away from The Square when it suited. Nothing full on, just two people enjoying each other's company.

I'm not about to leave her to face this alone, not if she doesn't want to.

I arrive to find Flora seated in the alcove, staring at her information board. The post lady has long gone yet the large padded envelope remains unopened on the bar table in front of her. Annie stands tentatively behind her bar polishing a tray of glasses.

'I'll go and put the kettle on,' says Annie, quickly departing.

'Flora?' I approach and can see she's all of a dither, her hands are twisting in her lap, her eyes are fixed on the coloured flags stuck into the map.

'Would you like some privacy?' I ask, approaching slowly for fear of crowding her and her thoughts.

'Not really. This is it... in there could be the answer I've been longing for or an incomplete answer – which means I've wasted everybody's sodding time and effort... including yours.'

I pull up a bar stool and settle myself at her table.

'No, you haven't... everyone has willingly helped and supported you... including me.'

She turns to face me, her features are gaunt, her skin looks sallow and waxy.

'You must think about you.' I point to the padded envelope. 'In there could be the answer you're seeking. Please open it.'

I nudge the envelope across the table, closer to her quivering hands.

Annie joins us with a tray of teas and begins to hand out the mugs.

'Joel's right, you can't think of others right now, think about yourself.'

Flora's tears well and glisten. Annie settles at the table and we sit in silence as Flora slowly retrieves the package and her index finger works at the seal.

My heart is beating ten to the dozen; who knows at what rate hers must be pumping.

She suddenly stops, and exhales deeply.

'What if it's someone I don't like?' she asks.

'It won't be,' soothes Annie, sipping her tea.

I shrug. What can I say? I can't predict anything.

Her hands drop into her lap along with the envelope.

'No, seriously, what happens if it's...' she looks up at me, her doleful eyes almost pleading.

'What?' I ask.

'Veronica.'

'Veronica... she's a pussy cat... *seriously*, don't go there.'

Flora's shoulders sag.

Annie's hand reaches for my forearm and rests on it gently.

'I don't think she means that, Joel... do you, Flora?'

Flora shakes her head and looks away.

The penny drops.

'Hey, we're history. Seriously, I'm done with that chapter of my life.'

'I know, but you and her... were a couple,' she says. 'If this turns out to be confirmation that she's my... where does that leave...?'

'Us?' I finish her sentence.

The enormity hits me like a sledgehammer.

'Flora, this,' I point to the envelope, 'makes no difference to us and anything that might develop, I promise you. If the result says that Veronica is your biological mother, seriously we'll deal with it – we will.'

'But you can't... a mother *and* her daughter!' stutters Flora.

'Annie tell her,' I beg.

Annie shrugs.

'She's got a point.'

Not helping, Annie.

'She hasn't... Flora, I'm telling you whatever result is in that envelope will not change what we have, seriously it won't.'

'OK,' she says, her voice flat and lifeless.

'Please open the envelope and put this to an end,' I add, my nerves jingling at my throat.

Her index finger slices through the remainder of the envelope seal.

Annie and I exchange a nervous glance; Flora brings the paperwork into the light.

Her hollow eyes scan back and forth before she switches papers and a deep sigh is exhaled.

'You OK?' I ask.

'Yep, I have my answer.' She clutches the paperwork to her

chest and the tears spill over her lashes. 'I have an answer. I know who my birth mother is.'

'For certain?' I prompt.

Flora nods, rolling her lips inwards, as her eyelids lower. 'Mmmm.'

'Are you pleased with the result?' asks Annie, discarding her mug.

'I don't know...'

Flora gives a blubbery smile as her entire body slowly morphs into a wracking mess of sobbing as we sit and witness a lifetime of anxiety disappear.

48

Flora

'What the hell do you expect me to say?' he shouts, jumping up from his seat. 'You waltz in at Christmas stirring the village up with this witch hunt and for what?'

'To find *my* birth mother – you may describe it as a witch hunt, but never have I said a bad word about any of the women in this village.'

'You've screwed my old man's head for a start... the poor sod's only just lost his wife and now... thanks to you, he's got a damn sight more to think about!'

'Scott, I have a right to know who my birth mother is!' I glance towards the alcove display over which Annie has kindly hung and pinned a red tablecloth to cover the details for the time being.

'You have no frigging right. If she made a decision at the age of fifteen... that was her choice! All you've done is sullied the memory of *my* mother in this village. The locals are going to crucify her now, gone are the memories of the gentle woman who had a kind word for everyone. She'll be the cruel bitch who dumped a baby on a doorstep... that's what you've done!' rants Scott, leaning over me as his words spit venom.

I sink into the nearest bar seat. Joel jumps up, stands close to his buddy and places a reassuring hand on Scott's shoulder.

'Look, mate, she has every right to know... cool down and we can talk about it.'

'She has no right in my book... my mother's name is going to be dragged through the mud because of her!' he continues to rant, while pointing at me and shrugging Joel's hand from his shoulder.

I get a chance to breathe, this wasn't the reaction I was expecting. It has been a few days since I called round their house to share the test results. I hadn't expected Scott to invite me in for tea or welcome me with open arms, but surely they recognised that I was trying to be respectful. Surely Scott and his dad should be the first to know, after me. My visit had lasted all of ten minutes; I've waited several days for Scott to come to The Peacock.

'Mate, you need to calm down – *this* isn't helping,' says Joel, putting his arm round his buddy.

'I never meant to cause you *or* your father any upset.'

'I'll never forgive you for what you've put my father through, *never*!'

'Scotty, there's no getting away from the fact,' starts Joel. 'It's there in black and white.'

'Don't. Even. Say. It.' He turns and scoots from the pub, the door slams shut behind him.

Joel seats himself next to me and takes my hand.

'Are you OK?'

I shake my head as my eyes well up.

'He came through the door like a bull...'

'I saw him from The Square. Can I get you anything?'

'No, I wanted to talk to him... explain why I've had to do this.'

'Now's not the time, Flora. Scott needs space to get his head around the details... give him time – he'll calm down and then a civilised conversation can actually take place.'

'But *will* it?'

49

Scott

I avoid her for another two nights, but when I walk into The Peacock, a sea of faces turn, stare and fall silent. I stride to the bar; Annie pulls my usual.

What the hell? If one more person gives me that hound-dog expression suggesting my mother was the local bike of eighty-six – I swear I'll kick off and willingly spend a night in a cell.

My mum was the sweetest woman ever to live. The kind of mum that baked butterfly cakes every Sunday so my packed lunch contained home baking. She hid Easter eggs around the garden and created rhyming clues for birthday treasure hunts. *And*, she was devoted to me and my dad. My mum, Tracey Hamilton, would *never* walk away from a baby. *Never*.

'You OK?' whispers Annie, as she places the pint on the bar.

'Grand, Annie, just grand. Any sign of Joel?' I take a sip from the pint.

'Upstairs with Flora, she's not too good today, but if you want me to call her…'

I feel the entire bar inhale.

'Why would I want to see *her*?'

'I thought that…'

'Well, you thought wrong, didn't you?' I turn and face the crowd. 'And you lot, you nosey bleeders, you can sod off with your sympathy looks. My mum *never* had a child before me.'

'Lad, we all know this is difficult for you... and your dad but...' calls Mick, from the far end of the bar. 'We do understand.'

'What the hell would you know? You didn't even speak to my mother, so do me a favour and don't mention her name now!' I slam my pint glass down, spilling the majority on the bar top, and walk out.

'Scott!' is the distant cry I hear as the pub door closes.

I'm across The Square before I know it, heading who knows where, but anywhere is better than The Peacock right now. My feet pound the cobbles and, before I realise it, I'm striding along the pathway to St Bede's Church.

What the hell?

I'm inside the church door before I can think.

'Scott, are you all right?'

His voice brings me to. I stare into the calming blue eyes of Father Maguire.

My mind reels. My body ceases to be mine as he steers me into the end pew and forces me to sit down. My knees bump against the wooden pew in front adorned with an embroidered kneeling cushion hung from a gold hook.

'This is a difficult time for you and your father but you must take a few days to digest the information... if you need to talk to anyone, or contemplate the changes that this will bring... please don't hesitate.'

I look around the church, its high arched ceiling, its elaborate decorations carved in stone and the large wooden crucifix suspended above the altar.

'Father?'

'Yes.'

'What am I supposed to do?'

'Accept the facts, Scott.'

I shake my head. I understand his kindness; his words are calming, but how? How do I accept that she is supposed to be my sister?

'Did my mum ever tell you about Baby Bede?'

'I've known your mother since she was a small child, I married your parents at that altar and baptised you within the year. She *never* mentioned the other baby to me.'

'I knew it,' I mutter. 'Father, of all the people in this village my mother would have told you... for sure!'

'Don't be so quick to judge her – she was just a child herself.'

His words run round in my head.

I stand.

'Thank you, Father.' I shake his hand as I depart.

There's only one place I can go: Gran's house in Windmill Road.

Kathy

'Scott!'

'Up here, Aunty Kath,' his voice comes from the open loft hatch on the landing area, before his taut face appears in the ceiling's square gap. 'I'm on a mission.'

'*Really*?'

'Come up, you can give me a hand.'

Phew, he seems in a better mood.

I was closing The Posy Pot when Annie nipped round to say he'd mouthed off in The Peacock. My nephew can be loud and brash but he rarely makes a scene.

I straddle the window ledge and bannister rail with some difficulty before gripping the wooden loft lip – one swift but cumbersome heave launches my body up into my mother's dimly lit loft space.

'It's been years since I came up here. How can you see anything using that tiny torch?' I ask, as Scott scoots about the wooden eaves in a crouching style, holding a torch.

'I've found enough, believe me... look.' He points to several long travelling trunks adorned with silver press locks. 'I've prised the locks open.'

'And you're looking for what exactly?'

'Anything.' He begins wrenching at another lock with a long-handled screwdriver.

'Scott?'

I watch his shoulders pump forcibly at the lock before it springs open.

'Open sesame,' laughs Scott.

'Seriously, should you be doing this?'

He turns, screwdriver held high, his face instantly twisted in anger.

'Are you serious? The whole village is gossiping about my mother, *your* sister, and you have the nerve to ask me if I should be doing this?'

I shrug, as words fail me.

His hands are frantic as he sifts through the medley of forgotten items within the trunk.

'Got them!' he yells.

He sits back, hauling a pile of tiny plastic padded books onto his lap. The sight brings old memories flooding back. Christmas morning, we always received a box set of matching address book and diary. Each had a gaudy picture cover with a tiny gold latch and padlock attached. The tiny keys never lasted five minutes.

'*Diaries*… Mum always kept a diary.'

Shit!

Mine was ditched by January fifth, but Tracey religiously kept hers up to date all year through.

'This might seem like the greatest idea, but nothing good is ever learnt from reading a diary, Scott.'

'Quit the lecture, I need to know for certain and these…' he lifts the pile into the air, 'are *her* words.'

I have two choices: leave or support him.

I choose the latter, sinking onto my haunches to be alongside my nephew as he piles each plastic-covered diary on top of the other.

'What's with the tiny locks… they are hardly security-force standard, are they?' he laughs, flicking one tiny gold padlock.

'To keep nosey people out of private matters – we thought they were great,' I offer.

'1989, 88, 87...' Scotty works through the diary pile, discarding each based on the large foil numbers emblazoned on the front cover.

My hand reaches for his shoulder as the countdown continues.

'Scott... scientific tests have revealed the truth. Me and your Gran also confirmed that the silver rope ring was identical to the one Tracey had and lost... so surely there's nothing else you need to know?'

He stops and looks up at me. There's an intensity about his features, his hazel eyes drill into mine. I can see my younger sister looking back at me.

'I need to know the truth... not through science, a squashed piece of jewellery or village gossip, but the truth from her, my mum.'

'But once you know, will it be enough?'

'It's been enough for Flora, hasn't it? Nobody seems to have stopped her in her quest for the truth.'

I remove my hand from his shoulder. There's nothing else for me to say, he needs to do what he needs to do, just as young Flora did.

He returns to his countdown.

'1986, got it!'

I stare at the tiny blue flowers and tiny gold lock swamped by Scott's hand. My heart rate pounds as the tip of his screwdriver wrenches the lock and half the padded cover from the diary.

Scotty's fingers busily flick through the lined pages filled with neat schoolgirl script.

Friday, 10th October 1986

I never meant for this to happen. Seriously, I didn't. If my mam knew, she'd have my guts for garters. I thought she'd told me everything during our birds and bees chat – she said she was being honest. She must have forgotten to mention the pain of childbirth.

I sat watching my radio alarm click around to six forty-five. I couldn't go any earlier, as it was pitch-black outside. I'd waited for an hour then crept down the stairs, grabbed my green parka and quietly clicked the front door behind me.

Thick fog filled the street. I walked along Windmill Road then along North Street, heading under the archway into The Square. I lowered my head each time I reached a lamp post. I didn't see anyone, not even Tommy Duggan's dad who he reckons walks to work early, just a black cat walking the fence by Melanie Delaney's gran's.

I knew where I was heading. I'd already made my choice.

In The Square, I turned right towards the row of houses beside the church. All their lights were off. Everything looked eerie in the fog – only the phone box on the corner stood out in the mist.

I didn't hesitate once I reached Doc Fowler's gate, I tiptoed along the path. I didn't need to go up the steps, I could reach from where I was.

Their front door had fancy stained glass panels cut into the dark blue paint. Ours doesn't. I looked up at the brass knocker. Should I knock? Or just leave? Had I got time to run and hide if they answered straight away? I looked about The Square; they'd see me, unless I hid in the telephone box. But what if I was caught? Mam would go spare.

I gently put her down. She didn't make a sound as I pulled the towel away from her face. I expected her to cry, do something, anything, but she didn't. Her face was puffy yet squashed, with a tuft of reddish brown hair. She smelt brand new. Stupid, she is!

'Bye Danielle,' I'd whispered, kissing her tiny fore-head. I didn't know what else to say, so said the one thing Mam always says to me and our Kathy when she leaves us at Nan's for the weekend – 'Be good.'

I turned and walked, as quickly as I could.

I quietly let myself back in with the key Mum had given me so I can come home from school for dinner – she says I'm old enough to be trusted. Ironic!!! I snook up the stairs and darted into my bedroom. I leant against my closed bedroom door, crumpling the corner of my Smash Hits *Wham! poster and cried.*

Please be good, Danielle x

Scott's voice quivers as he reads the page aloud.

He looks up, tears rolling down his face.

'Oh babe.' I grab him in a bear hug like only an aunty can.

*

'To think it's sat in that loft for all these years – well, I never,' mutters Scott's gran, my mother, staring at the diary entry, having helped two tear-stained relatives down from her loft space.

'Did you never suspect?' I ask, having drunk half my tea.

'Never. I honestly thought it was one of the Delaney girls from around the corner... they were always up to no good with men. That Melanie was beyond her years thanks to her older sisters, but our Tracey? *Never.*'

'So how did she conceal it, Nan?'

Mum shakes her head, returning the diary to Scott's shaking hand.

'I've asked myself the same question for the last few days.

School uniform, P.E. lessons, roller discos – you name it, our Tracey was there, wasn't she, Kathy? All dressed up, and yet... I honestly can't say.'

'Are you shocked, Aunty Kathy?' asks Scott, flipping through the pages.

'*Absolutely*, we told each other everything, secrets and shared talk about boys, but our Tracey didn't say a word about a baby.'

Silence descends as Scott flips the pages back and forth, Mum stares into the fire and I sip my tea.

'What does that say?' Scott pushes a diary page under my nose, his finger pointing at three scrawled letters.

I twist my head to view it from various angles, squinting my eyes, but I can't make out the letter shapes. The date he is pointing to is 2nd January, 1986.

Scott jumps up, his eyes wide.

'I bloody knew it!' shouts Scott, dashing from my mother's back kitchen, our Tracey's diary still clutched in his hand.

50

Joel

'I've spoken to Scott.' I watch as my words rouse the figure curled in a foetal position on her tufted bedspread. 'He needs time to adjust, Flora... this is as much a shock to him as it is to you.'

She lifts her head, tear-stained eyes peer from a blotchy face, gulps and resumes her position.

I perch on the edge of the double bed, as Annie's words race in my mind 'right now, finding her mother is the biggest thing in her life. If you can step back and allow her to satisfy that... that need... she'll be putty in your hands.'

'We didn't know how this would turn out, did we? You came here looking for answers... and now you need time to take in the results – I know it isn't the ending you'd hoped for.'

I hear a snort.

'I imagine you wanted to meet her, dreamt of chatting, asking questions, understanding why certain things happened... and her death has put a stop to all those possibilities,' my mouth is on autopilot. 'But some good has come out of it... you have a younger brother. OK, he's as shocked as you are, but give him time and who knows what will come of it.'

'He hates me! He arrested me!' she snarls.

Fair point.

'At the minute he does, and yes, he did just that... but for good reason, you broke my nose remember. He didn't arrest you for being his sister, did he?'

'You'll never understand,' she mumbles into the pillow.

'I'm trying to.'

'Can you hear your mother's voice in your head? Can you smell her hand cream? Have you heard the songs she sings while cooking the evening meal?'

I can't bring myself to answer; she has a valid point.

'Well. I. Can't!' A fresh burst of wailing fills the room. I scoot along the edge of the bed, placing my hand on her back as her shoulders rise and fall in a sporadic manner, and wait for her tears to subside.

'I'll never... get to... speak to her – *ever.*'

We're going round in circles, and I'm not convinced I'm helping to lift her mood.

'Come on, you can't lie here all night crying, how about we go for a walk? It's late I know, but even so... it was trying to snow earlier.'

'I don't want to.'

'Something to eat then? Annie said you've been up here for several hours.'

She shakes her head, matting her hair even more.

'Flora, you can't stay like this, it isn't good for you... what do you want to do?' the words have barely left my mouth when she launches up from the bed, her hands clamp either side of my face and her lips roughly plant themselves on mine.

What the hell?

I pull back from her passion.

'Flora, this isn't the time or place.' I wrangle my face from her hands.

'I don't care. I want you to hold me, make love to me.'

'No.' I grasp both her hands and hold tight, raising myself to standing. 'Not like this, babe.'

'Joel!'

'I know... but you're upset, you're not thinking straight... right now all you want is comfort, and *this*...' I shake her clutched hands, 'is not the right thing to do.'

She yanks her wrists from my clutches and flops back onto the bed, her back twisted against me.

'*Great*!'

'Hey, don't *great* me... I'm doing it for your own good... if I was some kind of heartless player I wouldn't refuse, would I? But that's not me, Flora. I don't take advantage of women in any situation, least of all... ones I actually care about.'

Her head slowly swivels round to look at me.

'Yes, if you hadn't noticed, I do actually care about you... and what happens to you... and yes, as hot-headed as you are, *and* you broke my nose *and* gave me two black eyes – I am interested in building a future with *you,* but you as a person, Flora, not some casual fling.'

Her cheeks flush, a wry smile dawns.

'You think we have a future?'

'Yes, very much so... and so this is not an option. So up you get... we're going for a walk.'

Scott

The door chime announces my entrance. I stride to the end of the bar and lean across to speak to Mick, quietly. The usual crowd stand and stare – instinct warns them there may be trouble ahead.

'You dated my mum as a teenager – get up to a bit of slap and tickle, did you?'

Mick's blue eyes grow wide; I have his attention.

'I'll speak to you outside in five minutes,' I growl, before leaving the bar to wait in The Square. It's beginning to snow and I'm pacing like a madman on the cobbles; my grasp tightens upon the tiny diary.

Mick joins me within seconds, his face is ashen and his awkward gait suggests his back is still playing him up.

'I don't know what you're harking on about, young man... we were kids messing about after a few swigs of cider. We weren't sweethearts or anything serious.'

'That's you!' I jam my finger at the three initials scrawled on 2nd January's page. It's badly written, whether on purpose to disguise them or teenage excitement, but there is a definite MO'N. 'Your initials, I believe.'

Mick peers at the page and slowly shakes his head.

'You got her pregnant, didn't you?'

Mick shrugs.

'I wouldn't know,' he adds, his voice dropping.

'Don't know? It isn't difficult to work out... did *you* sleep with my mother around New Year?'

Mick's brow furrows, his fingers twitch as he counts the

months. I can't wait for his slow calculations, I've already worked it out, so I interrupt.

'I suspect you did and *that's* why my mother never spoke to you again... she was never rude to anyone but she avoided you like the plague, didn't she? One teenage dalliance with you and she regretted it for the rest of her life!'

Growing up in Pooley there were plenty of village events where the evening would finish up back at The Peacock – BBQs, summer fetes, Christmas parties and New Year celebrations, but she never spoke to Mick, *never*. With his loud mannerisms I assumed she simply disliked him, but now, looking back, she avoided any contact at all.

'She wasn't unkind, she was a warm, loving person... but if you shared a night of teenage kicks... then dumped her shortly afterwards for whatever reason, she's hardly going to be chatty with you... especially as she's walking about consumed with guilt by your behaviour *and* her actions.'

My voice has risen, passers-by turn and look before continuing on their way through The Square.

'I've got a fecking good mind to...' The possibilities whir in my mind.

'She never said a word, I swear. I took her to the cinema one night, we didn't speak much after that date. Tracey was a nice gal but a bit too quiet for me... I suppose, girls don't forget stuff like that, but she never said a word about a baby.'

'You dumped her for being quiet?' I mock. 'Cheers, man.'

Mick looks round for encouragement – there isn't any.

'Mick, what's going on?' shouts Annie, dashing from the pub, tea towel in hand.

'Nothing, love, I'll be inside in a minute,' says Mick, not turning his head to speak, his eyes lock on mine, muttering, 'Now look what you've started?'

'But, Mick,' Annie marches over and joins our discussion, 'what's with the shouting?'

'He's Flora's father.'

A deep groan is expelled from Mick's chest.

Annie's face freezes as she stares at her husband, before distorting in instant agony.

'You and… but you never said that you and Tracey…' her words stumble. '*Mick*?'

'We were kids messing about one night, but she never said a word, *honest.*'

A painful wail fills the air, Annie dashes back into the pub like a rocket.

'What a mess!' mutters Mick, before chasing after her. 'Annie!'

Unsure where to go, I stop pacing and stare around The Square. I've known this square since childhood: The Corner Café where mum bought me mugs of hot chocolate, the summer fetes and the Christmas markets. Everything revolved around this place, but now… it's all changed so quickly. *Nothing* will ever be the same again.

Flora

He likes me. It's not me thinking he likes me based on a look or a smile – he actually said the words '*we* have a future.' My mind spins through the memory of various boyfriends, at this stage not one had ever looked ahead towards the future. It was always the kissing, the date, the clinch, the sex that had snared me deeper into a relationship, but Joel actually said it, straight out.

'And now that you've dried your eyes... can we get the hell out of here, because as quaint as Annie's bedrooms are they're not where I think you should be, OK?'

I take his outstretched hand and raise myself from the bed, which has been my nest for numerous hours.

'Excellent, the woman is upright and walking.' He plants a tender kiss on my forehead.

'I think a walk around the village would be good... it's been hours since I left this room.' My sentence is interrupted by a commotion outside.

Joel races to the window, pulling the drawn curtains aside to show the first flurries of snow.

'Is that Annie shouting?' asks Joel, peering into the twilight.

'Sounds like it... but who's that?' I stand alongside him, cupping my hands over my eyes connecting with the glass pane.

'Mick and... Scott!'

'What does he want?' I retort glumly.

'Oi cut it out, he may well have come to see how his big sister is doing. Be nice, come on.'

He takes my hand and pulls me from the room, my face remains blotchy and my hair matted, and we head to the bar.

Annie

I dash into the bar, brushing the beginnings of snow from my hair and pump a glass tumbler up to the whisky optic several times. I neck it in one. A deep burn fills my innards as an audience of startled customers watch.

I want another double but that would be unwise.

Never before have the customers seen me drink on duty. *Never*. The jukebox may be playing but a silence descends as tongues and glasses are suspended in motion.

I don't know whether to shout and scream at him for having the one thing I can't ever have: a daughter. Or hug him for gaining the one thing I always wanted: his daughter.

And now the truth unravels for us, despite all those fertility tests, all those sleepless nights. The truth always comes out however much *they* try and hide it.

How is Flora going to react when she hears this? Love or loathe him? And what about me... does our relationship change from this point onwards? Officially making me her step-mother... I think I prefer being her friend.

A lump knots at my throat.

I have two choices: burst into tears or repeat the double action on the optic. I choose the latter and pump the optic for a second time before necking it as swiftly as the first.

'Annie?' Gene's voice breaks the spell.

'The usual, Gene?' I spring back into my role.

'Annie... love... what's happened?' Gene approaches,

placing his half-filled pint glass on the bar before coming round to our side.

The door chime sounds; the audience turns to witness Mick's return, his face pale, brow puckered, brushing snowflakes from his shoulders. He walks to the bar, simply gives me a woeful look and disappears through to the back room.

'Whatever it is...' continues Gene, having paused for his brother, '...let it go, for now.'

'*Sure*, can't a woman get a drink around here!' I snap, pushing my tumbler towards the dirty glass rack.

Joel and Flora appear at the bottom of the staircase, interrupting the silence.

'Usual, is it?' I shout, grabbing Flora a large wine glass from the back shelf.

Gene steps back from me, shakes his head and returns to the correct side of the bar.

'I was only trying to help,' he mutters.

'Joel, what's it to be?' my vision locks onto the pair as they make their way towards the bar, every eye taking in her dishevelled appearance.

'Nothing thanks, Annie – we're heading out for a walk and a bite to eat,' he says, viewing the audience of faces staring at them.

'We heard a commotion,' adds Flora, staring from me, to Gene and back to me. 'Outside, Mick and Scott were having words.'

I shrug nonchalantly.

'Nope, not as far as I know... Scott's gone, Mick's in the back.'

Joel gives a swift nod before leading Flora towards the exit.

'Enjoy your walk, it's just started to snow,' I shout, trying to sound casual and cover up the commotion.

*

Mick

'What the hell!' I slump into the armchair and stare at the ebbing fire. 'What the hell?'

Tracey didn't breathe a word of it, then or since. One teenage date to the pictures to see *Back To The Future* and thirty years later... I have a daughter who the entire village has talked and speculated about for the last three decades.

It was simple. We'd bought a bottle of cider on the way home, both got a bit excited after a quick snog, then gone the whole way as stupid kids do because that's what we thought you did.

Why couldn't I have walked her to the door, pecked her on the cheek and been done? But no, I didn't want to look like a prat in maths if she told her friends that I'd got aroused and then bailed out.

I peel myself from the armchair, grab a glass and pour a large whisky from the sideboard.

'Tracey, why didn't you say?' I mutter into the fireplace. 'My poor Annie... *this* will break her heart.'

51

Dr Fowler

It's gone midnight but the hammering on the front door is frantic. I jump up from the fireside armchair certain there's a medical emergency.

'You bastard!' screams Annie, as soon as I open the front door. 'All these years you let me think it was him and it was me!' Her body propels into my hallway without an invite or a response, bringing a flurry of snowflakes inside. I understand in an instant; Annie knows the truth.

'Annie, please...'

'Don't you Annie-please me... you and him have known all these years... all these bloody years!'

'Let me explain... Mick asked that I went along with his suggestion... he thought it was kinder.'

'Kinder? We put our faith in doctors... we're brought up to trust and listen to what they advise and then I find out you've lied... lied to me for all these years!'

I step backwards, the bannister handrail nudges my lower back. Annie crumples to the floor sobbing.

Where the hell is Mick? What do I say? I knew this would happen one day.

'Annie, please hear me out... I know what it's like to watch a wife be twisted and taunted every day of her life knowing she can't have what others have – I've lived it. My poor Nina tortured herself for years with the guilt of not giving me a child... she was torn apart by it – Mick knew that you would be the same... so he asked me to say it was him that was infertile... he knew you could live with that *and* cope.'

Her sobbing face looks up at me in a desperate manner.

'Please believe me, he asked because he loves you... I lost my Nina... she was never right after that baby was left on our doorstep – she begged me to lie and I let her down that morning, Annie. I let her down by being honest.'

'Annie?' Mick stands in the open doorway, politely peering through at his wife, crumpled between my radiator and my mail table. 'Sorry, Jeffery.'

'Come in, Mick, please come in...' I watch as he gently collects her from the floor, wrapping his arms around her, and she falls into his chest. 'I'm so very sorry... I knew you could bear it if it were me, so I asked him to lie... to save us.'

I quietly move from the bottom of the staircase back into the lounge and resettle in my armchair. Within five minutes, I hear my front door gently click shut.

Flora

I tiptoe down the staircase, feeling for the light switch, the tufted bedspread slung around my shoulders and clasped to my chest.

'Hello?' I say, reaching the final step. I peer into the muted darkness of the bar. 'Annie? Mick?'

No answer.

My bare feet gingerly touch the cold tiles of the bar, the bar fridges illuminate the area which reflects in the mirrored wall of optics. I survey the room, nothing is out of place, every stool is upturned, every surface cleared and wiped, the fruit machine and jukebox are dead. Everything is just as it should be, except for the front door: wide open.

I knew I'd heard something.

Have they been burgled? I glance at the till, its protruding bottom lip displays its plastic innards, Annie's usual routine before the cash is locked away. I wish Joel was here; he'd know what to do. I'd best call for Mick.

With my eyes locked on the far end of the bar, certain that masked men with baseball bats are crouched in the darkened corners, I sneak my way towards the back room and their private domain.

'What the hell were you thinking? The poor guy...'

I stop as Mick's voice sounds from outside.

'How dare you even question my actions when you and him have colluded for years to deny me my *own* medical knowledge?'

Annie? Are they both outside?

Feeling braver, I tiptoe across the bar towards the open door and see them both standing outside in the snow, her facing The Square, Mick staring at her side profile as plumes of breath surround them.

'Hi,' I whisper. 'Is everything OK?'

They spin round in surprise.

'Yes, Flora, sorry if we woke you. Everything is fine, lovey,' assures Annie. 'You go back to bed, don't let us keep you up.'

'You said that earlier when we came into the bar… but it didn't seem like nothing,' I say, not convinced by Annie's tone.

Mick turns away to stare at The Square.

Is he being off with me?

'You sound upset, Annie,' I add.

'You'll catch your death standing around like that,' soothes Annie. I can see her taut smile is pulled up from her boots.

'Can I get you anything… make a drink for us all?'

'*Flora…*' says Mick.

'Mick don't!'

'Annie, I have to.'

'What's wrong?'

'*Mick?*' I can hear the plea in Annie's voice. 'Not here, not like this.'

'I won't have the courage in the morning.' His voice cracks as he answers.

'Tell me, please?' I ask.

Mick inhales deeply, before turning towards me. Annie lowers her head.

'There's a strong possibility that I might be your father.'

Annie

Now it was my turn to ask, if there was anything I could get her?

For the third time in one night I double-pump a glass tumbler to the optics for medicinal purposes, rather than recreational.

'You're lying!' was her first reaction. I think the stunned silence that surrounded us confirmed he wasn't.

'Why on earth would I suggest such a thing, if it wasn't true?' says Mick, breaking the silence.

'Come on, love... he needs to explain.'

I'd led her inside, already she was shaking and not from the freezing temperature, we seated ourselves near the fire and her alcove.

I left them to fetch tumblers of whisky, when I return they are as I'd left them, staring into the hearth's embers.

'All I can say is that we were foolish teenagers. I asked her for a date during a science class, we broke up for the Christmas holiday so I didn't get to see her or make an arrangement to take her out. Christmas came and went but a few days after I saw Tracey in The Corner Café. It seemed best to do it before going back to school, so we went to the pictures.'

I watch Flora's face, eyes wide and fixed, as she absorbs his every word.

'We watched a film, shared some popcorn, I tried it on a bit in the pictures as young lads do but she wasn't standing for it, kept brushing my hand away...'

'And?'

'We shared a bag of chips on the walk home, I bought a bottle of cider from the Spar and we sat at the side of the church swigging it back... we didn't have much in common so everything was a little stilted and awkward but...'

'As the cider went down, your inhibitions eased,' murmurs Flora, sipping her drink.

Mick nods.

'Something like that... she was a good girl was Tracey... she might have wanted to be like Melanie Delaney but she wasn't cut from the same cloth. Melanie was anyone's who wanted a quick thrill in return for some attention but Tracey was different, more reserved, too reserved probably, which made for an awkward date. It could have been one of her first dates, I couldn't name anyone I'd ever seen her out with before... anyway, things got heated, by the end of the night she wasn't brushing my hands away and we ended up... over by the church.' Mick looks up briefly. 'Sorry.'

'I get it, don't worry,' mutters Flora graciously.

Silence descends.

'I walked her home afterwards... I think we both knew that it meant nothing. She never spoke to me again, school pals probably thought we'd left it at the date request in science and never got round to going on the actual date. I take it she told no one – which suited me. I put it down to experience; I never bragged about it to my mates.'

'Then I turn up like a bad penny, and bingo the whole village is speculating once again.'

'Flora, you are no bad penny.' I jump in before she can continue. 'You've brought me a new friendship and possibly more, if Mick's suspicions are correct.'

'How long have you known?' she asks.

'I didn't. Scott explained his suspicions based on her diary, and knowing Tracey as I did throughout school... yep, he could be right. I think the timings fit.'

'But the testing results didn't show a positive, did they?' she asks.

'I was laid up in bed with my bad back, I didn't have one taken.'

'But you'll need one!' I add. 'She needs to know for sure.'

Flora sits back and stares at the fire grate.

'So why were you pair arguing?' She suddenly turns to me with a questioning stare.

'Nothing, don't you worry about us.'

'Come off it, something's happened for you both to be outside at this time of night.'

I inhale, now it's my turn.

I explain my unplanned visit to Doctor Fowler, the fertility tests from long ago, the hopes, the dreams and the results: truth and lies.

Her arms reach for my shoulders in a warm embrace, just what I need.

'It's deception, yes, but I wanted to avoid what happened to his Nina,' says Mick, stroking my arm.

'Do you think that's why Tracey placed me on Doctor Fowler's doorstep?'

'Possibly. Nina was desperate for kiddies, maybe Tracey childishly thought they'd raise you as their own. We'll never know. Who knows what teenagers think?'

'How hard must that have been when her plan went wrong and the police and ambulance were called instead?' says Flora.

'One lie turns into another though, doesn't it?' I say, not daring to look up at Mick.

'Sadly, my darling, it does,' whispers Mick.

52

Joel

In the station's locker room, my mobile rings as I change clothes to begin my morning shift – Annie's name illuminates the screen. I depress the answer button.

'Hello, Annie.'

'She's gone!' I can hear the panic in her voice.

'*What?*'

'Flora… she's bolted during the night. She's left a pile of money on the bedspread as payment and taken her clothes, the car has gone – she's left us, Joel.'

'Did she leave a note?'

'Nothing… just the pile of money and an empty room.'

'I don't understand… yesterday *was* a tough day but she saw it through.'

'We had an awful night here at The Peacock… lots of wild accusations have come out and understandably she's upset but they make for a difficult situation. I'm so sorry but I think she's gone back home.'

'She can't go home, not yet!' I can hear the panic rising in my voice, other officers who were changing alongside me, spin round to stare. 'I'll be right over.'

I snap the mobile shut and ignore my colleagues' questions.

'Where's Scotty?' I demand.

'I think you'll find he's called in sick due to personal reasons,' explains one officer.

'Bullshit! He hasn't a choice but to face it,' I say, striding from the changing room.

My mind is whirring into action.

Flora can't have gone home, not after everything we said. I haven't strung her along, I've been honest. She agreed. So why bolt? And what did Annie mean it was a difficult night at The Peacock? Surely, they can calm her and handle things when I'm not there. Common sense is all that's needed.

I sign in for duty, giving little thought to the orders of the day or Kylie, my stand-in duty partner.

'You seem distracted,' is all she says as I march across the snow-covered yard to collect our patrol car. 'Hey, I thought I'd be driving in Scott's absence.'

'Not today, Kylie.' I swing the driver's door open and climb inside. She quickly occupies the passenger seat before protesting some more.

It's going to be one of *those* days.

I swing the car out of the station and head for The Square, I'll get the whole story from Annie first before beginning our search.

*

Within minutes we're parking outside The Peacock: everything looks as it should before opening time.

'Kylie, stay here and fetch me if anything comes through on the radio,' I ask, slamming the car door.

Annie and Mick are like glum statues behind the bar; neither looks surprised to see me enter in full uniform.

'Any news?' I ask.

'Last night, Mick told Flora that there's a high possibility that he is her father,' says Annie, pronouncing each word slowly and deliberately for my benefit.

'Sorry, repeat that again?' I ask, as clearly my ears are deceiving me. 'How can that be?'

'It's a long story.'

'Well, make it quick – I've got to find her!'

It took Annie another ten minutes to fill me in on what happened last night, Scotty's unexpected arrival and accusation, the everything-is-fine-cover-up sending us out on a walk, the doctor's doorstep drama and the early morning father-daughter introduction in The Square.

'Is that it, there's nothing else to tell me?'

'Nothing more,' mutters Mick, his head in his hands.

How stupid are these people? Wasn't it clear how distressed she was last night prior to our walk and then to learn the truth. Who knows where she is now, probably bombing down the motorway towards Bushey in the same hurry as she arrived in.

I muster a polite voice.

'Thanks, Annie, I'll be in touch.'

'You don't think she'll do anything stupid, do you?' asks Annie.

'Unlikely, but you never know,' I add, glancing between the pair.

'Please find her, Joel... this has to end well, for her... for all of us,' says Annie, wiping her eyes.

'You're too right, some of us more than others!'

*

We confirm that her Mini has definitely gone from the car park from the oblong of dry tarmac so distinguishable in the snow.

'Now what?' asks Kylie, picking at her thumbnail.

'We get Scotty.'

'He's off sick.'

'No, he isn't. He's drained and confused about everything, but right now, that can all wait – I *need* him.'

I glance at Kylie hoping she isn't offended, but I need my duty partner, not a stand-in.

Within ten minutes we are pulling up outside his dad's house. The lounge curtains remain closed and the mail is poking out of the letter box.

I run along the pathway and hammer on the door until Scotty climbs from his pit.

'What the hell are you doing, man?' he mumbles on opening the door, wearing a pair of grey boxers and a baggy T-shirt. 'I'm off sick.'

'Get dressed, Flora's done a bunk.'

'*Good.*'

My hand grasps his T-shirt, pushing him off balance and against the hallway wall quicker than I thought possible.

'Woo, Joel man – cool it!'

'I'll fecking cool *you* in a minute... you have your feelings and I have mine... now get dressed before I start showing you some more of mine.' I release his T-shirt, which he nonchalantly tries to straighten before following my request.

I watch as he drags his sorry ass up the staircase.

What am I doing? In full uniform, I've just manhandled my duty partner when he's called in sick. Let's hope his neighbours are all late risers and didn't witness my behaviour.

'Scotty mate, I have to find her... you understand that,' I shout after him.

He reaches the top stair and bends down to view us past the hallway ceiling.

'No, I don't frigging get it, but I've got a funny feeling I'm going to have to get used to it!' Scotty disappears from sight.

I turn apologetically to Kylie.

354

'Sorry!'
She shrugs.
'I saw nothing.'

Scott

I pull my uniform on as fast as I can, not for *her*, but for Joel. I can't remember the last time I saw him flare like that. Though, I'd have preferred not to have been on the end of it.

I traipse down the staircase and rejoin them in no time, shout a farewell to the old man – who remains warm in bed.

'So where are we heading?' I ask.

'Shouldn't we tell the Chief?' asks Kylie, glancing between us.

'No!' comes our answer in unison.

'Thanks, buddy... I owe you one.'

'Believe me, after *that* in there... you owe me more than one! Kylie, you're in the back seat, now hop in!' I order, as I snatch the keys from Joel.

'I thought you were ill?' snaps Kylie, removing her hat.

'I was, but suddenly I feel a lot better... so get in!' I retort. I'm not in the mood for banter.

Seatbelts fastened, I take the wheel and spin out into the street.

'Am I allowed to put on the blues and twos?' I ask, knowing full well what he'll say.

'No!'

'Isn't it an emergency?' comes Kylie's voice from the rear seats.

'No!' we shout in unison, before we exchange a grin.

This is when I love being Joel's duty partner, when the pair of us are singing from the same sheet, and come what may, we've got each other's backs.

'What time did she leave?' I ask, swinging the patrol car towards Pooley village.

'Sometime after three, that's when Annie and Mick finally went to bed and they saw her go upstairs,' explains Joel.

I grimace.

'Don't ask, seems like it was an awful night all round at The Peacock after you left!'

'And as a result – she's gone?'

'Not quite… her emotional state is pretty low after the DNA result, to be fair your outburst hasn't helped matters. I hear you proved who her father was thanks to a teenage diary.'

I stamp on the brakes as if all our lives depend upon it.

'*My* mother's teenage diary, *actually*!'

'What?' screams Kylie.

'Don't ask, as it isn't my place to say,' Joel answers.

'Tread carefully, it's my mother we're talking about,' I say, staring straight ahead.

'*Scotty*, please?'

My heart is racing. Why? Knowing that my mother's daughter is so distressed that she could be in serious danger? Or the fact that my sister is missing? I can't say which, but I can feel the anxiety growing.

'Where to first?' I ask.

The silence is deafening.

'Seriously, man, where am I heading?' I ask.

'Her parents live in Bushey.'

'Big Chief *will* notice if we take a day trip down South!' screeches Kylie.

Joel

'A red Mini abandoned at Pooley Point, can a patrol car attend and assist, copy,' comes the voice from control.

We exchange a look and copy back.

'Secluded spot, isn't it?' Kylie says, from the rear seat.

'We had a winter picnic there a while back,' I say, fastening my seatbelt.

Scotty gives me a stare.

'Oh, like that, was it?' he adds.

I switch on the blues and twos. Never have we driven to Pooley Point so fast. Scotty screeches around the corners, nips between the morning traffic and narrowly avoids a near miss on the spinney bridge – but we turn into Pooley Point in no time.

'Holy moly!' is the only comment from the backseat, as Kylie uncovers her eyes.

On arrival, we see her red Mini, beside which Big Tony straddles a police motorbike parked at the rear of the vehicle.

The Mini's driving seat is empty.

Scotty kills the engine.

I'm out of the patrol car in a flash.

'I'll stay here with Kylie, shout if you need assistance,' calls Scotty.

I approach the car with caution and walk around the snowy perimeter, peering inside it.

I scour the area looking for the tiniest detail, but the snow around the car is scuffed, providing no definite tracks.

What the hell has happened to her?

Big Tony takes the left side of the road; I take the right, peering over the hedgerows into the barren field: nothing. There's nothing for some distance before the village erupts from the country lane along which we've driven. There's nothing in the car to suggest she's fallen ill, no handbag left unattended or scribbled note – nothing out of the ordinary.

So why did she come here, park and then decide to leave the vehicle? Hers are the only set of tyre tracks in the freshly fallen snow until you arrive at Scotty's patrol car and Big Tony's motorbike. So she hasn't been collected by taxi, or hitched a ride in a passing vehicle or even been collected by friends.

'Joel, quick,' shouts Big Tony, hoofing it across the ditch into the spinney area.

I dart over the road and follow, unsure of what he's seen, not sure I want to know.

My boots sink in the crunch of snow covering the ferns and bracken as I dodge the tree stumps and roots, charging behind his bulky body. For an overweight, aged copper he can certainly shift in top gear.

A clearing appears, the blue sky opens and when Big Tony moves aside I see her. Seated on a tree stump staring ahead across the open fields, with the village nestled amongst them, like a statue dressed in leggings and a granddad shirt, without a coat or a blanket.

'Flora!' I shout, overtaking the bulky figure of Big Tony. 'Are you OK?'

She doesn't move but continues to stare ahead. I stand in front of her blocking her line of vision but her features remain unchanged. Her lips are blue and her green eyes are glazed.

I want to touch her, but instead I kneel in the snow.

'Flora, listen to me. You're quite safe, nothing is going to happen to you. We'll fetch a blanket to wrap you up in and when you're ready... we'll walk you to the car.'

There is no reaction to my words. Big Tony goes to fetch a blanket.

My beautiful girl, what the hell have we done?

Her hair falls across her shoulders and drapes down her back. She's like a pale Pierrot doll staring at her moonbeam.

What am I doing? The question hits me like a thunderbolt. Thirty-three years of age, single, chasing a signature from a woman who didn't want to be with me. Kneeling in the snow in front of the most amazing person I have ever had the good fortune to accidently clash heads with.

It's as if the universe has suddenly made sense and fallen into place, someone has turned a small dial and the fuzzy, blurred life of this thirty-three-year-old man has become a sharp, high-definition image.

All around, the diamond glint of snow twinkles in the sunlight.

I know, without doubt, what I want. I love her.

I ignore the rules and gently take her left hand in mine.

'Flora? This may seem like the most ridiculous thing in the world, but believe me, this is possibly the most clarity I have ever had...' Shit, I'm babbling. Focus.

I raise her hand and gently squeeze.

'Flora Phillips, despite our unfortunate beginnings... will you marry me?'

I jump as she swiftly turns and stares into my eyes.

'Joel!'

Her surprise at seeing me makes me smile. Has she heard my question?

'Flora... hi... we were worried about you.'

'How come you're here?' She looks around in a frantic fashion, an alarmed expression on her face.

'Don't worry, you're quite safe.' I squeeze her hand, gently raising it to my lips. If she hasn't heard, I'll ask her later.

'Why am I here?'

'Shhh!'

Big Tony returns, handing me a blanket collected from the rear of the patrol car. I wrap it around her shoulders and secure it at her neck, before helping her to her feet. She's unsteady and stumbles several times before I pick her up into my arms and carry her across the spinney towards the waiting patrol car.

Scotty

Joel carries her from the spinney, she looks like a frozen child suspended in his arms.

'How long has she been there?' mutters Kylie.

'Who knows, but it doesn't look good,' I add, muttering to myself. 'She looks so frail.'

Joel gently lowers Flora's feet to the ground and she takes a few tentative steps.

Joel leans forward, she moves forward. Bang! Her forehead connects with Joel's face, *again*!

'Jesus, she's done it again!' I shout, banging my hand hard on the steering wheel.

Joel doubles over in the blink of an eye, as blood bursts upon the surrounding snow, the blanket falls from Flora's shoulders as she staggers backwards. In slow motion I leap from the car, leaving the door wide open, and dash to my buddy's aid for the second time.

'What the hell's she doing to you, man?' I ask, supporting Joel as he clutches his bleeding face.

'It was an accident, Scotty,' his speech is distorted by the blood and rapid swelling.

'Love, you can't assault a police officer, you can't do that,' says Big Tony, rushing to handcuff Flora. 'I'm arresting you on suspicion of assaulting a police officer, you do not have to say anything but...'

'Tony, you aren't listening! Joel said it's an accident like last time.'

'Last time? ... Of course, this is the gal that nutted you on Christmas Eve!' He shakes his head. 'And you're still chasing her? Son, you've definitely lost it!'

I walk Joel back to the patrol car, beckoning to Kylie to help Flora into the rear seat while Big Tony radios the station to let them know what has happened.

'Isn't this cosy?' I chime sarcastically, once the patrol car doors are locked, with Big Tony preparing to follow on his bike.

'Hardly,' snorts Joel, his eyes beginning to bruise. 'This'll be another hospital job, for sure.'

53

Joel

'Name and address?'

'Gareth, it was an accident, she didn't mean it,' I say, charging towards the desk sergeant, a cold compress held to my face.

'She did!' interrupts Big Tony, flipping open his pocketbook to relay the details. 'Once is unlucky, but *twice*? The woman's not right!'

'Flora, speak up for yourself,' I say, turning to her.

'I've asked her to remain quiet until she's checked in… so please, Joel,' says Gareth, from behind his plastic security wall.

'I'm not leaving!'

'You are if you keep this rattle up while I'm checking her in!' retorts Gareth. 'So, name, address?'

'Flora Phillips of The Peacock Pub, The Square, Pooley,' her voice is calm, unfazed by the commotion.

'She needs to see a doctor,' I say.

'Where's Scott?' shouts Gareth. 'Anyone seen Scott to take his buddy up to the hospital before I plant him in a cell to calm down?'

'I'm trying to help!'

'Shut up then?' snorts Big Tony, looking up from his notes.

I feel deflated as Gareth enters her details in the log and Big Tony smirks at my swollen features.

Within minutes, they lead Flora to cell eight, a corner cell with the usual decor of plastic mattress and stainless-steel en suite.

'Joel, Chief wants you upstairs,' shouts another officer from the front desk. 'And he said, make it quick!'

I take the stairs two at a time, dash through the main office heading straight towards the Chief's office, ignoring the roar of catcalls and wolf-whistles from the other police officers – news travels fast around this place.

I rap on the glass door panel.

'Come in!' he barks. 'What the hell has happened to you?'

'She didn't mean to do it, Sir.'

'Don't tell me it was Baby Bede... *again*!'

'Sir.'

He stands and grabs his jacket from the back of his chair.

'Come on, I need to see this one... Is she in the cells?'

*

I watch as the Chief slides the bolt on cell eight's door hatch and peers in at Flora.

She sits on the plastic mattress, her knees bent beneath her chin, arms wrapped around her shins – the epitome of glumness.

The Chief grimaces before locking the hatch and stepping aside for the door to be unlocked by the detention officer.

'Well, well, well, young lady... haven't you got yourself into a right pickle?'

Flora looks up, her expression remains frozen beneath the tear stains.

I remove the compress from my face, fighting every urge to sit beside her and offer comfort.

I have to respect that I'm a police officer on duty. But by God it's hard.

'Chief, can I say...'

His hand lifts; I fall silent.

That told me.

'Yet again my officer has a damaged face caused by your forehead... is there anything you want to say to him, or me for that matter?'

Her eyes stare, taking in his haggard features and rotund spread.

Flora remains silent.

The Chief waits patiently, then he turns to me.

'Anything you'd like to add?'

I fight the urge to mention my proposal, but know that now is *not* the time.

'I'd like to confirm it was an accident... and that Flora and I are actually...' I don't know how to finish the sentence. We are what? Dating? Together? Why was *this* so complicated?

'I see, like *that* is it?' he shakes his head.

Shit, that came out wrong. Whatever we are he now thinks it's cheap and tacky.

'Acquaintances, sir,' I try to correct his opinion.

'*Cheers!*' retorts Flora, coming to life and switching her stare to my bruised features.

'No, what I mean is...'

'I heard what you *mean*, thanks!' replies Flora.

Seriously, am I dreaming or is this actually being played out in front of my boss?

'I'll leave you two to sort out your private lives, and when you're done we'll be having a quick chat in interview room three... don't take too long, Joel.'

The Chief spins on his heels and leaves as Flora launches from her bunk.

'Are you for real? You say you like me one minute and then start denying it when it sodding suits,' she spits.

'Hey, hey, hey, lady – you've hardly been forthcoming in

defining what *we* are. I wasn't going to let my Chief think it was a sordid little affair, was I?'

'Oh great, you now move from embarrassed to sordid.'

'Embarrassed? Me?'

'Yeah you. The other night, at the picnic when we...'

'Made love?'

'Well... yes, afterwards you couldn't bring yourself to even look at me, you fiddled with your shirt buttons instead.'

'I wasn't embarrassed about us. I was annoyed with myself for acting that way without protection or even a discussion. But I wasn't embarrassed by *us*.'

Flora stares at me, her tear-stained face looking drawn and tired.

'You looked ashamed – that's why I said what I said.'

'Now that *did* annoy me, suggesting it was... meaningless.'

'Guys don't always want committed relationships, planned or unplanned – I said it to give you a get-out clause!'

Her words plunge like a knife to my chest. I step backwards from her, wounded. Have I not explained myself? She obviously missed my question at Pooley Point.

'I'm not most guys, *OK*?'

She blushes, averting her gaze.

I shift my stance, reposition the ice pack across my face and watch her. I know she's tired, I can see she's upset and incredibly hurt by recent events. How was this helping?

'So why didn't you kiss me and hold me close afterwards?' Her voice cracks as she speaks.

'Flora, please. We're going around in circles. I know you're hurting... you're tired and not in a good place, but seriously, I need medical treatment, my nose is swelling, I can hardly breathe... can we talk about this later?'

'No, you need to be honest with me.' Her green eyes blur with tears and her face pales. 'Stop toying with my affections.'

367

'Joel!' Scotty's head appears around the cell's door frame. 'You ready to go?'

'Not quite, mate.' Scotty pulls a face and goes to disappear. 'Scotty, stay... you might learn something about me... maybe this façade of boring bloke is just a front I put on for the ladies or for my work colleagues.'

'Joel... you haven't got a front, mate, believe me, if anyone knows you, it's me... not *her*! So can't you pair call it quits and I'll nip you up the hospital to get your nose checked out, *again*.'

'She was in your bed waiting for you on Valentine's Day!' sobs Flora. 'We'd been together at the picnic only hours before. What am I supposed to think, Joel?'

'Shit!' sighs Scotty, 'I'm out of here... this one's turning nasty, mate.'

Her fingers grip the edging of the blue plastic mattress. I can feel her frustration.

'Did I ask or invite her into my bed? No!'

'You must have...' she mutters softly.

'She has a key, she let herself in – as you did.' She's not convinced.

'He was drinking at mine till the early hours,' says Scotty.

'I was at Scotty's... and do you want to know why?' I ask.

'It's none of my business,' she whispers.

'You're right it's none of your business, but I'm sure as hell going to tell you because otherwise you're going to carry on thinking I'm still sleeping with my ex, despite the fact that I've already explained I'm not.' I'm spent, there's nothing left to say.

'Joel!' The Chief's voice travels the length of the cell corridor. 'Now!'

'Call it a day, buddy – she won't believe you – women never do!' jibes Scotty, tugging at my shoulder. 'And you, lady... words fail me... he's a decent guy... he doesn't need this crap after the year she's put him through, but hey, what do you care? You've got what you wanted by destroying everyone's life. Come on, Joel, let's get you up the hospital.'

I get a taste of bile in my mouth and that sinking feeling in my guts.

'Flora?'

She closes her eyes and turns her chin away.

'Leave it, Joel, what did I tell you... women, they'll screw you up every time!'

54

Annie

'Toast!' I shout, grabbing one of the remaining glasses of champagne from the bar. 'Toast!'

I watch as Flora gingerly gets to her feet, it's clear to see that she's delicate in spirit and soul. Today's events were enough to flip her over the edge, thankfully she was released without charge. An impromptu celebration was the least we could do. I look round the gathered crowd, each clutching their pint or champagne flute, and witness a sea of empathy flowing towards her.

I might be annoyed with the locals for many things: drunkenness, gossip, nosiness, but when it really counts in our village, we always have, and hopefully always will, come together to support each other.

I brush a tear from my eye, this doesn't bode well if Flora's about to do a speech.

'I'm not good at these moments, so I'd like to say a quick thank you to you all… I arrived here nearly two months ago, and yet I feel I have always lived here. This village has definitely given me a sense of belonging – which, sadly, I've never truly known, but in recent weeks you've given me what I've needed the most… a background and roots,' her voice cracks on the final word.

A murmur of whispers circulates as Flora composes herself.

'I have so many people to thank... from my devoted parents who've shown me nothing but love,' she turns to blow them a kiss. I nod, pleased that Janet and David had made their way up from Bushey as the emergency unfolded to be here when Flora arrived back. 'And Annie and Mick... *Dad*...' her cheeks colour at her own subtle correction.

I raise my chin and smile, as all around me the neighbourhood pretend not to be shocked by the recent revelation disclosed so sweetly.

'I'd also like to thank Father Maguire, Major Matthews, Darren, Gene, Melanie, Kathy, Betty, Old Nancy... then there's Denny and Donnie, plus a whole host of others, such as my best friends Lisa and Steph who have supported my journey.' She pauses for breath, takes a swig of her champagne. 'Oh, I'm supposed to be keeping this for a toast, aren't I? Anyway, it goes without saying I am truly grateful for everything and I hope my quest hasn't caused *too* much trouble. I hope I can repay your kindness someday! So, could I ask you to raise your...'

I cough loudly to interrupt her, she's forgotten someone. Someone special.

'*Annie?*'

I nod towards the bottom end of the bar, where a young man stands listening to the proceedings, drink in hand, strapping across his cheeks and eyes as bruised as the corner shop's bananas.

'See... I said I was useless at such moments. I nearly forgot to mention and thank... my dear friend...' she stops mid-sentence; her final words linger in the air like a child's helium balloon.

I whip round to view his expression, ignoring the puffiness, swelling and purple haze, his eyes are locked on her. Time appears to have frozen.

'Excuse me...' Flora begins to move, easing through the silent crowd in his direction. Joel simply watches her approach, not a flicker changes in his expression or posture. Scott, standing beside him, becomes flustered, looking from Joel to Flora and back again, his gestures quickening as she nears their position.

Flora stands in front of Joel and places her champagne flute on the bar beside his pint glass.

'I've been foolish and utterly selfish. I never meant what I said earlier, honest. I was consumed by my own hurt... and I thought you were embarrassed about us and I tried to make you feel better and then... everything I said came out wrong. I acted like a petulant child.'

A tiny nod confirms he's listening, Flora continues as the rest of us hold our breath.

'I'm *so* very sorry, I nearly made the biggest mistake of my life by not thanking you... and that's probably because, unlike any other person in this room... words simply aren't enough.'

Her hands lift to his face, cradle his jawline and gently lower his face to hers – she kisses him.

The crowd go crazy. We watch in awe, he responds by changing her gentle kiss into a deep and passionate embrace made for Hollywood. In a crowded pub they are totally alone.

I blush, unsure what to do.

'Well, a toast to Flora and Joel!' I announce, as we watch the proceedings.

'Flora and Joel!' is chorused around the pub like a strange echo.

'Get a bloody room!' shouts Gene, from the other end of the bar.

Scott's face instantly drops.

'Oi, less of that, Gene – that's my...' Scott struggles to speak, as the crowd switch their attention to his outburst.

Flora and Joel release each other, looking suitably embarrassed to find a room full of onlookers.

'What was that you were saying, Scotty?' shouts Gene.

'That's my *sister*!' shouts Scott, as Flora launches herself in his direction for a sibling embrace. Joel looks on as proud as punch.

'To a new brother and sister!' shouts Gene, wrapping his arm around our Mick's shoulders and pulling him close. 'And daughter, and niece!'

'Get off, you soppy git!' chunters Mick, ducking his twin brother's affection.

'Oh, Mick, he cares about you,' I joke, averting my gaze from the sibling embrace. Scott looks on, trying to hide his smile behind a pint glass.

I scan the crowd for Flora and Joel but they're nowhere to be seen – the only clue is the swinging door chime.

Flora

As Scott lets me go, Joel grabs my hand and drags me through the crowded bar and out of the pub door.

'You're hurting my wrist,' I moan, as we arrive outside.

'Sorry, but I have to speak to you.'

Here we go again.

'Go on, say what you have to, though you know Annie will kill you if *that* was false.'

'I'm not on about that! That was real... that's what I've been longing to do since the first time I laid eyes on you, but you, being the deranged woman you are...'

I raise my index finger to his lips and silence him.

'OK, let's drop it. You were saying.' I slowly remove my finger from his mouth.

'As I was saying before you rudely interrupted... that I know you said you didn't wish to hear it but I need to explain about the other morning... the Veronica incident.'

Instantly, my good mood dissolves.

'Oh, *that*!'

'Hear me out, please... don't get stroppy.'

My mouth is firmly closed.

His finger now lifts to rest on my lips, he continues to talk.

'Hush please. I need to explain what has been happening, so please don't say a word, just listen... apparently she's been going to my flat whilst I've been on duty. It's been happening for months, you happened to turn up and catch her. Veronica has said you can confirm any of this with her later, should you wish to.'

'I see.'

'Do you *really*? There is nothing going on. I'm trying desperately hard to cut the remaining ties with this woman and yet she's doing all she can to remain in my life, though it's proving difficult for her... with you about.'

'Honestly, I get it. You talk as if you're the only one to have gone through this... I've been there too, you know?'

'I need to know that you trust me, there's nothing I wouldn't do to prevent you from being hurt.'

'OK.'

'So, please no more talk about *her*. The locks are being changed, the legal side is nearly complete and then... or rather now, we can focus on us without distractions.'

'Agreed.'

'Flora... earlier when you were sitting in the snow, do you remember me asking a question?'

I frown.

'I remember you putting the blanket round my shoulders... and carrying me across the snow...'

He slowly shakes his head.

'Nope, there was something else.'

His body lowers onto one bended knee and he takes my hand before I realise what is happening.

'Flora Phillips, despite our unfortunate start... and for the second time of asking... will you marry me?'

'Yes!' bursts from my throat before I can think.

In a second, he is standing, his arms wrapped around my shoulders, pulling me close. I breathe in the woollen mix of his jacket and aftershave. I lift my chin as he lowers his and we kiss like screen lovers in Hollywood.

I can hear the slight chuckle in his chest.

'What?'

'Next time I'm on shift remind me to tell Big Tony… maybe I'm not losing my touch after all,' he laughs.

Veronica

I sip my gin and tonic, watching the jovial scene unfold in The Peacock.

I stare at the finished alcove, now all the final pieces have been added to the jigsaw – it looks like a mishap from Tony Hart's Gallery.

I can't bring myself to join in with their celebrations... boy oh boy, such a frigging fuss over nothing. So what, she's confirmed who her parents are, whoopi-doo! Let's hope this all dies down when she goes back home. She's nothing but friggin' trouble.

'Truce?'

I jump as Flora speaks, staring down at me as I sip my drink. 'Pardon?'

Her hair looks blustered from being outside with Joel, a wispy strand is caught on her eyelashes.

'I said, is it a truce?' she pulls up the nearest bar stool and settles opposite me, trying to flick the annoying wisps away.

'I suppose so.'

Joel lingers by the bar, his ear cocked in our direction.

'Thanks for the enthusiasm. I had hoped for a little more...'

'Warmth?' I pout, my drink in hand ready to sip.

I watch as Flora's shoulders droop and Joel continues to watch from the bar.

'Look, Veronica, take it or leave it. I've tried my best to make amends... I understand what it feels like not knowing what you want and yet, knowing. But this...' she waves her hand back and forth between us. 'This rivalry, shall we call it, is futile.'

'We *were* happy.'

'I'm sure you were but...'

The silence hangs heavily and I know every eye is upon us.

'But life moves on, hey?' I whisper.

I hear her intake of breath.

'*Exactly*, life moves on.'

I look over to Joel, casually propped against the bar, watching. He must have put her up to this, offering a truce after the drama she'd been through today. I'd loved and lost him. Now, despite my own feelings, I need to walk away.

'We'll call it a truce then! And now, I think I'd better go home to Gordon. Goodnight!'

The entire crowd watches me stride across the bar and open the door, I just about manage to keep my head held high.

55

Flora

A gentle breeze disturbs the bare branches as we walk along the gravel path of the graveyard. In a few weeks, fresh young buds will spring into life, but for now the branches are empty, haunting. On either side are rows of gravestones: some leaning, some erect and some fallen, slabs of granite and marble poignantly inscribed with love. The lichen clings to each stone much like my arm does to Joel's.

My free hand tightens around the cellophane-wrapped bouquet, that bumps my thigh with each step.

Is it peaceful wherever she is? Is she watching us?

The yew trees loom and lean as a flock of cawing rooks circle above our heads.

'You are sure about this?' he asks, as we pass the rows at a steady pace.

I simply nod; emotion has quashed my ability to speak. I never knew you could grieve for a stranger but now I understand. I can't eat, drink or sleep. I've been lying awake each night begging for a single moment, yearning for her to whisper my name – consumed by the need to have known and be known.

I have no idea where her resting place is, but I know when Joel's pace slows that we are getting near. Joel releases and unlinks my arm, takes my hand and steps from the gravel path onto the overgrown grass. The tops of my feet are sodden with glistening dew, matching Joel's trouser hems.

'This way.'

I scan the inscriptions of the granite row: Townsend, Marsh, Walton, Jacobs, O'Dwyer... there she is, Tracey Hamilton – a grey stone angel, head bowed, hands clasped in prayer.

Beautiful, it's what I would have chosen.

An arrangement of brown crispy roses and ferns lie at the angel's feet.

'Do you think they'd mind me laying flowers?' I lift my bunch of lilies for his inspection.

'Of course they won't mind.'

'It's the only thing I can give, isn't it? Something bright and pretty, but it would replace their flowers.' I nod at their spent arrangement.

Joel nods and smiles.

'Did you know her?'

'Yeah, for a number of years after Scotty joined the force, she was always just Scotty's mum... if we saw her on duty we'd stop for a chat, she'd tell him off for being messy about the house and then disappear into the crowd. Nice lady – if *that's* what you're asking.'

'Do I look like her?'

'Not really, her colouring was more like Scotty's, she didn't wear much make-up... but she did have lovely straight teeth.'

'What a thing to notice about someone.'

A silence descends between us.

'Would you mind if I have some time alone?'

'Not at all... it's what I expected.'

Joel kisses my forehead before carefully treading his way back across the long grass towards the path.

I'm lost for words. I stare at the angel's bare feet before kneeling to replace the dried flowers with fresh.

'I'm sorry,' I whisper. 'Sorry I waited so long. Sorry that I missed you. Sorry that I was too selfish and wrapped up in my own silly world to think that time might be running out.'

I fall silent as a gentle breeze whistles, rustling the cellophane wrapping pushed beneath my knee, as my hands busily arrange the lilies.

'Sorry... Mum.'

There is nothing left to say.

Raising my fingers to my lips, I gently press a kiss onto the angel's bare feet and then turn to follow Joel.

56

Tracey

The day my son was born was the second worst day of my life. I lay in that hospital bed, with my baby boy asleep in my arms, and my heart broke. His father and the nurses simply smiled and patted my arm, assuming it was just a cocktail of emotions and hormones because I was holding my firstborn. He wasn't. He was my second.

I hadn't truly understood what I'd done that October morning. I was fifteen, what the hell do teenagers know about life and love? Nothing. They think they know everything, but in hindsight if felt more like delivering a doll. I can see her now, with her tuft of fluffy hair and squashed face wrapped in that towel.

I thought the towel would give me away, surely my mum would recognise it from her airing cupboard when it was plastered across the front page? She didn't. I'd grabbed it to mop up; thought I'd wet myself in fear. I realised later it was my waters breaking. How had I given birth alone? The PSHE films at school focused on conception, they never mentioned the labour. I could have bled to death cutting the cord – I'd never been so frightened, but prayed they wouldn't wake and hear my muffled cries.

I couldn't tell anyone. I just couldn't.

I stripped and remade my bed before breakfast, I stuffed the dirty sheet into my school bag, Mum thought I had a PE lesson by the size of it. I sat tight during breakfast, I slurped my orange juice alongside my Coco Pops, and said nothing. Dad was in a foul mood as his newspaper was late; I should have guessed there was a connection.

When Darren wasn't in school that day, the other kids said he'd bunked off. His mum was so proud of him for finding Danielle and giving a statement to the police. I once asked him what she'd looked like when he found her? He said she was waving, that made me happy – it was a risk, but everyone else was asking questions, so why shouldn't I?

I married a good man, who I spent twenty-seven years of my life loving. I should have told Jerry. I could have told him – but I didn't. He was the kindest man I ever knew, and yet, I simply couldn't tell him. Not because he'd judge me but because I was so ashamed of my actions. I thought about telling him many times. But when is the best time to announce to your husband you abandoned a baby? At the engagement party? Our wedding day? Before long, I was carrying our Scott. I couldn't admit it then. Jerry would have been frightened I'd harm Scott too; I'd never seen Jerry so happy.

I never found the right moment, *ever*.

Not a day went by when I didn't think about her, not one. The worst occasions were her birthday, Christmas and Mother's Day – I'd try to imagine everything she was doing. I'd take myself off into the garden for a good cry. Buy extra flowers for the front windowsill and watch as they bloomed and faded over the week. It was *my* secret, my little way of recognising her existence – it was the only gift I could buy her.

Jerry had wanted more children but I said I was happy with one. I couldn't face chancing it and having a girl. How could I raise a daughter knowing what I'd done? I was blessed with our Scott; I knew not to be greedy. Our Scott would have loved a brother, Jerry suggested adoption, but what if I cracked under the questioning. They'd have taken our Scott into care, I'm certain of it.

I'd ruined my life, I had to do everything I could not to ruin Jerry and Scott's too.

I was always so rude towards Mick. I couldn't bring myself to speak or be civil to him. Not because I was hurt by our date night, it's what kids do, but because he reminded me of what I had done that morning, alone.

My only comfort was knowing a family were loving *my* little girl. Had they told her she was special? Did she despise me? I hope she doesn't hate me.

I knew it was the end when the diagnosis came through; other people fight cancer – I simply accepted my fate. I was being punished for my actions. I deserved it.

I understand Jerry's confusion – he thinks I didn't trust him. Our Scott argued and rejected her in an instant. Bless him, I know he's only trying to protect my memory, my reputation. But I want him to embrace her. She's his half-sister. I hope one day he loves her too.

And, Danielle… I *always* loved you. Not a day went by that I didn't speak to you darling, not one day, even my last.

'Danielle,' my final word in life had been my favourite sound. Jerry had kissed my forehead as I'd slipped into a wakeless sleep. I'd taken my chance to say her name for what I knew was the last time. He hadn't heard or hadn't reacted, I'll never know… but finally with my last breath I found the strength to share her name, rather than the silent prayer that I'd said every day since our goodbye.

Epilogue

24th December 2017
Flora

Reader, I moved in with him.

I smooth the duvet across my warm body and settle back against the plump pillows, beyond the curtains the snow steadily falls.

Looking back, February seems so long ago.

It's amazing how quickly life changes: one moment we were outside The Peacock in a passionate embrace, the next we were heaving my belongings up three flights of stairs to his flat, despite the lack of Veronica's signature. Our cohabitation instantly altered her mindset and she signed the necessary papers within days. I believe she's thrown herself into renovating Major Matthews' home in the hope of securing a stable future alongside a lucrative sideline hosting children's party days within the maze. I wouldn't call her a friend, more an acquaintance, but Aunty Kathy was right – Veronica has a good heart.

I watch as Joel slowly moves around our bedroom, he doesn't make a sound as he treads back and forth.

Within weeks we'd settled into a routine and life was good. Mum and Dad arranged for my belongings to be sent up from Bushey, but they come and visit all the time.

I stayed on at The Posy Pot, working during the day to hone my floristry skills alongside my aunty Kathy and bantered with the locals while serving behind the bar at The Peacock on two nights a week.

As Annie kept saying, 'family looks after family' – which was confirmed when Mick's paternity results came back. I wasn't surprised by the positive result; I'd accepted it as given following Tracey's diary entry.

Scott and his dad, Jerry, are coming around to the idea of a newbie joining their little family, as hard as it was to accept that Tracey had kept such a secret. I wasn't prepared to push either of them to accept me, but within weeks of moving into the flat we had our own family news.

'Has the blue line appeared?' asked Joel, as I handed him the tiny plastic indicator. I couldn't answer him, words failed me as tears of happiness began to flow. Thankfully, Joel's delight matched mine.

In such a short time, I'd gone from being a singleton to a mum-to-be, much to the surprise of both Lisa and Steph – who celebrated in style on a brief visit to deliver yet more of my belongings from Bushey.

I pinch myself at how quickly my life has changed. And all because I chose to leave a nightclub queue on a snowy Christmas Eve, one year ago today! I recognise that wasn't the true start of my story, but everything's turned out for the best. There's still plenty of unanswered questions, which I've had to accept will never be answered, but what has disappeared are the nagging doubts, my age-old insecurities and my constant questions about who I am. I no longer link the circumstances of my birth to every negative aspect of my daily life: my bank overdraft, a missed train or a bad day at work. I know what I am and what I have become: a secure woman, with a loving partner and, as of today, having just sworn and screamed throughout a seventeen-hour home birth, a mother.

My own birth seems so inconsequential now.

From across the room, I watch my daughter sleep in the crook of her daddy's arm and know there's no way I could move an inch from this warm bed, let alone dress and carry her through the streets of Pooley searching for a specific doorstep. The last ninety minutes has answered my nagging self-doubt – could I ever do what Tracey did? The answer is a definite no. I could never leave my daughter, *ever*. And neither would Tracey, *if* she'd been any more than a child herself.

Joel's dark eyes are fixed on her tiny face. Her eyes are squeezed shut, her rosebud mouth glistens and rolls as Joel stands beside my bed, gently rocking our daughter from side to side. Not a hospital bed, as Joel had wanted, but *our* bed in our new home: number three, St Bede's Mews – the centre house in a row of five situated adjacent to the church of St Bede's. How could we stay in the flat knowing a baby was on the way? We couldn't, so Doctor Fowler's sudden decision to downsize felt like the perfect opportunity.

Outside, The Square is bustling with Christmas preparations. The community Christmas tree is decorated with coloured lights, garlands of holly and ivy dress the doorway of The Peacock pub and St Bede's Church proudly displays a straw-filled manger, complete with an infant doll.

The afternoon light squeezes through a gap in the closed curtains, a brightness only achieved when a blanket of snow covers every cobblestone, pavement and doorstep.

Below our bedroom window sits our doorstep – my beginning three decades ago, though today, in addition to the snow, a bunch of pink helium balloons bob and wave courtesy of Mick and Annie.

'Joel?' I whisper, not wanting to wake the baby.

'Hey, sweetie, how are you feeling?'

I raise an eyebrow.

Only a man could ask such a question.

I smile.

Joel nears the bed and sits on the edge rocking her gently. He struggles to reach into his trouser pocket but eventually retrieves a tiny velvet box, which he places on my duvet-covered lap.

'A little present from our daughter,' he says, tilting the baby slightly to show her sleeping face.

My fingers nimbly open it to reveal a silver ring with a twisted rope design identical to Tracey's.

'Thank you,' I mutter, as tears silently tumble down my face and he gently eases it onto my finger.

We sit in silence watching her sleep, as the rest of The Square busies itself for Christmas.

'What do you think?' I ask.

'She's perfect, beautiful…'

'*But* nameless.'

'She doesn't look like an Abigail or a Lydia, does she?' whispers Joel, recalling our chosen names.

'Maybe a Danielle?' I whisper, hesitantly.

Joel tilts his head, stares at our sleeping bundle.

'I believe she might be a *Danielle*.'

The End.

Acknowledgements

A massive thank you to my editor, Sarah Ritherdon – we both said we liked a challenge and we've succeeded in the shortest possible time.

An unreserved thank you to my agent, David Headley of DHH Literary Agency, for being the wealth of knowledge and reassurance that I need. Emily Glenister – you are a superstar! It's the experts that support each author that enable us to focus on our writing.

Huge respect to the Romantic Novelists' Association – midnight on 2nd Jan 2012, I hit the send button for my NWS application email, I never dreamt that my journey towards publication had begun. To my fellow RNA buds who have been so encouraging, witty and creative – thank you for your friendship.

Big thank you hugs to Helen Phiffer and Bella Osborne for being the best writing buddies a dreamer could wish for – you've both been amazing and truly inspiring over recent years.

My writing fairy godmothers, Jo Thomas and Katie Fforde, for your support and generous spirit, especially on 15th March 2017 when my dreams came true.

Thank you to Donna Ashcroft, with whom I was jointly awarded The Katie Fforde Bursary 2017. There had never been a duo until our year, so thank you for the beginnings of a wonderful friendship.

Alison May, Janet Gover, Miranda Dickinson, Rowan Coleman and Julie Cohen for organising such fabulous writing retreats where the advice and knowledge shared regarding the business of writing is the truth, the whole truth and nothing but the truth! Thank you to Lizzy Kremer for the opportunity awarded to me – I will never forget 'my moment'.

Thank you to English class 11En3 2015/2017 – apologies for boring you with the tales and snippets of my publishing journey during our two years of GCSE English. But your spontaneous reaction to my 'big news' was amazing and truly memorable.

Unconditional heartfelt thank yous are for those at the centre of my world, my husband Leo and my mum – your unwavering love and support is all I need.

And finally, thank you to my readers – I'm humbled that you've invested your precious time and hard-earned money to enjoy my book. Without you guys, my characters and stories are simply daydreams.